CHRISTMAS AT DOVE CREEK

This Large Print Book carries the
Seal of Approval of N.A.V.H.

CHRISTMAS AT DOVE CREEK

SCARLETT DUNN

THORNDIKE PRESS

A part of Gale, Cengage Learning

GALE
CENGAGE Learning·

Farmington Hills, Mich • San Francisco • New York • Waterville, Maine
Meriden, Conn • Mason, Ohio • Chicago

GALE
CENGAGE Learning®

LIBRARY OF CONGRESS CIP DATA ON FILE.
CATALOGUING IN PUBLICATION FOR THIS BOOK
IS AVAILABLE FROM THE LIBRARY OF CONGRESS

ISBN-13: 978-1-4104-9487-0 (hardcover)
ISBN-10: 1-4104-9487-X (hardcover)

Published in 2016 by arrangement with Zebra Books, an imprint of Kensington Publishing Corp.

Printed in Mexico
1 2 3 4 5 6 7 20 19 18 17 16

*To Cole and Kara with much love and
best wishes for an extraordinary future,
and
To everyone who believes in miracles.*

PROLOGUE

Wyoming Territory, 1868

The small-town one-room church was as hot as Hades. Though the pastor had opened both doors in hopes of lowering the searing temperature a notch or two, not one hint of a breeze filtered through. Thorpe Turlow stood ramrod straight on the make-shift altar, wearing a tailored black suit, a crisp white shirt, and a black string tie, looking more handsome than ever, if that was even possible. The pastor and the town doctor stood beside him, politely conversing as they waited for Thorpe's soon-to-be bride, Evelyn Tremayne, to make her appearance. One glance at the folks in the pews snapping their paper hand fans back and forth said they were as miserable as Thorpe was in the stifling heat. No doubt their patience was also running as thin as his while they waited for the beauty of the territory to bless them with her presence. As it was, patience had never been one of Thorpe's virtues, and after thirty minutes of waiting, his temper was simmering. Tugging at his collar for the umpteenth time, he was tempted to shed his confining jacket, rip off his tie, and unbutton his shirt. "Why does it always take women so da . . ." His eyes met the pastor's and he quickly amended what he was about to say. "Darn long to get ready?"

Considering the circumstances, the pastor overlooked Thorpe's testiness. To his way of thinking, the groom had every reason to be cross. There wasn't another woman in town, other than Evelyn Tremayne, who would have kept Thorpe Turlow waiting. The pastor's own wife had told him every single lady in town would give their eyeteeth to wed the tall, good-looking rancher. "Thorpe, don't try to understand women. One time I heard a pastor say that God offered to give him the desire of his heart. The pastor told God he desired to understand his wife. And do you know what God said?"

Thorpe and the doc both shook their heads.

The pastor leaned in close and whispered, "God asked him what his second desire was."

Eliciting a chuckle from both men, the pastor continued with his nervous chatter. "I can't understand women. They've planned their big day from birth, so you would think they would arrive on time if for no other reason than to make sure the groom hasn't changed his mind."

"It rarely fails," the doc agreed. "They harangue you to death, trying to get you to the altar, and then they make you wait forever once you're there. I think it's their way of making you think you are about to escape that noose." The doc joked, yet silently he hoped the bride didn't show. He'd been at odds with himself all week, trying to decide if he would be out of line to tell Thorpe the secret he held about his betrothed. Thorpe was a good man as well as a friend, and he didn't deserve what was about to happen to him.

While Thorpe appreciated their attempt to keep the mood light, in all truth, he didn't feel like laughing, and it was more than the heat getting to him. He'd nearly called off the wedding several times in the last two weeks. He couldn't put his finger on what was troubling him, but he had a deep-seated feeling he was going to regret this union. Only his sense of honor prevented him from doing what that little voice inside his head told him to do.

The pastor turned to look at the congregation wedged elbow to elbow in the pews. "I don't see that Englishman here, the duke or earl, or whatever his title. Did he go back to England?"

"Nicholas Ainsworth. He's still at the ranch. He'll probably ride to church with Evelyn and her father." Ainsworth had been a guest at the Tremayne ranch for several months. Evelyn's father told him Ainsworth was the son of a friend, and he came to Wyoming specifically to study cattle ranching. Evelyn had mentioned several times that Ainsworth was an aristocrat, but Thorpe didn't put a lot of stock in titles. All the same, he figured it was a good thing Ainsworth had inherited wealth because the man wouldn't make a good rancher if that was his aim. After spending some time with the Englishman, it was Thorpe's opinion he could sit a horse well, but he was scared to death of longhorns. And he wasn't inclined to work the long hours necessary to run a ranch.

Hearing the congregation begin to grumble about the heat and the wait, the pastor thought it was extremely rude of Evelyn not to arrive on time. He wouldn't dare state his thoughts aloud as Mr. Tremayne was a generous benefactor of the church and he could ill afford to offend him. "Thorpe, do you think I should ask everyone to wait outside under the shade trees?"

Thorpe looked over his shoulder to the entrance of the church. No buggy in sight. *What in heaven's name was taking the woman so long to get here?* "That might not be a bad idea. I would understand if they all want to go on about their business." It had been his preference to have a small wedding with Evelyn's father and the preacher in attendance, but Evelyn was adamant they invite everyone in town. Well, everyone Evelyn considered respectable, which didn't include the soiled doves from the saloon. Now here he stood facing the stewing guests and Evelyn was nowhere in sight. She didn't have a care if everyone in town was inconvenienced. It was all about Evelyn.

When the pastor stepped away, the doc thought this might be the only time he would be able to speak to Thorpe privately. "Thorpe, I need to talk to you."

"Ladies and gentlemen . . ." the pastor began, but was interrupted when Curtis Ryder, Thorpe's ranch foreman, entered the church and hustled down the aisle.

"Thorpe, I need to speak with you." Curtis quickly closed the distance between them.

Hearing the urgent tone in his foreman's voice, Thorpe said, "Excuse me a minute, Doc." Curtis's expression was serious and Thorpe knew something was wrong. "What is it?"

Reaching the altar, Curtis grabbed Thorpe's arm and urged him toward the back door so he wouldn't be overheard. He positioned his back to the now-silent assembly and spoke in a low tone.

Thorpe pulled back and stared at him with narrowed eyes. "When?"

"Before dawn."

"Tell the guests to leave, Curtis." Thorpe turned and stalked down the aisle, stripping off his tie before he hit the threshold.

"Thorpe, we need to talk," the doc yelled after him. When Thorpe didn't look back, he added, "It's important."

Curtis grasped the doc's shoulder as he started down the aisle after Thorpe. "Let him be right now."

Thorpe Turlow walked out of that church a changed man.

CHAPTER ONE

Missouri, 1868

This is a heck of a way to die was Thorpe's first thought when the arrow slammed through his left shoulder. Slumped over his horse, Smoke, he prayed the arrow tip wasn't laced with poison because it was stinging like the devil. Without any commands from Thorpe, Smoke was still moving fast, but the band of braves was staying with him. Smoke was a strong, stout horse and difficult to outrun, and right now he seemed to have his own plan. Thorpe trusted him to make it to the trees if the two of them were going to stand a fighting chance. He hated endangering Smoke's life; the horse meant more to him than a human friend. That single thought spurred him into action. He wasn't about to let anything happen to Smoke or himself as long as he was still breathing. *It wasn't in my plan to die today, you sons of Satan.*

Gripping Smoke with his thighs, Thorpe steeled himself against the pain, pulled his .45, and turned to fire at the eight warriors closing the distance behind him. His rifle might have been the best option, but the pistol only required one hand. By his third shot, he'd managed to hit one brave, knocking him off his horse. The remaining seven warriors were not deterred; they kept coming. He thought he might have winged another brave, but he'd emptied his gun and he needed to reload or pull his rifle. To keep from making himself a larger target for their arrows zipping by his head, he leaned over in the saddle as he deftly pulled cartridges from his belt.

Holding his .45 against his thigh, he was in the process of opening the chamber when he felt Smoke slow a step. Looking up to see what had alarmed his horse, he saw a black and white Appaloosa in front of the trees about two hundred yards away. The Appaloosa was facing him, standing totally motionless in the drizzling rain, but Thorpe didn't see a rider. The Indians chasing him were also riding Appaloosas. The thought that more braves could be waiting to ambush him in the trees filtered through, yet instinct told him his only option was to make it to the cover of the trees if he wanted to stay alive. He stayed the course.

"It's okay, son, keep moving." Smoke picked up his pace and Thorpe kept his eyes on the horse in front of him as he loaded his gun. He figured the horse would soon move out of the way with Smoke barreling down on him. Arrows continued whizzing by, but before Thorpe had a chance to fire again, he heard the report of a rifle. With the sounds of the horses thundering behind him, not to mention hearing his heart pound away in his ears from the pain, it was difficult to determine the origin of the shot, but he thought it came from the trees ahead. He prayed whoever was holding that rifle wasn't aiming at him.

When he turned to fire, he saw one brave fall from his horse. *Someone was lending him a hand.* Aiming as best as he could, he fired and another brave hit the ground. He looked ahead to see they were just a few yards from the Appaloosa, and he spotted a rider leaning over the side of the horse holding a rifle trained on the braves. Another shot rang out. *Thud.* Four warriors down. He gave thanks that the rider on that Appaloosa wasn't shooting at him because he was deadly accurate.

With a slight squeeze of his thigh, he signaled Smoke to pass the horse on the opposite side of the rider. Flying past the Appaloosa, three things struck Thorpe at once: There was no saddle on the horse; whoever was riding that animal was very skilled to make a perfect shot from that position, not once, but twice; and that was one very well-trained animal.

"Don't stop!"

Unless his ears were playing tricks on him, the voice belonged to a female or a very young man riding that horse like a brave.

The rider turned the Appaloosa and followed Thorpe into the interior of the dense thicket. Several minutes ticked by as they weaved their way through the woods until they happened on a felled tree surrounded by heavy brush. They both slid off their horses and when the rider reached for Smoke's reins to move him out of danger, Thorpe saw his rescuer was indeed a young woman. They took cover behind the cottonwoods, and the woman handed Thorpe his rifle she'd pulled from his boot. Positioning herself behind a tree, she held her rifle to her shoulder and scanned the terrain. Thorpe glanced at her. The determined look on her face said she was prepared to give anyone who appeared through the trees a lethal greeting.

Remaining silent, they waited for the warriors. Within seconds, soft rustling sounds told them they were no longer alone in the brush. The woman quickly dropped to one knee and took aim. Thorpe didn't see the braves, but he braced his rifle against the tree to hold it steady as he aimed in the direction of the sound. Right after she fired, they heard what sounded like a groan. Three braves remaining. Silence ensued. Minutes later, the woman stood. "They're leaving," she whispered. They listened until the sound of hooves grew faint.

Thorpe figured the warriors might be retreating for the moment, but he wasn't foolish enough to think they wouldn't be back. He slumped against the tree and slid to a sitting position. The woman approached him, propped her rifle next to the tree, and kneeled down beside him. When she removed her hat, long blond hair tumbled past her shoulders. Large, clear blue eyes met his. Thorpe thought he must be hallucinating, or he was already dead and in heaven, because he had to be staring at the face of an angel. Everyone always told him his ex-fiancée was a beauty, but compared to this woman she was downright homely.

She glanced at his shoulder and said softly, "Let me take a look."

His gaze met hers and he nodded.

She tore a small hole in his shirt to get a better view of his wound where the arrow was protruding from the back of his shoulder. "Why weren't you wearing a slicker?"

Thorpe chuckled. He hadn't expected that question. Now that his adrenaline had abated, he was really feeling the pain, and even though he was drenched from the rain, sweat was rolling down his face. He removed his Stetson and swiped his forehead with his shirtsleeve. "The rain came quickly and I had stopped to pull out my slicker when they surprised me." He noticed she wasn't wearing one either, and her clothing was so wet, it was clinging to her body, but he didn't point that out. She was wearing black trousers and a white blouse, and he figured that was the reason he couldn't see her on the Appaloosa — she blended in with the horse's coat. "Can you break it off and use my knife to push it through?"

"I'm afraid I'm not strong enough to break it off without doing more damage."

Thorpe noticed she was just a little thing, but her size didn't matter when it came to shooting. She was one heck of a deadly shot.

Seeing the perspiration on his face, she placed her palm on his forehead to see if he was feverish. She thought most men would have already passed out from such an ordeal.

The contact surprised Thorpe since he hadn't been touched in months. He might have jerked away, but her soft, cool hand felt good against his skin. Their eyes met again and held for several seconds. She definitely had the face of an angel, but her expression was serious. Her eyes flicked over his face and he wondered if she thought he was going to keel over. "I'm not going to pass out."

She smiled at his statement. She was worried about him losing consciousness. She didn't want to leave him alone, but she didn't know what else to do. That arrow needed to be removed and she couldn't do it without some help. But if she left him and those braves came back for a second bite at the apple, he'd be at their mercy, and she knew they'd make sure he died a slow, painful death for killing so many braves. Coming to a decision, she reached for her rifle and stood. "I'd best get Jed. It won't take but a few minutes, he's not far away. Do you think you can stay conscious until I get back?"

Thorpe didn't want her riding out of the trees alone. Granted, he might not be in good shape, but he could still pull a trigger.

He grimaced as he pulled himself to his feet using his rifle for support. Whistling softly, Smoke came trotting to him. "I'll go with you. They may be waiting for us."

She knew he was in a lot of pain, but he was obviously a strong-willed man. "We'll ride through the trees. Can you get on your horse?"

He wasn't about to ask her to assist him. She wasn't even half his size, but she sure had grit, he'd give her that. "Yeah." He figured Jed must be her husband, and he wondered why he'd allowed her to ride off alone. Thorpe handed her his .45. "Would you mind loading it for me?"

She placed her rifle against the tree. "Of course." She reached over, and without saying a word she started removing cartridges from his belt. When she realized she probably should have asked him before she touched his gun belt, she glanced up and found him watching her with intense dark eyes. She went very still.

Taking the cartridges from his belt was an innocent move, but somehow it felt very intimate to Thorpe. Her head was right at his chest, and when she looked up at him, much to his surprise, he had the urge to touch her face. He hadn't even thought about touching a woman in months. How long had it been? Five, six months? Thanks to his ex-fiancée, he'd found out just how deceitful women could be. He'd been angry with all women ever since, and he sure hadn't wanted to put his hands on one.

Lily's mind was racing. The man was so attractive he practically took her breath away. She forced her eyes from his handsomely sculpted face, past his wide chest, and tried to focus on his gun. Opening the cylinder, she inserted the cartridges with shaking fingers.

Thorpe noticed her delicate fingers as she pushed the cartridges in the chambers. It occurred to him he'd never seen a woman load a gun. Evelyn wouldn't have touched a gun, much less known the business end. This woman handled the revolver like an expert. She was an unusual woman. "Do you live nearby?"

"No, we're on our way to Wyoming." She snapped the cylinder on the .45 in place and handed the gun to him. Pulling a pistol from her waistband, she held it out to him. "If they come back, don't take time to reload, use this."

When she turned away, Thorpe heard her say, "Blaze." Her Appaloosa walked through the trees to her side.

Thorpe tucked her revolver in his belt and

reached for Smoke's reins. "You're headed to Wyoming this late in the year?" He was also going home, and he'd cursed himself for being the biggest kind of fool for not getting an earlier start. Having finished what he'd come to do in Missouri, he wanted to go home and he wasn't inclined to wait until spring. Before he set out for Wyoming, he knew the weather could change in a flash and it wouldn't be in his favor, but he was prepared. The weather wasn't the only challenge travelers had to consider. As he'd just experienced, there were other dangers that could prove far worse and fatal. It was one thing for a man to travel alone under such circumstances; he only had his own hide to consider, not a beautiful woman's. The way he saw it, her husband was plain irresponsible for risking her life on such a foolhardy journey. Right now, he was thanking the Good Lord that those Indians hadn't seen her long blond hair or he'd certainly have more trouble on his hands.

"It couldn't be helped," she answered. "I'm Lily Starr. Do you live near here?" She'd noticed he was traveling light; just a saddlebag and bedroll were on his horse.

"Thorpe Turlow." He braced himself for the pain he was sure to feel when he mounted. "I'm headed to Wyoming Territory. My ranch is there."

Lily didn't want to call him a liar, but he didn't have provisions for such a journey. "Where are your supplies?"

Not only could she ride and shoot, she was also an observant woman. "I imagine those warriors have them by now. I had to let my packhorse go when they gave chase. He's a fine animal and I didn't want him to be shot." He stroked Smoke's neck. "I figured the two of us would stand a better chance of outrunning them, and if we got lucky, all three of us might survive."

His answer satisfied Lily. She understood the way he valued his animals; she felt the same way about Blaze and her mule, Daisy. She jumped on Blaze in one fluid motion, and waited a minute for Thorpe to catch his breath once he was in the saddle.

When Thorpe could speak again, he said, "Thanks for helping me out. But what were you doing out here alone?"

"I heard the shots and thought I'd better check it out."

He wondered why her husband didn't come when they heard the shots, or another man in her party. "How many in your group?"

"Four."

He'd expected her to be traveling with a

23

much larger group. "And you haven't run into trouble?"

"No, we've been fortunate so far." She moved Blaze ahead, leaving Thorpe to follow. After winding her way through the trees, she pulled her horse to a halt to get her bearings and to see if Thorpe was staying with her. Considering the pain he was in, not to mention the blood loss, she was amazed that he was still in his saddle. "It's just a little farther."

Thorpe didn't want to lie to her about passing out, but he thought he was close. "We'd best hurry." By the time three wagons came into view, Thorpe was gripping his saddle horn to stay upright.

"Jedidiah!" Lily yelled as she hopped off her horse and ran to Thorpe's side.

A large man came running from one of the wagons with a huge dog beside him just as Thorpe started to slide from his horse.

"Help me with him," Lily instructed. "We need to get this arrow out."

Jedidiah was a muscular man, but he staggered backward from Thorpe's weight. "Mercy, Miss Lily, he's a big one."

"Yes, he is. Some braves were running him down, so we need to keep our eyes open. Let's get him to my wagon."

Together, they helped a nearly unconscious Thorpe into Lily's wagon and situated him on a feather mattress covered with hand-stitched quilts.

"Jed, I can twirl the shaft, so I don't think it lodged in bone. We can break off the shaft and push it through, or we can cut around the entry and pull it out carefully."

"Break it off and push the dang thing through." Thorpe could tell the arrow tip missed the bone and he wasn't about to let anyone cut on him.

The sound of his deep baritone voice made Lily and Jedidiah jump. Lily collected herself and pulled Thorpe's large knife from his scabbard and handed it to Jedidiah. "You can use the flat of the blade to push it through."

"Lily, do you need help?" Isabelle yelled from the back of the wagon.

"What's going on?" Dora asked.

Lily expected the two women would have a thousand questions, but there would be time to explain later. "Bring the whiskey, bandages, and make a yarrow poultice and boil some water. And bring a needle and some thread."

"You'd best be asking for that whiskey to pour down my throat," Thorpe said. He tried to stay alert by reminding himself he'd been hit by an arrow before and been shot a couple of times, so he could handle the pain. If those Indians came back with more braves, he didn't want these people facing them alone. *Did Lily say four were in her group?* One man was in the wagon with them and he heard two other women. That made four people, and that didn't make him feel a whole lot better.

Lily smiled at him. "You can have a hefty drink before we start."

Seeing that smile of hers nearly made him forget about his pain. Truthfully, it darn near made him forget his own name.

"Lordy be, I may take a swig 'cause I surely don't look forward to causing you more pain," Jedidiah said.

"Jedidiah, this is Mr. Thorpe Turlow. Mr. Turlow, meet Jedidiah Clarke," Lily said.

"Pleased to meet you, Jed," Thorpe said.

"Jed, can you get his shirt off?" Lily asked.

"Yes, ma'am." Once he helped remove Thorpe's shirt, he inspected his shoulder. "Mr. Thorpe, you sho'nuf got yourself in a real mess."

"That I did, Jedidiah." Thorpe figured Jedidiah wasn't Lily's husband after all.

"Miss Lily knew right away those shots we heard meant business. I thank God we was close by."

"I'm thankful to Miss Lily myself. I

thought the Lord sent an angel to help me."

"And he surely did. Yessir, he surely did. He sent this angel to help us all," Jedidiah replied.

Thorpe wondered what the big man meant by that statement, but he didn't have the chance to ask because the canvas flap opened. He whipped his Colt from his holster in an effortless motion and pointed it toward the opening.

In light of Thorpe's weakened condition, Lily was awed by the speed he pulled his gun. She placed her fingers on the barrel of his pistol. "It's okay. It's just Isabelle and Dora. They're traveling with me."

Thorpe holstered his pistol and looked at her. "Sorry, I guess I'm still edgy."

Isabelle shoved the bottle of whiskey and other items through the opening. "We're making the poultice now, Lily."

"Good. Would you see to the horses for me?"

"Sure thing," Isabelle said.

Dora leaned over, trying to get a look at the stranger, but Jedidiah was blocking her view. "Do you need some of my tonic? It'll help relax him."

Lily looked at Thorpe and he shook his head. He figured a tonic meant some sort of opiate and he didn't want to be unconscious for a long time. "Whiskey will do."

After removing the cap, Lily handed the bottle to him. "Here you go, Mr. Turlow."

Thorpe clasped the bottle and looked into her eyes. "Here's to avenging angels." He took a long swig and handed the bottle to Jedidiah.

"No, sir, I best keep a steady hand. I ain't much for spirits. But now you need to take another mouthful before we start."

Thorpe did as Jedidiah suggested, and after he drained a good portion, he handed the bottle back to Lily. "Let's get it over with."

Lily poured some whiskey over his skin and the shaft that was going to pass through his shoulder. After she placed the bottle aside, she positioned herself in front of Thorpe and braced one hand on his right shoulder and one hand on his chest over his heart to help hold him still. Her face was mere inches from his and she looked into his eyes. "Okay?"

Looking down at the small hand over his heart, Thorpe felt sure it skipped a beat. His eyes moved back to hers and he gave a nod. Jedidiah didn't hesitate taking the shaft between his strong fingers and quickly snapped off the end. He grabbed the knife and placed it against the shaft and pushed the arrow tip through Thorpe's muscled shoulder.

Thorpe didn't make a sound, nor move an inch when the tip of the arrow pushed through his flesh. He was staring into beautiful blue eyes before his head dropped to the curve of Lily's neck seconds later. His last thought was *Miss Lily smells better than any flower.*

Under Thorpe's weight, Lily fell backward with him landing on top of her.

"He's bleeding bad, Miss Lily," Jedidiah said.

Lily tried to push Thorpe aside, but couldn't budge him. "Help lift him off of me so I can take care of it." She'd noticed how tall Thorpe was, but when Jedidiah removed his shirt, she didn't think she'd ever seen a more powerfully built man. His chest was broad with well-defined muscles, as were his arms. She estimated he had to weigh over two hundred pounds.

Lily and Jedidiah finally slowed the bleeding just as Isabelle returned to the wagon with the poultice. Once they had Thorpe's shoulder cleaned and stitched, Lily held the poultice to his wound as Jed wrapped the bandage around his shoulder. Jedidiah tied off the bandage and together they lowered him to the mattress.

"I ain't seen too many men bigger than me, but Mr. Thorpe shor' is, Miss Lily."

"He's going to need every ounce of that strength considering the amount of blood he's lost." Lily unfastened Thorpe's gun belt and Jedidiah lifted his hips so she could pull it off. She placed the gun right beside him so it would be within reach if he awoke. The flap opened again, and Dora and Isabelle poked their heads through.

"Who have you brought back this time, Lily?" Isabelle asked.

"She done went and saved Mr. Thorpe here," Jedidiah answered. "Had an arrow through his shoulder."

"Indians are close?" Isabelle questioned.

"We shot all but three and they left," Lily said quickly so they wouldn't be alarmed.

"They'll be back with more," Isabelle warned.

"Oh my, would you get a look at him, Isabelle," Dora said, her eyes roving over the large man lying prone on the mattress.

It seemed to Isabelle that he filled the entire interior of the wagon. "Merciful heaven! Look how big he is!"

"He'll eat a ton," Dora added.

"I got a feeling Mr. Thorpe can be a big help," Jedidiah commented. He figured any man who pulled a gun as fast as Thorpe was a man who could probably deal with a whole lot of trouble.

"And he told me he was headed to Wyoming. He said he has a ranch there," Lily told them. "It would be helpful to have someone along that is good with a gun."

"You mean if he doesn't die," Isabelle said.

"He is not going to die!" Lily said. "Don't even say such a thing. Quick, say a prayer." She didn't know what it was about Thorpe Turlow, but she could tell he wasn't a man that one arrow could fell.

Dora and Isabelle rolled their eyes at her. "You pray enough for all of us," Isabelle said.

Lily gave them a stern look as if they were two misbehaving children.

"Okay, we'll pray for him," Isabelle said to satisfy Lily.

Jedidiah laughed. "You should know that Miss Lily has a direct line to the Almighty. Why, even Mr. Thorpe said he thought she was an angel that came to save him."

Dora couldn't take her eyes off the big man on Lily's bed. He had a striking face and the broadest chest she'd ever seen. "I'm happy this injured critter only has two legs," she commented. "And I have to admit he's much more handsome than Blue."

"I guess that's a matter of opinion," Lily

said. She wasn't really thinking about Thorpe's striking face. The comment about Thorpe's appetite forced her to consider their limited supplies.

"I have to leave for a little while." She glanced up at Jedidiah. "Look after him, Jed. Make sure he stays put if he comes around."

"I'll get those wet pants off him," Jed told her.

"You just said Indians are roaming around out there," Isabelle said, fear creeping into her voice.

"Keep your guns handy. If you see anything just start firing. I don't expect I'll have to go that far," Lily told them. "And I'll leave Blue here to alert you if trouble is coming. Start packing up camp because we need to keep moving for a few more hours." She didn't want to say she expected those braves to come back, just like Isabelle said, but that was what she was thinking.

"Miss Lily, it don't sound safe for you to be out there wandering around by yourself. Where are you going?" Jed asked.

"Mr. Turlow had a packhorse that he had to release and he seems fond of his animals. I'm going to see if those braves captured him."

CHAPTER TWO

Lily led the wagons until she found a spot that she thought would be easily defensible should they find themselves under attack. Before she helped Jedidiah with the animals, she jumped into the back of the wagon to check on Thorpe. He was either asleep or out cold, and when she placed her hand on his forehead, she thought he felt feverish. She nudged his shoulder. "Mr. Turlow." Receiving no response, she pulled another quilt over him before she left the wagon.

"Jed, would you help me unpack his horse? That poor animal needs some rest. We'll put the supplies in our wagon so he won't have to carry that weight tomorrow."

"Yes, ma'am. How is Mr. Thorpe doing?"

"He feels feverish. I hope he wakes up soon so we can get some fluids in him."

"He will be happy you found his horse. You didn't have any trouble, did you?" Jedidiah had listened for gunfire when she left to find the horse, but he hadn't heard anything. When she returned, she was in a hurry to get moving and they didn't have time to talk.

"That horse is one smart animal. I think he was following us. I didn't see Indians, but I think the two of us best keep watch together tonight."

"Yes, ma'am."

Once they cared for the animals, Lily took a pail of fresh water into the wagon with her. Blue jumped into the wagon behind her and plopped down next to Thorpe's side. It was unusual for Blue to take to strangers. He'd been with her a year and she'd never seen him show affection to anyone but her. He was young when she'd found him near death's door with a gunshot wound. She'd nursed him back to health and he'd been by her side from that day. Blue was wary of most people and generally people were afraid of him. "So you like him, huh?" She figured Blue recognized when someone cared for animals, like Thorpe.

She kneeled down beside Thorpe and felt his forehead again. He still felt warm so she dipped the cloth in the water and placed it on his forehead. She felt more comfortable observing his masculine features without him staring back at her. His weathered skin showed lines around his eyes and creases at the corners of his mouth. He had a few gray hairs at his temples, making him look older than she thought him to be. Without a doubt, he was the most attractive man she'd ever seen.

After she pulled her eyes from his face, she decided it would be a good time to check his wound. She picked up his knife and cut the bandage from his shoulder. She washed the front of his shoulder and gently scrubbed the blood from the hair on his chest. She was just about to yell for Jedidiah to help her turn him over so she could wash the back of his shoulder when Thorpe opened his eyes.

"That feels good." Thorpe awoke while she was washing his chest, and it felt so good he didn't want her to stop. He could barely remember the last time someone took care of him. It must have been when he was fifteen when he'd caught a fever and his mother tended him. That was just a year before she'd died.

"Your wound looks good. If you can turn on your side I'll wash the back of your shoulder."

When he turned on his side his eyes landed on the big dog lying next to him. "Who is this?"

"That's Blue, and you should feel flattered."

Thorpe reached out and rubbed the animal behind his ears. "Why is that?"

"Blue doesn't take to many people."

"Well, I'm glad he likes me. He's a good sized dog and I'm in no condition to tangle with him right now."

"He's a wolf."

Thorpe's hand stilled over Blue's head. "A wolf?" Blue was big even for a wolf.

"Yes, I found him nearly dead from a gunshot wound last year. I guess you could say he adopted me after he recovered."

Thorpe looked into his blue eyes as he stroked his head. *Intelligent eyes,* he thought. "I guess he's friendly."

"Sometimes."

"I've never seen a wolf with blue eyes."

"I hadn't either until I found Blue."

"How long have I been out?" He felt a bit foggy, as if he'd been asleep a long time.

"A few hours. I thought it would be best if we got out of that area and we just stopped for the night."

"Did you see any braves?"

"No." She soaped up her cloth again and started washing the back of his shoulder. Noticing the many scars on his back, it was evident that arrow hadn't been his first encounter with danger. "You aren't bleeding so I'll leave the bandage off for a while. I'm boiling some water for another poultice."

"Thanks for taking care of me." Thorpe had to admit that it was nice to have her looking after him, if for no other reason than he liked watching her.

"How do you feel?"

"Much better." His wound hurt, but he wasn't going to confess that to her.

"Dinner is cooking and I'll bring you some coffee." She dried off his back and Thorpe slowly turned over.

Lily reached for a quilt and folded it several times to make a pillow and placed it under his head. "How's that?"

"Good, thank you." Thorpe noticed she hadn't changed her clothes and his blood was on her white shirt. "I think I ruined your shirt."

In her haste to find his horse and get out of the area, she hadn't thought one thing about her clothing. "I need to get cleaned up."

"I must be in your wagon. I can sleep outside."

"That's not necessary. I'll clean up in one of the other wagons. You stay put. It's going to be a cold night." She moved toward the flap and turned back to him. "I found your packhorse. Actually, I think he was trailing us."

"Miss Lily, you are a surprise. But you shouldn't have put yourself in further danger." He couldn't believe she'd gone to the trouble to find his horse, especially not knowing if those braves would be waiting.

"I was very careful, and as I said, I didn't have to go far."

There was no way he could express what it meant to him that she'd found Shadow. "Smoke and Shadow are good horses and good friends. It means a lot to me that you found him."

"I could tell your animals are important to you. You don't have to worry about them. I've already brushed them down and fed them. Jed set up the makeshift corral right by the wagon so they can hear your voice. I figured they're used to your voice and it would calm them to know you're near. Jed and I put your supplies in our supply wagon so Shadow can take it easy for a while."

"Feel free to use whatever you need from my supplies." He thought that was the least he could do considering she'd done so much for him.

"Thank you. I'll be back in a little while with some food." She glanced at Blue, but he didn't seem inclined to move. In a way it hurt her feelings that Blue didn't leave with her; he always wanted to be by her side.

Seeing the direction of her eyes, Thorpe said, "I think he's warm. I put off a lot of heat."

"Yes, you do." She'd noticed that when she touched his skin.

When she left the wagon, Thorpe put his arm around Blue. The wolf rested his head on his chest. "You've got quite a lady there, boy." He appreciated Lily's thoughtfulness to corral his horses near him. She was right when she guessed his voice would calm them down. He was the one that always checked on the horses before turning in at night, so his voice was the last thing they heard. It was such a relief to know Shadow was unharmed. When the arrows started flying and he had to let Shadow go, he knew he would go back to find him once he was able. He wouldn't have left him behind even if it meant tracking down those braves. But Miss Lily saved him that trip.

He hadn't been delirious when he saw her earlier, because she was definitely a looker. He was curious to know why the four of them were making such a trek across country at this time of year. He didn't feel right plying her with questions from the start, but he wanted to know why in God's name they only had one man with them. And if he remembered correctly, Jedidiah wasn't even wearing a gun. Granted, Lily was an excellent shot with a rifle, but if they ran into trouble, they'd need a whole lot more than one person with a gun. He hadn't wanted to travel with other people as he preferred going at his own pace, but it seemed Providence had intervened. All things happened for a reason, and while Miss Lily might have saved his sorry hide, he had a feeling they might need him more than he needed them.

Thorpe was starving by the time Lily returned to the wagon carrying three plates. Jedidiah was standing outside the wagon holding cups of coffee for them.

"How are you feeling, Mr. Thorpe?" Jedidiah asked through the open flap.

"Much better, Jed. Thanks for getting that arrow out."

"You're much obliged. Here's your coffee, Miss Lily. And I have Mr. Thorpe's saddlebags here if there's something he might need." Jedidiah placed the saddlebags in the corner of the wagon along with Thorpe's bedroll. "Mr. Thorpe, your saddle is in the supply wagon."

"I'm indebted to you, Jed. You and Miss Lily have done more than enough for me. I'll be up and around tomorrow to help you out."

"There's no hurry, Mr. Thorpe. You just let yourself heal."

When Lily put a plate in front of Blue, Thorpe was surprised the wolf didn't start eating right away. He was eager to get started on his dinner, but Lily wanted to put a fresh bandage on his shoulder first. Thorpe noticed she had changed into a clean white shirt and she smelled so good, even Blue was sniffing her.

Lily handed him his plate and a cup of coffee when she finished with the bandage. "I bet you're hungry."

"Yes, ma'am, I am. And the coffee smells almost as good as you." It wasn't his intention to say that, but he wasn't sorry he did. He couldn't help but smile watching her cheeks turn pink. Glancing at the food on the plate she offered him, Thorpe knew he could eat twice that amount, but he didn't want to appear ungrateful. It made him wonder if they were low on supplies. He really liked the fact that she'd brought her plate to have dinner with him, but the small amount of food on her plate didn't seem sufficient for a woman who had been so busy all day. He took a large sip of his coffee. "Do you think I could have some of that whiskey in my coffee?"

She grabbed the whiskey bottle and poured some in his coffee. "It probably didn't help your shoulder bouncing around in this wagon, but I wanted to get out of the area. Are you in a lot of pain?"

"You did the smart thing. My shoulder isn't that painful. Besides, your bed is real comfortable."

Lily sat near him on a quilt and picked up her plate. "Isabelle made dinner, and when she cooks it's usually good, especially the biscuits." Lily had piled five biscuits on Thorpe's plate along with a huge helping of stew.

Thorpe started to pop a biscuit in his mouth, but when Lily bowed her head to pray over her meal, he dropped it back to the plate. He'd often finish his meal before he thought of saying a prayer. He noticed Blue didn't touch his food until Lily raised her head. It shamed him that the wolf had better manners. Picking up the biscuit again, he took a big bite and chewed. "These are good." He handed a biscuit to Blue. "What do you think, boy?" Blue made quick work of the offering, and Thorpe grinned at Lily. "I think he likes them."

Lily had a hard time keeping her eyes on her food; they seemed to drift to Thorpe's face or his bare muscled chest like they had a mind of their own. "Blue likes all food. I'm afraid I've ruined his hunting ability."

"He probably wouldn't be happy in the wild again or he would take off. You don't keep him tied."

"No, I don't tie him. I wanted him to do what he wanted once he healed. No animal or person should be forced to stay where they don't want to stay."

That statement made Thorpe wonder why she was leaving her home for Wyoming. "Where exactly are you headed in Wyoming?"

"Fort Steele. Isabelle is to be married to a soldier. She needs to be there before Christmas."

Thorpe knew the military was dispatched to the fort to protect the rail workers. "What does her future husband think about her traveling with two women and one man all the way to Wyoming?" He couldn't imagine any man worth his salt allowing his fiancée to take on such a journey.

"Ah . . . I'm not sure." She didn't want to reveal too much about the reason they were going to Fort Steele and have him think ill of Isabelle.

"Why does she have to be there by Christmas?"

Now she'd done it. She didn't know what answer to give him. "It's personal."

She doesn't want to answer, Thorpe thought. "Are you sisters?"

"No, we're all friends."

"Are you from Missouri?"

"No, I'm from Texas."

Thorpe knew there was a story here, more than she obviously wanted to reveal, but he wasn't going to keep asking questions. He wasn't a man to pry, and if she wanted him to know she would tell him. He just hoped this odd foursome wasn't wanted by the law. "My ranch is west of Fort Steele."

Lily was thankful he stopped asking so many questions. "Is Wyoming as beautiful as everyone says?"

"I think so. The weather can be harsh, and we get a lot of snow, but a man can ride for days and not see anyone."

"It sounds wonderful. Do you have a large ranch?"

"It's not the biggest, about one hundred thousand acres."

"Oh my, that sounds so large. What brought you to Missouri?"

Thorpe didn't want to discuss the reason he came to Missouri. "I needed to take care of some business."

Lily heard the change in his voice. She thought he might not feel like talking. When she finished eating, she scraped the remainder of her dinner on Blue's plate. Grabbing her coffee, she leaned back and took a sip. "Jedidiah makes the best coffee."

"It's good and strong, just like I prefer." He finished his dinner and put his plate aside.

"Mr. Turlow, you are welcome to travel with us if you are of a mind."

He wondered if that was what she wanted, and more importantly, how she knew she could trust him. "Call me Thorpe. You don't know anything about me. How do you know I can be trusted?"

"I assure you I am not an empty-headed female. I know a great deal about you."

Thorpe arched a dark brow at her. "How so?"

"It's been my experience that one can learn a great deal about a man by how he treats his animals. When I put your horses outside this wagon and they heard your voice, they both perked up. Then, there's the fact that Blue likes you. That tells me all I need to know, because Blue doesn't care much for anyone but me. If you have his trust, then I'm sure I can trust you."

Thorpe liked her thinking. He often judged people by the way they treated their animals. There was no denying he wanted to know more about Miss Lily and the reason she was going to Wyoming. "Are you married, Lily?" What on earth made him ask that question? As much as he told himself he was going to stay away from women, he wanted to know all about Lily. Still, he felt the need to explain asking such a personal question. "I was wondering what your husband would think of a man traveling with you."

Her eyes moved over his handsome face. "Jedidiah is a man."

Their eyes locked. "I'm a different man."

Was he ever! She'd never seen another man who was as physically appealing. "It won't be a problem. I'm not married."

He couldn't believe a beautiful woman like her wasn't married. Even though she came to the right conclusion that he could be trusted, he didn't think she should be so trusting of any man that happened along. A woman that looked like her should be more careful before she invited a complete stranger to join them. The wrong man could do what he wanted with these women once Jedidiah was out of the picture. Perhaps they thought Jedidiah offered enough protection by his presence, but he wouldn't be much of a deterrent if someone was intent on doing them harm. Miss Lily may not know it, but she definitely needed his protection.

CHAPTER THREE

After Lily left the wagon for the night, Thorpe poured himself another cup of whiskey to help him relax. He thought about the reason Lily gave him for their trip to Wyoming. What kind of soldier would encourage his fiancée to travel with two women and one man from Missouri to Wyoming? That explanation didn't make sense to him. Why did they leave Missouri so late? Couldn't they have waited until next spring? Was it possible Miss Lily was as duplicitous as his former fiancée?

He sipped his whiskey slowly and thought about the situation. He had no reason to jump to the conclusion that Lily was being deceptive. Was he judging her because of Evelyn? Maybe he hadn't been able to put Evelyn's betrayal behind him like he'd thought. She hadn't been on his mind recently and he considered that a good sign. And he wasn't happy that he was thinking about her now. Rationally, he knew it wasn't fair to compare every woman he met to his lying fiancée. It made him realize he was still harboring anger and he needed to let it go. Forgiving Evelyn wasn't for her benefit, it was for his. Evelyn hadn't asked for his forgiveness, but he knew it was important to forgive, or he would be the one to pay the price. *Easier said than done.*

He closed his eyes and the past filled his mind. He'd met Evelyn five years ago when her father purchased a ranch that shared a boundary with his. The first time he saw her she was sitting on her front porch wearing a yellow dress. At seventeen she was already a beauty with dark hair, golden eyes, and a figure that made a man take notice. Word spread as fast as a raging wildfire about the beautiful rancher's daughter, and she soon had her choice of men trying to court her. Thorpe hadn't staked his claim early on, running his ranch occupied most of his time, and he wasn't ready to marry and settle down. But Evelyn's father approved of Thorpe, and in an effort to encourage the relationship, he'd invited him often to the ranch for dinner.

The Tremayne ranch wasn't the only place Thorpe spent his limited free time. He wasn't as taken with Evelyn as she was with him, and he occasionally accepted dinner invitations from other single women in town. There was no denying Evelyn was the most attractive woman he'd courted, but Thorpe had a difficult time understanding why she wanted to marry a rancher when she seemed to hate ranch life. He couldn't quite figure out how she spent her days. She didn't cook; her father employed a cook. She didn't ride horses, because she said they were smelly, and she was adverse to chores, telling him that was why they had hired hands. Taking her own words into consideration, he didn't think she was the logical choice for a rancher's wife, if he'd been looking for a wife. Evelyn's mother had died when Evelyn was a young girl, and Thorpe thought her father spoiled her to make up for their loss.

Evelyn didn't have the same hesitation about Thorpe. She'd set her sights on him from the first day she saw him. Thorpe always thought she wanted him because he could offer her a comparable lifestyle to what her father provided. Her major complaint about Thorpe was that he was too much of a gentleman because he refused to succumb to her feminine charms. It took him over four years to agree to marry her even though she'd been bold enough to ask him several times. The very night he'd agreed to marry, she'd immediately set the date. Three weeks before the wedding was to take place, Evelyn came to his ranch and told him she had a surprise for him. It had been an unforgettable night. She told him to sit in his favorite leather chair and close his eyes. When she allowed him to open his eyes he was stunned to see she was nearly undressed. He believed her when she said she would be too nervous on their wedding day to enjoy their first night together. Maybe he just wanted to believe her. When she sat on his lap and started kissing him, he didn't resist. She'd stayed until the early morning hours. He'd regretted his rash decision that night, thinking he should have politely refused and taken her home before things got out of hand. But it happened, and wishing it hadn't was a waste of time. That one night sealed his fate. He was determined to do the right thing by her, and that meant showing up at the church three weeks later. His sense of honor wouldn't allow him to call off the wedding even though he was having doubts before she'd spent the night in his bed.

He'd never been as angry in his life as he was that day when his foreman walked into the church and told him Evelyn had left town with the Englishman staying at the Tremayne ranch. The fact that she'd chosen not to marry him wasn't the issue, but her dishonesty was what enraged him. It wasn't until the day after the wedding was to have taken place that he learned the reason Evelyn left with Ainsworth. The doc paid him a visit at the ranch and told him what he tried to tell him on his wedding day. Evelyn was with child. The doctor had seen Evelyn three weeks before the wedding. She'd seen the doctor the very day she'd shared Thorpe's bed. The doc said he thought she was about three months along and Thorpe knew it couldn't be his child. It was obvious she'd been with Ainsworth from the time he arrived on their ranch. At least, he figured it was Ainsworth's child. Evelyn had played the role of the innocent very well when she was with him that night. Her performance had certainly fooled him. Now that he had time to reflect, he had no one to blame but himself. He didn't want to recognize the signs of an experienced woman. He'd been so caught up in the moment that he had betrayed his own sense of right and wrong, and failed to control his desires. What he couldn't figure out was why she insisted on the wedding when she had been intimate with Ainsworth and was carrying his baby.

Why hadn't she insisted Ainsworth marry her? Thorpe wanted an answer to that question. He told himself it would be a waste of his time to find her and ask his questions; he doubted she would tell him the truth. After all, she'd lied to him for months. But other thoughts filtered through his anger. Thoughts like Ainsworth may have forced himself on her and she could have been afraid to tell him what happened. If that was the case, he would kill Ainsworth.

Thorpe knew he would never put this situation behind him until he knew the truth. Four days after he was supposed to be a married man, he left the ranch in the care of Curtis. He rode away, intending to track Evelyn down and get his answers.

Away from the pressures of the ranch, Thorpe had plenty of time on the trail to think about how his relationship with Evelyn had evolved. Facing his own shortcomings wasn't an easy thing to do. He'd spent most of his time building the ranch and had given little time trying to figure out what he wanted in a permanent relationship, not to mention a partner for life. It hadn't been fair to Evelyn not to settle those issues before their engagement. When he agreed to marry, he'd told himself it was time because he wanted children. Most men his age were married and already had two or three kids. Even though he was angry Evelyn had left him standing at the altar, part of him felt a huge sense of relief.

By the time he arrived in Kansas City, he'd come to realize he'd never been in love. Not with Evelyn, not with anyone. He cared about Evelyn's welfare, and he would have protected her with his life had they married, but it wasn't love. He would have been faithful to their vows, but deep inside he knew there was something missing in their relationship. The experience left him a wiser man, though he doubted marriage would be in his near future. It would ease his mind to know Evelyn had not been forced by Ainsworth. He could go on with his life and learn from the experience. If she had been forced, he would do what he needed to do.

After he settled his horses at the livery, he asked the owner to direct him to the finest hotel. The man directed him to a grand hotel and his guess paid off. The hotel clerk confirmed Mr. and Mrs. Ainsworth had registered a few hours earlier. Instead of going to their room, Thorpe took a seat in the lobby and waited. It didn't take long before he spotted Evelyn walking down the staircase alone. When her gaze drifted around the large lobby and landed on him, she stopped dead in her tracks.

Thorpe stood, ready to chase her down if need be. He could see her eyes darting around the room, looking for Ainsworth, or a way to escape; he didn't know. She slowly made her way toward him.

"What are you doing here?" she snapped.

"I want to talk to you. I think you owe me an explanation."

She turned and led him to an alcove out of view of the people entering the hotel. Thorpe figured she expected Ainsworth to appear. "I'm not going back to Wyoming."

"I'm not here to take you back." He'd told her the truth. That was the last thing he wanted. "I have one question for you."

She looked around to make sure they were out of earshot of other patrons. "What's that?"

"I want to know why you wanted to be with me when you knew you were carrying another man's baby."

Her eyes widened. She obviously thought her secret was safe. "What difference does it make? I didn't marry you, did I?"

No denial, no crying, no hysteria, no apology. He already had one answer. She hadn't been forced by Ainsworth to do something she didn't want to do. "I want to know, and if I have to stay here to talk to Ainsworth, I will." It wasn't an empty threat. He thought he might feel some satisfaction confronting Ainsworth.

That comment gained her full attention, and for the first time she looked into his eyes. "He hadn't asked me to go back to England with him until the night before the wedding."

"Does Ainsworth know you were in my bed?"

The look she gave him clearly stated she thought he was mad. "Do you really think I would tell him about that?"

No, he didn't credit her with that much integrity considering how dishonest she'd been with him. It was too much to expect her to be more forthcoming with Ainsworth. She'd even kept her own father in the dark about her relationship with Ainsworth. Mr. Tremayne came to Thorpe's ranch the night the wedding was to take place to apologize for his daughter. He wasn't aware of her plans to leave with Ainsworth. He'd been as surprised as Thorpe and he felt equally betrayed.

"Does he know this is his baby, or does he think it could be mine?"

Evelyn looked away, and Thorpe could see she was nervous about something. When he thought she wasn't going to answer, he said,

"Don't test me. I swear to you I'll ask Ainsworth."

She knew Thorpe well enough to know he wasn't bluffing. "He doesn't know about the baby yet. I'll tell him after we are married. I don't want him to think I'm trapping him into marriage."

That explanation rang hollow to Thorpe's ears. "Did he force himself on you?"

"Why would you think that? Don't you understand? I'm marrying a duke. I won't be living on a dusty ranch in the middle of nowhere. I'll be living in a castle, I will have servants, attend socials, and travel the world. I'll have everything I want. We will marry before we sail."

Thorpe stared at her, and for the first time he knew he was seeing the true Evelyn. All of his questions had been answered in her response. Yes, she was a renowned beauty, but she was empty on the inside. He didn't know her at all. He was dumb enough to think she'd already married Ainsworth because they registered as a married couple and were sharing a room. In his estimation she'd best hurry and get married. Even with her clothes on he could see she was gaining weight around the middle. He glanced at her stomach. "How do you hide it from him?"

"Women have their ways, Thorpe." She wasn't about to admit it was becoming more and more difficult to conceal her condition from Ainsworth. She was worried that if he knew about the baby he may not agree to marry her. Each time she broached the subject of marriage, he found an excuse to change the conversation. "You aren't going to ruin this for me, are you?"

"You didn't mind trapping me, but you don't want to trap him. Or do you think he wouldn't want you if you're with child? Perhaps he wouldn't believe he is the father." By her expression, Thorpe knew he'd guessed the truth.

That was exactly what she'd been thinking. Ainsworth hadn't been her first indiscretion, and she'd done everything in her power to hide the truth from him.

Thorpe gave her a hard look. He almost pitied her. "You were planning on having me raise another man's baby if Ainsworth didn't ask you to marry. Were you ever going to tell me the truth?"

She didn't answer, but he had his answer. "Good-bye, Evelyn."

Thorpe left the hotel and walked to the livery. After he loaded the supplies he'd purchased from the mercantile, he was ready to go home to Dove Creek. Evelyn might not like living on a ranch in Wyoming, but he couldn't think of a better life. That day in the church he'd had his mother's emerald wedding ring in his pocket. It was his mother's most treasured piece of jewelry and he'd been ready to place it on Evelyn's hand. He hadn't told her about the ring and he was thankful he hadn't given it to her before their wedding day. For the first time in months, he breathed a sigh of relief. He'd been spared a lot of heartache with a woman that couldn't appreciate having a home like Dove Creek Ranch.

CHAPTER FOUR

Lily couldn't sleep for the handsome Thorpe Turlow occupying her thoughts. She prayed he would decide to travel with them to Wyoming. Knowing that another man was with them, particularly a man who was as skilled as he was with a gun, would make her rest easier. It would be a blessing to have him along to share the responsibilities of protecting the others. Agreeing to travel this time of year wasn't the smartest decision she'd ever made, but after the confrontation with the people on the wagon train she didn't have a choice. Those people had professed to be Christian, yet they had little trouble passing judgment on Isabelle and Dora. Once they'd turned on Jedidiah, and she couldn't persuade them to change their mind, she'd lost her temper and gave them all a piece of her mind. There were times when a person had to stand on principle, even if it meant staying behind with the unwelcome threesome.

Isabelle and Dora told her they would be traveling to Wyoming with or without the wagon train, and she couldn't have their deaths on her conscience. She'd tried to recruit some men to accompany them as guards, but they refused to leave until spring. As her grandfather always said, *Sometimes you just have to have faith and do what God says: believe.* She couldn't help but think Thorpe Turlow was the answer to her prayers. Just as she believed Blue had been sent to help her, she also thought Thorpe was a godsend.

After adding branches to the fire, she placed the coffeepot along with some biscuits on the rocks. She stood near the fire, soaking in the warmth. Even though they had good weather since they'd left Missouri, the nights were getting cooler and she wasn't ready for the change. She wasn't accustomed to this kind of climate; she preferred heat and humidity.

In the middle of the night Thorpe awoke and he wanted to get out of the wagon for a while. He lit the lantern and pulled a shirt from his saddlebag. By the time he managed to get it on, he was too exhausted to bother with the buttons. He carefully climbed out of the wagon with Blue right behind him. As soon as he hung the lantern on the outside of the wagon, he saw Smoke and Shadow standing as close as they could get to the wagon. They whinnied when they saw him. "You missed me, did you?" He couldn't lift his injured arm, so they had to take turns getting stroked. "You boys did real good."

"You shouldn't be moving around," Lily said.

Thorpe heard someone moving near the fire, but he thought it was Jedidiah. "I wanted to see them and put them at ease. Besides, I'd been in that wagon so long, my joints were getting stiff."

Lily moved beside him and stroked Shadow's neck. Shadow hung his head down and sniffed her neck. "He's such a smart horse. He was following the trail we took through the trees when I found him."

"I'm really grateful you found him. Smoke and Shadow are stablemates and they don't like to be apart."

Lily understood what he meant. Her mule had to stay in the same stall with Blaze or she would raise a ruckus. "Blaze and Daisy are the same way."

"Who's Daisy?"

Just as Thorpe asked the question, a mule

pushed between the horses and nudged Lily's hand. "Daisy meet Thorpe, Smoke, and Shadow."

Thorpe scratched Daisy on the head. "A mule is a fine animal, intelligent and sure-footed."

Lily laughed when Daisy nudged Thorpe's arm when he stopped scratching her ears. "And loves affection."

Thorpe laughed with her. He noticed what a pretty smile she had, but he also thought she looked tired. "Didn't you get some rest?"

"Jed will relieve me in a while."

"I can take the watch."

"You don't need to be out here in this cool weather."

Thorpe saw her shiver and figured the cold was getting to her. "I'm used to the cold. Besides, this isn't cold. When you get to Wyoming you'll see cold. Do I smell coffee?"

"Yes, I just made some."

"Why don't we go sit by the fire and have a cup? That will keep both of us warm." He didn't want to go back in that wagon; he'd rather sleep outdoors.

They walked to the fire and Lily grabbed some blankets for him. Once he was seated, she draped one of the blankets around his shoulders and noticed he still hadn't buttoned his shirt.

"Thanks."

"I don't want you getting a fever." She reached for a cup and poured some coffee.

He took the cup from her and blew on the steaming liquid before he took a sip. "This is good."

"Thanks. Jedidiah taught me to make it like he does. His was better than mine." She handed him a warm biscuit and gave one to Blue.

"Thank you. I really like these biscuits. Tell me, Miss Lily, besides making great coffee, who taught you to shoot and ride like you do?"

"My grandfather."

Thorpe had rarely seen anyone but an Indian brave as agile on horseback. "Tell me about him." He really liked to hear her talk; she had a soft angelic voice that was easy on the ears.

"His family had a farm in Texas and when he was ten years old, they were attacked by Comanche and he was taken captive. He lived with the Comanche until he ran away at age fourteen. They taught him to ride and shoot like a brave."

"Comanche are known to be great horsemen."

"They taught him well. The Comanche called him Blue Wolf."

Her story piqued Thorpe's curiosity. "Why Blue Wolf?"

"My grandfather found a young wolf not long after he arrived at their village and they were inseparable. One of the elders in the village told my grandfather that he believed they were spiritual brothers. Wolves are revered by most tribes. They believe they are spiritual beings and have magical powers. Many believe that wolves will guide them to their spiritual world. My grandfather said the Comanche told him they learned the importance of family, and how to be such good hunters from wolves."

"Did the wolf come home with him?"

"No, he'd left the village some months earlier and my grandfather never saw him again. The elder told him they would be spiritually connected forever. Like Blue, my grandfather's wolf had blue eyes."

Thorpe looked at Blue. He wondered if she thought Blue was the wolf her grandfather had found years before. He wasn't sure how long wolves lived, but he didn't think it was over fifteen years. "Did the Comanche treat your grandfather well?"

"Yes. They told him he'd fought like a brave warrior when he was captured. He wasn't unhappy living with them, but he always wanted to return home and find out what happened to his family. When he left the Comanche, he learned his parents were killed in the raid, and his older brother had left Texas. He kept the farm going, married a few years later, and had a son . . . my father. It was a long time before he heard news of his brother, and by that time he had a family and couldn't leave Texas to find him. When I was sixteen my grandmother died, and it wasn't long after when my grandfather left the farm to find his brother."

Thorpe didn't ask, but he would guess Lily was about twenty. "Did he find his brother?"

"I don't know. The last we heard from Grandfather he was in Independence and he wrote that he was leaving for Wyoming. That was a couple of years ago."

"So that's what you are doing out here . . . looking for your grandfather?" Before he gave her a chance to answer, he asked another question. "What do your parents think about you taking off on such a journey?"

"Our farm was raided by Comanche last year and they killed everyone but me. I was helping a sick neighbor that day. My grandfather is all the family I have left, so I decided I would try to find him. I think Blue was sent to help me."

—"You think Blue was sent to guide you to your grandfather?" Thorpe noticed when he asked that question, Blue raised his head and stared directly into his eyes.

"Maybe to guide me, or to keep me safe." She shrugged as if she didn't expect him to understand. "It probably doesn't make sense to you, but I know Blue is here to help me. He always alerts me to danger. Let's just say I think of him as my angel." She didn't add that she thought it was another sign that Blue obviously liked him, and she also thought he'd been sent for a reason. Right now, Blue was glued to his side and that was the main reason she was placing her trust in Thorpe Turlow.

Either this woman had a lot of guts, or she was just plain loco to go on such a journey searching for a man she hadn't seen in years. But he couldn't say he wouldn't be doing the same thing under the circumstances. Having lost his family, he knew the importance of having those you love near while they were living. He didn't know what to think of her belief that the wolf was sent to help her. But then, during many difficult times on the ranch, he thought a guardian angel was watching out for him. He guessed it was possible she had a guardian wolf.

Lily jumped up and said, "I'll be right back."

Thorpe watched her climb into her wagon, and when she returned she was holding a large leather pouch. She sat next to him and emptied the contents on her lap. "My grandfather carved all of these." Rifling through the wooden pieces, she held out a hand-carved wolf.

Thorpe held the piece near the fire so he could see it clearly. He figured all wolves had similar features, but like all animals, they also had distinguishing traits. Blue had a small notch at the top of his right ear and so did the carving. After examining the carving from every angle, he was positive of one thing: It was a miniature wooden replica of Blue. "When did your grandfather carve this?"

"When he was twelve."

He could think of no explanation how her grandfather was able to do that. Unless . . . impossible. Blue was a young wolf. He picked up some of the other carvings and they were all skillfully made, stunningly life-like. "These are amazing."

"My grandfather believes that men and animals communicate through their spirits."

Thorpe thought her grandfather must have studied animals closely to make these pieces so authentic. He picked up one carving in particular that caught his eye. It was two doves sitting on a limb side by side.

Seeing the carving he was admiring, she said, "He said doves are spirit messengers between worlds, and are a symbol of love. He told me feathers are gifts from the sky and when you find one, they come with a purpose."

"Are you sure your grandfather is still alive?"

"I have no proof, but I think he is. My grandfather always told me I would have the answers to all of my questions if I would be still and listen. He told me God would speak to me." She looked into his eyes and added, "When I listen, I hear the answer here." She placed her hand over her heart.

Thorpe stared at her for a long moment. He understood that connection with a loved one. The day his younger brother, John, died in an accident, he'd been working several miles away on the ranch. A thought kept nagging at him that John was in trouble, so he jumped on his horse and raced to where he was working. It was too late. John's horse had broken his leg and Thorpe figured John had tried to jump clear, but he'd hit his head on a rock. At fourteen years of age, John took his last breath in Thorpe's arms. Thorpe was crazy about his little brother and he always looked out for him. He carried a lot of guilt that he hadn't been there to protect John that day. Since his brother's death, Thorpe had never felt such a close bond with another person. He certainly wouldn't question Lily's link to her grandfather. "Did you travel from Texas with your friends?"

"No, we met in Independence. We were all prepared to leave on a wagon train, but there were some problems and we didn't get to leave at that time."

He inclined his head in the direction of the wagons. "You didn't know any of these people before you arrived in Missouri?"

"No, we had never met."

The more questions she answered, the more questions he had. "What kind of problems prevented you from traveling with the wagon train?" Thorpe had the feeling she was trying to hide something from him.

Lily started to respond, but she saw Isabelle and Dora climbing from their wagon. The women carried their blankets with them and joined them by the fire.

Thorpe expected Jedidiah was more than likely lurking nearby, if for no other reason than to make sure he could be trusted with the ladies.

Lily made the introductions. "Thorpe Turlow, this is Dora Love and Isabelle Baker."

"Ladies."

"Why aren't you two resting?" Lily asked the women.

"We heard you talking and we couldn't sleep anyway," Isabelle said.

Lily knew Isabelle wasn't sleeping well. The poor girl was worried about everything. That was another reason she wanted Thorpe to stay with them; it might help to allay some of her fears. Lily knew it wasn't nerves that kept Dora awake; she just wanted to meet Thorpe.

Dora confirmed her thoughts when she said, "We thought it was time to meet our visitor. You seem to recover fast, Mr. Turlow." Dora's gaze traveled from his face to his unbuttoned shirt, all the way down the length of his long outstretched legs.

"It's not much of a wound." Thorpe saw the direction of her eyes and he knew she wanted him to notice her interest. This woman wasn't an innocent like Lily, unless Lily had him completely fooled. Dora was a comely woman, with dark brown hair and dark eyes. All three were fine-looking women. Another reason they should be

71

traveling with more protection.

"I'm glad you are feeling better. Lily was very worried about you," Isabelle told him.

Thorpe glanced at Lily. "Was she?"

"When's she's praying for you, that's when you know she's worried," Isabelle replied.

Thorpe figured no one had prayed for him since his mother died. Even though his heart had hardened toward women, the thought of Lily praying for him touched him. "Lily was just about to tell me what happened with that wagon train you ladies were supposed to be traveling with. Did you have the wagons and supplies ready to go?"

"Yes, we had everything," Lily replied.

If he decided he would stay with them all the way to Wyoming, he had to trust them. Trust worked both ways, and right now he knew nothing about them. "What happened?"

The three women exchanged a glance.

Thorpe wondered what they were hiding. "You three aren't outlaws, are you?" Though he asked the question in a teasing manner, he knew they were hiding something.

Lily shook her head. "Of course not."

"Then why didn't you travel with that wagon train? It would've made a lot more sense than what you are doing now."

"The fine people on that wagon train found out I worked at a saloon in Kansas City and they didn't want me traveling with them," Dora said. "Lily took up for me, but they wouldn't change their minds. Lily stayed behind because of me."

Thorpe took a swig of his coffee and looked Lily in the eye. "And you two had just met. That was kind of you to take her part."

"I couldn't believe they weren't going to allow her to go. They said they were God-fearing folks, but their behavior didn't seem very Christian to me."

Thorpe looked at Dora. "Miss Love, you didn't say why you are going west."

"Call me Dora, honey. I figure there are a lot of men out west looking for a woman. As a matter of fact, I heard the men out-number the women one hundred to one. I'm planning on finding me a husband."

Dora was plainspoken, Thorpe had to give her that. It wasn't difficult for him to believe Lily defended Dora, but he had a feeling there was more to this story. His eyes moved to Isabelle. "Were you taking Dora's part, too?"

"Actually, the ladies on the wagon train didn't want me traveling with them either, Mr. Turlow," Isabelle said. She hadn't wanted to tell him the truth, lest he judge her like those people on the wagon train, but Dora spoke honestly, so she could do no less. "You see, I am with child and I am an unmarried woman. The ladies on the wagon train thought it was unseemly for me to be in the presence of their young, impressionable daughters. It didn't matter that I was going to meet the father of my child so we could marry. You see, he's a soldier and he was sent to Fort Steele. The soldiers are protecting the men building the railroad from Indian attacks."

It seemed Evelyn wasn't the only woman that put the cart before the horse. But he wasn't one to sit in judgment of these folks. He'd made his own fair share of mistakes; he was in no position to throw stones. His eyes moved back to Lily. "Anything else?"

Jedidiah joined them at the fire and sat on a stump near Thorpe. "Mr. Thorpe, Miss Lily also gave those folks on that wagon train the dickens over me. I wasn't welcome either after I spoke up for Miss Dora and Miss Isabelle."

Thorpe shook his head. In addition to all of Miss Lily's other talents, it seemed she had a soft heart. He just didn't want that heart getting her killed. "Well, Miss Lily, I understand your reasoning, but it still isn't wise to travel this time of year. It's not only the weather that will more than likely present complications. What happened to me is just one of the problems you could face. If the braves did overpower your group, they might take you ladies captive, and well . . ." He let the thought trail off. He wanted to scare some sense into them, but some things were best left unsaid. "You could run into outlaws, and no offense, but they could easily overtake the four of you."

Lily had thought of all the things he said and more. "We knew it wouldn't be easy, Mr. Turlow, but we all agreed to give it a try."

"Jedidiah, you're the only one that hasn't told me why you are going west," Thorpe said.

"I have a brother in the Ninth Calvary and last I heard he was somewhere in Wyoming Territory. This is a big country, Mr. Thorpe, and I always wanted to see what else there was out there. I'm a blacksmith by trade and I figured there might be a need for a man like me out west. I didn't have a wagon, but the wagon master agreed to let me join the wagon train saying I could make repairs and care for the animals."

"There is definitely a need for a good blacksmith in any town, Jedidiah." He had a feeling the wagon master made a mistake by not taking Jedidiah. He was a man that could pull his own weight, and no man was more important to the success of a town or a wagon train than a good blacksmith. Thorpe thought about what they told him and he only had one more question. "What I don't understand is why you need to be there by Christmas."

Isabelle didn't hesitate to answer him. "The doctor said I would be having my baby around Christmas. I didn't want to give birth to this babe and not be married to the father. I didn't want my child to pay for my mistakes and be ostracized."

Thorpe wondered why this soldier didn't marry Isabelle before he left Missouri if he wanted her. He wouldn't be the first man to take advantage of an innocent woman and leave her once he got what he wanted. He prayed this wasn't the case because she was having his child. But a woman in her condition only added to the many potential problems they would face on this trip. "The wagon train had to leave months ago. Why are you so late in leaving? Why didn't you leave right behind them? They might have had a change of heart."

"Miss Lily got sick. She had typhoid fever and we weren't about to leave without her,"

Jedidiah said.

"They cared for me for two months," Lily added.

"When Miss Lily got well she tried to hire some men for guards, but none of them would take the job," Jedidiah said. "They wanted to wait until spring."

"That's right. She did," Isabelle confirmed. "She was even going to pay for them out of her own funds."

"And she's taught us how to shoot better. We may not be too good, but if someone is close enough, I reckon we could hit him," Dora added.

"We will make it to the fort by Christmas, won't we?" Isabelle asked.

"If the weather holds and we don't have unforeseen problems, we could make it by Thanksgiving." Thorpe had planned on making it to his ranch well before Thanksgiving and that was just a few days' ride from the fort, but it would take longer by wagon.

Everyone smiled at the thought of making it by Thanksgiving.

"Mr. Turlow, we could pay you to travel with us as a guard." Isabelle turned to Lily and added, "That is, if Lily thinks it would be a good idea."

Lily wished she'd thought of hiring him as

a guard. "Yes, I agree if he is willing. We will pay as much as we can afford." When Thorpe didn't immediately reply, she thought he might turn them down. "Our wagons are filled with mostly supplies, no heavy furniture like the folks on the wagon train, so we are traveling lighter and will be able to make better time. We have good sound mules."

Thorpe looked at the group around the fire. He saw the hope in their eyes, and that told him they were not ignorant of the fact they needed help for this journey. He did owe Lily for helping him, but that wasn't the only reason he wanted to stay with them. Lily was a unique woman, unlike anyone he'd ever met. Her story intrigued him, and maybe he just wanted to see if she would find her grandfather. Or maybe he was as loco as they were. "You won't have to pay me, Lily. I'll stay with you and get you to Fort Steele in one piece." His gaze landed on Lily and he saw the relief in her eyes. She was more concerned than she'd allowed the other three to see.

"Thank you," she said softly.

It tugged at his heart to hear the emotion in her voice. He figured she wasn't a woman to give in to tears. He winked at her, and to lighten the mood, he said in a teasing tone,

"Miss Lily, before you thank me, you should know I eat a lot of food."

"That's not a problem, Mr. Turlow. I'm a good shot."

CHAPTER FIVE

"My goodness, he sure is a handsome man," Dora said. The women were in the wagon early the next morning changing clothes, and Lily was forced to listen to Dora drone on and on about the good-looking Thorpe Turlow the entire time.

"I just thank God that he is kind enough to go with us. I'm sure he would make much better time without us," Isabelle said.

"Is he married?" Dora asked.

Lily had tuned them out; she was thinking she needed to go to Thorpe's wagon and check his wound and apply a clean bandage.

"Lily!"

Lily jumped and whirled around to face Dora. "What?"

"I asked you if he was married," Dora repeated.

"He didn't say."

Dora shook her head. "That is the first thing you should find out when you run across such a handsome man."

"I believe I had a lot of other things on my mind at the time," Lily reminded her.

Isabelle walked to Lily and started braiding her long blond hair. "Yes, Lily was busy saving his life. You know, Lily, I once read that if you save a person's life you are forever bound together."

Isabelle's comment reminded Lily of her grandfather. He'd said the same words to her before, but he also said the same holds true for animals. When she saved Blue's life, she thought they would be together forever.

"I'd like to be bound to Thorpe forever," Dora commented.

"Behave yourself, Dora," Lily said.

"Oh, I promise to be good, really good," Dora replied.

"You are incorrigible." Lily couldn't help but grin at Dora. She looked over her shoulder at Isabelle. "Are you finished?" She wasn't going to take time braiding her hair; it was much easier to shove it under her hat, but she didn't want to hurt Isabelle's feelings. "I need to check his wound to see if it is healing properly."

"Yes, go," Isabelle said.

"I'll check his wound," Dora said.

"You wouldn't even know what it was supposed to look like," Isabelle told her. "Come

81

on, we need to start cooking."

As Lily jumped from the wagon, she heard Dora mention Thorpe's muscles. She'd seen the way Dora looked at Thorpe last night. There was no doubt Thorpe had noticed Dora's obvious interest. She wondered if he was as attracted to Dora as she was to him. Reaching Thorpe's wagon, she tapped lightly on the wood.

Thorpe opened the flap and Blue jumped out. "Well, hello." She ruffled Blue's ears. "I wondered where you were."

Thorpe held his hand out to her. "I heard you women talking so I figured you'd want to take a look at my shoulder."

Lily hoped he couldn't hear what they were saying. "We need to keep it clean and that means a clean bandage twice a day." She took his hand and he lifted her off the ground with one hand.

"I already washed it as best I could."

In the close confines of the wagon, Lily couldn't help but stare at his bare chest. All she could think about was what Dora said about his big muscles. Realizing she couldn't see what she was doing if he was standing, she said, "Could you sit while I bandage you?"

"Sure thing."

Thorpe sat on the mattress and Lily

inspected his wound, trying to keep her eyes from drifting down his magnificent body. "This looks good. You do heal fast."

"I think it was that compress you put on there." Thorpe turned his head and his cheek was a hair's breadth away from hers.

"It was a poultice made of yarrow."

"How did you know that would help?"

"My grandfather taught me how the Comanche treat wounds."

She poked around the wound. "How does it feel?"

"My shoulder is a little stiff, but it'll work itself out once I get in the saddle."

"Oh no, you don't! You don't need to be riding yet."

Thorpe tugged on her braid hanging over her shoulder. "Miss Lily, if you think I'm going to ride in this wagon all day, you're wrong." He hated being in close confines, and unless he was unconscious or sleeping, he wasn't going to stay in that wagon all day.

"You can ride on one of the seats, but you can't handle a team yet."

Riding in the seat next to her didn't sound so bad. "Okay, I'll sit next to you today."

She finished bandaging his shoulder; all the while her thoughts were centered on him sitting close to her all day.

"Your hair looks real pretty like that."

His compliment flustered her. "Thank you," she said just above a whisper. She collected the things she needed and quickly jumped from the wagon.

They took one short break at noon and stopped for the night before dusk. Lily thought Thorpe had enough jostling around for one day.

Thorpe suspected Lily stopped because she was worried about him. "Don't worry about me. We can keep going."

"We didn't get much sleep last night, and to tell you the truth, I'm tired." Lily didn't want to tell him that she was on edge with him sitting on the seat next to her all day. Not that he did anything to make her feel uncomfortable; quite the contrary. He was a very congenial traveling companion. He'd asked her about her home in Texas and her life on the farm before her parents' death. They'd discussed several topics, but every time she looked his way, all she could think about was how handsome he was.

Thorpe jumped down and reached up and wrapped one arm around her waist and lifted her to the ground in one easy motion. "I'll help Jedidiah with the animals. You get some rest."

"You should take care not to lift anything too heavy."

"I'd say that doesn't include you. You barely weigh more than my saddle," he teased.

When he walked toward the team, Lily stared after him. It was more than his physical appearance that was appealing. He was a potent combination of masculine confidence and dogged determination. She'd never met a man quite like him.

After the nightly chores were complete, they were all relaxing around the fire when Thorpe saw Blue jerk his head up and stare intently into the brush behind them. Thorpe glanced at Lily and she nodded, indicating she saw the same thing.

Thorpe pulled his Colt and whispered, "Stay here." In a crouch, he slipped away from the campfire and made his way to the first wagon for cover with Blue right beside him.

Lily pulled her rifle to her side and whispered to the women to get their pistols ready. She had told them to carry their pistols tucked into their coat pockets so they could easily protect themselves if need be. Jedidiah picked up his rifle and placed it across his lap. They remained very still, their eyes searching the brush surrounding them, but they heard nothing, not even Thorpe's footsteps. Only minutes had passed, but it seemed like hours before Thorpe strolled back to the campsite followed by Blue and a scraggly-looking dog. Lily hoped it was a dog and not another wolf. The animal was not as large as Blue, but it looked like it had been in the wild too long. The poor thing was caked in mud, and so thin Lily could see ribs protruding through the skin.

"She's starving," Thorpe said.

Lily jumped up and grabbed Blue's bowl and dished out a healthy portion of stew along with some biscuits and placed it in front of the dog.

Jedidiah grabbed a pail, filled it with water, and set it beside the bowl of food. "I wonder what she's doing out here all alone."

"I don't know, but from the looks of her, she's been out on her own for some time. I guess Blue found himself a girlfriend," Thorpe replied.

Blue positioned himself near Thorpe again, but when the dog finished eating and drinking, instead of resting near the fire, it trotted back out through the brush. Blue jumped up and followed her.

Thorpe was just about to go look for Blue and the dog when they walked back to camp, each with a puppy clutched between their teeth.

"Oh my goodness, she's had new puppies! The poor thing!" Lily placed a blanket near the fire and the dog plopped down with her pup and Blue placed the puppy he was holding beside her. The dog and Blue exchanged a look, and Thorpe was certain something unspoken passed between them. The puppies immediately nuzzled their mother, but Blue turned around and walked back into the brush. Thorpe grabbed a lantern and followed him. When they returned, Thorpe was carrying two more puppies.

He leaned over and gently placed the puppies at their mother's belly so they could nurse. "That's all of them." He stroked Blue's head as they watched the puppies burrow into their mother. "You did a good job, boy."

Lily noticed how gently Thorpe had cradled the little puppies in his strong hands. "What are we going to name them?"

"You're going to keep them?" Dora asked.

"Of course she's going to keep them," Isabelle responded. "How could you ask such a thing?"

"We don't have the food to feed all of them," Dora snapped.

Dora's question angered Thorpe. "Which ones would you leave behind?"

"We're already sharing the supplies with Jedidiah," Dora said.

"Dora!" Lily said. "We are not sharing anything. Jedidiah earns his way."

"Miss Dora, I'll share my portion with them," Jedidiah offered.

"That won't be necessary, Jed. I have more than enough supplies to feed the dog and the puppies when they are old enough," Thorpe said.

Jedidiah walked to his wagon, and Lily confronted Dora. "Don't ever say anything like that again! I swear if you do I will leave you behind!" She couldn't really say at the moment it was an empty threat.

Thorpe looked at the two women, clearly confused by the underlying current. He couldn't imagine why Dora would object to Jedidiah riding with them. The man more than pulled his weight.

Isabelle looked at Thorpe and explained the situation. "Dora's angry because Jedidiah didn't have a wagon or supplies. Lily said he didn't need supplies since he would be such a big help."

"I'd say you ladies are getting the best end of that deal. Don't let supplies be a source of contention. As I said, I have enough for all of us."

"Lily purchased enough supplies for him with her own money, so Dora shouldn't be complaining about anything. It didn't cost her a thing."

"We had to buy our wagons and supplies. And even though Lily bought more supplies, they aren't limitless, especially if we run into bad weather. Plus, Jed's not even handy with a gun," Dora retorted.

"What business is it of ours if Lily bought extra supplies for him and lets him use *her* wagon?" Isabelle asked.

Thorpe was thinking the same thing. He didn't see that it was anyone's business but Lily's.

"We have plenty of supplies and I can shoot what we don't have," Lily said. "There's no reason to worry. Dora, you should be thankful we have him along. Do you really think the three of us could have handled everything? Would you have taken care of the animals? We would be even more vulnerable without him. I think you need to consider these things before you apologize to him." She glared at Dora. "And you will apologize."

Dora walked away without uttering another word.

Thorpe thought he didn't want to be on

Miss Lily's bad side. She was a little spitfire underneath that sweet feminine appearance. He thought he would redirect the conversation on a more pleasant subject. "Why don't you two name the pups?"

"Are they boys or girls?" Isabelle asked.

Thorpe leaned over and lifted a leg on each puppy. "Looks like we have two girls and two boys."

"Do you have a dog, Thorpe?" Lily asked.

"My dog died last year." It still saddened him to think about Sam; he'd been a great companion for twelve years.

"Well, then, you need another one. You name one of the boy dogs," Lily suggested.

"I want to name one Honey," Isabelle said.

"Which one?" Thorpe asked.

Isabelle pointed to the smallest female.

"Honey it is."

Jedidiah walked back to the fire and threw some more beans into the coffeepot.

"Jed, can you think of a name for one of these little critters?" Thorpe asked.

Jed squatted down and looked at the puppies. "They're just about the cutest little things I ever saw. How about we call a female Sweetie Pie?"

Thorpe grinned at the big man. "That sounds fine."

"What did you come up with, Thorpe?"

Lily asked.

Thorpe pointed to the smallest male dog, and while he thought it was possible the dog wouldn't make it, he didn't voice that notion aloud. "Lucky seems fitting. These little guys were lucky that we happened by. I don't think their mama would have lasted much longer from the looks of her."

"I like that name," Lily agreed. The dogs weren't the only ones that were lucky. She felt very lucky that they had met up with Thorpe. She walked over and ladled some more food in the bowl and placed it in front of the dog. "We need a name for her."

"You name her," Thorpe said.

"I like her spirit," Lily said. "Think about how brave she was to have her puppies out here all alone."

"That sounds like a fine name for her. Spirit it is," Thorpe said.

Lily smiled. "I like that. What about the other male?"

Thorpe looked at Jedidiah. "Any thoughts?"

"I can't think of what suits him," Jed replied.

"What do you think about Henry?" Thorpe asked.

Everyone nodded their agreement. "That's an excellent name for him," Lily said.

It was easy to see that Lily had already adopted them in her mind, and Thorpe didn't want her to be disappointed if the puppies didn't survive. "Lily, they probably haven't been nourished like they needed."

Lily held up her hand as if to stop him. She sat beside the dog and stroked her head. "Don't say it. They will be fine and Spirit will be fine. They just need love and food."

"I just didn't want you to get too attached," Thorpe said.

She gave him a quivery smile. "It's too late. I'm already attached."

"I think Spirit and her puppies need to sleep inside for a while, so where do you want them?" Thorpe asked.

"Your wagon is the only one with enough room. Do you mind?"

"Nope. I'll carry her."

"Mr. Thorpe, I'll carry that dog. You need to rest your shoulder," Jedidiah said.

"Thanks, Jed." Once they settled the dogs in the wagon, Blue snuggled beside Spirit and put his paw on her back. "It looks like they have their protector for the night," Thorpe said.

Once Thorpe and Jed returned to the fire, Thorpe said, "Jedidiah and I will switch off watch tonight. You ladies can get a full night's rest."

"You're the one that needs rest," Lily replied.

"I'll wake you in a couple of hours," Thorpe said.

Lily knew he had no intention of waking her. "Thank you."

When Lily walked to her wagon, Jedidiah laughed. "Mr. Thorpe, I know you don't plan on waking her."

"You're right, Jed. She needs some rest. I've noticed she doesn't sleep much."

"Mark my words, she'll be back out here in a couple of hours. The few times I tried to let her sleep longer, she still relieved me right on time. She told me God woke her."

CHAPTER SIX

Nicholas Oliver Edmund Ainsworth was lying in bed watching Evelyn stalk around the room in a fury, snatching up her clothing from the floor that he'd helped remove the night before. The delicate items she angrily tossed through the air landed in the vicinity of her trunk. Evelyn was a beautiful woman and that was one of the reasons he had relented when she begged to return to England with him. He hadn't been keen on traveling to Wyoming, but when he met Evelyn, he thought his time in the West wouldn't be a total loss. Nick's father was insistent that he come to Wyoming to learn all he could about cattle ranching since he was interested in purchasing a spread near the Tremayne ranch. Nick relented, mostly because he was tired of listening to his father harp about him finding a wife.

From the first day he arrived at the ranch, Evelyn spent most of her time flirting with him. By the end of the first week of his stay, Nick took her up on what she was offering. Even though she'd told him she was betrothed to Turlow, it hadn't stopped her from sharing his bed. When it was time for him to return to England, she'd begged to go with him. Finally, he agreed, though he hadn't considered marriage. Evelyn simply assumed he wanted to marry her, but marriage was not in his plans. He intended to establish her in a nice home with a sizeable monthly stipend for expenses, and keep her as his mistress.

She'd been a pleasant diversion up to this point, but he was growing less and less tolerant of her outbursts, and tiring of her litany of complaints. No one ever dared to tell him what to do and he wasn't about to start with Evelyn. Any woman who tried that tactic on him soon learned he would do the exact opposite. Over the last few days he'd even considered leaving her behind when he sailed.

Evelyn finally realized he had no intention of marrying her and now she was angry with him. No, not angry. She was livid. She'd traveled across country in miserable conditions on the stagecoach, and now he still refused to get married. While he hadn't actually asked her to marry him, she was confident he would eventually do the honorable thing. She stalked around the room once more to see if she'd overlooked anything she wanted to pack. The only thing left was the robe she was wearing, so she shrugged it off her shoulders and threw it at her trunk.

Ainsworth's gaze followed her progress around the room. He wished she would calm down so he could coax her back to bed and get her mind off marriage. But when she walked past the bed, he jerked his head from the pillows, his eyes fixed on her stomach. This was the first time in weeks that he'd seen her body in the daylight. Now he understood the reason she'd insisted on dressing behind the screen in the mornings. He hadn't given it a lot of thought, considering how moody she had been, but she'd never been hesitant to be seen nude in the daylight before. Actually, he'd enjoyed her lack of modesty. From the start she'd used her body to seduce him and it worked like magic. How could he have missed her thickening waistline? "My dear, I thought you were simply gaining weight from all of the desserts you've indulged in over the last few weeks, but I think it is something else altogether."

If Evelyn hadn't been in such a rage, she

might have denied her condition. But she was tired of his excuses and dithering about. She wasn't about to go to England unmarried when she wouldn't be able to hide her condition much longer. She refused to be humiliated. She'd whined, cajoled, pleaded, but to no avail. She could not persuade him to change his mind. Evelyn wasn't accustomed to being denied something she wanted, and Ainsworth was the first man she couldn't seduce into submission.

When he first arrived at their ranch, his refined deportment and handsome face had certainly turned her head. He was titled, extremely wealthy, and she wanted to live the kind of life he could provide. She waited impatiently for him to make the overtures, but he was slow to respond. Making a rash decision to take matters in her own hands, she slipped into his room one night after her father retired for the evening. She'd shared his bed many nights thereafter. The one night she'd spent with Thorpe, Ainsworth was out on the range with her father. It proved to be the perfect opportunity to set her backup plan in motion after she'd learned she was pregnant.

Now that she was unable to persuade Ainsworth to marry, she thought she'd made a mistake by turning Thorpe away.

He was more handsome than Ainsworth to be sure, with his perfectly chiseled features and beautiful dark eyes. He was also a better lover than Nick, but Thorpe couldn't give her a castle filled with servants. Yet she knew Thorpe would have married her even if he'd found out she was pregnant with another man's child. When Thorpe found her at the hotel in Kansas City, all she had to do was say Ainsworth forced himself on her and he would have married her then and there. He would also have killed Ainsworth. Of that, she had no doubt.

Evelyn jerked her underclothes from the wardrobe and turned to face Ainsworth. "Unless you are blind, I'm sure I don't have to tell you anything!"

"Tell me, love, how long have you known?"

She wasn't going to tell him she'd known before they had left Wyoming. "A few weeks."

Ainsworth fluffed his pillows and leaned back against the headboard. He'd seen a pregnant woman's body before, and he thought she looked to be quite far along. "You need to see the doctor today so we will know the date."

Evelyn turned and glared at him. "I've already . . ." She'd almost slipped up. She couldn't reveal she'd seen a doctor. "It's not necessary. I'm just a few weeks along."

"Still, we want to make sure it is safe for you to travel," he said.

"I'll be fine. There is no need to see the doctor before we arrive in England. The only person we need to see is a pastor."

Approaching the side of the bed, Evelyn placed her hands on her hips. "Do you want to take me to England like this?" She pointed to her stomach. "Unmarried?"

"If you are just a few weeks . . ." He didn't finish, Evelyn turned her back on him and stomped to the dressing screen. "We need to be married," she shouted.

Ainsworth didn't reply. Perhaps her situation explained her moodiness since they'd left Wyoming. Now he was in a quandary. It wouldn't do for his father to see her in the family way and be unmarried. Considering how petulant and demanding she'd become, he shuddered at the thought of spending his life with her. The whole situation was becoming so tiresome that he was inclined to give her money for her trip back to Wyoming. Yet he knew she wouldn't go now that she was carrying his child. He wouldn't be surprised if she followed him to England and made a spectacle of herself. If his family found out about her and the heir she carried, they would insist he marry her for fear of scandal. He weighed his alternatives. Evelyn could obviously give him the heirs he needed and he would be envied for capturing such a beauty from America. It wasn't what he'd planned, but as long as he could maintain a mistress on the side, he could live with the arrangement.

His father and mother spent little time together and they'd been married for years. They didn't even share a bedroom, and aside from social engagements, the only time he saw them together was at the dinner table. It was common knowledge his father kept a mistress, and he was confident his mother was aware of the woman, though she would never admit that fact. Nick could see his future; it mirrored his father's. He'd simply find a woman less demanding for a mistress and he could spend more time with her than his wife. There was no question in his mind that he would need a welcoming reprieve from Evelyn's constant carping. "We will see the doctor, and then go to the church to have the pastor marry us before the stagecoach departs."

Behind the screen, Evelyn smiled to herself. She would insist on seeing the doctor alone and Nick would never know how far along she was. He didn't need to know she was pregnant before he arrived in Wyoming. If she'd known how quickly he would agree to marry once he learned of her condition, she would have told him weeks ago and saved herself so much agonizing over the situation. Well, no matter, they were going to be married today and she would finally have everything she wanted.

The doctor completed his examination and gave Evelyn privacy to dress before he spoke with her. "Mrs. Ainsworth, you are over four months along and everything looks as it should. And you will be sailing to England in a few weeks?"

Evelyn had led the doctor to believe that she was already married. "Yes, my husband and I are going back to his home. He was worried I might be too far along to leave."

He smiled at her. "I think you will be fine. No doubt his family will be pleased as punch to have a new grandchild on the way. Children are such a blessing."

A blessing. Indeed! This pregnancy had caused her nothing but problems from the moment she saw the doctor in Wyoming. She didn't particularly want children; they didn't fit into the life she wanted. She consoled herself knowing they would have nannies to care for the child in England, which would make things much easier for her.

The doctor helped Evelyn with her cape and wished her a safe journey. She'd told Nick she would meet him in time for tea at the hotel, but she was sidetracked when she saw a fetching hat in the window of a dress shop.

Nick was growing irritable by the time he finished his second cup of tea and there was still no sign of Evelyn. He walked to the window and looked down the street. His patience at an end, he grabbed his coat and hat and left the hotel. Entering the doctor's office, he didn't see anyone in the outer room. "Hello?"

The doctor walked from the back room. "May I help you?"

"Yes, I thought Evelyn . . ." Ainsworth started.

Hearing the gentleman's accent, the doctor said, "You must be Mr. Ainsworth." He extended his hand. "Congratulations are in order, sir."

Ainsworth politely, albeit impatiently, shook his hand. "Thank you. But where is Evelyn?"

"Oh, she left a few minutes ago."

"I didn't see her," Ainsworth said.

The doctor opened the door and looked

down the sidewalk. "I bet she stopped in the dress shop. Maybe she needed a few new dresses since she will need some larger clothing. The ladies tell me by the time they are four months along, their clothing seems ill suited to the changes in their girth."

"Four months?"

"As I told her, I think she is past four months." Seeing Ainsworth's stunned expression, the doctor thought he was concerned about traveling. He patted Ainsworth on the back. "Now, there's no reason for concern. As I told her, she is strong and healthy. Her condition should present no problems on your trip. Of course, sometimes seasickness is a problem, but that can happen to those not in the family way as well."

"Thank you, Doctor." Once he was out the door, he saw Evelyn leaving the dress shop carrying a hat box.

He caught up to her in a few strides and when he grabbed her arm, Evelyn jumped. "I told you I would meet you at the hotel."

"I didn't expect it would take you so long." He took the box from her and took hold of her elbow and ushered her to the hotel.

He was walking briskly, making it difficult for her to keep up with his long strides. "Why are you walking so fast?"

103

"We have some things to discuss and I'd rather do it in the privacy of the room."

Evelyn didn't like the sound of that, nor the set of his jaw. "What do we need to discuss? Did you see the pastor?"

He didn't respond. They entered the hotel and he practically dragged her up the stairs.

When they reached the door to their room, Evelyn jerked her arm from his grasp. "What is wrong with you?"

He opened the door and motioned for her to enter. Once she was inside, he slammed the door and dropped her hat box on the table. "I think you need to tell me the identity of the man who fathered your child. Was it that cowboy you were going to marry?"

She tried to remain calm as she walked to the mirror and pretended to be interested in arranging her hair. "What are you talking about?"

He walked to the sideboard and poured himself some brandy. "I saw the doctor. You can drop your act."

Met by silence, Nick drank the brandy before he slammed the glass down on the table. "He said you are four months along."

She had never seen Nick angry, but she wasn't going to allow him to intimidate her. Taking a deep breath, she turned to face him. "He's mistaken."

He stared at her stomach. He'd been ready to marry her when he thought he'd fathered the child, but now he was having second thoughts. "I don't think he is mistaken. Is it Turlow's?"

"No, it's yours! You know I was an innocent!"

"My dear, let's not lie to each other. You gave an adequate performance of playing the innocent, but it didn't quite hit the mark. Your ranch foreman hinted to me that the two of you had a relationship before I arrived in Wyoming." He had played poker with the ranch foreman and the man talked too much when he was drinking. He hadn't really believed the foreman at the time since Evelyn was with him every night. But she could have been in his bed, or Turlow's bed before he arrived in Wyoming.

She wasn't surprised Travis boasted about his conquest if he'd been drinking — he was known for his loose tongue — but she tried to act surprised. "He must have been drunk to say such a thing." She'd known all along the baby she was carrying was conceived with Travis.

Nick gripped her by the forearms and shook her. "Were you intimate with Turlow, too? Are you trying to pass his seed off on me?"

"It's your child!" She pulled away from him and walked to the door.

"You were engaged to him. Why should I believe you didn't give him the same thing you so freely gave me?"

"We need to see the preacher before the stagecoach gets here." She opened the door and walked out without saying another word.

Ainsworth was right behind her and before she reached the staircase, he clutched her arm in a bruising grip and turned her to face him. "I want the truth for once. Is this Turlow's child?"

"I've told you, I didn't share Thorpe's bed." She struggled to pull away from his grasp, but this time he didn't release her.

"I don't believe you, and I refuse to make a common trollop my wife."

Enraged, she balled her fist and started pummeling his chest. "How dare you! I'll have Thorpe kill you for slandering me!"

Shocked by her outbursts, Ainsworth released her arm and stepped back. When he stepped away, her fists struck air as she continued to strike him. She lost her balance, and when Ainsworth reached out to steady her, he was too late. She tumbled backward down the staircase.

CHAPTER SEVEN

Thorpe checked on the puppies several times through the night to make sure they were still breathing, and each time Blue let him know he was keeping watch over them. He'd just taken more food for Spirit in an effort to fatten her up quickly so she could nourish her pups. The temperature had dropped so he wrapped more blankets around the little family. When he jumped from the wagon, he almost knocked Lily over. She was bringing a full bowl of food for Spirit.

Thorpe smiled at her. "I guess we're thinking the same thing. I just fed her again. That gal can eat, but I think she already looks better."

"Why don't you get some rest? I'll take watch," she told him.

"I'll sleep by the fire. I sent Jed to sleep in his wagon about thirty minutes ago." Thorpe followed Lily back to the fire. When they sat down, he noticed the dark circles around her eyes.

"You didn't sleep well?"

"I couldn't go to sleep for some reason." She knew the reason, but she wasn't going to tell him. Everything about Thorpe enticed her and she couldn't sleep for thinking about him. On the surface he was a large, imposing cowboy, but after watching him with the puppies, it was obvious there was a softer side to him, which she found very appealing.

"I can stay awake if you want to try to sleep," he offered.

"No, really, I'm fine. Go to sleep."

Thorpe leaned back on his saddle and poured some whiskey in his cup. He held the bottle up to Lily and asked, "Want some? It'll help you sleep."

"No, thanks."

"Have you ever had whiskey?"

"No. Is your shoulder hurting?"

"Some." He didn't want to talk about his shoulder; something else was on his mind. "Why is Dora so concerned about the supplies? Don't you have enough?"

"I purchased what I could afford and it should be enough. Isabelle and Dora couldn't afford more. Perhaps she's worried we will run into bad weather and supplies may run low."

Thorpe thought she was being generous trying to make an excuse for Dora's behavior when none was warranted. He smiled at her. "Would you really leave her behind?"

Lily made a face at him. She'd spoken in anger and she felt bad about that, but she wouldn't allow Dora to be rude to Jedidiah, particularly after he'd defended her to those people on the wagon train.

Thorpe held up his hands. "Hey, you had me convinced."

She laughed. "Drink your whiskey and get some sleep."

Thorpe thought she was even more beautiful when she laughed. "Yes, ma'am." He finished his whiskey, leaned back on his saddle, and pulled his hat over his eyes. He didn't know if he could sleep with Lily near him, but he was tired and his shoulder ached, so he'd give it a try.

Another week passed and they hadn't run into any problems. Thorpe's only complaint was Dora. She tried to corner him whenever he was alone. He didn't know if she thought he needed a wife, but if that was what was on her mind, he needed to set her straight and pronto.

He'd spent the last few hours riding well

behind the wagons to make sure they were not being followed. Blue left Spirit and the puppies in the wagon and was walking beside him. The little puppies were doing well, and Thorpe no longer worried that they might not survive. Jedidiah had told him Miss Lily had a fast track to the Almighty, and he was beginning to believe the truth of that statement.

Seeing Blue lag behind, Thorpe looked back to see him staring into the trees some distance from the trail. He turned Smoke around and trotted back to Blue. "What is it, boy?" Thorpe gazed over the landscape, but saw nothing amiss. They waited a few minutes, listening for any sound out of place, and when Smoke's ears flicked forward, Thorpe instinctively knew they weren't alone. "Come on, boy, let's get to the wagons."

Thorpe pulled beside Lily's wagon and said, "Pull over near that rocky ledge ahead. We may have company."

Lily didn't question him; she wasted no time directing the team to the area that would offer protection from a rear attack. Once Lily pulled the wagon to a halt, she jumped down and ran to tell everyone what was going on. While Thorpe and Jedidiah unhitched the teams, Lily pulled out extra cartridges and passed them around. Once the animals were moved safely away, Thorpe told the women to go about their normal routine as if they were stopping for the night. He instructed them where to take cover if trouble came. It was dark by the time he got a fire going, and he knew he wouldn't be able to see anyone until they were on top of him. He would have to pay attention to any sounds not commonplace to the night. But he also knew Indians could sneak up on them before they heard a thing.

Lily walked to the fire and set the coffeepot on a rock. She saw Thorpe's Winchester resting beside a large boulder near the fire. "Indians?"

"That would be my guess. I don't want you out here in the open. Why don't you go back by the wagons?"

"You're here," she said simply.

Thorpe didn't have time to argue the point. He heard the horses before he saw them. "Get down!"

Jedidiah was at Thorpe's side within seconds, his rifle at the ready.

"Lily, go back by the wagons," Thorpe instructed. "Jed, get behind that rock."

Lily ignored him and kneeled down behind a boulder. "I'm fine right here."

Thorpe kneeled down next to her and

aimed his rifle. "You're one hardheaded woman, Miss Lily." He glanced behind him to make sure Dora and Isabelle were out of sight. The only thing he could see were the barrels of their pistols sticking out from the interior of the wagon. "See there. They do what they are told."

She smiled at him. "They can't shoot as accurately as me."

Thorpe didn't respond. The first arrow zoomed over Lily's head and he started firing. Seeing that arrow so close to her put his heart in his throat, and he was thankful he could still react with precision. As he was firing, a quick count told him there were about a dozen braves, and just as quickly he shot three off their horses. Lily easily equaled his count, and Thorpe admired her for her calm in the midst of total chaos. He knew how difficult it was to stay focused with men trying to kill you. Jedidiah wounded one brave and he fell from the saddle, but another brave pulled him on his horse and they rode away with the remaining braves. Thorpe thought they would wait a few hours before they came back to collect their dead. He wasn't inclined to kill them all, but he hadn't started this fight. And he knew if he didn't kill them, they wouldn't hesitate to take the women if they got the upper hand. "We can wait for them to come back tonight, or we can pack up and keep on moving for a few more hours."

"Do you think they will bring more braves back with them?" Lily asked.

"It's possible. They've lost so many, they may just give it up. I say we should move on for a few hours."

Lily's instincts told her Thorpe was right. "Let's go."

It was past midnight before they stopped for the night. Thorpe could tell the women were exhausted and their nerves were on edge. Every little noise made them jump. He brought the puppies from the wagon, hoping they would take their mind off of the Indians for a while. His plan worked until the puppies were ready to go to sleep and the women were still wound tight.

"Are you ladies about ready to retire?" Thorpe asked.

"Not yet," Isabelle responded.

"Do you think those braves will come back?" Dora asked.

Thorpe wanted them to relax, but he didn't want them to be caught off guard so he wasn't sure how to respond. "I think they've lost enough men, but it won't hurt to be prepared."

"And Blue will be alert," Lily added.

"Why don't you tell us about your ranch, Thorpe?" Isabelle suggested.

Thorpe was tired, but he understood what they were feeling, so he indulged them. "I drove cattle up from Texas some years ago and started my ranch."

"Was Texas your home?" Dora asked.

"Yes. When my father died I decided to go west."

"You don't have any brothers or sisters?" Isabelle asked.

Thorpe thought about John daily, but he didn't talk about him often; it was too painful a memory. "My younger brother, John, died when he was fourteen."

Lily could hear the change in Thorpe's voice when he spoke of his brother. "What about your mother?"

"She died a few years before my pa."

"I'm sorry." She wondered if he felt the same loneliness she felt with her family gone.

"How can you be away from the ranch so long?" Isabelle asked.

"I have reliable men who have been with me from the start."

"You must have a lot of land," Isabelle said.

"Yes, ma'am. Wyoming is a big place."

"What's the name of your ranch?" Lily asked.

"Dove Creek."

Lily remembered the way he looked at her grandfather's dove carving. "That's beautiful. Did you name the ranch?"

"Yes, ma'am. My mother was partial to doves, particularly white doves, so that's how the name came about."

Lily wondered if he thought doves were symbols of love. "Do you see many doves in that part of the country?"

"People say they rarely saw so many doves until I named my ranch. Now we see them all of the time, but we don't see white doves often."

"Don't you get lonely on that big ranch all by yourself? Or do you have a wife?" Dora asked.

"No wife. The ranch keeps me busy. As I said, I have men who work for me, so there's always plenty of people around." The nights did get lonely, and he couldn't deny that was part of the reason he'd ask Evelyn to marry. At the time, he'd thought it would be nice to have a soft warm body next to him at night. Thanks to Evelyn, he'd decided he would be better off spending his nights alone.

"Are there many females in your town?"

Dora asked.

Thorpe knew where she was going with this line of questioning. "I expect there are as many as in most towns."

"Is there a saloon?" Dora asked.

"Yeah. The town is not as large as some, but we have everything we need. It's growing now with the railroad."

"Do you visit the saloon?" Dora asked.

"Yeah, we go to play poker once or twice a month."

Dora smiled at him. If he was like most men, she expected he did more than play poker. If she had to resort to working at a saloon, she wouldn't object to seeing him a few times a month. And a growing town meant more men, and she was sure there would be many men like Thorpe who had been alone too long. "Are the men that work for you married?"

"Three of them have wives and children. Their homes are on the ranch."

"Is it beautiful in Wyoming at Christmastime?" Lily asked.

"We always have snow, so it's quiet and peaceful." Generally, he didn't look forward to snow as it made it difficult to care for the animals, but having a snowy Christmas was an exception. He loved the silence on the range on Christmas night. But that first

117

Christmas had been difficult for him. He felt the loss of his family more than ever. He'd kept busy all day to take his mind off his family and the sadness he felt without them. When his work was finished, he didn't want to return to an empty house, so he rode Smoke around the ranch. Before he called it a night, he decided to ride to the entryway of his ranch to see how his new log gate looked in the falling snow. Just a few months earlier he'd installed the massive lodgepole pine posts, and had the blacksmith forge the letters for *Dove Creek Ranch* that were mounted on the connecting rail. Seeing the sign that Christmas night made the ranch feel more like home. He'd missed Texas, but he knew it had more to do with his family than the place. He reined in at the entryway and stared at the gate, allowing the memories of the last Christmas with his family to fill his mind. The last Christmas present he'd given his mother was a brooch that had two white doves designed in little mosaic tiles against a midnight sky. He'd worked any job he could find for six months to earn the money to buy that small piece of jewelry. It was worth it though. His mother had loved that brooch, and she wore it every day until the day she died. He'd even pinned it to her dress the day he and his father buried her under the large oak tree on their land. His mother would have loved the name of his ranch.

He didn't know how long he'd sat there that night, reminiscing, when he saw something extraordinary. At first, he thought he'd fallen asleep and was dreaming, but Smoke reacted, so he knew he was fully awake. He'd never experienced anything like it, and what he saw gave him a new perspective on life. After that Christmas night, he knew he wasn't alone. He believed he was in the presence of his family and his Creator. He'd never shared what happened that night with anyone. He figured his men would think he'd done too much celebrating. Every Christmas since, he'd ride to the entryway late at night and wait for his Christmas miracle. "When I'm out on the range, it seems like even the animals know it is a special night."

Lily understood what he meant. She'd often thought Christmas night was the perfect night to go for a ride on Blaze and enjoy the peacefulness. "It will be nice to see snow for Christmas," Lily said. "We don't see that often in Texas."

"Having a new little baby for Christmas will be a blessing," Jedidiah said.

"You think everything is a blessing," Dora said.

"Miss Dora, life is a blessing. A new baby at Christmas is special."

"My life has been anything but a blessing," Dora commented.

"You were blessed to meet up with Miss Lily," Jedidiah reminded her.

"Jedidiah, I'm tired of your preaching," Dora said.

"Jed wasn't preaching, and you might do well to hear what he has to say. Sometimes it's best to remember the things you have to be thankful for," Isabelle said.

"He's right. A new baby is a blessing indeed," Lily said. In many ways she was envious of Isabelle. To plan a future with a man she loved and to have his children had to be a thrilling prospect, no matter the hardships at the moment.

"I guess all of you have more to be thankful for than I do," Dora said.

Lily was tired of hearing Dora complain, so she redirected the conversation. "Thorpe, how do you celebrate Christmas at Dove Creek?"

"I'm afraid holidays on a ranch aren't always exciting because the work goes on. A few days before Christmas, I cut a tree, and the wives of the ranch hands and their children add the little decorations. It looks real fine. On Christmas Day, the women come to the house to cook a big dinner while we're out working. The house smells real nice when we come in. I swear you can smell the pies they bake a mile away." Thorpe did enjoy coming home to the mouthwatering aromas of a home-cooked dinner, and his house filled with joyful people.

Lily thought Thorpe's description of Christmas on his ranch sounded lovely. She envisioned him all bundled up, dragging a tree behind his horse in the snow. He'd said he didn't have a wife, but she wondered if he had a woman who shared those special moments.

"Maybe we can all celebrate Christmas together at the fort," Isabelle said.

"That would be nice," Lily said. She'd celebrated last Christmas alone. While she was thankful she had him, she'd missed her family desperately. Before she became emotional thinking of her family, she stood and said, "Right now, I think it's time we got settled for the night."

"Lily, I will stay up if you and Isabelle want to go to bed." Dora thought Thorpe was going to be the one taking the first watch and she wanted to spend some time alone with him.

That was a first, Lily thought. Dora never offered to take a watch before. She knew it was because she thought Thorpe was taking first watch tonight. "Thanks, Dora. I'm sure Jed will appreciate the company." Earlier, Jed told her he would take the first watch. He thought Thorpe needed some rest since he'd been up most of the night before.

Thorpe had planned to tell Jed he'd take first watch, but after Dora's offer he was glad he hadn't said anything. He decided to go to the wagon. "Jed, wake me in a couple of hours."

"Mr. Thorpe, why don't you rest four hours? I'll be fine right here," Jed suggested.

"Thanks, but two hours will do. I'm used to this." Thorpe was accustomed to sleeping with one eye open, and tonight would be no different. While he trusted Jed to stay awake, he'd spent a lot of years taking care of business himself. If the braves came back with a greater force, Jed might be overpowered quickly.

Lily pulled the warm water from the fire. "I'll clean your wound and put on a fresh bandage before you go to sleep."

Once they were in the wagon and Thorpe had removed his shirt, he asked, "Don't you think I can leave the bandage off now?"

"I think we should keep it on for just a few more days." Lily unwrapped the bandage and started washing the back of his shoulder.

"Miss Lily, I'm beginning to think you just like the look of me without my shirt," Thorpe said lightly. Even though he'd sworn off women, there was still a part of him that wanted to know if Lily found him attractive. There was no question Dora was interested, but Lily wasn't Dora. It occurred to him that Lily might have a special beau in her life waiting for her.

Any woman would like the look of him, but Lily wasn't about to say her thoughts aloud. Everything about Thorpe was beautiful; even his skin was a lovely golden brown. "I'm not the one you need to worry about."

He turned to look at her, and when their eyes met, he arched his brow. "You mean Dora? Yeah, I had the feeling she'd like to know me better."

So he had noticed the way Dora flirted with him. Lily waited to see if he would say whether he would like to know Dora better, but he didn't comment further. Dora was experienced with men, an area where she was seriously lacking. She had been kissed a few times and she couldn't say the experience thrilled her. But she wasn't so ignorant that she'd missed the comment Thorpe made about going to the saloon on occasion. She had heard what went on in some of those places, and even Dora told her that she provided services for lonely men. Perhaps Thorpe enjoyed the services of women like Dora. "Dora is a lovely woman."

"She's pretty enough. Is her name really Dora Love, or is that her saloon name?"

"It's the name she gave me." Moving in front of him, Lily dried his shoulder. She wondered what Dora would do if she was alone with Thorpe in the wagon. She figured there must be many men that preferred women as experienced as Dora.

Thorpe almost told her he could wash his shoulder, but he liked the way her hands felt on his skin. Then there was the fact that he just liked to watch her expressions as she concentrated on her task. Dora was a pretty woman, but Miss Lily was an uncommon beauty, and she was an innocent. She was a woman no man would ever forget. Of course, at one time he'd thought Evelyn was an innocent. He couldn't forget appearances could be deceiving. Evelyn was proof of that fact.

Two hours later, Lily jumped out of her wagon, ready to take the second watch, and she saw Dora leaving Thorpe's wagon. She guessed that answered her question whether Thorpe was interested in Dora.

"Jed, go on to bed," she said when she reached the fire.

"I was going to wait on Mr. Thorpe."

Lily watched Dora walk to her wagon. "I'm sure he'll be along. I'll be fine."

"Yes, ma'am." Jed looked in the direction of Lily's gaze. "That ain't what you're thinking."

"I'm not thinking anything. Now go get some rest. You've been up too long." Lily didn't have to do much thinking about the situation. Dora let Thorpe know she was interested, and Thorpe wasted no time responding.

CHAPTER EIGHT

A week after the encounter with the Indians, Thorpe saw a thin stream of smoke rising above a clump of trees about a mile ahead of the wagons. Even though the Indians hadn't made another appearance, he couldn't ignore the possibility they might be waiting for them. On the other hand, if it wasn't the Indians, once they saw the smoke, he figured they'd be sniffing around soon enough. He rode back to Lily's wagon and it didn't surprise him that she'd already spotted the smoke. "I'll circle in behind the area from the ridge above and see what's going on."

"I'll ride with you."

"I think you should stay with the others in case it's those braves. You will be needed here if they are trying to separate us. I'll take Blue with me."

Lily didn't argue with his reasoning. She'd quickly learned that Thorpe was a savvy trail man and he didn't take unnecessary risks. Still, she didn't want him riding into a dangerous situation alone. Other than a few polite words here and there, it was the first interaction they'd had since the night she saw Dora leaving his wagon. It didn't make sense to her why it upset her so much to think of the two of them together, but it did. After that night, she'd arranged to take watch with Jed, and Dora had made a point of joining Thorpe on his watch.

Thorpe made his way to the ridge and tried to remain out of sight as he rode the crest until he was directly above the area where he could still see the smoke. From his vantage point he saw a small campfire, but little else. He dismounted and tied his horse to a tree and quietly made his way down the slope. With his Colt drawn, he crouched behind a rock with Blue at his side. Scanning the campsite below, he saw one man sitting with his back against a boulder near the fire. He couldn't actually see the man, only his hat. He kept his eyes focused on the hat for a few minutes and saw no movement. He smelled a trap. "Blue, I don't like the looks of this."

"Howdy. Come on into camp," a voice said from below.

Thorpe cocked his Colt, and Blue scampered away through the dense brush.

"I know you're alone," the man said.

Thorpe knew the voice wasn't coming from the man sitting behind that rock, if there was a man there. "How do you know I'm alone?" The words barely left his mouth when he saw movement near a tree a few feet from the fire. A hand holding a pair of field glasses came into view.

"These told me you were alone. I saw the three wagons and a couple of women so I didn't figure you were the killers coming back." The man walked from behind the tree with his own pistol cocked. "Name's Stone Justice and I'm a U.S. Marshal." He pulled his coat to the side so Thorpe could see the star on his shirt.

"Thorpe Turlow." He holstered his pistol and walked toward him. He inclined his head as if he wanted the marshal to look behind him. "Meet my partner."

Stone smiled as if he thought Thorpe was bluffing about a partner. Then he heard the low growl behind him.

"That's Blue."

Stone turned slowly to see the large wolf standing directly behind him. "I thought you were bluffing. Tell me he's friendly."

"That depends. He's friendly enough with me. Depending on your answers, he might or might not be friendly with you."

Stone glanced back at the large wolf baring his sharp teeth. "What are the questions?"

"What are you doing out here without horses?"

"I was with two other marshals and we were taking our prisoner" — he pointed to the man on the ground — "Bryce Harlow, to Fort Smith to stand trial in Judge Parker's court. We were ambushed by Harlow's gang a few days ago. My partners were killed, and a bullet grazed my head, but I was able to grab Harlow and pulled him in front of me so they couldn't finish me off. They hightailed it out of there when they saw Indians riding our way. They took our horses, and after I buried my friends, we started walking. The only thing I was able to take was my saddle, and I had darn few provisions in my saddlebags."

"He's lying, mister. I'm the marshal and he got the best of me," the man on the ground said.

Thorpe moved closer and studied both men. The man calling himself Stone Justice was a big man, near his height, with a lean and rugged appearance. Even though Thorpe judged him to be just a few years older than him, right now he looked like he'd tangled with an angry grizzly and lost. Something about his countenance told Thorpe he was indeed the marshal, but he'd withhold judgment until he saw how Blue acted. He turned his attention on Harlow, and while he had an affable smile plastered on his face, Thorpe didn't like the looks of him. His gut told him he was the criminal. He glanced back to Justice and asked, "What'd he do?"

"He's part of the Black Hills gang. They robbed several stagecoaches, and they killed three people on the last one they robbed."

"Mister, you need to listen to me. I'm telling you I'm the marshal and he's lying."

Ignoring Harlow's declaration, Thorpe noticed Stone limping to the fire. "Blisters?"

"Yeah, it's been a long time since I had to hoof it anywhere carrying my saddle."

"We're headed to Wyoming and you're welcome to travel with us. It's too late to turn around now to go back and we can't spare two horses to give you. We've had a couple of run-ins with Indians, so you wouldn't be safe alone."

"Wyoming is fine by me. I'm not sure I can even ride right now until my feet heal. I just need to get to a town so I can put Harlow in jail, send a telegraph, get provisions, and go after those killers. I'm grateful you happened by, but why are you folks on the trail this late in the year?"

"Couldn't be helped," Thorpe replied. "Just stay put and we'll bring the wagons to make camp here tonight."

"Sounds good to me. I won't even complain about riding in a wagon."

Thorpe chuckled. He figured the marshal didn't like being in a wagon any more than he did. "You'll have time to rest up, that's for sure." Thorpe rode back to the wagons and told the group about the marshal and his prisoner.

"How do you know for sure which one is the marshal if the other man says he is lying?" Dora asked.

"Justice seemed like a man accustomed to authority. But I figured I'd keep a close eye on both of them until we're positive."

"I know how we will be able tell who is lying," Lily said.

Thorpe smiled at her. "Blue. That's what I was thinking."

When they reached the men, Thorpe made the introductions.

"I think I've died and gone to heaven," Bryce Harlow said, eyeing Lily before moving on to admire Dora and Isabelle.

"Mind your manners, Harlow," Stone

warned in a no-nonsense tone.

Thorpe glared at Harlow. He didn't like the way he was leering at Lily. "Mister, you show respect to these ladies or I'll tie you behind my horse and you can walk all the way to Wyoming."

"That was a compliment." Harlow grinned at the women. "Ladies, I tried to tell your man here that he's believing the wrong man. I'm the marshal."

The women stared at Harlow. He was tall and trim, with coal black hair and a thick mustache, and the most unusual light gray eyes. His easy smile and flirtatious manner said he was a man confident in his appeal to women.

Jed gave Harlow a hard look. "And maybe you are just full of the devil."

"Your name is Justice and you're a law-man?" Isabelle commented to Stone.

"Yes, ma'am, and you're not the first to make note of that."

"I'm sorry about the other marshals," Lily told him.

"I just buried two of my friends back there a few days ago." He pointed toward terrain they would be traveling. "I rode with Riff Carson for five years and he was a fine man. Joe Martin was a man you could always count on to do the right thing. I'll track

132

those hombres to Hades for killing them, and I won't have to take them back to Fort Smith to be tried for murder. I can hang them as horse thieves. That'll be faster."

"Did they have wives and children?" Lily asked.

"No, ma'am. Like me, they understood this is no life for a family man."

"Sit down, Mr. Justice. We'll get some coffee going and have supper ready soon," Lily said.

The women walked back to the wagons and Thorpe approached Stone to speak privately. "Are we going to have trouble from Harlow?"

"It's possible. He's a mouthy son-of-a-buck."

"Do you expect his partners to come back for him?" Thorpe asked.

"To tell you the truth, I thought they would come back before now. Maybe the Indians got them. I can't say for sure I'm not endangering you folks."

"I've considered that," Thorpe replied.

"At least you'll have an extra gun hand now. How come you folks don't have more guns with you?"

"I wasn't traveling with them when they first started out. Indians were chasing me, and Lily came to help me out."

"Lily?" Stone thought he didn't hear him right.

"Yeah, she's one heck of a shot."

Stone's gaze found Lily working at the back of a wagon. "Who would expect someone who looks like her being skilled with a gun? I guess what my pa said about looks being deceiving fits in this situation."

Thorpe saw the direction of his eyes. "She's a woman to be reckoned with, that's for sure."

"What in holy heaven were they doing traveling alone?" Stone couldn't believe three beautiful women and one man would have taken out across country without considerably more firepower.

"They need to get to Fort Steele by Christmas," Thorpe told him.

"Why do they need to get there by Christmas?"

Thorpe didn't want to betray a confidence. "They have personal reasons."

"Thank the Good Lord you happened on the scene to help them out. Why were you out here?"

"I have a ranch in Wyoming and I was going home." Thorpe figured it was no one's business why he'd traveled to Missouri, so he didn't explain.

Lily returned with the coffeepot, and

when she glanced Stone's way, she saw the wound on his forehead when he removed his hat. "Let me have a look at that."

"It's just a scratch, nothing serious," Stone said.

"A scratch can get infected. It needs to be cleaned. I'll get some soap."

Stone stared after her as she walked to the wagon. "She's the prettiest woman I've ever laid eyes on."

"There aren't many like her; that's for sure."

"Is she spoken for?" Stone surprised himself asking that question, but it wasn't every day he met a woman as beautiful as Lily.

"I've not asked." Thorpe had asked if she was married, but he hadn't asked Lily if she had someone special waiting for her.

"Too bad I'm never in one place long enough to settle down. All three of these women are real pretty. You married?"

"No."

"And you haven't tried to get to know that little lady any better? Or are you interested in another one?"

"Nope. I'm not looking for a wife."

"I'm not either, but looking at these ladies might make me change my mind."

"Well, these women are the marrying

kind." Even though he might be stretching that statement considering Dora's past, he thought he would set Stone straight on that score. "Unless you have matrimony on your mind, you'll have to steer clear."

Stone didn't reply because Lily returned with Dora and Isabelle right behind her carrying pans to place over the fire.

"No doctor that ever tended me was as pretty as you," Stone commented when Lily kneeled beside him to take care of his wound.

Lily blushed, but she didn't respond. She pushed his dark blond hair from his forehead and scrubbed his wound. "This doesn't look bad now that it's clean."

Thorpe wasn't sure why it irritated him to see Lily tending Stone, but it did. He walked to the wagon to pull out a bottle of whiskey from his supplies. He thought Stone could use a stiff drink after what he'd been through. Once he returned to the fire, he filled two tin cups to the brim and offered one to Stone.

"Thanks. I appreciate this," Stone said.

"Jed, how about you?" Thorpe asked.

"No, sir. I don't believe I do."

"How about me? I could sure use some whiskey," Harlow said.

"No," Stone said.

"You're gonna have to untie me so I can eat dinner. Of course Lily could feed me and I wouldn't mind."

"I told you once to mind your manners. Unless you want a bandana tied around your mouth, you best heed my warning," Stone said.

Thorpe settled himself near Harlow and leaned back on his saddle. Blue and Spirit nestled beside him. He ran his hand along Spirit's back. "You're putting on some weight, girl."

"Mr. Thorpe, my dear mother always said you should never say that to a lady," Jed teased.

Thorpe laughed. "Sound advice."

Lily was placing some corn bread over the fire and heard Thorpe's comment. "She is looking much better. Her eyes have life back in them."

"And she looks real pretty since Mr. Thorpe brushed the mud off of her," Jed said.

Isabelle explained to Stone how they came to find the dog and the puppies.

"Seems like you folks have picked up a lot strays on your journey."

Lily didn't comment, but she wondered why Stone and Harlow had been sent to them. Her grandfather always told her people came into one's life for a reason. He'd said all you needed to do was wait and the reason would be revealed. Just like Thorpe had come into her life to help her on this journey, she was certain these new strangers had arrived for a reason.

When their dinner was ready and the ladies were filling the plates, Stone untied Harlow's hands. "Don't push your luck with me," he warned.

Lily passed out the plates of food, and when she handed a plate to Harlow he latched on to her wrists. "Why don't you sit down by me, honey? It's been a long time since I had a pretty gal beside me."

Before Thorpe got to his feet, Blue leaped to Lily's side and clamped down on Harlow's hand, not hard enough to break skin, but with enough force to let Harlow know he'd better not move. Thorpe was beside Blue in an instant, ready to haul Harlow to his feet and beat him senseless.

Lily shook her head at Thorpe. "One word from me and Blue will rip your arm from your shoulder, Mr. Harlow."

Harlow's eyes shifted from Blue to Thorpe. He didn't like what he saw in either set of eyes. He opened his fingers, releasing Lily's wrist.

Blue maintained his hold until Lily said,

"No." Blue opened his mouth and Harlow jerked his arm away from Blue's sharp fangs.

Blue listened to Lily and walked away from Harlow, but Thorpe wasn't so inclined. He grabbed Harlow by the shirt, jerking him off the ground. "There won't be another warning. I won't be like Blue and let you go." When Thorpe released his shirt, Harlow dropped back to the ground. It was hard to say if he was intimidated by Thorpe because he was laughing, but the way Thorpe looked at it, he'd given him fair warning.

Thorpe sat back down and listened while the women peppered Stone with questions, much like they had done to him. He noticed Dora sat beside Stone, and he wasn't going to complain if she redirected her attention on the marshal. Thorpe recalled the first night she'd come to his wagon under the pretense of waking him for his watch, she'd made it clear she was interested in getting to know him better. He told her in no uncertain terms that he wasn't interested in what she was offering. But she hadn't given up, and anytime he was in the wagon alone, she made it a point to invite herself inside. It also hadn't escaped his notice that Lily wasn't taking watch with him any longer. He wondered if Dora told Lily that she was interested in him and that was the reason she'd avoided him like the plague. Perhaps Lily thought he had a mutual interest in Dora. He found himself missing his nightly conversations with Lily. Now that his shoulder had healed nicely, he rarely had a few minutes alone with her. Just as he was formulating a plan to get Lily alone so they could talk, he heard her say she'd take first watch and he saw his opportunity. "I'll stay up with Lily."

"I can take a watch," Stone offered.

"You rest up tonight, I'll take second," Jed said.

"Jed's right. You need a good night's sleep," Thorpe told him. "We'll see how you are doing tomorrow."

Lily didn't comment, but she was surprised Thorpe offered to stay with her. She'd thought he'd been trying to spend time with Dora.

"Well, you're probably right. Since I've eaten so much I'd probably fall asleep in five minutes. I'll make sure you folks are reimbursed for our food when we get to the first town that has a telegraph. If it makes you feel any better, I'm mighty handy with a rifle, so I can shoot what we need."

"Lily is very handy with a rifle," Isabelle said.

"Thorpe told me she is an excellent shot." Stone directed his gaze on Lily. "I see you use a Spencer repeater."

"Yes, my grandfather gave it to me," Lily replied.

"It's an unusual woman who is handy with a gun."

Thorpe thought Stone was showing Lily too much attention, so he asked, "How many men bushwhacked you?"

"Ten. I winged one, but I don't know if I killed him. Joe Martin killed one before he was shot dead."

"What did they do?" Dora asked.

"They held up a stagecoach and killed three passengers. That's just the latest in a long line of robberies they've committed."

"That's terrible," Lily said.

"Yeah. They killed a woman and little girl on the stagecoach."

"I keep telling you people that I'm the marshal. I never killed anybody," Harlow said.

Thorpe glared at Harlow. It was evident the man was bad news, and Thorpe didn't like having him around the women. Knowing the crimes these killers committed worried him. The list of dangers they might face on the way to Wyoming was growing by the day. He hoped Harlow's gang stayed well ahead of them. "Stone, you can sleep in the wagon where I sleep."

"Thanks, but I don't mind sleeping by the fire."

"You can do that once you've rested up." Thorpe wanted time to speak to Lily alone to see if she had any misgivings about Stone and Harlow traveling with them. At least that's what he told himself was the only reason he wanted to talk to her.

"What about me?" Harlow asked. "One of you ladies want to share your wagon?"

"I'll tie you to the wagon wheel," Stone replied.

"It's too cold to sleep on the ground," Harlow retorted.

Stone stood and scowled at Harlow. "That lady and that little girl are cold in their graves. Those two marshals are cold in their graves. You'll get no sympathy from me."

Before Stone walked away, Lily handed him two blankets.

"I know you think I'm a hard man, ma'am. And maybe I am. But he killed a woman and her little girl. The woman's husband showed me a painting of them. The little girl was the sweetest little thing I ever saw. The locket the killer pulled from the woman's neck had a miniature of her husband and her little girl inside. The stagecoach

142

driver described Harlow as the one that pulled the trigger. Frankly, I don't give a hoot if he freezes to death out here."

Lily could tell the marshal was hurting. She couldn't imagine hunting down a man that had killed a little girl and her mother. She put her hand on his arm. "I don't think you are a hard man, Mr. Justice. I think you've seen things that I haven't. You do what you want with ~~that~~ those blankets."

They looked at each other for a long time. Stone wondered if she realized just how beautiful she was. He didn't think her outward beauty told half the story of the woman she was. He wanted to tell her, but he'd forgotten how to say sweet words to a lady.

"The puppies are in the wagon, but I can move them," Lily finally said.

"They won't bother me. It'll be nice to see some pups." After some of the things he'd seen recently, Stone thought it would do his soul good just to see little newborn critters. He'd been on the trail of those killers for months, and it'd been a long time since he enjoyed the simpler things in life that other people took for granted. Dealing with killers was taking a toll on him, and he knew he'd developed a hard edge. In his line of work he rarely had time to spend with real ladies. Under the circumstances, he thought meeting up with these folks was just what he needed.

CHAPTER NINE

Riding ahead of the wagons, Thorpe found two graves and he knew they were the graves of the two marshals. Not far from the graves he found two saddles that were still beside the burned-out fire pit. He could clearly see the hoofprints leading away from the area. Stone said he thought one man in the gang was killed, but he didn't see a body.

When the wagons reined in at the gravesite, Lily and Stone jumped down to join Thorpe.

After inspecting the graves, Stone said, "Looks like the rocks are doing the job."

"You did a fine job here," Thorpe replied.

"Let's put the saddles in the wagon." Thorpe turned to grab a saddle, but he stopped when he saw Lily kneel before the graves. He watched as she bowed her head in prayer. Both he and Stone removed their hats and remained silent until they heard her softly whisper, "Amen."

"Thank you, ma'am. That means a lot to me. And I know Riff and Joe would be real pleased to know someone prayed for their eternal souls." Stone grabbed the other saddle and carried it to the wagon.

Thorpe settled his hat on his head and walked with Lily back to the wagon. "The weather has been fairly warm, so I thought we'd stop early today closer to the river so we can all have baths."

"That would be wonderful," Lily said.

"It'll be a mite frosty in the river, but we'll heat the water for you ladies. I know you're hauling that large tub around for some reason," Thorpe teased. He thought it was interesting that the women had no furniture, but they had brought that big tub with them.

"Right now I wouldn't mind jumping in the river even if it is cold," Lily replied.

Like Lily, Dora and Isabelle agreed a bath would be delightful under any conditions.

"I've yet to meet a woman that didn't like a nice long bath," Stone commented.

"I think the men get as much enjoyment out of it as we do," Dora added. In the past she'd had many men who paid good money just to watch her bathe.

Stone chuckled at Dora's comment. "I expect you are right about that."

146

Thorpe knew Dora was right. He didn't often have the pleasure of seeing a woman bathe, but he would have to say it would be high on his list of pleasurable pastimes. He didn't have long to dwell on that thought because Harlow spoke up.

"One of you ladies can give me a bath like they do in those bathhouses in Deadwood."

Harlow was sitting beside Jed in the wagon and Jed pushed him off the seat and Harlow hit the ground hard. "Mr. Thorpe told you to mind your manners, and if you want to ride instead of walk, you'd best listen to him."

Thorpe smiled at Jed. "You saved me the trouble."

Having found a suitable place for the night near the river, Thorpe held true to his promise of a warm bath for the ladies. Along with Jed, they heated water and carried it to the wagon to fill the tub. When one woman finished with her bath, they repeated the process.

The men took turns bathing in the river so two men would be near the women at camp at all times.

Stone stood by the fire after he came out of the river. "I'm glad you got that fire going before I left. That water is too cold to stay in long."

"But we'll all smell a whole lot better," Jed said.

When Jed returned, Thorpe walked to the river, stripped down, and jumped in. Stone was right when he said he wouldn't stay in the water long. It was freezing, so he quickly scrubbed his body, washed his hair, and dunked under long enough to get the soap out. He hurried to the bank and grabbed his towel. He'd just pulled his pants on when Dora walked toward him.

"I thought I would bring you a towel."

He pulled his towel from his shoulder. "I brought one with me." He wondered if she'd taken a towel to Stone during his bath.

Dora moved closer and hooked her arms around his neck. "We have some time before we need to get back. We won't be missed."

Thorpe pulled her arms from his neck. "I told Harlow to treat you like a lady. Now I expect you to act like one."

"You know I worked in a saloon," she said.

"Yeah, I know, but Stone and Harlow don't. They won't unless you tell them."

"You can't tell me you don't find me pretty." Dora was convinced men wanted her; she'd never had one say *no.* More men than she could count had told her she was pretty.

"You're pretty, but that still doesn't mean I'm interested."

"Why not? Is there someone at home?"

Thorpe thought of his almost marriage to Evelyn, and that was the last thing he wanted to think about. "Not anymore."

"Then what's the harm?"

He was losing his patience. He'd made an effort to be polite about his lack of interest, but she wouldn't take no for an answer. She obviously wasn't hearing him when he tried to politely refuse her attentions. Before he spoke more bluntly, Blue startled him when he nosed through the brush and walked to the bank. When Blue looked down the bank he lowered his head and growled low. Thorpe pushed Dora to the brush. "Quiet." Quickly strapping his holster around his waist, he drew his Colt, crouched low, and made his way to the bank next to Blue. He heard the voices before he saw the men. He put his hand on Blue's back. "Shhh. I see them, boy." He counted nine men watering their horses. He turned to Dora as he slowly backed from the bank. "Get back to camp." He threaded his fingers in Blue's fur. "Come on, boy."

Lily saw Dora walk from the trees and before she could ask her what she was doing wandering off by herself, a shirtless

Thorpe appeared behind her with Blue.

"Jed, douse that fire," Thorpe whispered.

Hearing Thorpe's serious tone, Lily and Isabelle quickly pulled the pans holding their dinner away from the fire so Jed could kick dirt into the flames.

"Stone, nine men are just upriver." He glanced at the women to see if they were carrying their pistols. "Get your guns and take cover. Lily, take Blue to the wagon with Spirit and tell him to stay put."

Stone grabbed his rifle. "It has to be the Black Hills gang."

"I don't think they know we're here. At least not at the moment," Thorpe said. "Let's get the animals behind the wagons."

Overhearing the conversation between Stone and Thorpe, Harlow let out a loud yell. "I knew the boys wouldn't leave me behind."

Thorpe stalked to Harlow and leaned over and untied his hands.

"What in the Sam Hill are you doing?" Stone asked.

"Untying him."

"Why?"

"Because I can't knock the meanness out of a defenseless man." With that said, Thorpe pulled Harlow to his feet.

Harlow drew his arm back ready to throw

a punch at Thorpe. Thorpe blocked his arm and landed his massive fist in Harlow's jaw, knocking him to the ground.

Seeing Harlow was unresponsive after one blow, Stone dragged him back to the wagon wheel, tied him again, and wrapped his bandana around his mouth. "Think I should tie him behind the wagons?"

"Nope. Leave him there. If we are going to get shot at, then by heaven, so is he," Thorpe said.

They waited for any sign of the killers for thirty minutes, but nothing happened. "I'll go back to the river and see if they are still there," Thorpe said. Slipping silently through the brush, Thorpe made his way to the river. Just a few feet from the bank, he removed his hat and stayed low as he moved to the river's edge with this gun drawn. No one was in sight, so he remained still and listened. Hearing no sounds other than the birds and the water lapping gently against the shoreline, he decided to move down the bank to see if the men rode to his side of the river. Reaching the area where he'd spotted the men on the opposite bank, he saw the tracks where they had crossed. He waited and listened. Still, he heard nothing. He followed the tracks through the trees and saw they were headed west. He wondered why Harlow's gang would be hanging around. They'd already killed two lawmen so they knew they would certainly hang if they were caught. Logic told him they were looking for Harlow. They hadn't left him behind. But why? Was Harlow the leader of the gang? That's the way most outlaws operated; one man was in charge until the day came when someone questioned their authority.

On his way back to camp, Thorpe thought about the last night Lily was on watch with him. He'd told her that by allowing Stone and Harlow to travel with them, they were adding to their likely problems the rest of the way to Wyoming. She agreed with him that it didn't make sense to turn back. They'd already been traveling over a month and either way, they'd surely face bad weather. They couldn't be certain the outlaws would be back. Well, now Thorpe was certain. They wanted Harlow. He might not know the reason yet, but it had to be fairly enticing for them to risk hanging.

"We'll have to do without a fire tonight. Their tracks led away, but they won't get far enough before dark to chance a fire. My gut tells me they know we are here," Thorpe told them.

"You sure there were nine?" Stone asked.

"Yeah."

"Dinner is cold, but it was cooked before we doused the fire," Lily said as she handed the two men their plates.

Thorpe asked Lily to eat with them some distance from the others so she could hear his conversation with Stone. "Why do you think they would come back for Harlow? Is he the leader of the gang?"

"I'm not sure," Stone replied. "All I know is he kept telling us that the men would come for him. He seemed confident of that."

"How did you catch Harlow?"

"We got word they were headed south from Deadwood and we found their trail. The gang split up, and Riff, Joe, and I followed Harlow and two of his men. As it turned out, the three of them rode in separate directions, so we were each following one man. I had a shootout with the one I was following and killed him. Joe Martin lost the trail of the man he was following, and Riff came back with Harlow. We didn't know why they split up, but Riff said he thought two men were riding one horse, but he only found Harlow."

"You said they robbed a stagecoach. What did they take?"

"There was a large payroll on that stagecoach. Besides killing that woman and little girl, they killed a rancher who had just sold his cattle, and he was traveling with a sizeable sum. They shot the driver, thankfully he lived and he told us what was in the strongbox. He also told us those killers took the jewelry off the dead woman."

"You say they split up, so it's possible Harlow had the money with him," Thorpe said.

Stone looked at him for a minute. "We thought they had already stashed the money when they split. That might explain a few things if they still had the money when we got on their trail. When Riff brought Harlow back to meet up with me, he said Harlow was backtracking."

"Maybe he was hiding the loot," Thorpe said.

"Could be. Harlow didn't have anything on him. If he hid the money, then the rest of them don't know where to look," Stone said.

"That would account for the added weight on the horse," Lily commented.

Thorpe admired Lily's sharp mind. "She's right. If it's the money they're after, they don't want Harlow dead. He may be our ace in the hole."

"Yeah. To tell you the truth, when I pulled Harlow in front of me and told those hombres they'd have to shoot him to get to me, I half expected them to ventilate him. If we meet up with them again, we definitely need to put Harlow out front," Stone said.

"As long as he's alive, they'll keep coming." Thorpe looked at Lily. "Stone and I could take Harlow and ride out. Of course, that would leave the four of you in the same position you were in before I came along." He wanted to give her the choice, but he thought it was best if he stayed with them.

"I could take Harlow and light out on our own. Thorpe, I don't need to involve you in this," Stone said.

Thorpe shook his head. "I couldn't let you do that. You wouldn't stand a snowball's chance in Hades with those men after you. And no offense, but I go with my horses."

"I think it's best if we all stay together," Lily said. She was afraid that both of them might get killed with that many men gunning for them.

"That's my thinking." Thorpe was relieved that she came to the same conclusion he had. He didn't like the thought of leaving her. He'd given his word he would see them to the fort in one piece, and he aimed to keep his word.

"It took Riff a day to catch up to Harlow. I know the general direction he rode, but it might take some time to find the exact place."

"Why do you think Harlow's partners rode in the opposite direction tonight?" Lily asked.

"I'd say they are waiting to see how many are in our party. Men like that want to make sure they have the upper hand before they attack. I expect they will be making their way behind us by morning," Thorpe answered.

"I was hoping those Indians took care of them for me," Stone said.

They walked back to camp and the first thing they noticed was Dora sitting beside Harlow, feeding him his dinner like a baby.

"What's going on here?" Stone asked.

"We didn't want to untie him without your say-so," Dora replied.

"He kept hollering about being hungry, but I told her to wait for you," Isabelle said.

Jed was sitting on a nearby rock cradling his rifle, and Blue was beneath the wagon keeping a close eye on Harlow.

Stone looked at Jed and nodded. "Thanks."

"Yessir, I don't trust this polecat."

Stone approached Dora and offered a warning. "That was real nice of you, ma'am, but I'd rather you stay away from him. He's dangerous, and besides, he can hold a fork with his hands tied."

Thorpe thought Stone offered sound advice. He worried Dora might take up with any man, law abiding or killer. He leaned over and whispered to Lily, "She might listen to you if you tell her to stay away from him."

Lily wondered if Thorpe was jealous that Dora was paying attention to Harlow now. Dora had told her she thought Harlow was handsome even if he was a criminal. Lily supposed he was handsome enough, but there was something about him that made her want to keep her distance. "I'll tell her, but Dora's not one to listen."

Stone stood in front of Harlow when Dora walked away. "I know your friends will keep coming back until they get their hands on you. Either way, when the shooting starts, just know you will be the one out in front of us. You might as well tell me where you hid the money. It could help you at trial if you make it that far."

Harlow smiled. "Why, Marshal, what makes you think I have any money?"

"Those boys aren't hanging around this area for nothing. There's no stagecoaches out here to rob. They want you real bad for some reason."

"I don't know what you're talking about."

Thorpe noticed Harlow had dropped the pretense that he was the true marshal. "Stone is right. We will put you right out front when the bullets start flying."

"You mean he hid the money from his gang?" Isabelle asked.

"He killed a lot of decent people to get at that money. Tell me, Harlow, was it worth it? How did it make you feel to kill a little girl?" Stone ground out.

Harlow grinned at him. "You've got it all wrong, Marshal. I didn't kill anyone."

Stone had to walk away before he was tempted to put his boot in Harlow's mouth.

CHAPTER TEN

Thorpe was awake most of the night thinking about their situation. He had never found it necessary to think like a killer, but right now that was exactly what he was trying to do. He figured the killers wouldn't go about things in the smartest way, but in the most expedient way. That meant they wouldn't go to the trouble of searching for the money. It would be faster for them to get to Harlow. They'd already killed so many, what difference would another six lives make?

The little voice in his ear told him to go with what he knew. And if he was skilled at one thing that might help him in this situation, it was tracking. He was an excellent tracker. When he'd left Texas for Wyoming Territory years ago, he learned if he wanted to eat, he had to be skillful at following a trail.

As he did every morning, Thorpe left

camp early to ride ahead a few miles to make sure they weren't riding into trouble. But this morning he was trailing the killers. Just as he expected, they were circling back behind the wagons. He figured they were planning an attack, or maybe they thought Harlow would bribe the marshal, offering him a cut if he'd let him go free.

After Thorpe rode back to the camp, they headed out and made excellent progress. By nightfall, Thorpe figured they'd covered about fifteen miles. When the men were caring for the animals, Thorpe had a chance to ask Stone some more questions.

"How long had you been traveling with Harlow before the attack?"

"Three weeks. Why do you ask?"

"I found their trail this morning, and just as I expected, they circled around and are following us. I was wondering why they haven't attacked, and nothing makes sense. Surely, they don't think Harlow might try to cut a deal with us."

"You mean for a percentage of the money if we agreed to let him go?" Stone asked.

"Yeah. But I have trouble with that theory. There are too many of us that would have to agree to that arrangement. I tend to believe killers would be too greedy to want to share."

"Enough incentive will make people do some mighty strange things. Besides, he'd just have to offer cash to one of us."

Thorpe looked at him and nodded. "Good point. Did he hint at cutting a deal when he was alone with you?"

"No, he didn't. Even that killer had enough sense to know that after my friends were killed the only deal I want is seeing him swing from the business end of a rope."

"They are laying back for some reason."

"They might think he will find a chance to escape," Jed offered.

"Jed, you may be right about that. We can't let down our guard."

"Mr. Thorpe, I don't know if it's my place to say anything about this, but I worry Miss Dora is getting mighty friendly with that killer."

"How's that?"

"Every time she thinks nobody is watching, she makes a point to go talk to him."

Thorpe didn't question Jed's word. "We need to keep an eye on her."

"What are you not telling me about that gal?" Stone asked. "I have a feeling she's not the same sort as Lily and Isabelle."

Thorpe and Jed exchanged a look. Thorpe figured Stone might as well know the truth. "She worked in a saloon in Kansas City. I guess you've noticed she's partial to men."

"Yeah. I had that much figured out on my own." Stone had noticed Dora wasn't shy about her interest in men. "After I saw you two coming back from the lake together I thought you . . ." He didn't finish because Thorpe shook his head.

"Not interested. I hope she finally heard me that day."

"She's been after Mr. Thorpe from the start," Jed teased.

Thorpe grinned at Jed. "I'm glad you think it's funny, Jed. She's like a dog with a bone."

"I think she's just lonely," Jed said. "She wants a husband in the worst way."

"How do you know?"

"I heard her talking to Miss Lily and Isabelle."

"What did you say was her given name?" Stone asked.

"Love, at least that's what she is going by now," Thorpe answered.

Stone thought she looked familiar, but he hadn't been able to place her. He'd seen her before, but it was a long time ago. She had quite a reputation in Kansas City. "I saw her in a saloon once and I've heard of her reputation."

That news surprised Thorpe. "Really?"

"You mean you didn't know who she was?" It'd been Stone's experience that word of a pretty soiled dove made the rounds pretty fast in the cow towns.

"I hadn't left Wyoming for a few years until recently."

"Dora Love is a well-known soiled dove in Kansas City. Do you think she could be a problem with Harlow? Or do you think she knows him?"

Thorpe thought about his question. "I honestly don't know." Dora told them she wanted to go west to get married, but that didn't mean she wouldn't change course if a better opportunity presented itself. And it was possible she'd met Harlow somewhere along the line.

"Why did she leave Missouri?" Stone asked.

"Like Jed said, she told us she wants a husband and she thought she'd stand a better chance of finding one out west."

"I don't think she would do anything to betray Miss Lily after what she's done for her," Jed said.

Thorpe didn't say it aloud, but he wasn't as convinced Dora would be as honorable as Jed expected. He hoped he was wrong. "I hope you are right about her, Jed."

"Well, I don't think Harlow is the marrying kind," Stone added.

"If he is, he'd best get at it if hanging is in his future," Thorpe commented.

Just as Jed had warned them, when they walked back to camp they saw Dora talking to Harlow. Lily and Isabelle were preparing dinner and not paying attention to the pair.

"Ma'am, as I said before, I want you to stay away from my prisoner," Stone told her.

"It don't hurt to be friendly," Dora snapped.

"I realize you are just trying to be nice, but it's just not safe."

Lily overheard the conversation between Stone and Dora. "Dora, we could use your help." She'd told Dora to get the blankets out for the evening and hadn't noticed she stopped to converse with Harlow.

Lily followed Dora to the wagon to speak with her about Harlow. "Dora, please listen to Stone. He has every right to tell us to stay away from Harlow."

"I don't think Harlow did the things Stone said. He seems like a decent sort," Dora replied.

"It doesn't matter. He's Stone's prisoner and that's all there is to it."

After dinner, Thorpe went to check on the

horses and Dora followed him.

When one of the horses walked her way for some attention, Dora pushed him away. "Why is that marshal so touchy about talking to Harlow?"

Thorpe stroked the horse that she'd rebuffed. He thought she'd just shown what kind of heart she had. In his estimation, she didn't deserve Lily's goodwill. "He knows he's a dangerous man. He just doesn't want you to get hurt."

"I've handled men like him before. Harlow doesn't scare me."

Thorpe thought he would ask her straight out why she wanted to know Harlow. "Why are you so intent on keeping him company? Have you met him before?"

When she looked at him, she had a smirk on her face. "No, I've never met him. Are you jealous? I didn't think you were interested."

Thorpe stared at her. On the surface she was a pretty woman, but the more he got to know her, he found her far less attractive. "Are you wanting to take a killer into your wagon?"

"I don't see anything wrong with talking. Harlow's an interesting man."

"He's interested in using people." Thorpe didn't know if his words hit home. "He's a killer. You heard what Stone said about him killing a little girl."

"That's what Stone said. We don't know that for sure."

"We've no reason to doubt the marshal."

"Well, I like Harlow, and if I want to talk to him, that's my business." She turned and started to walk away.

"After Lily stuck her neck out for you, don't betray her trust in you."

Dora whipped around and glared at him. "So that's it. You're just concerned about Lily."

Thorpe was surprised by her angry outburst. He looked into her eyes and he saw more than anger. He saw hate. "I don't want any of you getting hurt."

"Yeah, I'll just bet you're thinking of all of us. I'll do what I want."

It was a few minutes before Thorpe walked back to camp. He stopped by the wagon to grab a clean shirt and Dora was waiting for him.

She moved within inches of him and lowered her voice. "Thorpe, I'm sorry."

Thorpe didn't say anything; he was waiting to see what she was going to say next.

"I think this trip is getting on my nerves." She stared into his eyes and placed her hand on his chest. "And I guess I'm getting lonely."

Lily was walking to the wagon to get the puppies, but she stopped when she saw Dora and Thorpe talking by her wagon. She watched as Dora ran her hand over Thorpe's chest. It looked as though they were having an intimate encounter and she didn't want to intrude, so she turned and walked back to the fire.

Hearing a noise, Thorpe glanced around and caught a brief glimpse of Lily walking away. He guessed Lily saw them together, and probably saw Dora's hands all over him. He looked at Dora, wanting to put an end to whatever was on her mind. "Just stay away from Harlow." He forgot about his clean shirt and hurried toward the campfire. Isabelle was there, but he didn't see Lily. He wanted to tell her about the killers he saw that morning, and to explain the encounter with Dora.

"Where's Lily?"

"She said she didn't feel well so she went to lie down in my wagon. She said she would take the second watch with Jed. I volunteered to stay up with Jed, but you know how she is. Plain stubborn. She'd insist on taking watch if she was half dead."

"That won't be necessary. Stone and I are

going to take first watch and I'll stay up with Jed. You ladies need the rest."

Stone and Thorpe were alone on the first watch and Stone decided to ask some of the questions that had been on his mind for days. "Who is the father of that babe Isabelle's carrying?"

Thorpe arched a brow at him. He knew Isabelle wore her coat day and night, trying to hide her condition.

Stone chuckled. "Don't look so surprised. She has that coat on all the time, and some days it's been downright warm. But even I can see she's starting to fill it out and can barely button the darn thing. And she rarely fills her plate, so she isn't gaining weight from eating too much."

Knowing Isabelle couldn't keep the secret for long, Thorpe figured he might as well answer Stone's question. "I'm not the father, if that's what you are thinking. I told you I met up with them on the trail." If Stone wanted more details about the father, he'd have to get answers from Isabelle.

Stone grinned. "I didn't think you were the father. I guess that explains why they need to get to Fort Steele before Christmas. I'm guessing the father must be a soldier. He should be mighty pleased to have a babe coming into the world. Isabelle is a sweet little thing and I'm thinking that soldier is a lucky man."

Thorpe remained silent.

Stone glanced at Thorpe. "I see. The soldier doesn't know about the babe, does he?"

"It's not my place to discuss Isabelle's circumstances."

He admired Thorpe for keeping confidences to himself; he liked that about him. "Thorpe, you'd make a first-rate marshal. You've got integrity and a clear way of thinking through problems."

Thorpe smiled at his compliment. "I was just about to tell you that you'd make a fine rancher if you ever get tired of wearing that badge. You're good with animals, and we have a lot of land in Wyoming Territory that needs filling with cattle and decent men brave enough to strike out on their own."

Stone didn't think Thorpe knew how close he was to the mark. "I've been thinking it's time I settled down. I worked ranches before I became a lawman. It might be time for me to stay in one place, maybe take a wife and have some sons."

Great! Now I've done it. Isabelle was going to be married, and Stone didn't seem to like Dora. But he sure looked at Lily like he wanted to know her better. And Lily seemed to like him. She sure as heck talked to Stone a lot more than she talked to him lately. "If you've thoughts of taking a bride, not many women would take to the winters in Wyoming." He thought of Evelyn and how much she hated Wyoming. He wondered if the winters got to her.

"You're looking at it the wrong way. I see it as an opportunity to keep a woman nice and warm. Heck, she might even look forward to the cold."

"You mean, *if* you have the time to keep her warm. Running a ranch is a full-time job. You can go days without seeing a bed, particularly in the winter," Thorpe countered.

"You make it sound downright romantic spending all that time with cattle."

"Yeah, it's real romantic. Though we do get an occasional Saturday night to release a little steam at the saloon."

Lily walked to the fire to take her watch with Jed; instead, she found Thorpe and Stone conversing.

"Go on back to bed. Stone and I are just getting comfortable," Thorpe said.

"I'm fine. You get some rest." She picked up a cup and poured herself some coffee.

He wasn't going to argue; if she wanted to

spend time with Stone, that was fine by him. He told himself he didn't care. Instead of walking to the wagon, he leaned back and pulled his hat over his face. "I'll just rest right here." He'd just listen for a while and see what they had to talk about every night. That was the last thing he remembered until Jed was shaking him.

"Mr. Thorpe, wake up!"

Groggy and disoriented, Thorpe tried to get his bearings as he struggled to a sitting position.

"What is it?"

"Miss Lily is gone!"

Thorpe jumped to his feet. "Gone? What do you mean? Gone where?"

"I don't know. She said she was going to check on the horses, but she'd been gone so long, I got worried. I went to look for her and I saw Blaze was gone."

Thorpe ran to the corral and threw his saddle on Smoke with Jed right behind him. "How long ago?"

"About thirty minutes," Jed said.

"What about Blue?" Stone asked.

"He's in the wagon."

"Blue!" Thorpe shouted.

Instantly, Blue was at his side. "Let's go, boy." He looked back at Jed. "Wake Stone and get everything ready to leave. I'll be back with her soon."

He told himself Lily was a sensible woman. For the life of him he couldn't figure out why she would take off by herself knowing that killers were near, not to mention the Indians could still be around. Blaze's tracks were leading right in the direction of the gang. He hadn't told her how close the killers were to the camp.

It didn't take long for Thorpe to figure out Lily was tracking two men, and he was incensed that she was being so careless. She knew darn well what she was doing. What was she thinking? His anger, not to mention, his fear for her increased the longer he followed her tracks. An hour later he thought steam was probably coming out of his ears. He was so furious that he didn't notice when Blue stopped moving. He felt Smoke slow and that caught his attention. He looked back and saw Blue staring into the thicket. "What is it, boy?" Just as the words left his mouth, Smoke's ears twitched and turned to the brush. Thorpe glanced down at the tracks and he saw Blaze's hoof-prints were veering off in that direction. Quickly dismounting, Thorpe and Blue slowly moved through the trees.

After he tied Smoke off to a tree out of sight, he darted quietly through the scrub.

He surveyed the area and spotted what he thought was the crown of Lily's hat between two boulders on the crest of a rocky ledge. It was very hard to see unless you were looking carefully. She was one smart woman. She'd picked the best spot to watch someone in the basin below without their knowledge. Crouching down, he removed his hat and slipped toward the rocks. Reaching the first boulder, he was surprised he'd been able to sneak up on her. She didn't even turn around. But when he moved closer to the rocks, he saw her hat was placed on top of a stout limb holding it in the air and not her head. "Well, I'll be," he muttered, snatching her hat from the limb.

"Why are you following me?" Lily asked softly, moving from another outcrop of rocks with her rifle in her hands.

"Why am I following you? Just what in heaven's name do you think you are doing?" Thorpe ground out as quietly as he could muster under the circumstances.

She used her rifle to point to the men below. "I heard a noise at camp, and when I checked it out, I heard horses riding away."

She sounded so calm while his heart was about to pound out of his chest. Thorpe thought the men were far enough away that they wouldn't hear him yell. *Good.* He wanted to yell. Wisely, he didn't, but his voice was gruff. "Couldn't you have awakened me before you did something so harebrained?"

"Why are you so angry?" She didn't know what had him so upset. She snatched her hat from his fingers and slammed it on her head.

"I can't believe you would ride off like that without a word to anyone. What if something happened to you?" It made him even angrier to see that her long blond hair was down. She hadn't even tried to conceal the fact she was a woman. Now wouldn't that be just perfect if those men saw her. Or what if those Indians were still lurking about? She'd be in a fine fix then out here all alone. They would have her well away from the area before he could spit.

She gave him a puzzled look. "It's not anything I haven't done before. I'm perfectly capable of taking care of myself."

"That may be, but there were never killers around before."

She didn't think now was the time to remind him of the braves that were trying to kill him. "Those men are following us," she said.

"Yeah, I know. I meant to tell you last night, but you were in the wagon. Isabelle said you didn't feel well. Then when you came to take watch . . ." He forgot to tell her because he was aggravated when she made it so obvious she wanted to take watch with Stone and not him. She might not have said those exact words, but the meaning was clear all the same when she told him to get some rest. He shook his head as if he couldn't understand why he was giving the explanation when it should have been her explaining. "But that's beside the point. You shouldn't be out here alone."

"They didn't know I was behind them."

Dang it all! Isabelle was right; she was hardheaded. "That's beside the point. *Again.* It's plain stupid to check things out by yourself!"

She couldn't believe he'd just called her stupid. "If I didn't check things out, you might be wearing a few arrows in your grave!"

He put his hands on his hips and glared at her. Unable to find an acceptable retort that didn't include a string of cuss words, he turned and stalked back to his horse. By the time he mounted, she was beside him on top of Blaze and leading a horse.

He eyed the horse and glanced back at her. "Are you a horse thief now?"

"I found him wandering around. Look at

175

him. He's in bad shape. I'm not going to leave him here."

When Thorpe didn't respond, she thought she would be as irrational as he was being. "Do you want me to ride down there and ask those outlaws if he belongs to them?"

"I'm surprised you didn't already do that." He turned Smoke around as if there was nothing else to be said. "And put that hair under your hat. If you can't keep it that way on this trip, then cut it off!" He couldn't believe he'd said that. What if she did cut it off? Her hair was beautiful and he'd hate to see her do something stupid like that. Sometimes his temper just got the best of him.

"I don't know why you are so upset." She removed her hat and twisted her hair on top of her head.

"And I can't believe you don't understand how dangerous it is for you to be out here alone."

"I was alone when I shot those Indians chasing you!" She galloped Blaze in front of him.

"Why didn't you at least take Blue with you?"

Lily turned in the saddle and gave him a look that clearly stated she thought he'd lost his mind. "I don't want him to get hurt."

If that didn't beat all, he didn't know what did. She worried about Blue, but not about her own hide. "And you're not even wearing a coat. It's freezing out here. We won't stop if you get sick."

"And I wouldn't ask you to stop if I did get sick." She wasn't an idiot and she wasn't going to allow Thorpe Turlow to treat her like one. She ignored him the rest of the way.

Thorpe muttered to himself all the way back to camp about women being the bane of his existence. He didn't even offer her his coat. If she got sick, then it would be her own darn fault.

CHAPTER ELEVEN

"What's going on?" Harlow asked Dora as she was collecting the blankets around the campfire.

"Lily left and Thorpe went to find her. Stone and Jed are getting ready to hitch the teams and Isabelle is putting the pans away." She ignored the warning about staying away from Harlow. Harlow made it clear he found her attractive and she liked his attention.

"Come over here, honey. We can talk now."

Dora walked over to him. "What do you want to talk to me about?"

"I like talking to a beautiful woman, Dora. Did I hear you say you worked in a saloon?" While he thought Dora was a pretty woman, she wasn't as lovely as Lily. But he didn't think he'd stand a chance with a real lady.

"Yeah, I worked in a couple of saloons."

"Sit down here beside me," Harlow urged. Dora sat close to him. "We don't have long, Harlow. They will be ready to hitch the teams in a minute."

"Honey, call me Bryce. Where did you work?"

"Kansas City."

"Did Lily and Isabelle work in the saloon with you?"

Dora laughed. "Those goody-goodies? No way."

Harlow realized he'd heard of the pretty soiled dove from Kansas City. "Are you Dora Love?"

"Yes. Have we met before?" Dora didn't think she had met him; she had a reliable memory, especially for patrons as handsome as Harlow.

"No, darlin'. If I'd met you before, I would've taken you with me. What I don't understand is why are you going to Wyoming? I bet you had a booming business going in Kansas City."

"I want to get married. I hear there are plenty of men who are looking for women out west."

"You won't like that life, honey. A woman as pretty as you would get bored in no time tucked away on a ranch."

Dora had thought the same thing, but she knew what was in store for her if she stayed in a saloon as she aged. "I got tired of the saloon. I want more out of life."

"Why don't you go to Mexico with me, darlin'?"

Dora looked into his unusual gray eyes. Too bad, she thought, it was a waste to hang such a handsome man. If he wasn't going to hang, she'd gladly go with him to Mexico. "I don't think you will make it to Mexico. You killed those people and Stone is going to make sure you hang."

"I didn't kill those folks. One of the other guys did it, but I was there, and they are going to pin it on me and hang me if they can."

"Is that the truth, Bryce? You really didn't kill that mother and her little girl?"

"Yeah, it's the truth. One of my partners looks a lot like me. That stagecoach driver got us confused. I might be an outlaw, but I don't have no reason to lie to you, honey." He leaned over and kissed her neck. "I don't want to talk about that now. I want to kiss you, Dora."

Dora didn't move away, and when he kissed her, she wrapped her arms around his neck and pulled him closer.

"I wish I didn't have my hands tied so I could really enjoy our kisses," Harlow said when he pulled back. "We could have a lot of fun together. I know how to make you

180

happy and you'd be a rich woman."

A man who kissed like he did would definitely know how to please a woman. Men rarely kissed her when they paid for her time, and the ones who did were nowhere near as handsome as Harlow. "You might know how to make a woman happy, but why would I be rich?"

"I hid that money from the holdup. My partners don't know where to look. If you help me out, I will take you anywhere you want to go. We could get married if that's what you want."

"How much money did you take?"

Harlow arched his brow at her. He knew he had her attention now. Obviously, money was more important to her than finding a husband. "I didn't take time to count it all, but I'd say there's over thirty thousand dollars. If I hang around here until my men come for me, then it'll be split ten ways. And your friends will be dead. You don't want that to happen, do you?" With his hands tied, he reached up and stroked her cheek with the back of one hand. "I don't want you to be killed, Dora. I want to be with you. The two of us could share that money."

Dora could hardly believe her ears. Even if she worked in a saloon the rest of her life, she'd never see that much money, not even half. "There couldn't be that much money!"

"Shhh . . . they'll hear you." He gripped her chin and kissed her again.

Hearing Jed's voice, Dora jumped up and grabbed the blankets on the ground.

"Let me know if you're interested, honey. Remember what I said about showing you a good time. With that kind of money we could have anything we wanted in Mexico," Harlow whispered.

"I was just about to go look for you," Stone said when Thorpe and Lily rode into camp. Thorpe didn't respond, and Stone glanced at Lily. Seeing the horse she was leading, he rushed to her. "Where did you find him?"

"Contrary to what Thorpe thinks, the horse was on the loose." She turned and gave Thorpe a frosty glare. "I didn't steal him."

Stone stroked the horse's neck. "This is my horse, Captain."

The horse was so excited to see Stone that he nearly knocked him over. Lily couldn't tell who was the happiest — man or horse. "He's not injured, but he hasn't been cared for."

"Thanks for bringing him back, Lily. I knew he would get away if he could. He's a smart animal."

Lily was pleased that the horse belonged to Stone. "I'm glad he's where he's supposed to be."

When Lily walked away, Stone looked at Thorpe and said, "You didn't really think Lily stole him?"

Thorpe looked frustrated. "It's a long story. There's no hurry to leave, so take care of your horse."

"I guess you saw the gang again," Stone said.

"Yeah, they know we're here. Lily was following two of them. For whatever reason, they are waiting to make their move." Thorpe's head was pounding, probably as a result of getting so angry at Lily for being a dang fool woman. "I'm going to make some coffee."

Dora was near the supply wagon when Thorpe pulled out the coffeepot. "Thorpe, I'll make coffee for you. Would you like me to warm the biscuits?"

"Thanks, Dora. I could use some breakfast."

"I'll have it ready in no time." Dora pulled out the supplies and went to ask Jed to start the fire again.

Lily overheard the conversation between Thorpe and Dora. He was certainly pleasant enough with her, and Dora was more than willing to see to his comfort. She walked over to the wagon to pull out a cup for herself, and Dora surprised her when she said, "The coffee will be ready in a few minutes, Lily. I'll bring you a cup."

"Thanks. I'm going to the wagon to get my coat." She was shivering, but she didn't want Thorpe to notice.

"I think it's going to be colder today than it has been," Dora said.

"Do you think I could have some more coffee?" Harlow asked Dora after Lily walked away.

"Sure. I'll bring you a cup when it's hot."

Harlow winked at her. "Thank you, honey. It gets cold sitting here doing nothing, but I know what I'd like to be doing to stay warm."

"Shhh," Dora whispered. "Someone will hear you."

Once the coffee was hot, Dora took a cup to Harlow. She leaned over to speak to him quietly. "Are you telling the truth about that money?"

"Yes, there could even be more than I think. You know we could have a lot of fun, honey."

Dora heard footsteps so she hurried back to the fire. Thorpe and Lily appeared by the fire at same time.

"The biscuits are warm and I put some bacon on them," Dora told them.

"Where's Isabelle?" Lily asked.

"She's lying down until we leave. I don't think she's feeling well."

Lily took her cup of coffee and walked to Isabelle's wagon. "Isabelle, are you awake?"

"Yes, come in."

After she climbed into the wagon, Lily was surprised by Isabelle's pale face. "You want some coffee?"

"No, I had some earlier. I'm just so tired." Isabelle opened her coat and looked at Lily. "Just look at me! I can't even fasten my coat now. All of a sudden it seems like I just exploded. And I'm tired all of the time."

Hating to agree with her, Lily had to admit that she did look huge. "Well, you are due in less than two months, so I think that's normal." She had no idea what normal was, but she wanted to comfort Isabelle. It was unimaginable how she would cope in Isabelle's position traveling in that blasted wagon all day while carrying a baby.

"I feel like the baby is kicking my ribs out of my body."

Lily wished they had someone with them that had helped birth a baby before in case this one decided to come early. "I think it's an encouraging sign that he's so active."

"You said *he.* Do you think it will be a boy?"

"Oh my, I have no idea. But I've always heard that boys are active." It seemed like she'd heard that somewhere. "Do you want a boy?"

"I think his father would like that." Isabelle wondered if her soldier, Ethan Horn, would prefer a baby boy. She'd thought of nothing else but Ethan for months now. They'd only been intimate the one time, but she'd carried the wonderful memory of that night in her heart. Ethan was so dashing in his uniform, and he'd promised he would marry her upon his return. How could she resist the handsome soldier who proclaimed his love before he departed for Fort Steele? A baby was the last thing on her mind during those passionate hours she'd spent in his arms. The next morning Ethan left for Wyoming with sweet promises for the future. Weeks later, when her morning sickness started, she knew their special night had produced a child. She was frightened, and too embarrassed to reveal the truth to anyone. She hadn't received a single letter from Ethan. She told herself that once he saw she was with child, he would do the honorable thing and marry her. Surely, he would be pleased to have a son.

"You've never told me the father's name," Lily said.

"Ethan Horn."

"You could name the babe after him. I'm sure any man would be pleased to have a son to carry his name."

Isabelle's face twisted like she was in pain, and she started sobbing loudly.

"What is it, Isabelle? Are you hurting?" Lily moved to her side and hugged her. "Tell me."

"I'm so ashamed," Isabelle said. "I don't even know if Ethan wants me. I haven't heard from him since that one night we were together."

Lily was stunned at her revelation. The poor girl had to be scared to death. "Of course he wants you. Didn't you know him a long time?" Lily couldn't imagine a man not wanting anyone as sweet as Isabelle.

Isabelle shook her head from side to side. "No, we hadn't known each other very long before . . . before . . . you know." She tried to wipe her tears away, but they continued to fall. "Mother warned me not to give myself before marriage and I didn't listen. She was so disappointed in me when I told them of my condition."

Lily assumed that Isabelle and her soldier

had known each other for years. She wasn't sure what she should say, but she wanted to reassure her. "I'm sure Ethan wants you. As soon as he sees you, he will want this baby."

"But he hasn't written one letter. He told me when he came back to Missouri we would marry. He was so handsome and he said such sweet things to me," Isabelle wailed.

"Shhh, don't you worry. I'm sure he is an honorable man." Lily thought he'd better be an honorable man or there might be a shotgun wedding. Following that thought, she wondered if Isabelle's soldier might have found someone new. What would she do then?

"I believed him, but when he didn't write, I didn't know what to think. I'm such a terrible person for allowing this to happen. My father told me he never wanted to see my face again and Mother agreed with him. I had to leave my home and I will never see my family again."

"Stop that right now. You are not terrible! You simply allowed your emotions to take charge." Lily wasn't speaking from experience; she'd never been tempted by any man. Lily's mother had also warned her not to be with a man outside the bounds of matrimony, or she might end up in Isabelle's predicament. Her thoughts drifted to Thorpe. What if he pursued her? Would she be strong enough to avoid temptation with him? Would her parents have disowned her if she was in Isabelle's condition? No, they were much more loving and forgiving. She didn't understand people that would turn their daughter away for such a transgression, particularly in her time of need.

Isabelle collected her emotions and dried her face on her skirt. "I guess we'd best get ready to leave."

"Do you feel up to traveling?" Lily didn't want her to be miserable and they could depart a bit later if necessary.

"Yes. It doesn't help to sit in here and cry. What's done is done."

Sitting by the fire, Thorpe drank his coffee and tried to calm down so his head would stop throbbing. He glanced over at Harlow drinking his coffee with a smug look on his face. Typically, the man was flapping his jaws about something, but right now he was unusually quiet. And Dora was acting strangely, too. He couldn't put his finger on it, but there was something different about her. Maybe it was because she wasn't flirting with him or Harlow. Whatever was going on, it was nice to sit there for a minute in peace and quiet. But every time he thought about Lily's ill-conceived adventure this morning, he found himself getting upset all over again. It was inexplicable why she would put herself in danger. He understood she thought she could defend herself, and maybe she could under most circumstances, but not against so many men. He didn't even want to think about what would have happened if those killers got their hands on her.

When he'd calmed down somewhat, he realized he shouldn't have been so gruff with her and he should probably apologize. But he'd for darn sure wouldn't apologize today. As much as he hated to admit it, he'd been frightened, and he couldn't remember the last time he'd felt that way. Not even Indians shooting arrows at him scared him like that. Until he saw that she was not harmed, he felt like his heart was going to pound out of his chest. A man didn't like to admit that he couldn't protect a woman. And Lily was making it darn tough to protect her. He'd be glad to get these people to the fort, and he prayed he could live up to his word that they would all arrive safe and sound. Then he could go home. With all that had happened over the last six months, Dove Creek sounded like paradise to him. The sooner he got there, the better.

CHAPTER TWELVE

Dora wanted to believe Bryce Harlow when he said he didn't kill those people on that stagecoach. If he was telling the truth, he shouldn't hang if all he did was ride with the gang and take the money. All she could think about was that thirty thousand dollars. She couldn't imagine that much money, and she'd spent the entire day wondering how heavy thirty thousand dollars would be. Not that she was thinking of finding it by herself. Even if she thought she could find it by herself, she couldn't make it out here in the wild.

Bryce was going to need her help if he was going to go free. She liked Bryce and she knew she would have an exciting time with a man like him. He was handsome, maybe even as handsome as Thorpe Turlow. The marshal said Bryce was an educated man, and he'd certainly been smart enough to hide all that money from his partners.

Bryce had told her his friends would come for him, and he said they wouldn't hesitate to kill everyone, and she didn't want that. Not to mention, if the gang came for him, the money would be split between them, and Bryce's share wouldn't last long. If they left before his partners showed up, they'd have all of that money for themselves. And she'd never been to Mexico. That much money could buy them a beautiful spread and she'd have everything she'd always wanted.

The way she looked at it, there were no guarantees that she'd find a husband in Wyoming, and she couldn't work in a saloon forever. Women that aged working in a saloon didn't come to a pleasant end. What would happen when she got old and no one wanted to pay for her time? What would she do then? She wondered if Bryce was the kind of man who would stay with her, or if he would take off after a while. She'd just have to make sure he didn't want to go anywhere. That shouldn't be too difficult since she had spent her life pleasing men.

Thorpe was carrying his saddle to his horse when Lily climbed from the wagon with Isabelle behind her. He reached up to help Isabelle to the ground. "Why is Dora being so agreeable?"

"Maybe she likes you," Lily quipped.

Thorpe frowned at her. "I'm serious. Haven't you noticed a change in her attitude today?"

"I think she took some of her tonic. She's always in a more agreeable mood when she's had a dose. I don't know what's in that medicine, but it must work. She asked me if I wanted some, but I wasn't sure I should take it in my condition," Isabelle said.

"No, I don't think you should," Lily agreed. She didn't know what was in Dora's tonic either, but she didn't think it wise for Isabelle to take a chance if it could be harmful for her baby. "You need to think of the baby right now."

"I just hope she listens to Stone and stays away from Harlow." Thorpe walked away thinking about Dora's tonic. He'd bet some spirits were included in her *medicine* because he'd noticed her eyes looking glassy on more than one occasion.

They'd ridden several days and Harlow's gang did not appear. Each day they expected the gang to make their move, but nothing happened. Thorpe lagged behind most days to see if the gang was getting closer. He figured they would keep a respectable distance so no one would be the wiser when they attacked. He wasn't too far from the wagons today when he heard a shrill whistle. Racing to the wagons, he saw Stone waving to him from the front wagon.

Thorpe rode up beside the wagon where Stone was riding with Isabelle. "What is it?"

"Thought you might want to see this before we got too close."

Thorpe looked to where Stone was pointing and saw four wagons off the trail ahead of them. "Did you see those when you came this way?"

"No. I didn't get on this trail until just a few days before the attack. I never liked this trail — too open for peace of mind."

Thorpe agreed with Stone on that score. Trees were scarce and they were pretty much out in the open now. "Stay here. I'll ride ahead and see what's going on." Before Thorpe reached the wagons, Lily rode up beside him. "You should have waited with the others."

"You didn't want me riding off alone. Why should you do the same thing?"

"Miss Lily, I'm learning you are one hardheaded woman. To answer your question, I don't think Harlow's gang would hardly be as happy to capture me as they would to have you."

She had no reply.

They dismounted and walked to the first wagon. No one was moving about, not even animals, so Thorpe looked inside the wagon. "They left a lot of things behind."

"Thorpe."

Thorpe turned to Lily and she pointed to an area away from the wagons. He saw five crosses lined up in a row.

Lily looked inside the wagon. "This is Mr. and Mrs. Craig's wagon. I recognize their things."

"They may have been ill and the other folks left them behind. That's probably why nothing was taken." Thorpe walked to the other wagons and the next two were much like the first with all manner of items left intact as if they'd just stopped for the night. He walked to the last wagon and found what was left of a body lying half out of the wagon. The man had been dead for a long time and the animals had gotten to him. "Lily, don't come back here." He didn't want her to see a sight that was difficult for him to handle. Thorpe figured the man had buried the five people before he succumbed to whatever had caused their deaths. The man probably knew he was going to die and freed the animals that had been pulling the wagons. It was sad that the man had to die alone after burying his friends.

Not knowing what disease the man might have carried, Thorpe didn't want to endanger the women by touching the man to bury him. There wasn't much left of the body, so he thought the kindest thing to do was to burn the wagon with the man. He struck a match and held it to the canvas top. "Lily, don't touch anything." When the fire took hold, he walked to the other wagons and set them ablaze.

"What was it, Thorpe?"

"The last man didn't get buried. I'm not sure what killed them, so I decided to burn the wagons. If it had been an attack, items would have been taken. Let's get out of here and stay clear."

Lily didn't question him further. She knew he was trying to spare her from seeing something she wouldn't soon forget. "I'm sorry for them. I hope they didn't suffer long."

Thorpe thought she was being very gracious considering those people hadn't wanted her group to travel with them. "I'm glad you didn't go with them." He didn't like the thought that he could have found Lily on the side of the trail.

Lily looked at him. She wondered if he

said that because of Dora, but she didn't ask.

That night while they waited for their dinner to cook, Thorpe explained why he burned the wagons.

"They got what they deserved, if you ask me," Dora said.

"No one deserves to die out in the middle of nowhere with no help on the way," Lily said.

"They said they was God-fearing people, so why did your God let this happen to them?" Dora asked.

"Dora, we may not have all of the answers about why things like this happen, but that doesn't mean we should lose faith, or blame God when things go wrong," Lily said. The one thing she'd learned about Dora was her mind was made up about God and she wasn't inclined to change.

"Dora, haven't you ever done something that you knew you shouldn't, but you went ahead and did it anyway?" Isabelle asked.

"I've always done what I wanted," Dora said.

"But it doesn't mean you were doing the right thing. I don't think you would want to be judged by the things you've done wrong. I know I wouldn't want to be," Isabelle said.

Dora didn't respond and Isabelle continued. "Maybe that's why you've never been happy. You've never given God a chance to work in your life. It doesn't mean that God is responsible when things don't turn out the way you want, especially if you are doing things you shouldn't. Believe me, we all must take responsibilities for our own actions, right or wrong." Isabelle knew what she was talking about. She didn't want to be judged by her mistakes, and she certainly didn't blame God for her situation. It was her choice to do the things that she did.

"We shouldn't be so quick to judge anyone," Lily said.

"Like I told Jed, you people preach too much." Dora turned and walked away.

"That's what's really wrong with Miss Dora. She don't want to let God in her life," Jed told them.

Stone overhead the conversation and thought Isabelle was wise beyond her years. "Miss Isabelle, you make a lot of sense. Too bad she doesn't want to listen."

"My pa was a preacher and a lot of what he had to say made sense. He probably wouldn't believe this, considering my condition, but I did listen."

Lily thought about what Isabelle said about her father. The man certainly didn't practice forgiveness. It was inconceivable to her how a preacher could turn his back on his daughter and demand she leave her family home in her situation. She had a notion that one day Isabelle's father was going to regret his decision. If not, he was going to miss out on a sweet grandchild.

⟶ Stone didn't know what had transpired between Isabelle and her father, but he heard the heartache in her voice. He'd had the pleasure of driving Isabelle's wagon today since Jed had been kind enough to put up with Harlow on his wagon. Jed figured Stone could use a break from Harlow's smart mouth. Stone was truly grateful for the reprieve; it was a pleasure to have Isabelle to converse with all day. As much as he wanted Harlow to tell him where he hid that money from the stagecoach robbery, he couldn't take much more of his attitude and his bellyaching.

Talking to Isabelle made him feel normal, something he'd missed riding the territory chasing outlaws. In his estimation, Isabelle was a remarkable woman. Not once did she complain or ask to stop on the trail. He didn't think there were many women in her condition that would have ridden that many miles without being cantankerous at the very least. But she asked for no special consideration. He noticed she could no longer button her coat, so he gave her a blanket when the temperatures started dropping later in the day.

He'd given a lot of thought to her situation, and he admired her for her courage to travel to Wyoming to find the soldier and hold him responsible. But if that soldier had some character, he would have married Isabelle once he'd bedded her, if not before. She was young and not what he would call worldly, and he figured that soldier had taken advantage of her naiveté. Before the day had ended, Stone vowed to himself that he would make sure that soldier did the right thing by this lovely young woman.

Isabelle thought Stone was the most considerate man she'd ever met. He'd asked her several times today if she needed to stop and see to her needs. He didn't pass judgment on her and she appreciated the way he treated her with true kindness. He'd told her the same thing Lily had told her that morning: Any man would be proud to have a child, boy or girl. The time passed quickly as she listened to Stone's stories about some of the places he'd traveled and the outlaws he'd captured. Before she knew it, she'd forgotten all about how uncomfortable she'd been that morning.

She didn't know how much older Stone was than Ethan, but he seemed much more mature and wiser than she remembered Ethan to be. It probably wasn't fair to compare the men because she had come to realize that she knew very little about Ethan. He was such a dashing figure in his military uniform that she never once stopped to consider if he was a decent, honorable man. Now it frightened her to think about how little she knew about him. Soon she would be responsible for another life; she could no longer afford to be so foolhardy in her judgment.

Ethan was young and handsome, but would he make a suitable father to their child? Would he be a good husband? Would he be as patient and kind as Stone had been with her today? She didn't even know what Ethan's plans were once he left the military. What if he didn't want to be a farmer? What would they do? How would they survive? If he didn't want her, how would she support a child alone? What would become of them? She had so many fears and she didn't want to burden anyone. One thing she'd learned, everyone had their own problems to deal with. The last thing she wanted to do was be a burden to someone else.

■ ■ ■ ■

Lily and Isabelle filled the plates when dinner was ready, and Dora took that opportunity to take the coffeepot and a cup to Harlow.

"How are you doing, honey?" Harlow whispered. "I've missed talking to you today."

Dora handed him the cup and poured his coffee. "I'm sick of these people preaching all the time."

"Honey, we don't have to stay here. You know what we can do."

Dora looked around to see if anyone could overhear her. "I've been giving that some thought. What do you plan to do if we get the money?"

Harlow smiled wide. She was saying what he wanted to hear. "I told you we could go on down to Mexico."

"How do I know you wouldn't leave me there with no money once you get what you want?" Dora had a difficult time trusting anyone, but she wanted to believe Harlow.

"Why would I leave you? I told you, we'd make a good team. You're a smart gal, and together we could have anything we want. I've never met a woman I wanted to marry, but I'd marry you, Dora. You've got my word on that. We could settle in Mexico where no one would find us. Wouldn't you like that? You wouldn't have to look for a husband when you have a willing man right here with money."

Before Dora responded, Harlow held his tied hands up to her. "Take this ring off my finger. You hold on to that as my promise to marry you."

Dora looked around to make sure no one was watching before she set the coffeepot down.

"If you don't want to help me, I want you to keep the ring. It is real gold and I didn't steal it. If you decide to go with me, then I'll buy you a ring with a diamond for your wedding ring."

She pulled the ring off his finger. It was a heavy gold ring that bore his initials. No one had ever given her such a nice present. "It's beautiful."

Harlow knew she was going to help him. He'd always been able to read women, and he had Dora hooked. He would take her to Mexico with him if she didn't slow him down. Since he would have to spend several months hiding out, Dora could be a pleasant diversion. Thirty thousand would last awhile, but he knew he wouldn't stay in

Mexico indefinitely. He craved the excitement of his profession and he knew he would go back to robbing once the law had given up trailing him. He figured the bloom would be off the rose where Dora was concerned by that time and he'd leave her in Mexico. "Here comes Stone," he whispered.

Stone walked up and handed Harlow his plate of food. "Dora, everyone else would like some coffee."

Harlow winked at her. "Thanks, ma'am."

"Anytime, sugar." Dora gave Stone a defiant look and held the coffeepot toward him. "Where's your cup?"

"By the fire."

Dora walked away making plans to help Harlow escape. She didn't tell him she planned on helping him; she was waiting to be convinced that he wanted her and that he would share the money. He'd convinced her when he gave her such an expensive ring. Now she just had to figure out the best time to implement her plan. The next time she was alone with Harlow for a few minutes she would tell him what she had in mind. She wished she could talk to him at night, but there was always someone around. She'd have to ask Thorpe how much longer before they reached Fort Steele so she would know how much time she had. But she figured she should act soon because she didn't want the gang to come for him and possibly kill her along with everyone else trying to free Harlow.

Later that night, Dora had her opportunity to speak with Thorpe while he was checking on the animals. She poured a cup of coffee and carried it to the corral. "I just made some fresh coffee and thought you would like some."

"Thanks." Thorpe wondered if she'd taken some of her tonic again.

Dora stood beside him as he drank his coffee. "I don't know how you get by on so little sleep."

"You get used to it working a ranch. You learn to get by."

"Thorpe, who does your cooking on your ranch?"

"I have a cook who handles those chores for the men."

"Is it a man or a woman?"

"Man." He didn't want to ask her why she wanted to know. He had a bad feeling about the direction of this conversation.

"Why don't you hire a woman to do the cooking?"

"My cook can go out on the range with

the men."

"I see. I bet you will be relieved to get home."

She had no idea. It was situations like this that made him uncomfortable. "Yeah, real glad."

"How long do you think it will be before we get to the fort?"

To his way of thinking, they'd made great progress. Of course, much of that good fortune had been due to the fair weather for this time of year. "Barring other complications, if the weather is on our side, we should be there in three weeks." It looked like they were going to make the fort before Thanksgiving, well before Isabelle's deadline of Christmas Day.

Dora knew he was thinking they could have problems from Harlow's gang. The gang probably figured out they were going to take Harlow to the fort, so they knew when they needed to make their move. The sooner she told Harlow of her plan, the better. But for now, she had to make everyone think that she was still interested in finding a husband. "Thorpe, I never said thank you, but I want you to know I do appreciate all you have done for us on this trip."

Thorpe was surprised that she'd expressed her appreciation. He'd noticed she rarely had a pleasant word to say to anyone. For a minute, he thought she was going to volunteer to be his cook at the ranch. He was thankful the conversation didn't head down that road. Maybe Jed was right, and there was more to Dora than met the eye. "You're welcome."

Dora reached out and placed her hand on his arm. "I still wish you were in the market for a wife. I'll make someone a fine wife, and I know how to please a man in ways that a real lady doesn't know."

Thorpe looked her in the eyes and he thought of Evelyn. There was a time when Dora could have easily convinced him she was sincere. Thanks to Evelyn, he was no longer as trusting, and he couldn't bring himself to trust Dora completely. He had a nagging suspicion that she was up to something. Maybe she was trying to change his mind about her, maybe not. "I don't doubt you know how to please a man, Dora. And you will probably have your fair share of men willing to take you up on your offer. But if you marry a rancher or a farmer, you'd best really like him because he may be the only person you see for weeks at a time during the winter months." Some women weren't cut out for the isolation of ranch life, and he thought Dora was one of those women. By the way she flirted with men, he doubted she would be faithful to a husband. Just like Evelyn. "And you need to stay away from men like Harlow. I don't think they'd be looking for a permanent union."

CHAPTER THIRTEEN

"What are you doing out here?" Thorpe was riding a mile behind the wagons and Lily surprised him when she rode up with Blue beside her.

"Dora said she could handle the team for a while, so I decided to give Blaze some exercise. I think Blue wanted to run, too. He hasn't left Spirit's side and she won't leave the pups."

He started to say something about Dora's change of attitude, but he remembered Lily's last comment when he mentioned Dora. "I'm sure Blaze appreciates a break from riding behind the wagon."

"Dora said you thought we would arrive at the fort in three weeks."

"As I told her, if all goes well and the weather holds."

"Why do you think those men haven't come for Harlow?"

"I don't know. Maybe they know the

general area where he hid the money is somewhere between here and the fort." Thorpe thought that was the most likely reason, or they were waiting for them to reach an area that would be more advantageous for an attack.

"How long will it take for you to get to your ranch from the fort?"

"Just a couple of days."

It saddened Lily to think in a few short weeks she would never see Thorpe again. "I bet you will be happy to get there."

"Yes, ma'am." He did look forward to getting home, but he knew he would miss seeing Lily daily. "You should come visit my ranch when you find your grandfather."

Lily looked at him, clearly surprised that he'd ask her to come to Dove Creek. "I'd like to see your ranch."

Thorpe gathered the courage to ask a question he'd wanted to ask for weeks. "Do you have someone waiting for you back home in Texas?"

She was puzzled by his question. "I told you my family was killed."

"I thought you might have a beau."

She blushed. "No, I don't. Unless my grandfather wants to go back to Texas, I doubt I will ever go back. I'll live wherever he wants to live."

She didn't mention marriage and a family. And what would she do if she didn't find her grandfather? "Don't you plan to marry someday?"

"Maybe. I would like to have children one day." He hadn't mentioned any woman in his life and she was curious. "Do you plan to marry?"

Evelyn's face appeared in his mind. "I came close to getting married, but the bride didn't show up at the church. She left town with another man."

Lily couldn't believe her ears. What woman in her right mind wouldn't show up to marry him? "That's hard to believe."

"Why?"

It wasn't a difficult question to answer, but she didn't think she should tell him all of the reasons she thought he'd be a wonderful husband. "Well . . . you have an agreeable disposition, you are hardworking, and you're trustworthy." She figured the woman he'd asked to marry must have been very special.

He grinned at her. "Maybe I should have had you to sing my praises."

As far as she was concerned, any woman who didn't recognize his fine qualities didn't deserve him. "Does she live near your ranch?" She thought it would be difficult for him to see a woman he loved frequently who chose another man over him.

"No, I imagine she's in England by now, married to a duke." The thought of Evelyn married to Ainsworth didn't bother him at all. Actually, he felt like laughing. He felt as if he'd dodged another arrow.

Lily thought he must have had his heart broken by the woman. "I'm sorry."

It took Thorpe a minute to realize she was talking about Evelyn marrying another man. "Everything worked out for the best."

Lily didn't want him to think about his heartache, so she asked, "You really think we will make the fort by Thanksgiving?"

Thorpe nodded. "That's my plan."

"I hope we will have a proper Thanksgiving meal." She glanced his way. "I mean sitting at a table and not around a fire."

Thorpe chuckled. "There's a way station where we will stop in a few days, so we can have a meal inside at a table at the very least."

"That would be nice."

Thorpe couldn't disagree; he missed sitting at his table at home. He really enjoyed the peacefulness in the early morning hours when he'd have his first cup of coffee at the kitchen table.

They were forced to stop a few hours later to work on a wagon wheel, and since the men were busy, Dora was able to speak with Harlow as she made the coffee.

After she explained her plan, Harlow realized Dora was more devious than he'd given her credit. "We need to do this soon. The gang will make their move when we get closer to the area where the marshal found me."

"Thorpe said we will be at a way station in a few days, so it should be no later than day after tomorrow." Now that she'd set things in motion, she wanted to get it over with before the gang made their move. The money, and going to Mexico with Harlow was all she could think about. She was nervous and excited at the same time. She had everything planned out and it was going to be difficult for her to wait another day.

"Sounds good," Harlow agreed. "You won't regret this, Dora. We'll have more fun than you ever dreamed."

Dora saw Lily and Isabelle bringing the food to the fire. "Shhh."

"What have you lovely ladies made for

supper?" Harlow asked.

"Beans and corn bread," Isabelle replied.

"I've made the coffee." Dora smiled again at Harlow as she walked away.

After dinner, Lily was playing with the puppies near the wagon under the watchful eye of Spirit and Blue when Thorpe walked over and handed her a cup of coffee. "Thought you might like this."

"Thank you."

Thorpe removed his hat and sat beside them. Today was the first time he'd spent more than just a few minutes alone with Lily in weeks. He'd missed talking with her more than he wanted to admit. At times, it seemed like she was intentionally avoiding him. "These little guys are growing like weeds."

Lily yelped when one of the puppies started chewing on her finger. "And their teeth are getting sharp."

Thorpe pulled a leather glove from his back pocket and handed it to her. "Use this." He took his other glove and started a tug-of-war with Henry. Thorpe laughed at the little puppy as he took the glove in his mouth and planted his rear end on the ground to gain leverage in the struggle. "They are strong little critters. When we found them I was worried they might not make it."

"I know, but I knew they would."

Thorpe leaned back against the wagon wheel and two of the puppies crawled on top of him and walked in a circle on his chest until they plopped down. "Miss Lily, I don't think I would ever want to play a hand of poker with you. I think you have an unfair advantage of seeing the future."

"Look." Lily pointed to the two puppies who were climbing inside Thorpe's hat lying on the ground. "They are so cute."

"They better not hike a leg in there." He tried to sound serious, but he couldn't help laughing at the sight of those two pups squirming around inside the crown of his Stetson. They promptly rolled up into little balls and fell asleep.

Lily didn't think she'd ever seen a more charming scene than Thorpe with the puppies on his chest and in his hat. She watched as he stroked the puppies; his hand was larger than they were. One of the puppies made his way to Thorpe's face and started licking his chin.

"I like the way you kiss." Thorpe's eyes met Lily's when he turned his face to keep from getting licked on his lips. He thought she looked lovely with the light from the fire behind her. He'd never seen a more beautiful woman. "Lily, how come you don't have a beau? You must have had a number of men waiting in line to court you."

Lily avoided his eyes. She leaned over and plucked one of the pups from his chest. "I guess I've never met one that I like that much."

Thorpe reached for her braid hanging over her shoulder and tugged her closer to him. "You haven't liked one fellow?"

She was inches away from the only man she thought was almost irresistible. Her eyes flicked over his handsome features. She knew she should be sensible and move away . . . but she didn't. She didn't know if he was teasing her or flirting with her. Finally, her eyes met his. She thought of what Isabelle said to her the day she brought Thorpe to her wagon. *If you save a person's life you are forever bound together.* Could that possibly be true? Would he ever feel bound to another woman after his experience with his fiancée? And what about Dora? Did he have feelings for her, or was she just a distraction to pass the time on a long journey? "Why do you ask?"

"As I said, you're a beautiful woman, and I would expect men to be clearing a path to your door."

"Thank you, but no, there has never been anyone. I'm not experienced like . . ." She didn't finish because he said it for her.

"Dora. I don't know why you keep bringing Dora up to me." He released her braid and Lily straightened.

"I just thought . . . well, I've seen her leaving your wagon several times. I guess I thought . . . it doesn't matter what I thought."

So that was what she'd been thinking all of this time. That was why she'd been so cool to him for weeks. She'd assumed he was seeking Dora's company. He tried to remember the first time Dora came to his wagon. It was a few days after he joined them, so Lily must have thought he worked fast. Maybe he should feel flattered. "She's made her interest known, and yes, she hasn't given up easily, but nothing has happened between us. I'm not interested."

While she was surprised by his denial, she didn't doubt his word. Maybe he'd spurned Dora because he was still in love with his fiancée. "Why aren't you interested? She's a lovely woman and she's definitely interested in you."

"I'd say she's set her sights on Harlow now. I don't think Dora knows what she really wants."

Lily couldn't disagree with him, particularly after the way she'd been flirting with Harlow. "You were right, she does seem more agreeable lately."

Thorpe smiled at her. "It's probably her tonic."

Lily laughed. "At least she appears to be listening to Stone when it comes to Harlow." She picked up her cup of coffee and took a sip. "And her coffee has improved."

"Her coffee has definitely improved." Thorpe enjoyed talking with Lily, and he'd even considered kissing her when she was so close to him. He wasn't sure why he didn't, other than he told himself he didn't want to get involved. To keep himself from reaching over and pulling her close again, he pulled the puppies from his hat and placed them on his chest. "I've never asked you how you got to Missouri from Texas. Stagecoach?"

"I rode Blaze."

"Alone?"

"Of course, along with Blue and Daisy. I purchased the other mules when I reached Missouri, along with the wagon."

He shook his head. The woman continued to surprise him by her resourcefulness. He was closer to understanding why she'd ridden off alone tracking those two men. She had been on her own for a long time. But as far as he was concerned, she'd been lucky to this point. She would be no match for men intent on doing her harm. "Miss Lily, you are a wonder. You've been fortunate that you haven't had problems."

Lily leveled her gaze on him. "I guess you could say that, or you could believe God's promises and not allow fear to hinder you."

Thorpe arched his brow at her. "Maybe God doesn't think we would be so foolish as to risk our lives needlessly."

"Maybe so, or perhaps that's why Blue was sent to me." She looked him directly in the eyes. "And you."

He wanted to remind her she took off without him, but he didn't want to cause friction between them again. "Was your grandfather a religious man?"

"He *is* a religious man. His first six months in captivity were difficult. He was subjected to routine beatings, mostly from the other boys in the tribe. They didn't like him and didn't want him there. He told me the only reason he survived was repeating all of the Bible verses he could remember. Over and over, he repeated God's promises, and that was what gave him the strength to keep going. After a while they started treating him like one of their own. He came to respect their spiritual beliefs, but he didn't forget his own faith."

Thorpe didn't intend to speak of the man as if he were deceased, and he felt bad about that. He wouldn't intentionally do anything to question Lily's belief that he was alive. Lily had been through a lot in her young life. He knew what it was like to lose your family and to be on your own. Without her family to help protect her, she wouldn't have survived on the farm alone in Texas. It was understandable how she'd made the decision to search for her grandfather. Either way, she was bound to face a lot of danger no matter the choice she'd made. He admired how she'd handled difficult situations with determination. He'd never once heard her complain about anything. "Your grandfather sounds like an amazing man. I look forward to meeting him."

Lily thought Thorpe was a remarkable man. He'd taken on their small wagon train as though they were his family, looking out for everyone's welfare. She didn't know why he'd agreed, but she was happy he did. It wasn't lost on her that they would not have made it this far without him. He'd gone out of his way to make sure they were safe. He rarely slept more than an hour or two at night, yet he was the one that left every morning before they broke camp to scout the area. He didn't make them feel indebted to him in any way. She had witnessed his many fine qualities over the passing weeks, and she doubted she'd ever meet another man like Thorpe Turlow. He was a man of integrity, much like her grandfather. "I'm sure my grandfather would like to know you."

CHAPTER FOURTEEN

Two days later, when everyone gathered around the fire for their meal, Lily ladled food on the plates and Dora poured the coffee. Lily watched closely as Dora approached Harlow with his cup and was pleased to see that she didn't appear to talk to him. If she did, it was a brief exchange.

When Lily sat down to eat with the others, Blue walked to her and started pacing in front of her. He was panting like he was winded, but he hadn't been running. "What is it, Blue?"

Blue moved to Lily's side and nudged her arm.

"What's wrong?" Thorpe asked.

"He acts like he doesn't feel well," Lily responded.

When Dora handed Lily and Thorpe their coffee, Blue growled at her. "What's wrong with him?"

Lily ran her hand over Blue's head. It

wasn't like him to growl unless he sensed danger. "He's been acting strangely since he ate." She looked into his eyes. "Sit beside me, boy."

Blue circled a couple of times and finally sat down. But when Lily picked up her coffee to take a drink, Blue nudged her arm again, causing her to spill the contents of her cup.

Lily set her cup and plate aside and pulled Blue to her. "Put your head in my lap."

Blue laid beside her and placed his head in her lap and allowed her to rub his stomach.

Thorpe didn't like the way Blue looked. He put his own plate aside and leaned over and felt his nose and looked at his eyes. "I didn't notice anything amiss with him earlier today."

"He seemed fine and he ate the same thing we are eating, so I know he didn't eat something bad."

"Maybe he picked up something earlier today and it didn't agree with him," Thorpe said.

Minutes later, Blue closed his eyes and fell asleep. Dora returned with the coffeepot and refilled Lily's cup. "Well, at least he's asleep now." That wolf scared her to death when he growled.

■ ■ ■ ■

As soon as Dora untied him, Harlow removed Stone's holster and buckled it around his waist. He checked the pistol to make sure it was fully loaded.

"What are you doing?"

"We need a gun; we can't survive out here without one." He grabbed a saddlebag and walked to the wagon and started shoving supplies inside.

"I have a pistol," Dora said.

Harlow looked over his shoulder at her. "Great. Shoot that wolf."

Dora wasn't so foolish to do something like shoot Blue. Lily would follow her to the ends of the earth if she harmed that animal. "I'm not shooting him. Besides, we can't take a chance on anyone hearing a gunshot. Thorpe said your gang was close behind us."

"I guess you're right about that. You have everything you need? Where do they keep the cartridges?"

"I got everything together before dinner, but I don't know where Jed keeps the cartridges."

Harlow searched through the food supplies and found one box of cartridges. "This will do. Let's grab two horses and get out of here." Harlow tried to throw a saddle over Thorpe's horse, but the animal reared, missing his head by mere inches. He wasn't going to waste time fighting the horse, so he moved on to Stone's horse. Once he tied the bundle of supplies to the saddle, he helped Dora saddle Lily's horse.

"They'll come after us for sure for taking their horses," Dora warned.

"If you gave them enough of that opium, we'll have the money and be well on our way to Mexico before they even wake up. The men won't leave the women, and we'll make better time on horseback."

"I gave them all a healthy dose of my tonic. They won't wake up for a long time." Dora gave less opium to Isabelle, thinking in her condition she wouldn't give them any trouble even if she was awake. She wasn't sure how much of the tonic she should give to Blue, but she gave him a sizable dose to make sure he stayed asleep. She told herself she didn't want to kill any of them, but she wanted that money and they weren't going to stand in her way. The deed was done now and she wasn't going to worry about them.

Harlow helped her on the horse. "Let's get out of here."

Dora had never spent much time in a saddle, but she was determined to keep up

226

with Harlow. He was her ticket out of an uncertain future and she wasn't about to let that money slip through her fingers.

Even though Thorpe thought he felt snow-flakes on his skin, he didn't want to open his eyes to see if it was really snowing. His head was pounding and his throat felt like he'd eaten a pound of dust. What in the world was wrong with him? He felt fine yesterday . . . before. Before what? He remembered eating dinner but nothing after that. He blinked several times before his eyes focused on his surroundings. What in the world was he doing lying down on the ground in the middle of the day? He thought he might have fallen off his horse and hit his head. Raising up on one elbow, he looked around and that's when he saw everyone lying on the ground. Spirit was whining and licking Blue's face. His gaze landed on Lily. She was so pale, he thought she was dead. Scrambling to her on his hands and knees, he held his finger to her neck. His fingers were so cold that he couldn't feel anything. "Lily!" He shook her, but she didn't respond. He put his hand on her chest and expelled a deep breath when he felt her heartbeat. *Thank God.* Blue was right beside her, so he placed his hand on

227

his rib cage. He was alive. He staggered to his feet, ran to Isabelle, and gently shook her by the shoulders. "Isabelle, can you hear me?"

"What?" Isabelle mumbled.

Stone was lying next to Isabelle and Thorpe shook him. "Wake up, Stone!"

Stone rolled to his side. "What is it?"

Thorpe picked up a cup beside Isabelle and sniffed the contents. He looked around and Harlow was gone and so was Dora. He threw the cup aside and ran to get some water. After washing the cups, he filled them with fresh water. He helped Isabelle to a sitting position and held her head and told her to drink. "Stone, sit up and drink some water."

Stone raised up and tried to focus on Thorpe. "What's going on?"

"I'd say we were drugged." He handed him a cup. "Drink, and help Isabelle. I need to check on Jed." He filled another cup and hurried to the wagon. Jed was lying facedown inside. "Jed!"

Jed turned over and looked at Thorpe. "Mr. Thorpe, what's wrong?"

Thorpe thrust the cup of water at him. "Drink this, Jed. I think Dora drugged us. She's gone and so is Harlow."

Jed drank the water in one gulp. "Why

would Miss Dora do such a thing?"

"I don't know, but if you can, get out of the wagon and have more water. Lily's not awake yet."

"I'm right behind you."

"Would you check the puppies? I don't think Spirit was drugged. Hopefully the puppies weren't either." Jed hurried away and Thorpe ran to check the horses. Daisy was whimpering and Thorpe took a moment to check her over. She wasn't injured, but she was definitely upset. He filled their pans with water and talked to Daisy in an effort to calm the poor animal. He glanced around the corral and saw that Blaze and Captain were missing.

When Thorpe returned to Lily and Blue, he saw the wolf lift his head. After Thorpe placed a bowl of water in front of him, he said, "Drink, buddy." Blue lifted his head over the water and started drinking. Thorpe pulled Lily into his arms and tapped her lightly on the cheek. "Lily, wake up."

Stone and Isabelle moved beside Thorpe as he tried to wake Lily. Jed came from the wagon with all of the puppies squirming in his hands. "They're okay, Mr. Thorpe."

"Thank God."

"Yessir. He was looking out for us. I'll get the fire going and make us some fresh coffee," Jed offered. He placed the puppies beside Spirit. "You'd best feed your babies."

"Jed, wash that pot out before you make the coffee. I think Dora put her tonic in the coffeepot and in Blue's food," Thorpe said.

"You think Dora drugged us?" Isabelle asked.

"Yeah."

Isabelle looked at Stone, her eyes filling with tears. "What will that do to my baby?" She placed her hands on her stomach. It was the first time in days she couldn't feel the baby moving. "I don't feel anything."

Stone didn't hesitate to pull Isabelle into his embrace. "Don't think the worst. Maybe he's just sleeping. Let's wait and see what happens after you've had enough water to get this stuff through your system. Let's get you some more water, honey."

As soon as the words left Stone's mouth, the baby kicked. Stone felt it. "See there. My voice must have awakened him."

Isabelle laughed through her tears. "He likes your voice." She hugged Stone, and Stone held her in his arms for a brief moment. When she pulled away, she turned to see Thorpe still hovering over Lily. "Why do you think she won't wake?"

"Maybe Dora put more tonic in her coffee," Stone said.

"But I saw Dora give a cup to Harlow," Isabelle said.

"She probably put the tonic in the pot after she gave him a cup," Stone replied.

"Why would she do such a thing?" Isabelle asked.

"I guess the money was just too tempting," Stone said.

After Jed placed the coffee over the fire, he walked to the supply wagon to see what was missing.

Thorpe looked at Stone. "They took your horse and Blaze."

"I'm going to kill that horse-thieving son of a . . ." He didn't finish his thought out of respect for Isabelle. He couldn't remember being as angry as he was at that moment. Harlow and Dora had not only endangered their lives, but also the life of an innocent baby. He vowed he was going to hunt down Harlow if it was the last thing he did.

"Miss Dora is going to regret taking off with that no-account," Jed said. "They took some supplies and a box of cartridges."

"Dora is really going to regret her decision if Lily doesn't come around," Thorpe said. Lily looked so pale and fragile that it scared him. Blue came to his side and nosed Lily's arm, much the way he did the night before. Thorpe remembered the way Blue acted last night. "That was why Blue growled last night when Dora handed Lily a cup of coffee. He must have known Dora was up to something."

"I heard him," Stone said. "I just thought he didn't feel well."

"Blue knocked Lily's arm and the first cup spilled. Dora poured her another cup after he fell asleep," Isabelle reminded them.

"Does everyone still feel a bit groggy?" Thorpe asked.

Everyone nodded. "I'll get something for us to eat," Isabelle said.

"Get into some dry clothes first. We don't want you coming down with a cold," Stone instructed. Everyone had awakened with damp clothing from the light snow falling. He pointed to the sky and added, "I think this snow is going to really start coming down soon. I'll put the tent up so we can all sit around the fire and stay dry until we get our wits about us." Stone waited for Isabelle to walk away before he spoke to the men. "I can go after them."

"We can make the way station by tomorrow. Let's get there and then we'll go after them together," Thorpe replied. "We can't be sure the gang knows Harlow has left and we need all the firepower we have if they come for him. I'd bet my ranch that Harlow and Dora are going to try to get to his hiding place before the gang shows up. They don't want to split that money."

"That's what I was thinking," Stone agreed.

They all sat under the tent Stone and Jed constructed and ate as they watched over Lily. Blue and Spirit wouldn't leave her side. Thorpe thought Lily was such a small woman that maybe the dose of opium was just too much for her. It appeared that Dora didn't bother with Spirit since she was always in the wagon with her puppies and wasn't much of a threat. Blue was the one that would have caused Dora and Harlow problems. Thorpe was thankful the opium didn't kill him. He glanced at Isabelle and asked, "How are you feeling?"

"Fine, now that I've eaten. I just wish Lily would come around."

"She hasn't been sleeping much before this, so maybe she just needs a nice long rest," Jed said.

"I pray that's all it is. I don't know how Dora could have done this to us, particularly Lily. After everything Lily has done for her, this is how she repays her," Isabelle said.

"I tried to think the best of Miss Dora, but she makes bad decisions," Jed said. "I was hoping she had changed, seeing how kind Miss Lily was to her. She owed Miss Lily better than that."

Thorpe had to agree that Dora should have felt indebted to Lily, but he'd seen for himself that Dora didn't care much for anyone but herself. He wondered how long it would take Harlow to leave her stranded somewhere, or worse.

"Maybe we shouldn't travel until she wakes up," Isabelle said.

"We'll stay here." Thorpe didn't want to leave Lily's side. He looked at the sky, thinking Stone was right, the snow was increasing and he had a feeling they were about to see the beginning of a real snowstorm. "Let's pray the weather doesn't get worse. If we leave before dawn we can be at the way station by tomorrow night."

"When we get there, Thorpe and I will leave and track Dora and Harlow." Stone looked at Isabelle and figured she was worried she wouldn't make it to Wyoming in time for her to get married before the baby came. "If it looks like it will take too long, Thorpe can come back and take you to Fort Steele, and send a telegram for me so I can get some help."

Isabelle wanted to get to the fort by Christmas, but she didn't want Stone going

234

after those killers alone. She looked at Stone, and in that moment she realized how fond she was of him. He'd been so kind to her, always seeing to her comfort, and he made her feel safe. She'd come to depend on his even temperament and his courage. Even if it meant she gave birth before her wedding, she was willing to pay that price to keep Stone from harm. "No, I don't want you to go on alone. We can wait, but you come back with Thorpe. If we don't make it to Wyoming in time . . . well, so be it. It's more important to me that you two stay together." She was confident Lily would feel the same way.

Thorpe didn't like the sound of Stone going after them alone either, particularly with the rest of the gang on their trail. "We've made excellent time, so we have a few days to spare. It would be best to stay together in case the gang shows up."

It was a few hours later when Lily finally awoke. Thorpe was sitting beside her near the fire with Blue lying next to her. After Thorpe gave her water, he explained what happened. Lily's first concern was Isabelle and her baby, but Thorpe assured her everyone was okay, and Isabelle's baby was still kicking. Lily was visibly distraught, and she wrapped her arms around Blue and held him to her for comfort. When she collected her emotions, she turned to Thorpe. "Are we going after them?"

"Stone and I will go after them once we get you to the way station."

Lily gave him a mutinous glare. "They took Blaze. They could have killed Blue. I want to go."

Thorpe understood how she felt; he would be out for blood if they'd taken Smoke. "Lily, I will bring Blaze back to you. You know it's more important for you to stay with Isabelle. She can't stay at that way station alone." Thorpe knew he said the one thing that would sway her.

She didn't want to leave Isabelle at a time like this. Still, she was angry, and she couldn't remember ever feeling the way she felt right now. She had never expected Dora to betray them. And to take her horse was an insult. Dora had to know she would come after her for taking Blaze. If Thorpe didn't bring her horse back, she would go after him whether Thorpe liked it or not. "Then let's get moving. The sooner we are at the way station, the faster you and Stone can leave."

Thorpe surprised Lily when he jumped up

on the seat of the wagon and took the reins from her. "You're still looking a little groggy."

She didn't disagree with him. It was probably a good idea for him to handle the team because she was so angry, she didn't think she could keep her mind on what she was doing. "I checked my wagon and Dora took my money."

"Everything?"

She nodded. "All of the money from the sale of the farm. We'll be in a fine fix when we get to the fort."

Thorpe heard the concern in her voice. "I'll find them and get it back."

"The money is one thing, but Blaze is another. If you don't find him, I'll go after her."

He placed his hand over hers and squeezed. "I'll find them, and you have my word I will do what I can to bring Blaze home." She'd found Shadow for him, and he intended to keep his word to her.

"The three of us will keep moving since the station master will expect payment if we stay. You and Stone can catch up with us."

"I'll handle the expense of the way station. And the three of you will stay put." He may have sounded heavy-handed, but he wanted to make it clear she wasn't going one mile without him there.

CHAPTER FIFTEEN

The station master, Slim Mason, and his wife greeted them warmly when they pulled in the station later that day. Stone and Thorpe explained the situation to Mason, and Thorpe gave him money in advance for the three who would be staying until he returned. Thorpe liked Mason and he felt he was leaving them in capable hands.

"Thorpe, you and Stone need to have dinner before you leave," Lily said.

"We can't take the time. We're going to need all the luck we can get to find their trail in this snow." It had snowed the entire way to the way station, and Thorpe knew they probably wouldn't see any traces of their trail. They'd have to depend on other signs to find the pair. It helped that Stone knew the general direction they were headed. Thorpe would do everything in his power to keep his promise to Lily and bring Blaze back to her.

"You can take Daisy to carry the supplies since Stone is going to ride Shadow. She will do well in the snow and if she is near Blaze she will let you know."

"Thanks. I'll take care of her." He'd thought to take one of the other mules, but it might prove handy to have Daisy, considering her special connection to Blaze. He'd seen for himself how upset the mule was when Blaze was missing.

"You might want to take Blue, too."

"No, I want him to stay here. You never know who might ride in here. I'd rest easier knowing he is with you."

Thorpe and Stone walked to the stable where Jed was already packing Daisy with provisions. "How much do you want to take, Mr. Thorpe?"

"Enough for a week, but don't tell Lily. I don't want her worrying that we will be gone that long."

They were all packed and ready to leave when Lily walked into the stable and handed Thorpe a bundle. "Here's something for tonight. Mrs. Mason thought you and Stone might enjoy some home-cooked food." Lily had looked forward to sitting at a table enjoying a fine meal with Thorpe and the others. She hadn't sat at a table since she'd left Texas, and she didn't want to forget what it felt like to dress like a lady. She'd found parlor manners served little purpose out on the Plains, but she didn't want Thorpe to think she didn't know how to be feminine.

"It smells delicious." Thorpe stored the bundle in his saddlebag. "Thank Mrs. Mason for us. We'll stop in a few hours and enjoy her fine meal."

Lily gazed into his eyes. She had mixed emotions about him leaving, and was at a loss how to express her feelings. "I'd like to go with you," she said.

Thorpe gave her a stern look. "I know, but we've covered that. I'll have your word that you won't try to follow us."

"You have my word. I wouldn't want to leave Isabelle and Jed alone." She hesitated, then added, "Do be careful and come back in one piece without any arrows."

Smiling, Thorpe said, "Yes, ma'am."

"I plan on celebrating Christmas in Wyoming with you and Miss Isabelle, so you can be sure we'll be back," Stone said. Stone had powerful feelings for Isabelle, and he'd come to that realization when she told him her baby liked the sound of his voice. Her words made him feel like he was the proud father.

Isabelle was standing in the doorway of the stable and had overheard Stone's statement. "You'd best live up to that promise."

Stone grabbed Shadow's reins and led him out of the stable. "You take care, and take care of that babe. Rest up. We still have a ways to go when we get back."

Isabelle didn't want him to leave, and her strong emotions confused her. She told herself she loved Ethan; he was the man who had fathered her child. But having spent day after day with Stone, she couldn't deny she'd developed tender feelings for him. "Please hurry back."

Stone reached down and took her hand in his. "Don't you fret, honey. We'll be back as soon as possible."

Thorpe turned to Jed and shook his hand. "Thanks for your help, and I'm counting on you to keep Lily and Isabelle out of mischief."

Jed laughed. "That'll be a tall order, Mr. Thorpe, but you have my word they'll be on their best behavior."

Thorpe glanced at Lily and added, "Don't let her go wandering off on her own."

"Yessir."

"I gave you my word," Lily reminded him.

"I know, but I figure Jed is the one to make sure you remember your promise."

He leaned down and told Blue to keep an eye on Lily, too. He knew if anyone could keep her close, it would be Blue. "Stay with her, boy." Before he jumped on Smoke, he tugged at the braid over Lily's shoulder and winked at her.

Lily and Isabelle watched until the men were out of sight. When they turned toward the house, Lily placed her arm around Isabelle's waist as they walked. "You're quite fond of Stone, aren't you?"

"He's a very nice man."

"Yes, and handsome," Lily said.

Isabelle felt her face turning pink. "He is handsome. So is Thorpe."

"Hmm." Lily noticed Thorpe didn't promise to spend Christmas with them. He was anxious to get to Dove Creek, and she knew he would be leaving soon after they arrived at the fort.

"I wonder why Thorpe isn't married," Isabelle asked.

Lily didn't want to reveal that Thorpe told her his fiancée left him at the altar. "I'm sure he'd have no trouble finding a wife."

"I guess he hasn't found the right woman," Isabelle said. "Do you ever think about marrying, Lily?"

Lily was evasive in her response. "All I've wanted was to find my grandfather."

Isabelle hugged her. "You'll find him." Lily was the kindest person Isabelle had ever met. She always saw to everyone's needs above her own. Isabelle was confident God would see to it that a person as wonderful as Lily would have her prayers answered. "Lily, I'm sorry about Dora. I never expected her to do something like that."

"I have to admit I didn't expect her to deceive us and take up with a man like Harlow. I thought she really wanted to change her life." Not only was Lily surprised by Dora's betrayal, she was disappointed. "I think Jed was right when he said she was bitter over the past. She couldn't let go of the bad things that happened to her."

"Jed is a wise man," Isabelle said. "I started to question if Dora truly wanted to change. She didn't act like a woman who wanted to find a husband, or maybe she thought Thorpe was a possible husband for her. The way she blatantly flirted with him you would've thought he invited such behavior."

"I thought Thorpe was as interested in her," Lily admitted.

Isabelle couldn't believe what she was hearing. "Oh, Lily! Thorpe has no interest in Dora."

"That's what he told me. But Dora is a

lovely woman and experienced, and I thought it would be difficult for him to turn her away."

"I think she was jealous of you."

Lily furrowed her brow in confusion. "Of me? Why on earth would she be jealous of me?"

"She thought Thorpe was attracted to you. When Harlow expressed his interest in her, she was vulnerable to his honeyed words. She thought Thorpe rejected her because of you and it made her angry. I think she was afraid she wouldn't find a husband in Wyoming, and she knew when her beauty faded she would no longer be in demand in the saloon business." Isabelle stopped walking and turned to face Lily. "That's not all. She told me Harlow gave her his gold ring."

Lily was stunned. "Why didn't you tell me she was getting that close to Harlow?"

"You know Dora. I thought she was just flirting like usual. Plus, she didn't like Stone telling her what to do, so she was bound and determined to do the opposite. The last few days I didn't even see her paying attention to Harlow. I never expected her to help him escape." Isabelle's eyes filled with tears. "I'm sorry I didn't tell you about the ring."

"Don't cry. It's done and we can't change anything."

"It may not make sense to you, Lily, but I know how it feels when someone seems to want you when you know you are nothing but a burden to everyone else."

Lily knew Isabelle was speaking about her father. "You have a bright future before you, Isabelle. Don't let words of the past keep you prisoner. Your father will come around one day and realize what a mistake he has made by banishing you and your child."

Isabelle gave her a brittle smile. "I wish you were right, but you don't know my father. He's very judgmental, and I doubt he will ever admit he is wrong about his decisions."

"If that's the case, then you will go on and build a happy life with your new husband."

Thorpe and Stone rode for several hours before they stopped for the night. After they got the fire going, Thorpe pulled the bundle Lily had given him from his saddlebag and placed the contents in a pan to warm.

"This dinner is sure going to be welcome tonight," Stone said as he placed the coffee over the fire.

"Looks like we're having beef and corn bread. A fine meal." Thorpe pulled out the plates and cups while they waited. Working around the fire made him think of Lily and how much he liked watching her move around the campfire.

"It's not the same without the women around." Stone had a feeling he knew what Thorpe was thinking.

"No, it's been a real pleasure having them around. A man absent a woman's presence forgets his manners."

"You seem right fond of Lily," Stone said.

"I'd say you're taken with Isabelle," Thorpe countered.

Stone wasn't hesitant to tell him the truth. "You'd be right. She's a fine woman, but she has a man waiting for her. Lily doesn't have a man."

"I told you when we first met that I'm not looking for a wife, and I haven't changed my mind." Thorpe dished the food onto the plates as Stone poured the coffee.

"I reckon that don't keep you from enjoying her company."

"Lily's a friend, just like you." Thorpe looked at him and grinned. "She's just one heck of a lot prettier and probably a better shot."

Stone chuckled. "Amen to that."

"Have you thought about what you'll do if Isabelle's soldier doesn't want her?"

Stone gave him a serious look. "I can't imagine a man wouldn't want her."

"Well, there is that. But I have to admit I've wondered why he didn't marry her before he left."

Stone had thought the same thing. If he'd compromised a woman like Isabelle, he would have taken her to see the preacher before he rode out of town. "Yeah, I've thought the same thing. I would have married her before I left."

That statement confirmed what Thorpe had been thinking. He wasn't sure when he recognized that Stone was smitten with Isabelle, but when he saw him say good-bye today, it was obvious he was crazy about her. "So does that mean you would marry her if her soldier doesn't?"

"I'd need to settle down because I'd never want to leave her."

Thorpe figured he had his answer. "Do you see yourself roaming all over the country chasing outlaws when you're older?"

"No, and I'm of an age where I need to make some decisions soon."

Thorpe respected Stone and felt like they were becoming good friends. "You told me you'd done some ranching. There's some land next to my ranch for sale and I could help you make a go of it."

Thorpe's offer was more than generous and too tempting not to be given serious consideration. "I don't have a lot of money."

"You don't need much. The property is owned by the bank and I know Mr. Bowles will work with you."

"I may just take you up on your offer. When I get everything settled with Harlow and his gang, I'll ride your way."

"I hope you do." Thorpe was sincere; it'd be a pleasure to have a man as trustworthy as Stone as a neighbor.

"I know if I was in your position I'd find me a beautiful woman to marry and have myself some children. Your ranch sounds like the perfect place for a family." Stone couldn't understand why Thorpe wasn't trying to corral Lily. She'd make him a fine wife.

Thorpe explained what had happened with Evelyn at the church. "She's ruined my appetite for marriage."

After Thorpe's explanation, Stone had a better understanding of why he wanted to steer clear of women, at least for a while. "I can see why that experience might make you more cautious, but you can't judge all women by her."

Thorpe grunted. "You do remember we are out here in the snow chasing Dora. Anyway, my ranch keeps me busy and I don't really have time for a family."

"I understand you want no part of marriage right now, but you'll come around. One day you will meet a woman who you just can't let go."

Thorpe laughed. "You haven't had the same experience with a woman."

"True enough. But you have to admit it's a real pleasure to look at Isabelle and Lily. And you can't tell me you don't enjoy the way those ladies expect a prayer to be said before they eat their meals. Just being around them makes me want to be a better man. Spending time in that wagon next to Isabelle made me recognize I've been alone too long."

—Thorpe agreed that he enjoyed being around the women on the trail; they made the most mundane task pleasant because you knew you were working for someone besides yourself. Like Stone, he appreciated the way the women made him want to brush off his dormant manners and clean up his language. He'd never seen Lily take a bite of food until she'd prayed. The many times he'd dined at the Tremayne ranch, he'd never seen them give thanks before eating. Evelyn probably never prayed. There she was again. He figured Evelyn's betrayal was too recent for him to envision trusting another woman no matter how much he liked her. "Do you think you will recognize the area where you met up with Harlow?"

With Thorpe's question, Stone figured the discussion about women and marriage was at an end. "Yeah, we should be in the general area late tomorrow. It's a real shame Dora betrayed her friends. I'd say she owed Lily more than she could ever repay."

"You're right about that. Dora doesn't understand friendship." Dora was another reason Thorpe couldn't forget about Evelyn. It was easy to be deceived by a pretty face, but thanks to Evelyn, Thorpe had misgivings from the moment he met Dora.

"I'm surprised Harlow didn't kill us while we were out."

"The shots would have alerted the gang."

"Yeah. But I bet he gave it some thought." His expression was serious when he asked, "Do you think Dora would have stopped him?"

Thorpe had pondered that very question. "I honestly don't know the answer to that question. But I know one thing; I sure wouldn't give her another opportunity to double-cross us."

"I just hope we don't run into the whole gang at one time."

They broke camp before dawn and had ridden through the deepening snow for hours, stopping occasionally to give the horses a rest. Each time, Stone would pull out his field glasses and scan the territory, but they hadn't seen any signs of riders. After six hours, they stopped and unloaded the horses, allowing them to rest for a couple of hours while they had something to eat. Under different circumstances, they might have appreciated the beauty of the pure white snow covering the terrain, but right now all they could think about was how it was slowing them down.

"I think if we keep going, we'll make the area by nightfall," Stone said.

"We've pushed the animals hard. Let's rest them for a couple of hours. With this snow we'll be able to see where we are going tonight."

Stone agreed with Thorpe. "I have a feeling Harlow's gang is on their trail since we haven't seen them behind us."

Lying on her cot, Lily stared into the darkness of the small room she was sharing with Isabelle. Isabelle had fallen asleep hours before, but no matter how hard Lily tried, she couldn't keep her mind off Thorpe. She was confident Thorpe and Stone could handle themselves if they ran into trouble, assuming the odds weren't overwhelming. Her first thought was to go to the stable and saddle a horse and go find them. But she'd given her word.

She turned to look out the window and she saw Blue sitting there staring at the moon. Spirit and the puppies were curled up on a pallet in the corner. Lily left her bed and pulled the blanket with her. She spread the blanket on the floor and pulled Blue next to her. She had the feeling he wanted to go after Thorpe, too. "They'll be okay. Don't you worry, boy."

Thorpe and Stone rested for two hours and loaded up again. The snow had slowed considerably the farther south they traveled. And the moon provided enough light for the horses to navigate the terrain safely. Stone reined in when he recognized the area where his partner had met him with Harlow in tow. "This is it." He pointed in the direction they needed to go. They rode another hour before Thorpe finally spotted tracks in the snow.

"I guess we found Harlow's gang," Thorpe said. "Looks like they might have been this way a few hours earlier."

"Yeah."

They pulled their rifles out and unbuttoned their coats so they would have easy access to their pistols. The gang was obviously headed in the same direction they were going. It wasn't long before they spotted more hoofprints.

"Not shod," Thorpe said.

Stone dismounted and kneeled down to closely examine the mishmash of prints. "None of these hoofprints belong to Captain, but I know we're headed in the right direction."

"We'll find them." Thorpe was determined to keep his promise to Lily that he would find Blaze.

CHAPTER SIXTEEN

Thorpe and Stone followed the tracks for hours, and it was late morning when they dismounted.

"The braves are right behind the gang," Thorpe said.

"Yeah. It makes me wonder if Harlow and Dora knew the gang was right behind them."

"I say we keep going." They were a day behind since they had been drugged and stopped at the way station. They'd be lucky to catch up with anyone before they reached Mexico.

"I agree." Stone just hoped they weren't too late, that the Indians hadn't caught up with them first.

They rode for another two hours and pulled to a halt to give the horses a brief rest. Both men poured water from their canteens into their hats to give the animals a drink. Thorpe stroked Daisy's neck and said, "You let me know if you think Blaze is near."

"I'm sure Harlow expects me to come after him," Stone said.

"I'm thinking he wasn't expecting a full house," Thorpe replied.

Stopping occasionally to listen, they heard nothing out of the ordinary. Moving slowly over uncertain terrain, Thorpe kept his eyes on Smoke for a signal that he heard something they couldn't. When his ears flicked up, Thorpe raised a hand for Stone to rein in. He glanced at Daisy, but she wasn't reacting. Hearing what sounded like an animal's low growl, they dismounted and tied the animals in the brush. Slowly, they made their way toward the sounds Thorpe recognized. Coyotes. By a large outcropping of boulders, they saw two coyotes in a standoff over something on the ground. The men didn't want to fire off a shot and alert anyone of their exact location if they weren't alone. Thorpe leaned over and dug through the snow until he found two large rocks. He handed one to Stone and pointed to one of the coyotes. They hurled the rocks at the same time, both hitting their intended targets with accurate precision. When the coyotes ran out of sight, the men pulled their pistols and made their way to the boulders. They found Dora lying facedown with a gunshot in her back. Thorpe knew she'd been there awhile by the snow that had accumulated on her body. When he turned her over, he saw that she was lying across a hole in the earth where someone had been digging.

Stone looked around to see if there were more dead bodies, but the only thing he saw was blood on the snow leading away from an area. "The gang was here and so were the Indians."

Thorpe holstered his pistol and lifted Dora out of the way. He noticed a little bag hanging from Dora's wrist so he pulled it off. After he opened it, he pulled out some folded bills and held it up for Stone to see. "I guess we found Lily's money."

Stone shook his head, at a loss for words at Dora's betrayal.

Thorpe replaced the cash in the reticule and tucked it into his coat pocket. He pulled his knife from his scabbard and started digging in the hard ground. Within minutes the tip of his knife hit something buried less than a foot from the surface. He looked up at Stone. "Could we be this lucky?"

Stone kneeled down to help him. "Let's see."

They unearthed a strongbox and pulled it

from the hole. The lock had already been removed, so Thorpe opened the lid. "I never expected this."

Stone whistled. "I guess the Indians ran them off before they could get to the loot." He saw a woman's gold locket on top of the money. When he opened the locket he saw the miniatures of a man and a little girl. It was the little girl that Harlow had shot. "I know where this belongs." He tucked the locket into his pocket.

"If the Indians didn't kill them, they will be back for this." Thorpe looked down at Dora. She may have deceived them, but she didn't deserve to die because she fell for Harlow's lies. She'd made some bad decisions and everyone had warned her off Harlow, but as Jed said, she wouldn't listen to anyone. "I wonder if Harlow killed her."

"I wouldn't be surprised. Either way, he was the cause," Stone said. He pointed toward the trail. "Someone was losing a lot of blood and I hope it is Harlow's. No one deserves it more."

Thorpe couldn't disagree with that sentiment. "Let's unload the horses and we'll bury her before we go after them."

They finished covering Dora with rocks to keep the animals away, and Thorpe and Stone removed their hats and stood over her grave. The spot was in an isolated area so far off the trail that Thorpe figured it was possible no one would ever see her grave. He wondered if she had relatives somewhere that should be notified of her death. Did she have anyone in her life that would mourn her passing?

"It's a shame it ended this way. I told her to stay away from him," Stone said.

Stone was right; everyone had tried to steer her away from Harlow. "It's not your fault. Dora wasn't one to take advice. Now she's paid the price."

"That's a fact." Stone settled his hat back on his head. "I reckon we'd best get at it."

"Yeah. Let's see where these hombres are headed."

They distributed the money from the strongbox to their saddlebags before they started following the trail of blood. The Indians were definitely chasing the gang.

"They were moving fast," Thorpe said.

"Yeah, and the Indians were gaining on them."

They rode at a pace that allowed them to carefully scan the terrain. It wasn't long before Thorpe spotted a boot heel sticking from the brush off the trail. They reined in and Thorpe dismounted to check it out while Stone cocked his pistol to be at the ready.

"Indians got him. It's not Harlow," Thorpe said.

Stone dismounted and walked to the brush. He turned the dead man over. "Corbin Ethridge. The Indians did the world a favor. He shot a bank clerk in Deadwood for no reason. Witnesses said the clerk had already given him the money, but Ethridge shot him in the head for moving too slow." Stone pulled the pistol from Ethridge's holster and tucked it in his belt.

"From the looks of it, no one stopped to make sure he was dead," Thorpe said.

"You can't credit killers with that much of a conscience." Stone wished he could say he was surprised, but after the evil perpetrated by the members of this gang on innocent people, nothing they did surprised him. "Let's see if we can find his horse." They followed the single set of hoofprints through the brush until they found the horse.

"I say we follow the trail a few more hours and then stop for the night," Thorpe said.

"If we don't see anything by noon tomorrow, let's head back. You know if the Indians don't kill them all, then they will come after the money. When they find it gone, they'll come after us. I've wasted enough time chasing Harlow. He'll come after me now that we have the money," Stone replied.

Thorpe didn't want to head back. He wanted to find Blaze. "I want you to head back alone with the money. I'm going to keep going."

"If anyone should keep going, it should be me," Stone told him. "I'm the marshal."

"You've got the money and Harlow may be dead, but I want to find Blaze. I promised Lily."

Stone understood what it meant to make a promise under most circumstances. Right now he felt certain Lily would understand why they had to go back. "Lily wouldn't want you out here on your own. We both should go back. You know they'll come for us if they are still breathing." He smacked Thorpe on the back. "Besides, I don't think we need to take a chance on having our scalps lifted."

Thorpe laughed. "No, I've had one arrow this trip and I sure don't need another one, but I gave Lily my word. If they got away from the braves, they'll circle back, find the money gone, and they'll head to the way station. It'd be best if you were there."

Stone didn't like his plan. "I think you need to come back with me."

"I'll follow them another twenty-four hours. If I don't think I can catch up with them, I'll turn around," Thorpe said.

"No, I'm not going back without you. That's final." Stone didn't relish the thought of either one of them being out here alone with outlaws and Indians. "Lily nursed you back to health once, and I for darn sure don't want her to have to do it again. We'll go together. No arguments."

It was late at night when Thorpe and Stone reached the way station a week later. Slim and Lily, with Blue standing beside her, met them at the porch with their rifles cradled in their arms.

"We didn't know who was riding in," Slim said.

Thorpe dismounted and gazed at Lily as he bent over and rubbed Blue's head. She looked so pretty standing there with that rifle in her arms, he was tempted to lean over and kiss her. He thought about her thousands of times while he was gone, and he thought she was even lovelier than he'd remembered. "Is Jed watching us from the stable?"

Lily was rubbing Daisy's nose. "Yes."

"Good girl." Instead of a kiss, he yanked

on her braid. "No problems while we were gone?"

Lily was so happy he was back that she could hardly speak. She'd missed him, and she hadn't realized how much until that moment. "No problems." She took hold of Daisy's reins and walked beside Thorpe to the stables. "You didn't find them?"

"Yes, and no. We found where Harlow hid the money. And we found Dora." Thorpe stopped walking and looked at her. "I'm sorry, Lily, but she was dead."

Lily's eyes widened. "No!" She had not expected this news and it saddened her beyond belief. Even though Isabelle disagreed with her, Lily still thought it was possible Thorpe may have some tender feelings for Dora.

"I'm sorry, Lily. We buried her proper." Thorpe expected hearing of Dora's death would be difficult for her to handle. Lily tried to see the best in Dora, and she'd been deceived for her effort. But Thorpe knew she would still be upset by her death.

"What about Harlow?"

"He was gone. The gang had caught up with Harlow and Dora, but so had the Indians. We figured the braves attacked just as they were digging up the money and they had to take off before they could get to the

263

strongbox. We followed their trail and found one of the killers with an arrow in his back."

"Did the Indians kill Dora?"

"I don't think so. She was shot in the back. I'd say it was before the braves attacked."

"You think they will come after the money?"

"If they got away from the Indians, I figure we'll see them again." Thorpe reached into his pocket and pulled out the bag that was on Dora's wrist. "This was on Dora. I figure the money inside is what she stole from you."

Lily examined the reticule her mother had given her. "This is mine." She reached inside and found the money. "Yes, this is what she stole. Thank you." She turned to lead Daisy into the stable and Thorpe followed.

"I'm sorry the way things turned out with Dora."

"Me, too. I know it must have upset you finding her like that," Lily replied.

Thorpe didn't catch her meaning. "After what Stone told me about Harlow, I can't say I was surprised. Dora put her trust in the wrong man."

Did he mean he was the right man? "Yes, she did."

Thorpe reached for Lily's arm and turned her to face him. He'd dreaded this moment. He'd given his word he would find Blaze and he'd let her down. He looked into her eyes and said, "I'm sorry I didn't find Blaze."

She hadn't asked, but when they were riding in, she saw that Blaze wasn't with them. She didn't doubt that he'd tried. "I know. I'll find Blaze once we get Isabelle to the fort."

He could see in her eyes how sad she was. She didn't place blame, but that didn't stop him from feeling like he'd failed her. Before he replied, she turned and walked inside the stable where Stone was waiting with questions of his own.

"How's Isabelle?"

"She's doing well considering the baby is kicking day and night. She'll be happy to see you," Lily replied.

"We're happy to be back." Stone wasn't a man to admit he worried about situations where he had no control, but he spent a great deal of time fretting over Isabelle's condition. When he sat beside Isabelle in the wagon, he'd felt the baby kick a time or two, and he didn't want that babe to show up before Isabelle was safely at the fort.

Jed walked over to help Lily unpack Daisy.

"Are you two hungry?"

"Yessir, and we'd sure like some of your coffee, Jed," Thorpe said.

"Well, you're in luck. Mrs. Mason just asked me to make some for her."

"Thank the good Lord," Slim uttered. When he saw everyone staring at him, he added, "My wife never could make good coffee, and we've been married for near thirty years." Then he waggled his finger at them. "Now, don't go tellin' her I said that. But I sure owe a debt to Jed for teachin' her how to make it right."

Stone smiled at the older man. "You mean you never told her you didn't like her coffee in thirty years?"

Slim smacked Stone on the back. "Son, I can tell you ain't married, because if you was, you'd know that if you said something like that to a wife, you'd be sleepin' in the stable for a few nights. I might not be the smartest man around, but I got more sense than that. I like sleepin' in a warm bed."

"Her cooking makes up for her coffee," Lily said as she pulled the blanket off of Daisy's back.

"No argument there, ma'am," Slim responded. "The first year we were married, I gained twenty pounds."

"I knew there was a reason I'm not married," Thorpe said.

Slim snorted. "You young bucks just wait. Your time is coming. You'll meet up with the right woman, and she'll have you chasin' your tails."

"Not me, Slim. Definitely not me," Thorpe said.

Slim moved his gaze to Stone. "What about you? You scared of getting hitched like this big galoot?" He hooked his thumb in Thorpe's direction.

"Nope. As a matter of fact, I could use a few pounds."

Thorpe turned to Jed. "What about you, Jed? You have a hankering to get wed?"

"Well, Mr. Thorpe, I ain't never met the right one, but I wouldn't be opposed to finding me a wife. She'd have to cook as good as Miss Lily and Miss Isabelle though."

Slim glanced at Lily. "And what about you? Why haven't you found a man and got yourself in the family way like your friend? You're so pretty, I know you have young bucks sniffin' around your door."

Lily felt her cheeks turning red and she thought about kicking Slim in the shins, but she didn't think that would be the polite thing to do. "I'm more concerned with finding my grandfather than finding a husband."

"Hmmph." Slim eyed Thorpe and Stone. "I don't know what's wrong with you young pups. She's the prettiest gal I ever laid eyes on. I guess you're just plumb blind and stupid." He turned and guided one of the horses to a stall, and Stone and Thorpe silently followed his lead.

Lily stood there for a moment stunned speechless. Judging by the lack of response from the men, she didn't have as much appeal to them as she did to Slim. Well, no matter. She wasn't looking for a husband anyway. She led Daisy to a stall and started brushing her down.

Thorpe couldn't disagree with Slim's assessment of Lily's beauty; he'd thought the same thing more times than he could count. But he still hadn't forgotten how lovely Evelyn was, and he'd learned the hard way that beauty didn't count for a whole lot.

Once the horses were in the stalls, fed and watered, the men grabbed their saddlebags and they all walked to the house.

"Let's see what we can find for you boys to eat," Slim said.

Isabelle was waiting for them when they walked through the door. "I'm so glad you're back. We didn't expect you to be gone so long. Did you find them?"

The men didn't know if they should tell

Isabelle the truth for fear of upsetting her, and they both glanced at Lily. Lily took Isabelle by the hand and led her to the bench to sit while she explained what happened.

Isabelle was sorry to hear of Dora's death, but not surprised. "She wouldn't listen to anyone. Lily told her Harlow was bad news, but she refused to take heed."

The men sat at the table and explained the possible scenarios they would be facing once they left the way station.

"If some of the gang are still alive, they will know we have the money. We're likely to have more trouble when we leave here," Stone said. "We stayed out longer than was prudent, but Thorpe was determined to find Lily's horse." Stone was certain Thorpe wasn't the kind of man that would expound on the lengths he'd go to keep his word. All the same, Stone thought it was important for Lily to know that Thorpe tried to bring her horse back to her.

Lily glanced at Thorpe. "Thank you for that."

Thorpe couldn't shake the feeling he'd failed to live up to his word. "Stone and I thought about asking you ladies to stay here until we get that money somewhere safe, but that might leave you vulnerable here."

Lily hated the thought of the men leaving

them behind. "They will definitely come for that money."

"If they are alive," Stone emphasized. He gazed at the two women. "We even thought about one of us taking the money ahead of the rest of you."

Before he could finish his sentence, Lily spoke up. "That doesn't make sense at all. There's no guarantee they would follow one man instead of coming after the wagons. They'd probably do both."

"That's why we decided against that option," Thorpe acknowledged.

"We are all going to the fort together," Isabelle stated flatly. She'd come this far and there was no way and no one that would keep her from getting to the fort before Christmas. Now that the men were back, she wanted them all to stay together.

"We just want you ladies to be safe," Stone added, looking directly into Isabelle's eyes.

"We've made it this far, I think we should stay together," Lily said.

Mrs. Mason placed the bowls of food on the table and Slim put plates and cups in front of Thorpe and Stone. "Now you men eat before it gets cold."

Slim grabbed the coffeepot and filled their cups. "And have some of my wife's fine coffee," he said, giving them a wink.

"He likes my coffee now that Jed taught me how to make it," Mrs. Mason said.

Slim's mouth dropped open.

Mrs. Mason laughed at his expression. "Close your mouth, you old goat. You think I didn't know you hated my coffee?"

"I'd say *hate* is a pretty strong word, Mabel," Slim replied. "It was . . . well . . ."

Mabel walked from the stove and patted Slim on the back as she passed. "That's okay, honey, at least you didn't tell me it was tolerable when it wasn't. Even I knew Jed's was a whole lot better." She looked at Lily and Isabelle and shook her head. "Why is it men always think they can fool their women? Don't they know that a woman knows when her man is keeping something from her?"

"Women are just as skilled at keeping things from men," Thorpe stated to no one in particular.

Mabel's comment was made in jest, but Thorpe's words held no levity. The older woman detected some bitterness in Thorpe's voice, and she figured someone had deceived him in the past. "If it's to spare their feelings over something as simple as coffee, then it doesn't hurt to err on the side of kindness. But there should be no secrets held between a husband and a wife

271

who love each other."

Lily knew Thorpe was thinking about his ex-fiancée. She wondered if he would ever get over the hurt of that failed relationship, or if he would ever trust another woman. Until Dora, Lily had never experienced betrayal. She imagined the pain was worse if you were betrayed by a person you loved. Thorpe must have loved his fiancée very much to have been hurt so deeply that he could never again envision himself married. He probably relived his heartbreak with Dora's deceit.

Lily prayed he would one day be willing to entrust his heart to another. She thought Thorpe was a wonderful man and any woman would be very fortunate to have his love. While he was gone she'd come to realize how much he meant to her. She'd be happy to reach the fort for Isabelle's sake, but she dreaded the day she would be forced to say good-bye to Thorpe.

CHAPTER SEVENTEEN

Instead of riding ahead of the small caravan, Thorpe had driven the wagon with Lily beside him since they'd left the way station four days prior.

"You see that?" Thorpe asked, pointing to an unusual rock formation in the distance. "That's Chimney Rock. We'll be there in a couple of days."

"Oh my, how beautiful." Lily stared at the infamous landmark she heard so much about, but she hadn't expected to become so emotional when she actually saw it for the first time. She felt it was the beacon that was leading her to her new life. There was an overwhelming sense of accomplishment in reaching this destination, and it was all due to the man beside her. Without him, their future would have been quite uncertain.

Thorpe understood this was a seminal moment for those seeing the landmark for the first time. He'd seen Chimney Rock before, but he could still recall how he felt. Even though many travelers still had a long way to go after they reached this point, some would travel to California, while others would go south, once they saw that landmark their spirits were renewed. "Some travelers climb that rock and carve their names."

"Just think, years after those people have died, their names remain as testimony of their life and their journey to those that follow." She turned to look at Thorpe. "I'd like to see some of the names if we have time." She felt a sense of responsibility to pay homage to those people brave enough to chance this journey. Somehow she knew her grandfather would have stopped for the same reason. She could envision him carving his name somewhere on the rock.

"Once we get there, we will only be a few days from Fort Steele."

Just as they stopped for the night, it started to snow again. Everyone surrounded the fire after dinner, but Isabelle could no longer sleep comfortably on the ground so she had to retire to her wagon.

"Lily, would you mind taking a walk with me?" Isabelle asked.

Lily understood Isabelle wanted to see to her personal needs. "Of course." She picked up her rifle and walked with Isabelle with Blue behind them.

"Now don't go wandering off if you need to go in the night. I'm taking first watch with Jed, so just yell for me," Lily told her.

"It seems like I have to go every thirty minutes," Isabelle complained. "I hate to bother you every time."

"It's no bother." She'd noticed Isabelle was needing to make more trips recently and she wondered if that was normal. She hoped this baby didn't decide to arrive before they reached the fort. "We'll be at the fort in a couple of days and you'll have no more bouncing around in that blasted wagon and that may help."

"I'm looking forward to that." Isabelle rubbed her protruding belly. "He probably won't know what to think being out of that wagon."

Lily had noticed Isabelle was always referring to the baby as *he* now. "I imagine he needs a rest just like his mother."

Lily returned to the fire after she made sure Isabelle was resting peacefully.

Stone had already fallen asleep, and Thorpe leaned back on his saddle and pulled his hat low over his eyes. "Wake me in two hours."

"Mr. Thorpe, you can sleep longer," Jed said.

"Two hours is fine, Jed."

Lily waited until she thought Thorpe was asleep before she spoke to Jed. "Have you ever delivered a baby, Jed?"

"No, ma'am, but I've seen my momma deliver a fair amount of babes."

"It seems Isabelle is getting bigger every day and she needs to go . . . well, to see to her needs every few minutes. I'm worried she won't make it to the fort."

"My momma said all women get real big in the last month, and as far as the other, I think that's the way things normally happen. I don't think Miss Isabelle will have that baby until Christmas."

Lily prayed Jed knew what he was talking about. She also prayed a doctor would be at the fort. "From your mouth to God's ears, Jed."

"Christmas will be mighty special with a new baby," Jed said.

Lily smiled at his childlike enthusiasm over the prospect of a new baby. "Yes, it will be very special."

"Miss Lily, we'll leave everything up to the Good Lord. He knows what He's doing. He'll help Miss Isabelle when the time comes."

Lily knew she shouldn't worry like she did, and be more like Jed, believing all would be well. She admired that about Jed; he lived his faith with confidence.

Thorpe wasn't sleeping, and he'd heard the tension in Lily's voice. He'd never delivered a baby either, but he didn't think it would be much different than delivering a calf. Still, he hoped Jed was right about Isabelle holding off until Christmas. He wanted something to go right on this trip. It would be better for Isabelle to have a doctor near and help her through the ordeal.

It was approaching the hour to wake Thorpe when Lily heard a noise that she thought came from the area near the horses. She glanced at Jed and he nodded, indicating he'd heard the same noise. She grabbed her rifle and walked swiftly toward the improvised corral. Blue was on her heels and growling low. Ducking under the rope to reach the horses, she moved among them to determine the cause of their restlessness. Blue would let her know if coyotes were about. Seeing nothing out of the ordinary, she ducked back under the rope and that was when she heard the sound of a pistol being cocked behind her.

"Drop that rifle." The voice came from the darkness.

Blue gave a menacing growl and started to move, but Lily grabbed him by the fur. She didn't recognize the voice and she feared Blue would be shot if he attacked. She wasn't about to drop her weapon. "No."

The man laughed. He liked Lily's spirit. She had to be the woman Harlow mentioned several times. "Maybe you better turn around and see where this pistol is pointed."

Lily turned and saw a big man holding Isabelle with one arm tight around her neck and he had a pistol pressed against her temple.

Tears were streaming down Isabelle's cheeks. "I'm sorry, Lily. I left the wagon without calling for you."

"Shhh. Don't fret about that. This is nothing I can't handle," Lily said.

The man grinned. "Shut up and drop that rifle. You must be the one that Harlow wanted. He talked about how pretty you was."

"Where is Harlow?"

"He took an arrow and we left him on the trail. He'd already told us you'd have the money."

Blue was growling viciously at the man, torn between pulling away from Lily's grip and attacking the intruder, or staying by her side.

"Unless you want a bullet in him, shut him up."

At Lily's command Blue stopped growling.

"Now drop that rifle," he ordered again.

Lily dropped her rifle. "Now what?"

"Walk back to the fire and no tricks or I'll put a bullet in her brain."

Lily laced her fingers in Blue's fur and held him firmly. They turned in unison and slowly walked back toward the fire. She heard the man tell Isabelle to move forward.

When Jed saw Lily approach, he started to ask if she saw anything, but he knew something was wrong by the look on her face. He stood and that's when he saw Isabelle with a gun to her head. Jed moved forward at the same time the man called out, "Come on in!"

"Leave Miss Isabelle alone," Jed shouted. Jed didn't wait for a response before he reacted. He hurled himself toward Isabelle and the man holding her captive.

Hearing Jed yell, Thorpe and Stone rolled off their blankets onto their stomachs with their pistols drawn just as a shot rang out.

The man had turned his pistol on Jed and pulled the trigger. The bullet slammed into Jed's shoulder, the impact propelling him backward and he fell to the ground.

"No!" Isabelle cried, trying in vain to pull away from the man's grip.

"Down, Isabelle!" Lily screamed as she pulled her pistol from her waistband.

Isabelle tried to move, but the man held her tightly to him and took aim at Lily. Four additional men raced into camp with guns blazing and total pandemonium ensued.

Twisting around, Isabelle was able to sink her teeth into the man's bicep. He automatically jerked his arm away and shoved her to the ground.

Lily dropped to her knee and fired at the man before he had a chance to react. He slumped to the ground.

Thorpe and Stone were blasting away at the four men advancing on them. One man turned and fired at Lily, and Thorpe unloaded a round at the exact moment Blue leaped through the air going for the man's throat. The man staggered backward from the force of Thorpe's bullet, which hit him in the chest just as Blue took him to the ground. Thorpe didn't know if his bullet found its target, or if he'd grazed Blue. Thorpe and Stone quickly dispatched the remaining killers.

The action was over within seconds, and Thorpe glanced at Lily to make sure she was unharmed. She was running toward Jed as Blue raced to her. He walked to the men on the ground and picked up their guns.

"I'm just hit in the shoulder, Miss Lily," Jed told her when she kneeled beside him.

Stone helped Isabelle to her feet. "Are you hurt?"

"I'm okay. I'm so sorry, Lily, this was all my fault."

Lily wasn't upset with Isabelle; she'd been frightened to death when she saw that gun flush against her temple. "They were going to attack us one way or the other. It's not your fault."

Lily hugged Blue to her when Thorpe kneeled beside her and inspected Jed's wound.

"Are you sure you're not hurt?" Stone asked Isabelle again. When he'd realized one of the gang was holding her at gunpoint, he'd felt his whole body tense. He wasn't sure he could have been as calm as Lily, or as precise a shot.

"I'm fine, but I should have listened to Lily."

Isabelle started to cry and Stone took her in his arms and let her cry on his shoulder.

281

"Shh, it's all over."

"Thorpe, if you'll help Jed to the fire, I'll get my herbs," Lily said.

"Jed, I'm sorry. This wouldn't have happened if I had called for Lily," Isabelle said between sobs.

"Don't trouble yourself about that. I'll be just fine," Jed assured her.

Isabelle stepped away from Stone and wiped her face on her skirt. "I'll heat some water to clean Jed's wound."

Stone walked over and looked down at the man who'd held Isabelle at gunpoint. He was lying on his back with a hole between his eyes. "I don't believe it. Thorpe, you have to see this."

Thorpe was supporting Jed's weight and they both turned to see what Stone was talking about. "What is it?"

"This is Kip Young, he's wanted for two murders. Lily made one heck of a shot. She got him smack-dab between the eyes." Stone was positive he couldn't have been as accurate under the circumstances.

Thorpe and Jed walked to the dead man to see for themselves.

"I knew she was skilled, but I didn't know she was that good, Mr. Thorpe."

Thorpe could hardly believe what he was seeing. "I didn't either. But nothing that woman does surprises me."

"Harlow wasn't with them," Stone said.

"That man told Lily that Harlow took an arrow and they left him," Isabelle said.

"I guess he must be dead," Stone replied.

Once Thorpe helped Jed to the fire, he pulled his knife and stuck it in the flames. After he tore Jed's shirt, he took a look at his wound. "Jed, it looks like it's my turn to dig into your skin."

"I expected as much."

"Stone, would you get me some whiskey?" Thorpe asked.

"Sure thing."

"Now, Mr. Thorpe, you know I ain't much for spirits."

Thorpe reached for a cup sitting on a rock and tossed out the coffee. "Consider it medicine. And it's the best we have right now since I don't think Lily kept any of Dora's tonic."

Stone returned with a bottle and Thorpe poured a generous amount of the liquor into the cup and handed it to Jed. "Drink this."

When Jed didn't immediately comply, Thorpe said, "Stop looking at that whiskey like it's a rattler and drink up."

Jed made a face, but he took a large swig and immediately started coughing. "Miss Lily, I think Mr. Thorpe is trying to kill me with this stuff."

"I know it's awful, but you'll thank him later." Lily urged him to finish drinking what was left in the cup. Once Thorpe cleaned Jed's shoulder and doused the wound with whiskey, Lily pulled the knife from the fire.

They waited a few minutes for the whiskey to work its magic on Jed before Thorpe started digging into his skin. Fortunately, the bullet wasn't deep and Thorpe quickly dislodged it with the tip of his blade.

Lily had her poultice ready to apply to Jed's shoulder and with Thorpe's help they wrapped the bandage quickly.

"Mr. Thorpe, that didn't hurt much at all."

Thorpe smiled at him, noting his eyes were looking heavy. "That's because the whiskey relaxes you." Thorpe knew from personal experience that whiskey didn't necessarily take the pain away, but it did help you relax. Considering Jed was a teetotaler, the whiskey would probably help him sleep for a few hours.

Jed's head was bobbing up and down and he mumbled, "It sure does that. Yessir, it surely does that."

Thorpe lowered him down to his bedroll and Lily covered him with some blankets.

Stone stoked the fire to keep it roaring so

Jed would stay warm through the night. "I guess we'd best get these bodies buried before the animals descend on us."

When the last body was covered with rocks, they walked back to the fire to see Isabelle sitting near Jed. "Where's Lily?" Thorpe asked.

"I thought she was helping you," Isabelle said.

Stone ran to Lily's wagon and looked inside. Spirit was alone with her puppies. "Blue is gone, too."

Thorpe grabbed his saddle, but before he walked a few steps, Lily appeared through the brush leading Blaze, Captain, and three more horses. She saw Thorpe glaring at her. "I knew they would be close by because Daisy was acting out," she said quickly before he scolded her for going off by herself again.

Thorpe didn't say anything; he was so happy to see the smile on her face from having found Blaze that he couldn't censure her. He tossed his saddle on the ground and helped her with the horses.

Stone took hold of Captain's reins and stroked his neck. "I'm real happy to see you."

Lily spent a lot of time with Blaze, reassuring herself that he hadn't suffered any injuries. Once the horses were cared for, they returned to the fire to have some of Isabelle's freshly made coffee. Stone grabbed the whiskey bottle and poured a generous amount in Thorpe's cup as well as his own before settling beside Isabelle. He glanced over at Lily and said, "Lily, you made one heck of a shot."

"My grandfather insisted I practice often." At the time, she hadn't questioned whether she could make the shot or not; she'd just reacted. Her grandfather always told her not to question her abilities, and not to waste a moment second-guessing what had to be done. He said there would always be time later to mull over the right and wrong of your actions. He'd told her his father was not handy with a gun and that was why the Indians were able to kill his family and take him captive when he was a boy. That was the very reason her grandfather had become an excellent shot, and he wanted to make sure she could defend herself. She'd practiced daily so she could make the tough shots if it was necessary in a life-or-death situation, and she'd become a very precise markswoman. One time she'd asked her grandfather if it was a sin to kill someone as she'd heard from the fire and brimstone sermons spouted by the town preacher. Her grandfather told her it wasn't a sin if you were defending yourself or your loved ones. The preacher never made that distinction; he believed in turning the other cheek. It was a question Lily grappled with.

"I'm glad your grandfather taught you so well," Thorpe said. He prided himself on being a fairly accurate shot under tense circumstances, but he'd never expected the same from a woman. She continued to amaze him.

"Hopefully, the braves killed the rest of the gang," Stone said.

"Do you think the Indians will be back?" Isabelle asked.

"I doubt it," Stone replied. "We're near the fort and they would be worried about the soldiers patrolling."

Lily and Thorpe exchanged a glance. There was no way Stone could be confident of that statement, but they understood he wanted to keep Isabelle from worrying, so they didn't voice an opinion.

Lily placed her blanket beside Jed and sat down. When Thorpe sat beside her, she asked, "Do you think he will sleep through the night?"

Thorpe grinned. "He drank a full cup of whiskey, so I don't think he will come around until morning. Fortunately, the bullet was lodged just below the surface and it will heal quickly. He might be a bit sore for a few days, but nothing serious."

"I'm thankful for that," Isabelle said.

Lily thought Isabelle looked very pale and tired. "Isabelle, why don't you go to the wagon so you can get some sleep? It's more comfortable than this ground."

"I don't want to be alone right now." Isabelle didn't want to say aloud that she felt safer just being close to Stone.

Stone walked to the wagon and when he returned he was carrying an armful of quilts and stacked them on the ground next to Isabelle. He grabbed his saddle for her to use as a pillow to make it more comfortable. "Here you go, this might work for a bed and you can stay warm by the fire."

Isabelle started tearing up again at his thoughtfulness. "This is so kind of you."

Lily was leaning back against her saddle with Blue, Spirit, and the puppies snuggled up beside her. She was staring into the fire as though her mind was a million miles away. Thorpe poured two fresh cups of coffee and offered one to her.

"Thank you." She was thinking how nice it would be to have a man like Stone care about her well-being. Isabelle seemed oblivious, but Stone showed his affection for her in so many little ways. Lily had never known that kind of affection from anyone other than her family. She questioned if Isabelle's soldier would be as kind as Stone. She hoped so. Isabelle had traveled a long way in grueling conditions for this soldier, and Lily hoped he was worth her sacrifice.

Thorpe sat near her with the animals between them. "Were you nervous?" Thorpe asked, interrupting her woolgathering.

Lily turned her gaze on him. "Pardon?"

"I asked if you were nervous making that shot."

"I didn't think about it." It was an honest answer. She'd intentionally avoided thinking about it then, and now. She was calm during the shooting, but afterward she felt like falling apart. She hadn't allowed her mind go there. Before she'd left Missouri, she'd never been forced to shoot anyone. She had never considered that she might be forced to kill another person. But what alternative did she have when men were trying to kill them? She figured her grandfather had been preparing her for that inevitable moment.

"I don't know many men who could have made that shot."

"I prefer not to shoot anyone. We are taught our whole lives to turn the other cheek, so it is difficult to understand how to justify taking another person's life. My grandfather said we will be remembered by the tracks we leave behind. I want to leave good tracks."

Thorpe thought about what she said. He'd never questioned situations where he was forced to defend himself or others. He didn't see it as right or wrong, just something that needed to be done. "We defended ourselves, nothing more. There was no vengeance in our hearts, and we didn't set out to kill them as they did us. I don't think *turning the other cheek* applies when there is a gun pointed to your head. Do you think he would have hesitated to shoot Isabelle? I don't see that you had a choice. I think you know that."

Lily didn't respond. He was right; she didn't regret saving Isabelle's life.

"Haven't you ever been forced to defend yourself before now?"

"I hadn't actually shot anyone before the day I saw you. On my way to Missouri two men were following me so I shot one of their hats off. I was just trying to scare them away."

Thorpe thought she'd been more than lucky traveling from Texas to Missouri alone and not run into more trouble than she did.

Her guardian angel was definitely watching over her. "Did it work?"

"Oh yes. They had followed me for several miles. But after I shot the hat, I never saw them again."

Thorpe chuckled. "I guess you didn't. That would persuade most men to steer clear of you. Don't saddle yourself with guilt, Miss Lily. You will leave nothing but good tracks behind." He saw her trying to stifle a yawn, so he said, "Why don't you get some rest? I'll stay awake the rest of the night."

Lily looked at him and whispered, "Do you really think the rest of them are dead?"

"Yes, I do." Thorpe wasn't sugarcoating his response. He thought Harlow would bring every man he had to get that money, and since he wasn't with them, he must be dead.

Satisfied with his response, Lily turned on her side facing Blue and started stroking his back.

Thorpe watched them as they stared into each other's eyes as though they were silently communicating. When Blue closed his eyes, Thorpe asked, "What will you do if you can't find your grandfather?"

She turned her large blue eyes on him. "He will find me."

291

Thorpe didn't comment. He stared at her until she closed her eyes and quickly fell asleep. She looked so young and vulnerable lying there, not to mention unbelievably beautiful. Thorpe had never seen her in a dress, but he didn't think she could look more beautiful than she did at that moment. He figured the pants she wore did more to display her figure than a dress, but for some inexplicable reason he envisioned her in something feminine and frilly. Evelyn was always dressed in lovely gowns as she frittered away her days. Evelyn was all-woman, and she made sure every man knew it. He couldn't imagine her sleeping on the cold, hard ground snuggled up to a wolf. And he couldn't imagine Lily living her life like Evelyn. For one thing, Lily didn't possess feminine wiles, and Evelyn had them in abundance. Lily was younger than Evelyn, and obviously much more innocent. No matter her age, he didn't think he'd ever met anyone — man or woman — with more courage. She sounded so confident that she would see her grandfather again, and he prayed she was right. She deserved that. He wouldn't go so far to say she wouldn't find her grandfather, but Wyoming was a large territory and her grandfather could be anywhere. It might take her years to find him. Still, when he left Texas, he'd done so on faith alone, and he wouldn't tell anyone faith wasn't an important component if that still small voice was whispering in their ear. Her grandfather sounded like the kind of man he'd like to know, and if he was in Lily's position, he'd be searching for him, too.

He smiled at the sight of Spirit and Blue lying next to Lily with the little puppies nestled beside them. He didn't know how long he'd sat there watching Lily, but when he saw her cuddle closer to Blue, he thought she might be cold so he took his blanket and placed it on top of her blanket. Blue looked up at him and licked his hand.

"You did good, boy. I was worried my bullet might have hit you instead of that varmint." He hadn't noticed Blue was ready to pounce on the man he was aiming at until he'd pulled the trigger. Blue was already in the air and he'd held his breath until he saw his aim had been true and Blue wasn't injured. He'd never forgive himself if he shot Blue.

CHAPTER EIGHTEEN

Three days later in the frigid temperatures they finally reached Chimney Rock. The terrible weather couldn't dampen their enthusiasm. It was early afternoon when they decided to stop for a meal and enjoy the views.

"The one thing that surprised me on this trail are the deep ruts in the ground the entire way," Isabelle said.

"So many wagons have come this way, it's to be expected," Stone said. "I imagine they will be there for eternity."

"I was surprised by how few trees there are," Lily said.

"I prefer trees myself," Thorpe said, standing and extending his hand to Lily. "But since there's only that rock, let's go see some of those names." He hadn't forgotten she'd mentioned seeing the names, and he wanted to make sure she got her wish. It might be the last time she passed this way and it would be a shame for her to miss the chance.

Lily took his hand and stood. "Do we have time?"

"In this weather we can't go too far, but we'll go up far enough to see some names."

Thorpe glanced back at Stone. "We won't be long, and I'll have a bird's-eye view to see if anyone is coming."

"We'll wait right here and watch you. Don't fall and break your fool neck," Stone told him.

"Miss Lily, you be careful," Jed said.

"Don't worry, Jed. I won't let anything happen to her," Thorpe assured him.

When Thorpe and Lily were out of earshot, Isabelle said, "They are perfect for each other."

Stone laughed. "Don't go thinking Thorpe is ready for marriage. He's not likely to get married anytime soon, if ever."

Isabelle turned her chin up at him. "Mark my words, those two will be married within six months."

Stone looked at her as if she was losing her mind. "Thorpe told me he didn't have his sights on Lily."

"Well, he might have said that, but his actions tell a different story. He is always looking at her like a man looks at a woman he wants."

"Lily is a beautiful woman and I'm sure that's the reason he is always looking at her. But believe me, he's not interested in her that way."

"I wouldn't be too sure about that, Mr. Stone," Jed said.

Stone turned to look at Jed. "You think Isabelle is right?"

"I know Mr. Thorpe acts like he's not interested in Miss Lily, but he likes her. I ain't saying it won't take him awhile to recognize it." Jed had seen the way Thorpe stared at Lily all of the time. Jed thought Thorpe cared much more than he was willing to admit to himself.

"Well, this should be interesting," Stone said. He thought it was remarkable Isabelle could see that Thorpe cared for Lily, but she couldn't recognize how he felt about her. It was for the best, he told himself. Isabelle cared for her soldier; she was carrying his baby and traveling across the country to marry him. He couldn't allow himself to forget that fact.

Thorpe stopped climbing and glanced down at Lily. "Be careful. The rock is smooth and the snow makes it slippery."

The words barely left his mouth when Lily lost her footing and started to slide, but Thorpe quickly reached out and grabbed her hand. He moved in her direction and wrapped his strong arm around her waist and pulled her close to him.

Lily looked up at him, surprise evident in her large eyes. "Thank you."

"Don't make a liar out of me, Lily."

Thorpe was holding her so close, she could feel the heat radiating from his body. Furrowing her brow at him, she asked, "What do you mean?"

His eyes roved over her face to her lips. Her lips were tempting, lips ready to be kissed, and he came dangerously close to forgetting his vow to avoid getting involved again. Giving himself a mental shake, his gaze flicked back to her eyes. "I told Jed I wouldn't let anything happen to you."

"Oh." He didn't release her and her eyes lingered on his mouth. She wasn't an experienced woman, but she thought he was about to kiss her. She wanted him to kiss her. She wanted to know what it felt like to be his arms and to be kissed by him. Her own thoughts surprised her. She'd never had such feelings about a man. She'd never wanted another man to touch her.

"Ready?"

Was he asking her if she was ready to be kissed? Yes . . . yes . . . yes. She blinked. "What?"

"Ready to climb a bit higher?"

"Oh yes." Her knees were shaking when she pulled away from him.

They found a flat ledge where they could stand side by side, and Thorpe held her securely with one arm around her waist. He pointed to some names on the rock. "There's quite a few names carved here."

It was an emotional moment for Lily, seeing the names of people that had traveled this way. People who may have made it to their destination, or some who may have died before they reached their dream, like Mr. and Mrs. Craig from the wagon train. She felt a kinship with those people who were brave enough to chance everything, including their very lives, to make a new start. Seeing the new land as she was seeing it for the first time was exciting and frightening. She wondered if they would have made it to this point without Thorpe. She didn't think so. It was because of him that she was standing here reading the names that would be here for eternity.

Thorpe watched her face as she reverently slid her fingertips over the crudely etched names.

Her gaze slid to Thorpe. "Thank you for making sure we made it here."

He smiled at her. "You're welcome. Are you too cold to stay here a few minutes?"

"No, why?"

"You'll see." He pulled out his knife and started carving. He finished etching Lily's name in the rock and started on his name. When he finished, he leaned back and looked at his work. He glanced at Lily with his brow furrowed. "Do you know the date?"

Lily understood how easy it was to lose track of the date. "I think it is November 25th."

Thorpe counted the days since they stopped at the way station and figured she was close enough, so he carved *November 25, 1868* below his name. Looking at his work once again, he thought he should connect the names to show that they were traveling together. Without thinking of the significance, he etched a large heart around both names.

Staring at the heart, Lily's first thought was their names would also be there for eternity. She liked the thought of being linked to this man for all time, if only by their names on a rock. They'd shared an experience traveling to this place that would remain in her thoughts for the remainder of her life. Someone might climb to this spot one day and see that heart and think this woman had a man who cared enough to inscribe her name with his. Isabelle's words echoed in her mind again. *If you save someone's life you are bound together forever.* Their names would be together forever on that rock.

Thorpe watched as she stared intently at his carving. He braced one hand on the rock and leaned over to look at her. "Don't you like my work?"

"Yes, it's lovely." She traced the heart just as she did the other names, then turned her eyes to him. "When we are gone, a piece of us will remain forever. People will look at our names, just like we are looking at the other names, and they will wonder who we were and if we made it to our destination."

Thorpe couldn't take his eyes off of her. Her cheeks were pink from the frigid wind, but the look on her face said she was more thrilled than if he'd given her a diamond ring. He wasn't sure why he'd drawn that heart, but he wasn't sorry he did. "They will know Lily Starr was one brave woman." If he hadn't given up women, he'd be honored to be connected to Lily in this life and beyond. She was a rare woman: a woman of courage, determination, and honesty. Their eyes locked. "Lily, if I was a marrying man, I'd be real honored to . . ." He didn't know what he was about to say, his thoughts were going in every direction. And before he knew it, his eyes moved to those kissable lips again. He tried to rein in his desire before it got the best of him. It had been a long time since he'd been with a woman and his heart was pounding like he was about to take a step off of a steep, slippery ledge.

He forced his eyes back to hers. "Well . . . I'm not a marrying man." He swallowed hard as he felt himself sinking in the depths of those blue eyes. Maybe one kiss wouldn't hurt anything. She was looking at him like she wanted to be kissed. He removed her hat and her long hair fell over her shoulders. He slid his hand behind her head and lowered his head until his lips were covering hers. His intention was to be gentle, a first kiss kind of kiss, but his honorable intentions floated away on a frosty breeze. He tightened his arm around her waist and he lifted her close to his body, pressing her back to the heart he'd just carved. He kissed her like a man who hadn't kissed a woman in months. He kissed her like he'd never kissed another woman. He kissed her like he'd never kissed Evelyn. Evelyn. There she was again. The very reason he didn't want another woman. Abruptly, he pulled back, but he couldn't go far because her arms were looped around his neck holding him to her. When did that happen? He lowered her to the ground and her arms dropped from his neck.

"I'm sorry. I shouldn't have done that." He was saying the words he wanted to say, but his baser instinct was to pin her against that rock wall again and kiss her some more. He took a step away, as far as he could go without falling off the ledge. It wasn't nearly far enough away to prevent him from giving in to the temptation of kissing her again.

Lily looked away as she settled her hat on her head. She wasn't one bit sorry, but she felt like crying because the look on his face said he regretted what had just happened. "Think nothing of it. We'd better get back." She turned and started to make her way down.

Their descent was quiet, and Thorpe felt bad about that. He didn't know what he'd been thinking to do something so hare-brained. Problem was, he wasn't thinking. Just like that night he'd allowed Evelyn to seduce him; his brain had stopped working seeing her without her clothes. Lily was fully clothed, bundled up in a coat, and his brain turned to mush. Oh yeah, he'd liked that kiss. Too much. But he figured he would like any woman's kiss right now since it had been so long since he had kissed one. If he was certain of one thing, he wasn't about to compromise a woman's virtue. Logically, he knew he'd spend some time with women in the future, but not one he'd have to marry. Maybe when Evelyn's betrayal faded, he'd be more inclined to think about marriage again. But that day was a long, long way off.

Lily couldn't get back to the wagons fast enough. She wasn't a woman who showed her emotions easily. But right now, she was on the verge of tears, and she didn't want to cry in front of Thorpe. All of these feelings were new to her and she needed to figure them out privately. She remembered her mother told her she knew her father was the man she loved because the first time she saw him he took her breath away. Thorpe definitely took her breath away. He evoked passionate responses she had never experienced. But he'd made himself perfectly clear that he didn't share her feelings. He was interested in her, but not for marriage. And she wasn't a woman that could give a man what was most precious to her without marriage. Isabelle had done that, and now she was setting her hopes and future on finding a man that may or may not want her. It was clear Thorpe might like her, and would take what she was willing to give, but he didn't love her. It was her misfortune that somewhere along the way on this trip she'd fallen in love with Thorpe Turlow. She couldn't blame him for that since he'd made his intentions clear from the start.

"Did you enjoy the climb, Lily?" Isabelle asked when she returned to camp.

"Yes, but I'm cold. I'm going inside the wagon." Lily didn't stop; she half ran to her wagon.

Thorpe stopped at the fire, grabbed a cup of coffee, sat down on a rock, and stared into the fire.

Isabelle and Stone looked at each other. "Thorpe, did you see a lot of names on the rock?"

It took a few seconds for Thorpe to realize Isabelle said his name. "Huh?"

"Did you see some names carved up there?"

"Yeah." Thorpe stood, tossed his coffee out, and walked to the corral to saddle Smoke. He needed to think and he did that best on horseback. He didn't ride far from camp; he just circled it, keeping it within sight at all times. He continued to berate himself for his impulsive actions with Lily. It was out of character for him. Evelyn had popped into his thoughts in time to prevent him from making matters worse. He didn't know why he kept thinking of her; he thought he'd forgiven her and moved on. Just because he was no longer angry didn't mean he'd forgotten her duplicity. At least it kept him from making the same mistake twice. He wanted to get home and put all of this behind him. Once he was back at Dove Creek, his life could get back to normal. Lily would go on to find her grandfather and she would no longer be a temptation. The routine of the ranch was what he needed. Hard work always helped him sort things out.

Lily was relieved to be in the privacy of the wagon. Blue, Spirit, and the puppies were inside with her so she wasn't totally alone, and she could cry in front of them. She wiped away the tears on her cheeks and Blue moved to her and put his head in her lap, offering her comfort. "I don't know why he did that, and then he apologized," she said to Blue. The corral was near the wagon and she heard Thorpe ride away. What if he didn't come back? No, she only heard one horse. If he planned to leave he would come back for Shadow, and he had supplies in one of the wagons. She didn't understand what was going on with him. The only thing that made sense was he hadn't forgotten the woman that left him at the altar. He was still in love with her. That was probably why he hadn't taken Dora up on what she was offering without a thought to marriage. If he didn't leave them, she would stay away from him. They'd be in Fort Steele in a few days and she wouldn't see him again after that.

CHAPTER NINETEEN

As soon as the newcomers rode into Fort Steele they were greeted by the officer in charge. "Hello, I'm Captain Wallace Anderson."

"I'm Thorpe Turlow." Thorpe pointed to his fellow travelers. "This is U.S. Marshal Stone Justice, Jedidiah Clarke, Lily Starr, and Isabelle Baker."

The captain nodded to the men, but reached up and tipped his hat when Thorpe introduced the women. His eyes moved over the group and zeroed in on Lily. "How may I help you?"

Thorpe answered for them, first explaining why Stone was with the group, and inquiring about the soldier Isabelle was looking for and Jedidiah's brother.

The captain invited the men to the post headquarters later to allow him some time to make the necessary inquiries. "I'll have a man show you where to put the wagons,

307

and they'll help you with the animals." He glanced back at Lily, and said, "You ladies can go to my personal quarters where you can freshen up and relax until dinner. It would be my honor to have you join us for our Thanksgiving meal." He motioned for one of the soldiers. "Sergeant Greene will escort you. We have a general store if you ladies are in need of anything."

"Thank you, Captain. We will be delighted to join you for dinner," Lily said.

The captain touched the brim of his hat again and smiled at Lily. "Until then."

Thorpe noticed Captain Anderson seemed to be taking a keen interest in Lily. And Lily seemed eager to join him for dinner.

Sergeant Greene stepped forward. "Ladies, if you would care to follow me. I will show you to your quarters."

"I need to send a telegram to my headquarters to inform them of the situation with Harlow and his gang, and the transfer of the money," Stone said.

"Of course, please come with me."

After Stone sent his telegram, and Thorpe sent one to his foreman informing him he would be home in a few days, they followed one of the soldiers to the building where they would bunk for the night. Once they cleaned up, they joined the captain at the headquarters building.

Stone told the captain about Harlow and his gang, and about the thirty thousand dollars. He asked if the captain could take charge of the money, guaranteeing its safe delivery to the designated bank. "I can assure you we will get the money to the bank." The captain walked to a table and grabbed a bottle of whiskey. "Gentlemen, would you like a drink?"

Thorpe and Stone accepted, but Jedidiah declined his offer. As they sipped their whiskey, they related the events that had taken place with the outlaws on their way to the fort.

"It sounds as though you've had an eventful journey," the captain said. "Are the ladies you're traveling with your wives?" He noticed the different last names when they were introduced, but it was a subtle way to find out if Lily was married.

"No, none of us are related." Thorpe wasn't surprised the captain found a way to inquire about Lily's marital status. He was surprised it had taken him so long, seeing the way he was gawking at her when he was introduced. Thorpe heard Jedidiah take up the story about Lily saving his life.

"That's some story," Anderson said.

"Sounds like you were lucky she came along."

Thorpe didn't respond to his comment. He wasn't in the mood to discuss Lily with the captain. He'd kept his distance from her since their kiss at Chimney Rock and she hadn't said two words to him either. "What can you tell us about Jed's brother?"

"Mr. Clarke, your brother's regiment was dispatched to northeastern Wyoming to Fort Kearny. It may be a few months before they return."

"Thank you for the information, Captain. I haven't seen my brother in a long time. It's good to know he's still alive."

"Of course, if you've a mind to stay here and wait for his return, we can always use a skilled blacksmith. Either way, I will get word to him where you are located," Anderson said.

"I thank you, sir, but I may just go on with Mr. Thorpe."

"What about Ethan Horn?" Thorpe asked.

"I'm sorry to inform you that Second Lieutenant Horn was killed two weeks ago. His battalion was in a skirmish with the Sioux. Everyone was killed."

"Are you positive, Captain?" Stone asked.

"Yes. No one survived. We've had some difficulty with the Sioux. If someone in your party is a relative, Mrs. Horn has not left the fort."

"You mean his mother is here?" Thorpe asked.

"No, his wife," Captain Anderson replied. "It was an unfortunate situation. Horn's wife had just arrived the day before he left. They were planning on settling here. To make matters worse, she is carrying their first child. She will be having this baby in a few months, and when she is able, she plans to go back to Missouri."

Thorpe glanced at Stone and Jed. They were as surprised as he was to hear about Mrs. Horn. "We are not relatives. A member of our party had met Ethan before and we wanted to say hello while we were here," Thorpe said smoothly. "We'd appreciate it if you wouldn't mention his death to the ladies. We don't want to upset them."

"I won't say a word." Captain Anderson was curious to know if Lily was the one who had met Lieutenant Horn. He'd heard from his men that the lieutenant had been real popular with the ladies. It came as a surprise to the other soldiers to learn he had a wife. The captain stood and said, "Dinner will be in two hours."

Back in their quarters, Thorpe, Stone, and

Jed were alone discussing how they were going to tell Isabelle about Ethan Horn.

"We can't tell her right now. In her condition I don't think she could handle the heartbreak," Stone said.

Thorpe understood what Stone was saying, but they couldn't keep this information from her. "She can't stay here waiting on a man to return that will never come back. After she has the baby she needs to go back home to be with her family. She'll need help caring for that baby."

"Mr. Thorpe, Miss Isabelle has no place to go," Jed told him.

Thorpe and Stone stared at Jed. "What do you mean? She has a home. She told us about her family. Her father is a preacher," Thorpe said.

Jed shook his head. "I wouldn't say anything, but now with the father of that baby dead, I have to tell you."

"Tell us what, Jed?" Stone asked.

"Miss Isabelle's father told her she wasn't welcome in their home. He told her to leave when he found out about the babe," Jed told them.

Thorpe processed what Jed said. "That does change things."

"What kind of father would say such a thing to his daughter?" Stone asked. "Not only did Ethan Horn lie to her about marrying her, but her father didn't treat her any better."

"Yeah, I was surprised to hear Horn was married," Thorpe said.

Stone was livid at the man that had taken advantage of Isabelle. He was sorry to hear he'd been killed, but he was still angry with a man he didn't even know. It had been his intention once he met him to give him a piece of his mind about not marrying Isabelle once he'd compromised her. He'd also planned to give him a warning that he'd better treat Isabelle the way she deserved to be treated in the future. A real man didn't walk out on a woman like Isabelle.

"We should talk to Lily and ask her how we should tell Isabelle," Thorpe said.

Thorpe found Lily at the corral checking on the animals. She spotted Thorpe as soon as he walked to the fence.

"I need to speak with you a minute," Thorpe told her.

Lily walked to the fence where he was leaning on the rail, Blaze and Daisy following her. Her first thought was Thorpe came to say he was headed out. Now that they had arrived safely to the fort, he had no reason to stay with them. She waited for him to speak since the huge lump in her throat prevented her from saying a word.

"Where's Isabelle?" Thorpe asked.

"She's lying down. I just came out here to check on the animals. Why?"

Thorpe took his hat off and slapped it against the rail before he settled it back on his head. "Lily, we just found out that Ethan Horn was killed."

Lily stared at him and shook her head as if she wasn't going to accept what he was saying. "Surely not!"

Thorpe saw some soldiers nearby and he wanted more privacy to tell her the rest. He reached out and opened the gate to the corral. "Walk with me."

Lily walked beside him in the direction of the building where they were staying.

"Lily, I'm afraid his death isn't the only thing I must tell you. Captain Anderson said Horn was married."

"He must be thinking of the wrong man. Ethan told Isabelle he would marry her when he returned."

Thorpe stopped walking and turned to face Lily. "No, he didn't have the wrong man. That's not all. Ethan's wife is here at the fort and she is carrying their first child. She'd just arrived before he was killed. Once she has her baby she plans on returning to

Missouri."

Lily could hardly believe what Thorpe was saying. Poor Isabelle. What would she do now that she would be having this baby without a proper marriage? An unmarried woman with a child would not be welcome anywhere. How would she support herself? She quickly concluded she would have to find a way to help her. She could find a job and help support Isabelle and her baby. They would simply say the baby's father was killed, which was the truth. They wouldn't need to advertise that Isabelle was an unwed mother. "How will we ever tell Isabelle this?"

"I don't think we should. I asked the captain not to mention it."

Lily gaped at him. "You didn't tell him about Isabelle and Ethan!"

"No. I just told him a member of our group had met Horn and we wanted to say hello." Thorpe didn't say he sensed the captain was skeptical about his explanation.

"Thank goodness," Lily said. She wanted to spare Isabelle further embarrassment. Isabelle was in a fragile state right now and she was worried this news might be too much for her to handle. "How will we get her to leave if we don't tell her the truth? She won't leave if she thinks he will return."

Thorpe knew Lily was right. Isabelle had traveled all this way and she was determined the baby would have a father. "I guess we have no choice, but don't you think we should spare her the other details?"

"Oh, you mean how Ethan deceived her to get what he wanted? How he told her he would come back and marry her when he could? How he forgot to mention he had a wife and how she is also with child?" Lily had worked herself into a dither. It was all so unfair. Isabelle would be labeled a fallen woman for one mistake: being led with her heart. And no one would think the worst of the soldier. He was no doubt considered a hero.

Thorpe didn't respond. What could he say?

"Men!" Lily said.

"Lily, men aren't the only ones who deceive."

She'd forgotten about his fiancée. The woman that had stolen his heart. The woman who didn't appreciate the man Lily thought was wonderful. The woman that made it impossible for him to love again. She took a deep breath and collected herself. "Let me tell Isabelle after dinner when we are alone in the room. I'll tell her he was killed, but no more. We will have to leave here. She can't stay with Ethan's wife here at the same time."

Thorpe had already thought about that situation, and after what Jed revealed about Isabelle's father, he thought he had a solution. "You can go to Dove Creek with me. I think I've talked Jed into staying until spring. Instead of spending Christmas here, you can stay at Dove Creek."

His offer brought tears to her eyes. "That's generous of you. Do you think I could find a job in town so I could help support Isabelle and her baby? She's going to need help."

"Why don't we talk about that later? Our biggest concern is to get everyone to Dove Creek in one piece, and make sure she doesn't have that baby on the trail. We should plan on leaving in the morning."

He was right, of course. Isabelle was so huge that Lily feared she could have that baby at any moment. If they stayed at the fort, Isabelle was sure to hear about Ethan's wife and baby. "Yes, we should leave as soon as possible."

"How do you think Ethan managed to keep his marriage from Isabelle? She must have known him a long time since he'd . . ." Thorpe started to say *taken her to his bed,* but he didn't think that would be the best choice of words to say to a lady.

"She didn't know him that long. I'm afraid she was taken with his attentions and didn't stop to consider that he wasn't sincere in his affections. She isn't the first woman to be swayed by a handsome face and sweet words." There was no condemnation in her words. She had recently learned how easily one could be caught up in a tender moment. If Thorpe said sweet words to her before they kissed on Chimney Rock, she might have been tempted to be as reckless as Isabelle.

CHAPTER TWENTY

"Oh my, Lily, you look beautiful," Isabelle said when she walked into the room wearing a light blue dress. Isabelle had helped Lily with her hair earlier, arranging it on top of her head and she'd weaved a blue ribbon through her curls.

"Thank you." Lily wished she could look forward to the evening. When the captain invited them to dine at his table, she was excited sit down to a Thanksgiving meal. She looked forward to the opportunity for Thorpe to see her in a dress, and that was why she'd allowed Isabelle to play with her hair for an hour. She'd imagined Thorpe's ex-fiancée was probably a beautiful woman, especially if she ran away with a duke. She doubted the woman wore pants, or rode a horse bareback, or shot guns. It wasn't that she thought she could compete with Thorpe's ex-fiancée, but she could at least show him she knew how to look like a lady.

Instead of the night she'd dreamed of, the devastating news she would have to give Isabelle when they returned later tonight had placed a pall over the evening.

Isabelle had noticed Lily was unusually quiet. Actually, she had been quiet since the day she and Thorpe came back from Chimney Rock. She'd asked several times if the two of them had had a disagreement, but Lily said everything was fine. After she'd awakened from her nap today, Lily told her the captain was checking on Ethan and when he knew something he'd let them know. After that brief conversation, Lily seemed preoccupied. "Are you ill? You've been very quiet."

"I'm fine. I guess I should have rested more."

"That Captain Anderson seems like a fine gentleman and handsome, too. His eyes are just about the same color blue as yours. And did you see that smile of his?"

"He seems very nice." Lily had noticed the captain's beautiful smile. If not for her unresolved feelings for Thorpe Turlow, she might be inclined to pay more attention to the handsome captain.

Though Lily hadn't said as much, Isabelle suspected she was in love with Thorpe. But according to Stone, Thorpe wasn't ready to marry. Isabelle thought Thorpe would change his mind quick enough if he thought another man was interested in Lily. Talking about Captain Anderson gave her a spark of inspiration. "You know Lily, Captain Anderson couldn't take his eyes off you. I have a feeling Thorpe could be quite jealous of that man."

Lily turned to face her. "Why would Thorpe be jealous of the captain?"

"The captain was obviously interested in you, and Thorpe had to notice the way he was staring at you. We all noticed."

Lily rolled her eyes at Isabelle. "The captain was simply being kind. Why should Thorpe care if a man looks at me?"

"I don't think Thorpe is as indifferent as he thinks when it comes to you. And that captain didn't look at me the way he was looking at you while he was being *kind,*" Isabelle countered. "Lily, it's none of my business, but if you have feelings for Thorpe, it wouldn't hurt to do a little flirting with another man to see how he responds."

Before Lily could confirm or refute Isabelle's suspicions, their conversation was interrupted by a knock on their door. When Lily opened the door, Sergeant Greene told her he'd been sent by Captain Anderson to escort them to dinner.

■ ■ ■ ■

"Might I say it is a pleasure to have two such lovely ladies at our table this evening," Captain Anderson said as he met them at the door and helped them with their coats.

"Thank you for inviting us. Isabelle and I will enjoy sitting at a table as opposed to a campfire," Lily said.

"I trust my quarters are sufficient for your needs."

"Yes, and we thank you for your generosity." Lily had a feeling that the other quarters would not have been as nice as the captain's. It was generous of him to offer his accommodations to strangers.

Captain Anderson led them into the parlor where Thorpe, Stone, and Jed were seated. Stone and Jed stood when the ladies walked into the room, but Thorpe was too stunned to move, much less speak. He simply sat there staring at Lily. She looked like some sort of princess in her blue dress with all of her blond hair on top of her head. He'd imagined her in a dress, but he never expected her to look so beautiful. Jed was right all along; she was an angel. His eyes landed on Lily's hand resting on the captain's arm. Out of the corner of his eye, he saw Stone move toward Isabelle, and he remembered his manners and stood.

"You ladies look beautiful," Stone said.

"As pretty as flowers in the springtime," Jed added.

Thorpe still didn't speak; he simply stared at the captain as he took Lily's hand in his and brought it to his lips. After he placed a kiss on the back of her hand, he said, "Much lovelier than any flower." He spoke softly, but Thorpe heard him loud and clear.

Lily noticed Thorpe hadn't said a word. She'd longed to hear him say something about the change in her appearance, but he remained silent. Well, she was determined she wasn't going to spend the evening fretting about his opinion, she had enough to think about having to tell Isabelle about Ethan tonight. She intended to ignore Thorpe and try to enjoy the dinner as best she could.

"How are you feeling, Isabelle?" Stone asked.

"Much better, thanks to the captain's comfortable quarters. It was a real joy to sleep in a bed that wasn't moving."

"It was my pleasure to be of service," Captain Anderson said. Noting Isabelle was with child, Captain Anderson wanted to question why her husband wasn't traveling with them, but he refrained from asking something so personal. The men had told him they were not related to the women, so he questioned why a woman in her condition was traveling with this group. For that matter, why was a beautiful woman like Lily traveling with them?

Captain Anderson extended his arm to Lily and walked beside her to the dining room. Stone was chatting with Isabelle, and Thorpe and Jed followed behind them. The captain seated Lily next to his chair at the head of the table, so Thorpe quickly took the seat across from Lily.

Although Thorpe was quiet, everyone else conversed pleasantly until Captain Anderson asked, "Isabelle, is your husband a soldier? Forgive me for asking, but I thought that must be the reason he is not traveling with you."

"Ah . . ." The question caught Isabelle off guard. She was tempted to blurt out the truth and ask the captain about Ethan. Fortunately, she wasn't forced to respond when Stone intervened.

Stone placed his hand on top of hers and gave it a gentle squeeze. "She is traveling with us to meet up with her love."

Lily hurriedly changed the subject. "Captain Anderson, how long have you been at this fort?"

The captain knew they didn't want to discuss Isabelle's husband, and he was sharp enough to realize it had something to do with the soldier they had inquired about earlier. Ethan Horn. He remembered their surprise when he mentioned Ethan's wife was at the fort. Isabelle wasn't wearing a wedding band, and he had a suspicion Ethan Horn might be the father of two children. He responded to Lily's question and avoided asking Isabelle more personal questions. He wasn't as hesitant with Lily. He asked her many questions about her background and her plans.

The evening ended, and Thorpe had just about all he could take of Anderson usurping Lily's time. "I'll see you ladies to your room," he said when they reached the door.

"That's kind of you, but Captain Anderson has already offered," Lily replied without an ounce of regret in her voice, yet her feelings were at odds with her words.

"Fine," Thorpe responded testily.

They said their good nights and Thorpe walked away with Stone and Jed while the captain had a woman on each arm.

When they reached the captain's quarters, Isabelle said good-night and left Lily alone with Captain Anderson on the porch.

"Thank you for your kindness, Captain Anderson," Lily said.

"Please call me Wallace. When will you folks be leaving?"

Lily lowered her voice so she wouldn't be overheard. "In the morning."

"Lily, I want to ask you something."

Hearing a serious tone in his voice, she looked up at him. "What?"

"Were you involved with Ethan Horn?"

"Heavens, no. I've never met the man."

His suspicions were confirmed. It was Isabelle who had an interest in Ethan Horn. "I have a feeling I know what is going on and why all of you really came here."

"Thorpe told me Ethan was killed," Lily said.

"I didn't know Horn personally, but I did hear that his reputation with the ladies was legendary. Isabelle seems like a nice woman, and I want you to know that I regret her situation."

Lily was stunned that he'd been so perceptive figuring out Isabelle was the one looking for Ethan. She saw no reason to lie to him since he wasn't judging Isabelle. "Isabelle is a wonderful person, and yes, I fear Ethan Horn took advantage of her. I am going to tell her tonight that he died, but not that he has a wife. I see no useful reason to reveal that information. We will be leaving in the morning to go to Thorpe's ranch. Her baby is due by Christmas, and we've no time to waste. I want her to go on believing that Ethan would have married her."

"You could stay here," he told her. "You would be safe."

"If we stayed, Isabelle would certainly find out the truth about Ethan. She's been through enough."

Anderson couldn't argue with that point, but he hated to see Lily leave. "How long will you be staying at Turlow's ranch?" He didn't think Lily was romantically involved with Turlow. She barely even looked at the man through dinner.

"Until spring." Lily knew she might have to wait until then to continue on with her journey to find her grandfather, and to make sure Isabelle was settled with the baby.

"Do you plan on going back to Texas in the spring?"

"No, I will go north and see if I can find my grandfather."

She'd mentioned during dinner that she was looking for her grandfather. "Why north?"

"I'm not sure. I just have a feeling that is where I will find him." It was difficult for her to explain to a stranger how she felt God's guidance. Most people wouldn't understand how God had placed the right people in her life at the right moment, or how she sometimes felt a spark of inspiration to go in a certain direction. She understood God was leading her, but others might question her thinking.

"You didn't tell me your grandfather's name."

"His name is Ben Starr."

The captain stared at her. "Ben Starr?"

"Yes."

"Well, you are on the right track."

"What do you mean?"

"Your grandfather was with us for a period of time. His language skills with the Indians proved invaluable. Last I heard he was headed north. I could make some inquiries if you like."

Lily's heart started pounding. He was the first person she'd met in a long time that had seen her grandfather. "How long has it been since you've seen him?"

"It's been over a year. Your grandfather is an amazing man." He'd been awed by Ben's knowledge of the Indians and his resourcefulness. He was a man of uncanny mental processes. He also had a soft spot for the plight of the Indians, and he tried his best to have everyone work together.

"Yes, he is amazing. There's no one like him." But then she thought of Thorpe. In his own way, he was every bit as amazing. She was so excited to know for sure her grandfather was alive and well just a year ago. The captain was another person God had placed in front of her at exactly the right moment.

"I'll make some inquires first thing in the morning. If I hear any news of his whereabouts, I will send a message to Turlow's ranch."

"Thank you so much." This trip had provided encouraging news for Lily, and poor Isabelle's news couldn't have been worse. Sometimes it was difficult to understand how life unfolded.

He smiled at her. "It's my pleasure to help you, Lily. My men and I will accompany your party until tomorrow night."

"I'm sure it's not necessary for you to travel with us." Lily was grateful to him, but she didn't want to take him away from important business. He'd already done more than enough for them.

He took her hand in his and looked into her eyes. "I want to, Lily."

Lily liked him; not only was he charming, but he was considerate and thoughtful.

"Thank you for all of your help."

Removing his hat, Wallace lowered his head, fully intending to kiss her, but he heard someone walking up behind him. He straightened and turned around to see Turlow. "Ah, Mr. Turlow."

Thorpe felt as though he'd interrupted an intimate moment between them. He stopped and said, "I thought I would check on the animals." He didn't move.

Anderson looked at Thorpe, waiting for him to move on. When Thorpe didn't walk away, it turned into a staring contest between the two men.

Lily's gaze moved from the captain to Thorpe. She wasn't sure what was happening, but the silence was making her uneasy. "Well, I need to go inside and talk to Isabelle."

Both men finally looked at her.

She glanced at the captain and smiled. "Thank you again, Wallace."

So she was on a first-name basis with Anderson, Thorpe thought.

"Good night, Lily. I'll see you in the morning," Anderson said.

"We'll leave at first light," Thorpe said to Lily.

Lily nodded, said good night, and walked inside and closed the door.

The captain turned to Thorpe. "I'll see you in the morning, Mr. Turlow. We'll be escorting your party part of the way."

"That's not necessary," Thorpe said.

"It is my pleasure," the captain responded before he said good night and walked away.

Lily closed the door and shut her eyes. She tried to summon the courage to tell Isabelle about Ethan.

Isabelle walked into the front room and saw Lily standing at the door. "Are you okay?"

"Yes, I'm fine. Isabelle, I need to talk to you. Let's go sit down."

They walked to the parlor and Lily sat beside her on the settee. "Isabelle, I'm afraid I have very bad news for you."

"It's about Ethan," Isabelle said.

Lily hadn't expected that response, but she didn't hesitate. "Yes, it is. I'm afraid he was killed in battle not long ago."

Isabelle's eyes filled with tears. "I think I knew. I didn't want to say, but I knew somehow this was never going to work out for me."

As her tears started to flow, Lily pulled her into her embrace as she cried. "I'm so sorry. I wish this didn't happen."

"I don't know what I will do. I can't go

331

home. How will I take care of this baby?"

"Thorpe told us we are welcome at his ranch and we will leave in the morning," Lily told her.

Isabelle dried her eyes on her skirt and looked at Lily. "That is so generous of him, but what happens after this baby is born?"

Lily tried to give her a reassuring smile. "We'll work this out. You have friends, you are not alone, and Stone is going with us." Lily thought if Isabelle knew Stone would be going with them it would make a difference.

"Lily, you're the best friend I've ever had. What would become of me without you?"

"We are all your friends and we are here to help you."

"So everyone knows about Ethan's death?"

"Yes. We thought you'd want to leave right away. If you can handle a few more days in the wagon, we will leave at first light for Thorpe's ranch." If Lily had doubts about telling her about Ethan's wife, they quickly dissolved as Isabelle outlined all of her fears.

"You're right. It is best we leave. I will make it."

CHAPTER TWENTY-ONE

Lily ran into Captain Anderson when she walked outside carrying the four squirming puppies in a basket, with Blue and Spirit at her side. "Good morning."

"Good morning." He picked up her valise by the doorway. "Is Isabelle ready?"

"She left a little earlier to take her valise to the wagon. I think she needed some time alone."

"How did she take the news?"

Lily heard Isabelle crying softly throughout the night. "It's difficult for her. She needs time."

They started walking in the direction of the wagons. "We are ready to depart if your party is ready."

"Do you expect problems?" Lily asked.

"We've had some trouble, but with us along I don't expect anything to happen." He'd struggled with the decision to accompany them. He told himself that the last wagon train had been attacked and he wanted to make sure something like that didn't happen again. Of course, it wasn't necessary for him to go along with his soldiers. He could easily dispatch some men to ride with them, but he wanted to go. He wasn't ready to see Lily ride away. He was attracted to her and he wanted to spend more time with her. There were few available women in this part of the country and certainly few like Lily. It was more than her beautiful face that attracted him; she was a person of character. He glanced at the puppies she was carrying in the basket and reached in and pulled one out. "These little guys sure are cute."

"They are growing fast. When we found them they were very tiny, probably just a few hours old."

"You'd never know it now by their fat little bellies." He laughed at the squirming pup in his hand.

Thorpe heard their laughter as he was harnessing the mules, but he didn't acknowledge them as they approached.

"Good morning," Lily said.

"Where's Isabelle?" Thorpe asked, sounding none too friendly.

"I thought she was here," Lily replied.

Stone walked up and heard Thorpe's

question. "Isabelle told me she was going to the general store."

"We're ready to leave," Thorpe said.

"I'll go get her," Stone said.

Isabelle had spotted a bolt of cloth in the window of the general store when she'd passed by and thought it would be perfect to make some clothing for her baby. When she went inside to have a closer look, there was another woman examining the same cloth. She was a lovely young woman with curly dark hair and large dark eyes.

"Looks like you had the same idea," the woman said to her when Isabelle approached and touched the fabric. Eyeing Isabelle's open coat and her bulging stomach, the woman asked, "When are you expecting your baby to arrive?"

"By Christmas," Isabelle responded.

"I thought you didn't look like you had much longer to go." The woman opened her coat and lovingly ran her hand over her small protruding stomach. "My little Ethan is coming a few months from now."

"You're naming your baby Ethan?" Isabelle smiled, thinking it was a coincidence the woman had chosen the very same name she planned to name her baby if it was a boy.

The woman smiled wistfully. "I know we can never know if we will have a boy or a girl, but I'm quite sure my baby will be a boy."

"I think my baby will also be a boy," Isabelle confided.

"I'm naming my baby after my husband." The woman became visibly emotional and she pulled her handkerchief from her sleeve and dabbed at her watery eyes. "You see, my husband was killed recently in battle, and my son will never know his father. I think that's the least I can do to honor his name."

"I am so sorry," Isabelle said. She found herself becoming emotional as she could relate to the woman's situation. At least the woman had a husband; she was a widow and she wouldn't be living in shame like she would be for the rest of her life.

"I'm sorry. It is ill-mannered of me to be so emotional in front of strangers. I'm totally rude for not introducing myself. I'm Charlotte Horn. I do hope your husband is not a soldier like my poor Ethan. Of course, I am proud of him, but I don't want another woman to go through such a loss."

Isabelle couldn't speak, she couldn't move, she couldn't breathe.

"I'm prattling on, I realize, but I've no

one to share this event with since . . . well, since Ethan is gone. We were going to settle in Wyoming, but now I will be going back to Missouri after my baby is born."

Stone overheard part of the conversation when he stepped over the threshold. He hurried to Isabelle's side. "There you are, my dear. I've been looking for you. Everyone is ready and waiting on us to leave, honey." He glanced at Charlotte Horn. "I'm sorry, but we are in a hurry."

Charlotte looked at the badge on Stone's jacket. "Oh, thank goodness you are not a soldier, Marshal. I just lost my poor husband who was a soldier, and I was telling your wife I'm naming my son Ethan to honor him. She is so lucky to have you by her side."

Mrs. Horn had assumed exactly what Stone intended, and he hadn't told a lie. He tipped his hat, and said, "Nice talking to you, ma'am, but we must say good-bye." He quickly ushered Isabelle out of the store before she broke down. Once they were outside, she still didn't utter a word. Stone feared she was in shock. "Are you okay?"

She didn't respond.

Stone helped her inside the wagon that he'd driven to the store. The captain and his men were ready to ride, and Thorpe was in the saddle. Stone caught Lily's attention and motioned for her to come to the wagon. Stone spoke softly to her and told her what happened in the general store.

"Oh no! Of all the people to run into in that store. Poor Isabelle. Tell Thorpe to give me a minute. I need to make sure she is okay."

Lily crawled inside Isabelle's wagon as Stone went to explain the situation to Thorpe and Jed.

"Do you think we should leave? Is she in any condition to travel now that she knows?" Thorpe knew what it was like to be deceived, and he worried she might be so upset that she would have that baby early.

"I think it will be best to get her out of here," Stone said. "I think if I were in her position, I wouldn't want to be anywhere near this fort."

"Let's give Miss Lily a minute. She'll know what to do," Jed said.

Isabelle was lying on her pallet, but she wasn't crying when Lily sat down beside her.

"Are you okay?" Lily asked softly.

"He had a wife. He said he was going to marry me, but he had a wife. He lied to me and I believed his lies. I'm going to have the

338

baby of a liar."

"I'm so sorry, Isabelle." Lily didn't think there was anything she could say that would take away her pain.

"I don't want this baby. I don't want any part of Ethan in my body."

"Isabelle, stop that! You're just angry right now and rightfully so. But this is your baby and you will love him. This baby can't help what his father did any more than you can. He's an innocent like you, and he's going to need someone strong that will look out for him."

Isabelle sat up and looked at Lily for the first time. "If you want it, I will give it to you. If you don't want it, I will find someone to take it when we get to Thorpe's ranch. I don't want any part of it."

Lily took her by the shoulders and shook her. "Listen to yourself! Before you found out about Ethan's lies you loved this baby. You are not making any sense. This baby is not an *it*! He is your baby and you will love him more when he comes. You have to have faith that something wonderful will come of this situation."

"You're wrong. I no longer have faith that anything good will happen." She lay back down on the pallet and turned away from Lily. "I don't want to talk about this anymore. Please tell Thorpe to get us out of here."

Realizing Isabelle wasn't seeing things clearly at the moment, Lily left the wagon and told Thorpe they were ready to leave. She looked at Stone and shook her head. "Give her some time."

During the noon break, Captain Anderson approached Lily and asked her to take a walk with him. Blue jumped up to accompany them. "Is this your chaperone?" Anderson asked.

"He generally stays with me all of the time." She didn't mention that Blue spent an inordinate amount of time with Thorpe now as well. She told him the story of finding Blue injured and how he'd been with her ever since.

"I noticed Isabelle hasn't left the wagon. Is she ailing?"

"No, unless you count a broken heart as being ill. I'm afraid she saw Mrs. Horn in the general store."

"I am sorry," Anderson said. "But perhaps it's best to know the truth about Horn."

"I agree, but she's not taking it very well right now. I'm worried about her."

"I'm certain she has to be frightened, given her situation."

340

Lily thought it was unusual for a man to be so perceptive without judging Isabelle. "Yes, she is. But Thorpe has invited us to stay on his ranch until spring, and she will have people surrounding her that care for her."

"When she has that baby, her whole life will change," he said. He looked off in the distance thinking of his life before tragedy stuck. "I know mine did."

Lily thought he was unmarried. "You have children?"

He stopped walking and pointed to some boulders where they could sit. "I was married several years ago, but my wife and young son died of cholera three years ago."

"I'm so sorry." Lily could tell by the look on his face that he still felt the loss.

"My boy was a little character. He'd put on my coat and hat and salute me. He was only four when he died."

"You must miss them terribly." Lily could sympathize with him, having lost her family.

"Yes." He tried to work up the courage to ask her the question on his mind. "Do you want a family, Lily?"

"I haven't thought that far ahead. I will have time for that later after I find my grandfather."

It wasn't the answer he wanted, but she

341

was a woman who knew what she wanted. He stood and took her hand and walked out of sight of the wagons and his men.

Thorpe was sitting on a rock enjoying his coffee and watching Lily and Anderson as they strolled away from the camp. He figured the captain was trying to gain favor with Lily. And that was okay with him, as long as he didn't try anything inappropriate. When they walked out of sight, Thorpe thought about walking in that direction, but Stone sat down beside him.

He inclined his head to the couple. "I think the captain likes Lily."

"I'm not surprised," Thorpe said, trying to keep his eyes from following them.

"Yeah. He seems like a decent fellow with a good head on his shoulders."

Thorpe didn't want to talk about Anderson. "How's Isabelle?"

"She says she doesn't want to talk about it, and that she . . ." Stone hesitated, not sure if he should reveal what Isabelle was thinking.

Thorpe noticed Stone's worried expression. "What?"

Stone threw his hands in the air. "She says she doesn't want this baby."

Thorpe shook his head. "She's hurt right

now. She'll come around. Give her time."

"You haven't seen the look in her eyes. She's changed." Stone didn't like what he saw when he tried talking to Isabelle; she wasn't the same woman.

"It's not easy to understand unless you've been betrayed. It takes time to get over the hurt and anger."

"Maybe you should have a talk with her," Stone said. "I didn't seem to make any headway and neither did Lily."

"I think you need to leave her be right now. As my dad used to say, *Time heals all wounds.* When I was younger I didn't understand what he meant. But I now understand when you give yourself time, you are able view situations without anger clouding your judgment. Leave her alone, let her think about it, and she'll come around. Isabelle is a fine woman and she'll let go of her anger." Thorpe figured Isabelle felt like he did when he learned of Evelyn's betrayal.

"I'm afraid we don't have much time before she has that baby. With her present frame of mind I'm worried she might really give that baby away. That's what she told Lily."

"Give her a few days and see if she comes around."

■ ■ ■ ■

Captain Anderson found a private area and turned to face Lily. "Lily, I asked if you wanted a family for a reason."

Lily looked up at him, her brows raised in question.

"I'd like to get to know you better. I'm not sure how long I will be in Wyoming, but I want to know where you go after you leave Turlow's ranch. Would you consider writing me and let me know where you are located? I'd like the chance to court you proper."

Lily liked him, and she thought perhaps in the future he might be a man to consider marrying when she was ready. If she could forget about Thorpe. "Yes, I will let you know."

Wallace took her by the shoulders and leaned down and placed a chaste kiss on her lips. He raised his head and looked her in the eyes. "I want you to know I'm not a man like Horn. I'd be true to you if I ever got the chance to court you." He wanted to give her a real kiss, but he had nothing to offer her at the moment. He couldn't even tell her when he would see her again, and he wanted to be fair to her.

When the captain pulled his lips from

hers, Lily found herself thinking of Thorpe's kiss. The captain didn't kiss her like Thorpe. No one had ever kissed her the way he did. She couldn't imagine another man kissing her that way, and she couldn't believe she'd ever enjoy another man's kiss quite so much.

Looking into her eyes, Anderson forgot about being fair and leaned down to press his lips to hers once more.

His second kiss startled her. Her mind was on Thorpe's kiss when Anderson wrapped his arms around her. Just as she was about to push him away, his lips left hers at the sound of a voice behind them.

"We're ready to pull out," Thorpe said.

Lily stepped away from the captain and stared at Thorpe. She was so flustered, she couldn't speak when she saw the look of contempt on Thorpe's face.

"Let's go," the captain said.

Thorpe turned Smoke around and headed back to the wagons. He couldn't believe he'd found Lily in Anderson's arms, and she looked like she was enjoying herself. He didn't know why he was so surprised; he already knew he couldn't trust women.

When Lily and Wallace walked back to camp, Thorpe stole a glance at Lily. Her face was flushed and he wondered if it was due to the cold or the kissing. "Is your wagon ready to leave?" he snapped. He already knew Jed was hitching the team for her.

"I'll have it ready in a few minutes."

The captain nodded to Lily before he walked away to join his men.

Lily left Thorpe standing there alone. She walked to her wagon and found Jed harnessing the animals for her. "Thanks, Jed."

"You're welcome, Miss Lily. Mr. Thorpe sure seemed to be in a hurry all of a sudden."

She looked Thorpe's way and saw that he and the captain were riding side by side.

CHAPTER TWENTY-TWO

"Thorpe, do you have an interest in Lily?" Anderson asked.

Thorpe couldn't say he was surprised by Anderson's straightforward question. He admired his direct approach. "I have an interest in her well-being, and I intend to make sure she arrives at Dove Creek safe and sound."

"I appreciate that, but I'm asking if you have a more personal interest in her. Have you planned on courting her once she's at your ranch?"

Though Thorpe liked the captain, he wasn't inclined to discuss his plans, if he had any when it came to Lily. "What business would that be of yours?"

"As you probably figured out earlier, I'm attracted to Lily and I plan to court her once she's settled. I've made my intentions known."

Thorpe reined Smoke to a halt and stared

at Anderson. "What does Lily have to say about your intentions?"

Anderson pulled his horse around so he could look directly at Thorpe. "You could see she had no objections."

Yep. Thorpe had noticed she wasn't protesting when he was kissing her. "Then I reckon you have no need to worry about me or my interest."

Anderson gave him a half grin. "I didn't say I was worried. You're a smart man. I figured if you were interested, you'd have done something about it before now. With a woman like her, a man would have to be crazy not to stake a claim when he had a chance. If you had told me you were interested in courting her, I would have told you that I plan to give you some competition."

Thorpe was tempted to take that challenge, but he wouldn't toy with Lily. After that kiss he'd shared with her, he knew he could easily get himself in the same position he had with Evelyn. He wanted her. He wanted her more than he'd ever wanted Evelyn. But he didn't want a wife right now. "I'm not looking for a wife."

"That's the best news I've had in a long time. I'm looking for a wife and I want children." Anderson was relieved Thorpe had no interest in marrying Lily. He figured

Thorpe would have the advantage since he'd spent so much time on the trail with Lily, and she was going to be under his roof through the winter. Smiling at what he thought was his good fortune, he urged his horse ahead. He hated to say good-bye to Lily tomorrow morning, but he had the night to spend some more time with her. He hadn't kissed a woman in a long time, and he didn't call that peck he gave her earlier a real kiss. He wanted to give her a kiss that she would remember, and one that would last him for several months.

Thorpe didn't move for a few minutes, thinking about Anderson's comments. He wanted children, and he wanted Lily to be the mother of those children. The thought of Lily being married to Anderson and bearing his children troubled him. But why should it? If Lily wanted Anderson, why should he care?

Watching Thorpe and Captain Anderson riding together, Lily realized she couldn't escape the fact that her heart belonged to Thorpe. It was obvious he didn't want anything to do with her, yet that didn't stop her from loving him. She liked the captain, but she couldn't see herself ever feeling for him what she felt for Thorpe.

■ ■ ■ ■

Captain Anderson rode with his men for several miles until he realized he could spend even more time with Lily before nightfall. He rode back to her wagon and told her to stop. After tying his horse behind the wagon, he jumped into the seat beside her.

Lily gave him a questioning look. "I decided this would be a much more pleasant way to pass the miles." He took the reins from her. "I hope you don't mind."

Much to her surprise, she didn't mind. Her mind had been on Isabelle, and she wasn't quite sure what she could do to change her mind about the baby. It would be nice to have someone to talk with. "No, I don't mind."

"You know I will be riding north in the morning and I may not be back to the fort for several weeks." He'd told her about the Sioux attacking soldiers in Montana Territory.

"It sounds very dangerous."

"Nothing that we can't handle."

"I'm sorry to see you go." She didn't want anything to happen to him or his men.

He looked into her eyes. "Are you?"

Before she responded, Blue jumped from the back and sat between them.

The captain laughed. "I think someone is jealous of me sitting too close to you."

Thorpe saw the captain jump into Lily's wagon, and he couldn't help but notice they were sitting very close. He almost laughed when he saw Blue squeeze between them. He wondered what Blue thought of the captain. He had the remainder of the day to think about what the two of them were discussing. They talked nonstop until they made camp at dusk.

The next morning Captain Anderson and his men were saddled and ready to leave, but he instructed his men to ride ahead and he would catch up with them. He rode to Lily's wagon and started hitching her team for her.

"Thank you," Lily said when she walked up behind him.

"I wish I could go with you, but I have my orders. Duty calls." Once he finished with the mules, he took Lily's hand and walked to the side of the wagon. "I may not see you for several months, but when I return I will come visit."

"I can't say where I will be come spring,"

she replied.

He wrapped his fingers around her shoulders and moved closer. "Lily, I want you to know I'd like to see what could develop between us. I know you are not ready to make any decisions right now about your future, and I'm not asking for guarantees. All I'm asking for is a chance to get to know each other better. Just agree to let me come for a visit. We may find we don't suit, but we can be friends at the very least."

Even if she was able to stop thinking about Thorpe in the future, she wasn't sure she would ever have the same feelings for Captain Anderson. Still, it didn't make sense to rebuff him because he wasn't asking for a commitment. "You can visit once I'm settled."

He smiled at her. "I look forward to that day. I will wire you when I have word of your grandfather."

"Thank you for that. It means more than you know."

"I feel honored to have met you." He reached for her hand. "I want to give you a real kiss, but I know we are not alone." He brought the back of her hand to his lips.

Lily was touched by his declaration. "Please be careful. I will pray for your safety." Even if she didn't develop deeper feelings for him, she'd like to have him as a friend, and she wanted him to stay safe.

He couldn't help himself; he leaned over and kissed her cheek. "Until then."

Lily watched him ride away and tried to untangle her emotions. For some reason she felt like crying. She wasn't sure she'd made the right decision to let him walk away without offering more encouragement. Captain Anderson was a respectable man, and she might never meet another man willing to wait for her to make a decision about the direction of her life. She said a silent prayer for him and his men, asking God to keep them safe.

In the background she heard Thorpe tell everyone it was time to leave, so she jumped into her wagon. She was relieved to have the time to herself driving the wagon; she needed to sort through her feelings. Thorpe's face popped into her mind along with the kiss they'd shared. She didn't want to think about Thorpe's kiss, but she couldn't help herself. His kiss set her skin on fire. Captain Anderson's kiss wasn't the kind of kiss that stirred passion, but it wasn't altogether unpleasant. There were other differences between the men besides their kisses. The captain wanted a wife and children. Thorpe wanted what Horn wanted from Isabelle. She had no doubt Thorpe could find any number of women to give him what he wanted, but she wasn't willing to allow a man to treat her with such little respect. Not even Thorpe.

"Do you want me to take you back to the fort?" Thorpe asked.

Lily hadn't heard him ride up beside the wagon. "What?"

"I asked if you want me to take you back to the fort." After watching the two of them say good-bye, Thorpe thought she might want to go back to the fort and wait for Anderson.

Lily was stunned that he would ask such a thing. "Why would I want to do that?"

"You and the captain are pretty friendly. I thought you might want to go back and wait for him."

He'd been the one to suggest they go to his ranch in the first place, so why didn't he want her there now? "Are you saying you don't want me to go to your ranch?"

Thorpe wasn't sure what he wanted. He wanted to say yes. He wanted to say no. What was wrong with him? "I just thought you might want to wait for Anderson at the fort."

She tried to control her emotions; she wasn't going to let him know how much his words hurt. "If you don't want me at Dove Creek, I can go back to the fort by myself. I don't need you to take me."

"I didn't say that!" he shouted. "The way you were kissing yesterday, I just thought . . ." His voice was so loud, the mules sidestepped away from him, and Blue jumped from the back of the wagon to the seat beside Lily and gave him a strange look. *Dang it all.* "Just forget I said anything." He rode away before Lily could utter another word.

If it wasn't for Isabelle, Lily would have turned her wagon around and headed back to the fort. She didn't know why Thorpe was angry, but she'd given her word to Isabelle that she would help her. She wiped away the tears that were trailing down her cheek. Blue nudged closer to her. "Oh, Blue, why does he care if I kissed the captain? He made it perfectly clear that he regretted kissing me." Well, Captain Anderson didn't regret kissing her. He wanted to kiss her some more. She should have allowed him to give her a real kiss good-bye in front of everyone!

"Why have you had a burr up your butt for two days?" Stone asked Thorpe when they were constructing a corral for the animals.

"I don't know what you're talking about," Thorpe said, refusing to admit to Stone what was on his mind.

"Does your bad attitude have something to do with Lily and the captain?" Stone knew the answer to his question; he just wanted to see if Thorpe would admit why he'd been so riled since they'd left the fort. He'd noticed Lily had been keeping her distance from Thorpe, too.

"My attitude is just fine." As a matter of fact, he'd told himself he was going to put Lily out of his mind. What she did with the captain was her business. He didn't care. If she wanted to kiss him and a hundred other men, that was fine by him.

Stone wasn't going to let it drop. "I'd say the captain is taken with Lily."

Thorpe didn't comment.

"He sure took up most of her time at dinner. But who could blame him? She looked beautiful in that blue dress."

Silence.

"He only rode with us just so he could talk to her some more." Stone glanced at Thorpe and he could have sworn smoke was coming out of his ears.

Thorpe started working faster.

"Heck, I thought he was going to kiss her

good-bye right in front of God and every-
body."

"I don't know why he didn't since he'd
already kissed her." Thorpe spoke before he
thought.

Stone stopped working. He'd only been
teasing, but he could tell Thorpe was serious. "He told you that?"

"No, I saw them."

"I guess Captain Anderson moves fast."

"Yeah."

For a man that wasn't interested in Lily,
Thorpe didn't look too happy about the
situation between her and the captain. "You
did say you weren't interested in marriage."

"Yep, and I haven't changed my mind."

"Then I guess you have no objections to
the captain courting Lily?"

"Nope." Thorpe couldn't think of one
reason he should object.

"He seems like a fine man," Stone said.

Finally, Thorpe had enough. He stopped
working and glared at Stone. "Are you going to jaw all night or get this finished?"

Stone laughed. "I don't know. It seems to
me you're working fast enough for both of
us."

CHAPTER TWENTY-THREE

The snow was falling in large white flakes by the time the entrance to Dove Creek Ranch came into view. At first glance, it was an entryway like many others with large logs and the name of the ranch forged in iron. But when they rode closer Lily saw what made the sign unique. There were hand-forged doves sitting on the top rail. It was the most beautiful sign she'd ever seen. She remembered Thorpe told them he'd chosen the name for his ranch because of his mother's fondness for doves. There was a side to Thorpe that was warm and loving. She'd seen that side of him before they'd shared that kiss at Chimney Rock. He hadn't been the same since. He'd been distant and ill-tempered. They hadn't spoken since he offered to take her back to the fort, and she had mixed emotions about going to his ranch, knowing he didn't really want her there. She'd told Isabelle she would see that she was settled at the ranch and then she would find a place to stay in town. She hoped she could find a job to get her through the winter and be able to help Isabelle financially once the baby was born.

They reached the gate and pulled their wagons to a halt.

"Mr. Thorpe, that shor' is a pretty gate. I don't reckon I've ever seen anything as pretty as those doves," Jed said.

"Thanks, Jed." Thorpe saw Lily staring at the gate. "I can't take credit for making it, but I told the blacksmith what I wanted and he did a fine job."

"Yessir, he surely did. No one ever asked me to make something like that." Jed considered himself a competent blacksmith, but he'd never realized how he could use his talents to make something so pretty. Seeing those doves had his mind racing.

"Jed, the blacksmith that did the work died last year," Thorpe said.

"That's a shame. I'd like to have met the man that made those doves," Jed said.

"How far is your home?" Isabelle asked.

"It'll take us about thirty more minutes," Thorpe said.

Stone looked at Isabelle. "I bet you're happier than anyone to be here."

"Yes, I am. Thank you, Thorpe, for inviting us," Isabelle said in a monotone voice. It wasn't that she was ungrateful, but she couldn't muster the energy to be excited about anything. Since learning of Ethan's deceit, she didn't think anything would ever excite her again.

"You're welcome to stay as long as you like," Thorpe replied.

Lily appreciated the way everyone was making an effort to cheer Isabelle, but nothing was having an impact on her. Not even Stone had been able to get her out of her gloom.

"How far is town from here?" Lily asked Thorpe.

Thorpe wondered why she'd asked that question. "It's about eight miles east of here."

Curtis met Thorpe as soon as he reined in at the house. "It's about time you came home."

"I'm happy to be here." Thorpe introduced his foreman to everyone. Curtis took the men to the stable and Thorpe showed Lily and Isabelle inside his home. His home was larger than the women expected. It was two stories constructed of logs and stone. When they walked in the front door, Lily's first thought was it was definitely a man's home. The front parlor was large with a massive stone fireplace, oversized furniture, and bare of any colorful item. She wondered why his fiancée hadn't added some feminine touches to his home. Or perhaps she did and Thorpe removed everything that reminded him of her.

Thorpe carried the puppies inside, followed by Spirit and Blue. He placed them on a rug in front of the fireplace. "I'll get a blanket for them." He led the women upstairs and opened the door to the first bedroom. "Isabelle, you can stay in this room." He pointed to a room across the hall and said, "Lily, you can take that room if you like."

Isabelle looked inside the room and saw it was nicely furnished. "This isn't your room, is it?"

"No, my room is at the end of the hall. There are four bedrooms. There's a fireplace in every room and I'll come back and get them going after I meet with my foreman. This house gets mighty cold at night." He figured tonight would be the first time his home would be warm with all of the fireplaces blazing.

"I didn't expect your home to be so large," Isabelle said.

Thorpe explained he'd been adding onto

his home every year, but he didn't give them a reason. He didn't tell them that he'd built his home from his mother's description of her family home in England. She'd often described her childhood home and her stories stayed with him. He hesitated at the doorway a moment and before he turned to leave, he said, "We have a doctor in town, and one of the women on the ranch helps women with . . . well, when the time comes." He planned to ride to town to see the doc in the morning to tell him about Isabelle and have him come out to meet her before the baby came.

"I don't know how to thank you," Isabelle said.

"No thanks needed. I'll let you two rest and later we'll bring some water up so you can have baths and get those fires going."

"That sounds lovely," Isabelle said.

Thorpe walked to his room and grabbed a quilt for the puppies. He'd noticed Lily didn't say one word.

Lily didn't plan on staying in the room, but she would definitely take a bath. Isabelle asked her to stay in her room for a while and Lily thought something might be wrong. "Are you feeling ill?"

"No, just tired, but I don't think I can rest right now. I will be glad when this is

362

over." She plopped down in a chair and Lily did the same. "What's wrong between you and Thorpe?"

Lily told her about the captain kissing her and Thorpe witnessing their encounter.

"He kissed you! Did you like it?"

"It wasn't like . . ." She hadn't told Isabelle about Thorpe kissing her. "It was fine."

"Fine? That doesn't sound like much of a kiss. Do you like him?"

"Yes, I do. He's a nice man."

"I told you the captain would make Thorpe jealous."

"Thorpe's not jealous. I don't think he really wants me here."

"I would say you're wrong, but it's obvious I don't even know when a man is lying. I'm of no help to you. I thought after you saved Thorpe's life you two would always be together. What are you going to do?"

"I'm going to ride to town tomorrow morning and see if I can find a job and get a room where I can stay."

"Oh, Lily, I don't want you to go. What if I have this baby when you're not here?"

"I'll come out and check on you as much as I can. But I have to earn some money."

"What is going to happen to us?"

Lily reached for her hand and squeezed. "I will help you and the baby. Please don't

363

worry. We will work this out."

"I haven't changed my mind. I don't want this baby."

Lily had thought about offering to keep the baby until Isabelle came to her senses. "Well, whether you want him or not, he is coming. We will work everything out later."

Thorpe had to meet with Curtis and catch up on ranch business, so he was grateful for Stone and Jed's offer to cook dinner. The man who cooked for them was out on the range with the rest of the men. Isabelle came downstairs to find the men setting the table.

"Why didn't you come and get me? I would have cooked dinner," Isabelle said.

Stone pulled a chair out for her at the table. "We thought we would let you and Lily rest."

Thorpe came through the door and stopped at the dining room. "I'll wash up and be right back."

Jed was pouring coffee when Thorpe returned.

"Where's Miss Lily?" Jed asked.

"She said she wanted to rest," Isabelle said.

Thorpe figured she was probably pining for the captain. He'd noticed earlier Blue

364

wasn't in the front parlor with Spirit and the puppies, so he figured he was with Lily. "Let's eat."

After dinner, Thorpe asked Isabelle if she wanted to take some dinner to Lily.

"Of course." Isabelle walked to the door and reached for her coat from one of the hooks.

"Where are you going?" Stone asked.

"To Lily's wagon."

"Why are you going to her wagon?"

"To take her dinner."

"But why isn't she upstairs?"

Thorpe overheard their conversation and walked to the door, waiting to hear Isabelle's response. He'd thought Lily was upstairs resting.

Isabelle looked at Thorpe. "She said she didn't want to stay in the house." She hoped Thorpe didn't ask her why.

Thorpe couldn't believe Lily had been in that wagon the whole time. "She can't sleep in that wagon. She won't have a fire." He had the men put the wagons inside a large barn that was near the stable. Lily wouldn't be warm in that drafty old barn with no fire. The woman was driving him to distraction. What in the heck was wrong with her? He'd offered her a nice, warm room to sleep in and she'd opted to sleep in a wagon where she would freeze to death. It was infuriating. He stormed out the door without grabbing his coat.

Once inside the barn, he saw she had a lantern lit and she was moving around inside the wagon. Before he knocked, he heard her speaking and he knew she was talking to Blue.

Lily pulled the flap back and stuck her head out. "Yes?"

Thorpe didn't think before he spoke. "What is wrong with you?"

Lily was surprised by his question. "Nothing is wrong with me."

"Well, what are you doing out here in the cold? Why didn't you have dinner with us? Why aren't you staying in the house?"

"I'm where I want to be," she replied. "And I'm not hungry."

Blue jumped down from the wagon and stood by Thorpe. Thorpe was so angry, he didn't know what to say, but he said the one thing likely to sway her. "Well, Blue's probably hungry."

Lily wouldn't allow Blue to go hungry. She'd already planned to start a small fire so she could cook something for him. "He can go back to the house with you."

"Come on, you're going to the house,"

Thorpe said.

"No, I'm not."

"What's wrong with my home?"

Lily decided he wasn't going to leave it alone, so she told him what was on her mind. "Nothing is wrong with your home. It's lovely. I know you don't want me here. Tomorrow morning I plan to go into town and find a job and a place to stay until spring."

Her plans took the steam out of his anger. Almost. "Who said I didn't want you here?"

"You didn't say it exactly. It's more the way you've behaved since that day at Chimney Rock."

"If I didn't want you here, I wouldn't have asked you to come." *Were all women so darn confounding?*

"You asked me if I wanted to go back to the fort. I thought that meant you didn't want me at your ranch."

"You and the captain seemed to be getting pretty darn close and I thought you might want to wait for him there." He'd only asked her that because he was angry. He didn't like seeing them kiss, particularly since he'd kissed her just a few days before. And he'd stayed away from her because he didn't want to chance getting in over his head again.

"Captain Anderson and I are friends."

"Do you kiss all of your friends like that?" Thorpe snapped.

"He surprised me, but . . ." *Why am I explaining anything to him? He was the one that regretted our kiss. I don't owe him an explanation.* "It's really none of your business."

On that point, he agreed. "You're right, it's none of my business, and I intend to keep it that way." He held his arms up to help her from the wagon. "Just come on in the house. I'm getting cold out here."

"I told you I'm fine where I am."

Thorpe was cold, tired, and angry. He wasn't going to argue in his present frame of mind for fear of saying something he would regret. He reached up and wrapped his hands around her waist and lifted her from the wagon. "You are not staying out here in the cold and that's final." He placed her on the ground beside him. "Do you need anything from the wagon?"

Lily didn't have the heart to keep Blue from having his dinner. And the longer she bickered with Thorpe, the hungrier Blue was going to be. "Yes, my valise."

Thorpe reached inside the wagon and pulled it out. "Now about this harebrained idea you have about finding a job in town . . ."

"I told you that was my plan when you invited us here. You can't stop me from doing that," Lily retorted.

Thorpe vaguely remembered she mentioned looking for a job. "This isn't a town like Kansas City. It's growing since the railroad is coming through, and we are drawing all kinds of people. Some are rough-looking characters. The hotel is no place for a lady and the boardinghouse is no better."

"I'm sure somewhere will be suitable. As you remember, I can defend myself," Lily replied.

"Not against a couple of drunks. There won't be any jobs for you either, unless you want to work in the saloon."

"I'm not without skills. I can work in a mercantile, I'm adept with numbers," she told him.

"Mr. and Mrs. Eads run the mercantile and their son works there."

"Perhaps the boardinghouse or the hotel needs a cook," she said.

"I doubt it. As I said, neither place is safe for a woman." There was an older woman who cooked at the boardinghouse, but Thorpe felt sure she was safe from unwanted attentions.

Lily thought he was being obstinate. Maybe he was worried about Isabelle staying alone on his ranch. "I'm sure women cook at these establishments."

"None that look like you. Besides, Isabelle needs someone to stay with her. If you're so all-fired to work, I need a cook. My man who does the cooking is needed out with the men, and now that more people will be staying on the ranch, you can do the cooking in the house. Stone and Jed cooked dinner tonight. They won't have the time to do it every night and neither do I." When she didn't respond, he decided to pull out his ace. "Besides, we've been fortunate that we aren't already knee-deep in snow. What if you're stuck in town and can't get out here when Isabelle has that baby?"

"Do you really need a cook?"

"Yes." He told himself she had no business staying in town alone and that was the only reason he wanted her to stay at the ranch. Was she telling the truth when she said she was just friends with Anderson? He didn't kiss his *friends* the way they were kissing. He wasn't interested in her, so why did he continue to dwell on her kissing Anderson?

"In lieu of wages, I'll work for a place to stay until Isabelle's baby is born." That would solve her problem short-term. But after the baby came, they would need to find a place to stay and she would need to find a position.

"You don't think you and Isabelle will be leaving after the baby is born?" He couldn't believe she was thinking of taking off with Isabelle and a baby in the dead of winter.

"Yes, we can't be a burden to you forever. We will move to town."

"You will stay until spring." It wasn't a suggestion. He wasn't about to let two women go traipsing off by themselves with a little baby. "Let's get to the house so you and Blue can eat."

As they walked toward the house, Thorpe said, "In a couple of weeks the wives of my men and their children will be coming around to start decorating the house for Christmas. You and Isabelle will get to have some female company for a change."

Lily thought preparing for the holiday sounded fun. She had wonderful memories of helping her mother decorate their home for Christmas and preparing the meal. "It will be good for Isabelle to get her mind off her troubles." She wouldn't admit it to Thorpe, but she looked forward to Christmas on Dove Creek Ranch. She started thinking of gifts she could make for Isabelle's baby now that she wasn't going to be spending her days driving a wagon. If she could make a trip to town, she could buy some cloth with what little money she had left. She could even make some shirts for the men. Perhaps if Isabelle joined her in making gifts, it would get her out of her melancholy. "Thank you for letting us stay, Thorpe."

Thorpe reached for her arm to stop her when they reached the porch. When she turned to face him, he said, "Lily, I never meant that I didn't want you at the ranch."

She stared into his dark eyes. "What did you mean?"

He thought about dropping her valise and the lantern he was holding and taking her in his arms. He wanted to kiss her again, but that wouldn't be the smartest idea he ever had. "I meant . . . I didn't . . ." *What did he mean?* If she went back to the fort, he wouldn't be tempted to do what he wanted to do right now. Evelyn had been alone in his home, and what started out as an innocent kiss had ended up with her in his bed. That's exactly where he wanted Lily at this very moment. It wasn't going to happen twice. "I don't know what I meant."

CHAPTER TWENTY-FOUR

The next morning Thorpe awoke before dawn to the aroma of coffee and something that smelled so delicious, his stomach started growling before he reached the kitchen. When he walked into the kitchen, he came to a halt. Lily was standing at the stove wearing a yellow dress and talking to Blue and Spirit. Blue was nudged up against her thigh as though he thought she might walk away without him. The puppies were playing on the blanket in the corner. He envisioned himself walking up behind her, wrapping his arms around her, and kissing her neck. He shook his head, trying to erase that vision. "Were the pups unhappy in the front room?"

She turned at the sound of his voice. "Blue pulled the blanket in here and the puppies followed."

"He likes to keep an eye on them." He walked to the cabinet to grab a cup.

"Blue likes to keep an eye on everything." She'd noticed Blue wasn't letting her out of his sight the last few days. Last night Blue had awakened her with his restless pacing and he wouldn't settle down until she sat beside him on the blanket with Spirit and the puppies. She'd talked to him for what seemed like an eternity before he finally went to sleep with his head on her lap.

"Something sure smells good."

"I found some dried apples so I made a pie this morning."

Thorpe glanced at the pie sitting on the counter by the stove. "Can I have some of that?"

"For breakfast? I'm cooking some bacon now, and biscuits are in the oven."

"I'll have that too, but that pie smells too good."

Lily smiled at him. "I'll slice you a piece when it's cooled a bit."

He poured some coffee. "Do you want some coffee?"

"I've already had some."

He leaned against the counter and watched her cook as he sipped his coffee. He always preferred his quiet time in the kitchen. Until now. Looking at her in the morning beat the heck out of being alone with his thoughts. "I'm going to ride to town to tell the doc about Isabelle and ask him to come meet her when he has time."

Lily glanced up at him. "What made you think of that?"

"The doc is a friend of mine and a reasonable man. I know she is having a difficult time and I thought he might be able to help her in some way."

Lily felt herself becoming emotional. The man could be so frustrating at times, and then he would turn around and make the most thoughtful gesture. Isabelle insisted she wasn't going to keep the baby, so maybe the doctor could reason with her. "I think that is a fine idea."

Thorpe leaned over and grabbed a fork and stuck it in the pie. He saw her staring at him and he smiled wide. "I can't wait." He stuffed a big bite in his mouth.

Lily laughed. "I didn't know you were starving. Let me get a plate."

He stuck the fork in the pie again and this time held it to her mouth. "This is great. Try it."

Lily didn't move while he held the fork to her lips. She stared into his eyes and nibbled the pie off the fork.

Thorpe's eyes were on her lips and he really wanted to kiss her. *Calm down.* "Delicious, huh?"

Lily thought she had never seen a more handsome man. She looked at him and nodded. She forced her eyes from his face, and stood on her tiptoes to grab a plate from the shelf above the stove.

Thorpe's hand covered hers. "I got it." He felt like he was struck by lightning when he touched her hand. "I guess I need to lower those shelves for you."

"They are fine. I won't be here that long." Trying to ignore the tension between them, Lily pulled a knife from the drawer and focused on the pie. She hoped he didn't notice her hands shaking. After she made the first cut into the pie, Thorpe placed his hand over hers again and moved the knife to show her he wanted her to cut a big slice.

"I eat a lot more than you think," he told her.

"Did we starve you on the trail?" She always thought she gave him large portions, but now she was beginning to think it wasn't enough for him.

He grinned at her.

"You should have said something," she told him.

"I need more food now that'll I'll be working a lot harder," he told her.

She placed the pie on the plate he held for her. "The biscuits will be done in a few minutes."

Thorpe carried his coffee and pie to the table and sat in a chair where he could watch her move around the kitchen. He liked watching her work with the animals at her feet. She looked like she belonged there.

When she placed another plateful of food in front of him, he said, "Aren't you going to have breakfast with me?"

"Of course." She hadn't planned on eating with him, but since he was making an effort to be congenial this morning, she would do the same. She filled a plate for herself and sat across from him. "Do you think I could ride to town with you? I want to pick up some cloth."

Thorpe didn't respond immediately. He was asking himself how he could ride in a buckboard with her all the way to town and back and not be tempted to put his hands all over her.

When he didn't answer right away, Lily thought he was probably thinking it would take too long. She knew he had ranch business that needed his attention. "I can change my clothes and ride Blaze so we can make better time. I won't delay you."

"We'll take the buckboard. I need to pick up some supplies while I'm there." He just hoped he wouldn't have to fight off every man he encountered since they were all sure to gape at her. He'd bet no man in town had ever seen anyone as beautiful as Lily.

Before they left the ranch, Stone rode up beside them saying he needed to send another telegram, and he wanted to talk to the pastor. Thorpe wrapped two blankets around Lily on the seat of the buckboard and Blue wedged himself between them. When they reached town, Thorpe asked Lily if she would like to go with him to see the doctor before they headed to the mercantile. "You'll have plenty of time to find what you need at the mercantile since I'll have to load supplies."

Lily was so shocked that he asked her that she readily agreed.

"I'll meet you two at the mercantile," Stone said.

They reached the doctor's office and Thorpe held the door for her. The doctor walked from the back room and shook hands with Thorpe.

"When did you get back? We've missed you around here." There were many things the doc wanted to ask about Evelyn, but he refrained seeing Thorpe was with another woman.

"Just yesterday. Doc, this is Lily Starr. Lily

378

this is Doc Emerson."

Just as Thorpe predicted, the doc couldn't take his eyes off of Lily. When he finally spoke, he said, "Please call me Michael."

"Of course," Lily replied with a smile.

Thorpe gaped at him. He wasn't sure he'd ever heard the doc use his first name. Everyone called him Doc.

Michael looked at Thorpe and said, "Where did you find Miss Starr, or is it Mrs. Starr?"

"It's Miss, and she found me." Thorpe told him about the Indians chasing him and Lily coming to his rescue. "I wanted to ask if you could stop by the ranch to see a friend of Lily's. She's due to give birth sometime this month. She says it's going to be Christmas Day. We're concerned about her because she recently learned the baby's father is dead, and now she says she doesn't want to keep the baby."

Lily was grateful Thorpe didn't actually reveal Isabelle wasn't married to the baby's father.

"I'm sorry to hear of her circumstances — it must be a difficult time for her. Of course, I will be happy to visit. Would tomorrow be too soon?"

"Perfect. Why don't you come around dinnertime? I'd appreciate it if you didn't mention we told you how she feels about the baby."

"Of course." Michael had so many questions he wanted to ask Thorpe, but he couldn't with Lily present. He couldn't wait to get him alone tomorrow night to find out if he was courting Lily. "And who is this?" he asked, pointing to Blue.

"He belongs to Lily. His name is Blue," Thorpe replied.

"Isn't he a wolf?"

Thorpe grinned at him. "Yes."

The doc shook his head. "I never knew anyone to have a pet wolf other than the Indians."

"He's Lily's protector," Thorpe told him.

"I can see that." The wolf hadn't left Lily's side from the moment they walked through the door.

While Thorpe loaded his supplies, several people stopped to talk to him. When he stopped working to talk, he'd glance through the window of the mercantile and watched Lily as she perused the catalog on the counter. With Blue beside her, he didn't need to worry, but he liked looking at her.

Howard Bowles, the banker, stopped to talk to him about the many new arrivals to their town. Thorpe had noticed the town had done some growing since he'd been gone. New buildings were going up and there was a renewed vitality to the small town all due to the railroad.

"Do we have a new blacksmith?" Thorpe asked.

"Not yet. You know of anyone interested in taking over that business?"

"I may. I have to talk to him about it first."

"I will give him a fair price on the building. It's in the best interest of the town to have a blacksmith."

"What is the price for the building and equipment?"

After Thorpe discussed the particulars of the blacksmith business, he finished loading his supplies. Once he was done, he walked to the door of the mercantile. He stood silently and watched Lily examine the various materials on the table. She ran her hands over one bolt of fabric, and he heard her say, "How lovely."

"What about that pretty white material you were admiring?" Sadie Eads, the proprietor of the mercantile, asked when Lily placed her purchases on the counter.

"It is lovely, but I'm afraid it won't work for what I need," Lily replied.

"Have you ever seen anything so beautiful? It would make a lovely wedding dress."

"Yes, it would," Lily agreed.

"And that sapphire velvet would make a lovely cloak for you with those beautiful blue eyes of yours. I had ordered that material for another customer but she left town before it arrived," Sadie said. "It was expensive, more so than any other material I've ordered. I don't know if I will ever sell it, but it's a real pleasure just to see something so glorious. Not very practical for weather out here in Wyoming."

"It is beautiful, and if lined with wool it would make a very warm cloak for this climate. But it is much too costly for my budget," Lily replied. She knew she'd never be able to afford material so luxurious. Glancing at the shelves, Lily spotted some books and walked away to look at them. One book caught her eye and she pulled it down and placed it on the counter. "I will take this as well."

Sadie picked up the used book. "A gentleman came in the store needing to buy some food for his family, but he had no money. He only had a few books and my husband traded him food for the books."

"That was very nice of your husband," Lily said.

"Are you ready?" Thorpe asked.

She turned to see him standing inside the

382

door; his large frame seemed to fill the entire room. He looked so tall and handsome standing there with his black Stetson on, that he took her breath away. "I will be a minute. I'm paying for my purchases."

Thorpe walked to the counter and stood beside Lily. "Just put this on my bill, Sadie."

"Sure will, Thorpe. We've missed you."

"Oh no, you can't pay for this," Lily said.

"Sadie, this is Lily Starr. She's staying at the ranch. Anything she needs you just add it to my bill."

Sadie nodded to Lily before looking up at Thorpe. "She's staying at your ranch?"

"Uh-huh. How's Jacob?" Thorpe hadn't noticed, or intentionally decided not to explain, why Lily was at his ranch.

"He's just fine," Sadie replied. She hadn't noticed Thorpe standing at the door and she thought he might have heard her comment about the customer leaving town before the expensive material arrived. She'd ordered that material specifically for his fiancée, Evelyn. Sadie had been one of the guests in the church that morning when Evelyn didn't show up to marry the most handsome man in town. Sadie's eyes moved back to Lily. *Looks like Thorpe found himself an even more beautiful woman.* She hoped this one had more character than Evelyn.

There wasn't a woman in town who liked Evelyn; she was rude and so thoroughly self-absorbed that no one could figure out what Thorpe saw in her. But what was this lovely young woman doing at Thorpe's ranch? Maybe she was a relative he brought home with him. If not, it would be most inappropriate for them to be living under the same roof if they weren't married. *Just wait until the pastor hears about this! He will be fit to be tied.*

Lily looked up at Thorpe and repeated, "You can't pay for this."

"Of course I can." He picked up the book and looked at the title: *Great Expectations.*

"Jed likes to read. I thought that would make a nice Christmas gift for him. He told me his mother taught him to read, but they had to do it in secret. He said they didn't have access to many books."

Her thoughtfulness didn't surprise him. "I know he will treasure this." He handed her the book and picked up the material and placed it under his arm. "Are you ready?" He took Lily by the elbow and nodded his good-bye to Sadie. "Tell Jacob hello."

Lily was astonished by his generosity, but she was also concerned that Sadie may have misconstrued their relationship. When they reached the buckboard, she said, "I hope that woman understands I am a guest and not a . . ." She didn't know how to finish her thought.

Thorpe placed her purchases behind the buckboard's seat. "Not a what?" He hadn't considered he needed to explain why she was at his ranch, or why he was paying for her purchases. He knew Lily didn't have much money to spare and that was the reason he put it on his bill. Plain and simple.

"She may have gotten the wrong idea about us."

"I don't think Sadie would jump to any conclusions."

Perhaps he paid for women's purchases before and Sadie wouldn't think anything was amiss. "You must let me pay you back. These are my Christmas gifts."

He pushed his hat back and stared at her. Gazing at her lovely face, he had a strong urge to kiss her again. What was wrong with him? The same thing had happened last night on the porch. He'd tossed and turned all night thinking about her and how she was sleeping just a few feet down the hallway from him. Then, the first thing this morning he saw her standing at the stove in his kitchen. His urge to walk across the room and take her in his arms was nearly overwhelming. He had the same urge in the mercantile. He needed to keep his mind on business.

He was thankful Stone rode to town with them, or he might have stopped somewhere along the way and given in to his urge to kiss her. "Lily, it's a gift, that's all. Sadie won't think a thing of it."

"Thank you," she said softly. "But some of that material is for Isabelle. Stone gave me money and told me to buy something she would like. Isabelle didn't get to purchase anything at the fort and we need some soft material to make nappies."

"Give Stone back his money."

"But my items are for Christmas gifts. They wouldn't be from me if you pay for them."

"Of course they would. You'll be making them."

"What about the book for Jed?"

"You picked it out," he countered.

"But . . ." She stopped talking when he put his hands around her waist and lifted her to the buckboard.

"If it makes you feel better, you can tell Jed it is from both of us." He was about to jump in beside her when the pastor walked up and greeted them.

Thorpe shook hands with the pastor. "Lily, this is Pastor Sewell. Pastor, this is

Lily Starr."

The pastor removed his hat and nodded. "My pleasure indeed."

Once Thorpe gave him an abbreviated account of how he'd met Lily, the pastor said, "I trust you will bring your lovely guest to service on Sunday."

"I have another lady staying at the ranch that's ready to give birth any minute, so we'll probably stick close to home. But you are always welcome to come by," Thorpe told him. Thorpe was just about to ask him if he met Stone, when he reined in beside the buckboard.

"Stone, this is Pastor Sewell," Thorpe said.

"I was just at your church," Stone said.

"Did you need me?" the pastor asked.

"Thorpe, I'll catch up with you," Stone said, dismounting and shaking hands with the pastor.

"I need to make one more stop," Thorpe replied. "We'll be headed back to the ranch in ten minutes."

Stone nodded, and tied his horse to the post. "I need a few minutes of your time, Pastor."

Stone talked to the pastor about Isabelle and her situation. He told him Isabelle's father was a pastor and how he'd disowned his daughter.

Stone finished his story and the pastor put his hand on his shoulder. "You are doing the right thing and I admire you for that. It was a mistake, but the young woman doesn't deserve to be shunned by her father. I'm inclined to send him a letter to remind him of God's forgiveness. Apparently, he's forgotten we are all sinners."

Thorpe pulled the buckboard to a halt in front of the building that the blacksmith used before his death. "Be right back." He jumped down and walked inside.

It only took him a few minutes, and when he walked back to the buckboard he saw Lily and Blue face to face, just staring at each other. It reminded him of that night on the trail when they stared at each other for the longest time. "Everything okay?"

"Yes. Blue and I were just having a talk. He's trying to tell me something, but I'm not sure what he is saying."

Thorpe didn't think there was anything unusual about her response; he'd already figured out they had an unusual way of communicating. "Do you think Blue is happy to be at the ranch?" He had wondered about Blue since he hadn't spent as much time with him the last few days; he'd been glued to Lily's side.

"Yes, and so is Spirit. Blue likes you very much." Actually, she thought Blue cared as much for Thorpe as he did for her.

Thorpe ruffled Blue's fur. "Good. I like him as much." When he saw Lily cooking in the kitchen this morning with the animals around her, he thought his house felt more like a home. If he didn't watch it, he'd want them around permanently. He gave her a quizzical look. "By the way, what's a nappy?"

CHAPTER TWENTY-FIVE

Doc Emerson arrived early for dinner so he would have a chance to speak with Isabelle privately. Lily had already told Isabelle that the doctor was coming to the ranch to see how she was doing.

After the doctor completed his examination, he sat with Isabelle and Lily. "Of course, babies surprise us all of the time, and you could deliver early, but I'm thinking you may have a couple of more weeks."

"I always knew he would be born on Christmas Day," Isabelle said.

The doc smiled at her. "I'm certainly not one to argue with the woman carrying the babe."

Lily thought it would be the right time to give the two of them some privacy. "We will be having dinner soon. You will join us?"

"I'd like that," he replied. He really wanted to find out if Thorpe was courting Lily. No one had mentioned she had a husband.

"Please excuse me. I need to get every-thing ready in the kitchen." Lily left the room to finish preparing dinner.

Thorpe came through the kitchen door with Stone and Jed behind him. "I see Doc is here."

Lily turned from the stove to greet them. "He's talking to her now."

"I hope she listens to him." Stone lingered by the stove when Lily handed him a platter of meat to carry to the table. He lingered momentarily, debating if he should tell them of his plans, but he decided he should speak to Isabelle first.

"I think once that little baby is born, Miss Isabelle will come around. She'll love it more than anything," Jed said, picking up the bowl of mashed potatoes.

Lily smiled. "I think you are right, Jed. How could anyone not fall in love with a little baby?"

Thorpe saw Blue following Lily's every movement. He hadn't left her side all day. In many ways, Thorpe envied that wolf. Lily was always petting him, or talking to him. It was little wonder he never left her side. He figured she could twist a man around her little finger just like Blue.

Thorpe grabbed a bowl of beans along with the plate of biscuits and headed to the table. Stone volunteered to go upstairs to get Isabelle and the doctor.

The meal ended and Thorpe walked the doc to the front porch. "I'm not sure I was of much help," Doc Emerson said. "She's fairly adamant that she's going to give the baby away. I'm hoping once she delivers, she'll come around."

"Jed said once she sees the baby she will forget all about giving it away. Doc, I appreciate that you gave it a try. We were at a loss how to help her. I know you will keep her situation in confidence. I don't want her to have a hard time if she stays here permanently."

"You have my word I won't say a word about her situation."

"Thanks, Doc."

"She's a pretty woman. She'll be able to find a husband if she's interested." He looked Thorpe in the eyes. "I reckon you're not interested. What about Lily?"

"Don't go there. You know how my last relationship ended."

"Lily's not married?"

Thorpe was curious about his interest. "You interested for yourself, Doc?"

"I might be. I'm a mite older, but I still have a few good years left." Seeing Thorpe didn't offer more information, he moved on to his next question. "Did you find Evelyn?"

He figured the doc had a right to know what happened. He was the one that told him about Evelyn's pregnancy. "Yep. She wasn't married to Ainsworth yet, and he didn't know about the baby."

The doc couldn't hide his surprise. "How was she hiding it from him?"

"I asked her the same thing. She said women had their ways."

The doc shook his head. "That doesn't make sense. Why didn't she want to tell him the truth?"

"I don't understand why she hadn't told him. He has a right to know."

"Maybe she's worried he might think the baby was yours since you were engaged. There was no way he would know you hadn't been bedding her all along," the doc said.

"That's what I figured. She told me he didn't force her."

"I never thought he did."

Thorpe stared at him. It seemed like everyone had a better handle on what Evelyn was doing except him. "Did everyone know?"

"Thorpe . . ." The doc stopped when the door opened and Lily walked outside with the animals.

She noticed they stopped talking when she stepped onto the porch. "I'm sorry. It was time for the pups to go out."

"I was just leaving. Thank you again for the lovely meal."

Lily led the puppies off the porch to the ground. After the doctor rode away, she turned to Thorpe. "I apologize if I interrupted your conversation, but Stone wanted to speak to Isabelle, and I thought I should give them some privacy." Stone was unusually quiet through dinner and she knew he had something on his mind.

"You didn't interrupt." He stepped down from the porch and stood beside her. They watched the puppies chase each other. "They sure have grown."

"Yes, they have. Do you think they will get a lot bigger?"

"Yes, you can tell by their paws. They might be bigger than Blue."

Stone led Isabelle to the parlor and he sat beside her on the settee. "Isabelle, I've been giving your situation a lot of thought and I think there is only one thing for you to do."

Isabelle turned her hazel eyes on him.

"What is that?"

Stone hesitated, unsure of himself. He jumped up and started pacing back and forth in front of her thinking of all the reasons he shouldn't say what he intended. He was much older than the man she loved, his future wasn't stable, he could fail miserably with his ranch, and she hadn't known him that long. She was much too young and lovely to want a man like him.

Isabelle grew concerned as her eyes followed him back and forth. "Stone?"

Stone stopped, and when he looked at her, he knew he was making her anxious. He took a seat beside her again and took a deep breath. "Isabelle, I think you need to marry me." Seeing her stunned expression, he quickly explained, "I've already sent a telegram resigning my position as marshal. I've talked to Thorpe and I'm going to buy some land that shares a border with his and start ranching. We won't have much at first, but I'm a hard worker and I know I can make a go of it. Thorpe said he'd help me with anything I need. He told me he even had a cabin near the area and I could use that until I get my home built. He'll help me build and we would have friends around us. I know you don't love me . . . and I don't expect you to, but I vow I'd make you a fine husband. I'll give you and our baby a home, and take care of you forever."

"But you don't really know me," Isabelle said.

"I know you well enough. You're a fine woman and I know I care for you." He leaned forward and put his arms on his thighs. He could tell it was time for the complete truth. "I think I started caring for you the first time we rode in the wagon together, but I knew you loved someone else." He didn't want to bring Ethan Horn into this conversation. "I reckon I can't take his place in your heart, but I'd be loyal and I'll be a good father. I'll love our baby."

As she listened to him, tears started to stream down her cheeks. She admired Stone, respected him, and she liked him a lot, but she didn't know if it was love. She wasn't sure she knew what love was. He was the answer to her prayers, yet she thought it would be a difficult thing to care for another man's baby. She swiped at her tears. "You might resent working so hard to pay for another man's child."

Stone put his arm around her and pulled her to him. "I will love our baby. I will never resent him."

She looked up at him. "I want to believe you. I care about you very much."

"That's all I ask. I know we could be happy together. Just think, we could have more children to play with little Stone."

His comment made her laugh. "Yes, we could."

Stone gently cupped her chin and he gave her a light kiss. He leaned back to look at her and asked, "What do you say?"

Isabelle put her palm to his cheek and pressed her lips back to his. Clutching her to him, Stone kissed her tenderly. It was an effort for him to pull away. "Are you saying yes?"

"Stone, I need to tell you something."

He knew this had something to do with Ethan, and he didn't think he could stand to hear the particulars of their encounter. He really didn't want to hear about Ethan Horn. If the man hadn't died, it would have been difficult not to knock his teeth down his throat for using Isabelle for his pleasure and lying to her. "You don't have to tell me anything."

"You should know I never loved Ethan. I didn't know him long enough to love him. He was the first person that ever wanted me. He made me feel special, and I guess I wanted to think I must be in love. But I had my doubts about my emotions all along. I just couldn't accept that I gave myself to a man without knowing my true feelings."

"I don't believe for a minute he was the only man that ever wanted you. You're so pretty and such a sweet thing, I'm sure a lot of men have had thoughts they shouldn't. I'm glad you didn't love him. He didn't deserve your love. As long as you like me and will give me a chance, I will try to earn your love."

"From the first day you drove the wagon, I knew I liked being with you. I was beginning to care for you and I thought it was wrong . . . considering my condition. I thought I was supposed to love Ethan, and I felt I must be a terrible person like my father told me. What I'm saying is, I think in a way I already love you. You're the best man I've ever known."

"Aw, honey, you're not a terrible person. You make me so happy. Are you saying *yes*?"

"If you are sure you want me, I'd be honored to be your wife," Isabelle whispered, her lips quivering.

"I'm sure I want you, honey. I can't wait until you are mine. It's a good thing you said yes because the preacher will be here tomorrow."

She furrowed her brow at him. "How . . . when?"

He grinned at her. "I saw him when I was in town."

"But he will know my condition and he might not want to marry a fallen woman."

"I told him I was doing right by you. If he jumped to the conclusion that the baby is mine, then he's right. This is my baby and no one will ever dare to say any different."

She threw her arms around his neck. "I've never known anyone as wonderful as you."

Stone held her close to his chest. "I intend to keep it that way." He couldn't remember ever being as happy as he was at this moment.

Thorpe and Lily walked back to the porch and waited for the puppies to exhaust themselves before they went inside for the night. Lily had forgotten to grab her coat and she was shivering.

Thorpe started to tell her to go on inside and he'd bring the puppies in, but he had a better idea. He walked behind her, like he'd wanted to do this morning in the kitchen, and wrapped his arms around her. He leaned down and his lips were next to her ear, and he asked in a low voice, "Better?"

His big body put off so much heat and it felt wonderful to be surrounded by him, but she pulled away. "I'm not too cold."

Thorpe reached for her and turned her around. "Lily . . ." He didn't know what he wanted to say. Every time he got close to her, he lost his ability to think straight. It was happening again. Instead of talking, he pulled her in his arms and crushed his lips to hers.

Lily didn't want him to stop; she loved his kisses. But she remembered what happened the last time he'd kissed her. She pushed against his chest and he let her go. "No," she said, and stepped back from his embrace.

Thorpe dropped his hands. "I apologize. I forgot about Captain Anderson. I'm sure my kisses don't excite you like his." He told himself he was an idiot. He just needed to find a way to stay away from her.

Lily was stunned by his comment. "It's not the captain's kisses I was thinking about. It's how you regretted our last kiss. I was sure mine didn't measure up to whomever you haven't been able to forget." With that said, she opened the door, walked inside, and closed his own door in his face.

CHAPTER TWENTY-SIX

Thorpe stood there staring at the closed door. What was the woman talking about? He hadn't compared her kisses to anyone. Who was she talking about? Blue walked up beside him and nudged his leg. "Yeah, I guess that didn't go too well." He saw Spirit and the puppies standing at the door ready to go inside for the night.

Isabelle heard the front door and called out to Lily. "Lily, please come into the parlor."

Lily walked into the room and became concerned when she saw Stone sitting next to Isabelle. "What is it? Is something wrong?"

Isabelle looked at Stone and smiled. "Do you want to tell her, or shall I?"

"Go ahead," Stone said.

"Stone and I will be married tomorrow."

Lily felt herself tearing up at the wonderful news. She hurried to the settee and hugged Isabelle. "Oh, I'm so happy for you."

"Stone already spoke to the pastor and he is coming tomorrow," Isabelle said.

"How wonderful," Lily said.

Isabelle reached for Lily's hand, urging her to sit next to her. "You don't think it is wrong . . . considering my condition?"

Lily shook her head. She knew Stone cared for Isabelle, and given time, she felt Isabelle would come to love Stone. She already trusted him and considered him a friend, and to Lily's way of thinking, that was half the battle. "I think it's perfect."

"Where's Jed?" Isabelle asked.

"I think he went to the stable to see to the animals," Stone said.

They all turned when they heard Thorpe walk through the door with Blue and the dogs.

"Thorpe," Isabelle said. "Do you have a minute?"

Thorpe, followed by all of the animals, came into the room to see everyone smiling. "What's going on?" He glanced at Lily and his first thought was she looked a lot happier than she had just a few minutes ago.

"Stone and I are getting married," Isabelle blurted out.

Thorpe walked over to Stone and shook his hand. "Congratulations. I guess that explains why you needed to see the pastor." It didn't come as a complete surprise to Thorpe; he had a hunch when he saw Stone talking to the pastor that he had something like this on his mind.

"I wasn't sure she'd say yes, so I kept my plans to myself."

"Well, we'd best check on that land right away since you're starting a family. Lots of new folks are coming to town and I don't want you losing out on it." Thorpe preferred to have a friend rather than people he didn't know sharing a boundary with his land. "And we need to get that home cleaned up to be ready for you when the time comes. It's been vacant for a while and I'm sure it's going to need some work. In the spring we can start to build a new home for you."

"Thorpe, I don't know how to thank you for everything," Stone said.

"Believe me, we will be helping each other out a lot in the future." Thorpe smiled at Isabelle. "Isabelle, you're getting a good man here."

Isabelle reached for Stone's hand and squeezed it between hers. "I know. I'm a very lucky woman."

"I'm the lucky one," Stone replied.

Lily could see the love in Stone's eyes and she realized his feelings for Isabelle were much deeper than anyone knew. She stood and said, "I'm going to go bake a wedding cake for tomorrow."

"You're getting married tomorrow?" Thorpe said.

"Yes. I didn't want to give her time to change her mind if she said yes," Stone said.

"Is that okay with you, Thorpe?" Isabelle asked.

"Of course. We need some excitement around here," Thorpe replied. "Besides, I can't wait to have some wedding cake."

Lily couldn't help but smile at his response. The man did love his sweets. She walked to the kitchen with Blue tagging along, followed by Spirit and the puppies. A few minutes later, Isabelle joined her in the kitchen.

"Lily, tell me the truth. Do you think I'm being fair to Stone by marrying him when I'm carrying Ethan's baby?"

"I think if you didn't marry Stone you would break his heart. Can't you see how much the man loves you? If I had a man look at me the way he looks at you, well, I can't imagine a better feeling."

"I think I'm already falling in love with him. I thought I loved Ethan, but deep down I knew what I felt wasn't love. What I feel for Stone is different. I respect him and

I know he wants what's best for me. He is a wonderful man."

"Yes, he is. You make a perfect couple."

"Like you and Thorpe," Isabelle said.

Lily stared at her, unable to form a response.

"Thorpe looks at you like Stone looks at me," Isabelle said. "He just does it when you aren't looking."

Lily shook her head. "Thorpe hasn't forgotten the woman that left him at the altar. He may never open his heart again."

Isabelle patted her hand. "You're wrong. He already has forgotten her. Remember I told you when you saved his life that you would be bound together forever. I still think I'm right."

In the middle of the night Lily was awakened by Blue when he climbed into bed beside her. She didn't know what was wrong, but she knew he was trying to tell her something important. She wrapped her arms around him and held him close. "I'm sorry, I don't know what you are trying to tell me."

Blue licked her face and whined. He remained snuggled against her the rest of the night.

■ ■ ■ ■

Thorpe left his bedroom earlier than normal the next morning hoping to be the first one in the kitchen. He wanted to get the coffee going before Lily came downstairs, and he intended to ask her about her comment last night. As soon as he walked down the stairs he heard voices in the kitchen. Jed and Stone were at the table drinking coffee and Lily and Isabelle were at the stove chatting. Even the puppies were already bouncing around the room. So much for his plan to spend a few minutes alone with Lily.

"Morning," Stone said when Thorpe entered the kitchen.

"Everyone is up early," Thorpe said, trying to hide his disappointment. He walked to the counter and grabbed a cup.

"I was too excited to sleep," Isabelle said as she poured coffee into Thorpe's cup.

Thorpe leaned over and petted Blue, who was standing beside Lily. "Morning, Lily."

Lily didn't look at him. "Good morning."

He kneeled down and started playing with the puppies. "Stone, when will the preacher be here?"

"He said he would be here around one."

"I'll ride back in for lunch then," Thorpe

said. He had a busy day ahead of him, but he wouldn't miss the wedding.

"Miss Lily, that cake you baked sure looks pretty," Jed said.

Thorpe looked around and spotted the cake. "Is that what smells so good? I guess we can't have that for breakfast."

"I think you smell the cinnamon rolls in the oven. They are just about ready," Lily replied.

Isabelle carried the bowl of eggs and a platter of bacon to the table as Lily pulled the rolls from the oven.

Thorpe pulled a chair out for Lily and sat next to her. He didn't have an opportunity to say more than a few words to her as the conversation centered on the bride and groom and their big day.

The sun was just peeking over the horizon when Thorpe, Stone, and Jed rode out to the range together after breakfast. It was a cold crisp morning, and the horses were eager to run, but Thorpe took it slow so he could tell Jed about the building in town. "Jed, I talked to the banker about the blacksmith's property when I was in town. He's willing to work something out if you're interested. No one has taken over the loan yet and I'm sure he will give you a reasonable deal." He didn't mention that he would cover for the loan if Jed ever ran into trouble. That would be an arrangement between him and the banker.

"Mr. Thorpe, how do I know I could make enough money to pay the loan? I don't know any of the folks in town. They might not want to do business with me."

"Every growing town needs an experienced blacksmith. I'm sure you could make enough money, and everyone will welcome you."

"Think about how many customers you would have with the railroad bringing all those new folks to town," Stone said.

"More folk don't always make a town better. Some folk don't like to do business with people they don't know," Jed added.

Thorpe glanced Stone's way and he could tell Jed's comment also caught him by surprise. Thorpe had a feeling Jed didn't relish the thought of starting over in a new town full of strangers. After the situation with the wagon train, he understood his hesitation about strangers. But Jed was a decent man and a hard worker; people would come around once they saw those traits. Thorpe wasn't going to push him if it made him uncomfortable. He'd give him time to think it over. Maybe there was another way to make it work. "It's something to think about."

"I may just travel with Miss Lily come spring. Now that Miss Isabelle is marrying, she'll want to leave to find her grandfather," Jed said.

There it was again. The thought of Lily leaving in the spring. After she found her grandfather, he wondered if she would go back to Fort Steele to be with Captain Anderson. Captain Anderson had been straightforward about his intentions. The man was so taken with Lily that Thorpe wouldn't be surprised if he showed up on his doorstep in a few weeks. Thorpe thought about what it would be like come spring when everyone left the ranch. His home would be as before. Nice and quiet. Stone and Isabelle would have their own home. Lily and Jed would be gone, and of course, Lily would take Blue. If Blue left, then Spirit would leave with him, and the pups would be gone, too. His house would be empty. For a man who had long cherished the solitude of his home, suddenly it didn't seem all that appealing. He'd grown accustomed to conversations with Stone and Jed over the weeks on the trail. Of course, he had Curtis and the other men on the ranch he considered friends, but a man couldn't have too many friends. He enjoyed the sound of women's voices in the house, not to mention how wonderful the house smelled with the freshly baked goods. He liked saying grace before his meals and minding his manners around the ladies. He didn't even object to taking extra care with his appearance, knowing a beautiful woman would be seeing him every morning. Maybe he didn't like shaving every morning, but it was worth it if Lily thought he looked handsome. And the plain fact was he liked looking at Lily, talking to Lily, kissing Lily. Heck, he liked everything about Lily. Well, almost everything. He didn't like her kissing Captain Anderson.

He needed to keep his mind on business, he reminded himself again. "We won't be working too far from that house I was telling you about. Why don't we ride that way this morning? We can see what we are going to need to fix it up nice for Isabelle."

"I'd like that," Stone said.

"Mr. Stone, just think, this is your last morning as a single man," Jed teased.

"That's just fine by me, Jed. I've been rambling all over the country since I was a young man and its past time I settled down. Thank God Isabelle agreed to marry me. I think I have enough years in me to have a fine family and leave something good behind."

"Yessir, you should thank God for your blessings," Jed said. "We've all been blessed to get here safe and sound."

Thorpe had to agree with Jed. He'd never given enough thanks for his blessings. What had seemed like a curse standing in a church of all places on that hot summer day less than a year ago, turned out to be the biggest blessing of his life. His mother and father used to tell him all things worked out for the best. Little did he know at the time how right they were.

"It's not as bad as I thought it would be," Thorpe said as they were walking through the small cabin on the north side of his ranch. "We'll need to do a little work, but it won't take long."

"It's a fine place to stay while we are building," Stone agreed.

They walked back outside and Thorpe pointed to the boundary. "This is the best place to build and it's the closest point to my ranch. It would be wise to stay in close proximity if there's ever trouble."

"I'd like that. Isabelle will be alone with the baby when I'm out working," Stone said.

Thorpe could appreciate how he'd worry

leaving a wife and young child all alone out here in the middle of nowhere. "We'll make it a point once you are out here to have men working nearby as much as possible. There's also a couple of cabins where my men live, not too far away. I'm sure the women will all become friends and can visit each other from time to time. Isabelle and Lily will meet them soon when they come to the house in a few days."

The men arrived back at the ranch at the same time the pastor reined in at the front porch. The pastor greeted them and said to Stone, "Are you ready to get married?"

"Yes, I am. Just give us a few minutes to get cleaned up. I don't want to scare away my bride."

Once the men washed and changed their clothes, they joined the pastor and the ladies in the parlor. Stone walked over and grasped Isabelle's hand. "Are you ready to take on this cowboy?"

She smiled and nodded at him. As much as she wanted to marry Stone, she was still nervous. "Could we talk for a minute?" she whispered.

"Only if you aren't going to tell me you've changed your mind," Stone said.

"No, I just need to speak with you about

something that's been on my mind all day."

Stone led her to the hallway so they could speak privately. "What is it, honey?"

She didn't immediately say what was on her mind, so Stone placed his hands on her shoulders and looked into her eyes. "It can't be that bad. Tell me."

"Considering my condition, you know we can't really have a wedding night," she said softly.

Stone hadn't even thought that far ahead. But now that she'd said something, he couldn't say he wasn't disappointed. But he'd waited this long to get married, so he could certainly wait a little longer for a wedding night. "That's okay, honey. It will give us that much more time to get to know each other better." He wanted to ask exactly how long he'd have to wait, but he didn't know if that would be a gentlemanly thing to ask.

Isabelle threw her arms around his neck. "You are so wonderful." Tears filled her eyes and she tried to keep them from falling. "I'm so emotional right now. I don't know what's wrong with me."

Stone handed her his bandana to wipe her tears. "Don't you worry about a thing, honey. We have all the time in the world to have a wedding night." He smiled at her and kissed her forehead. "You sure look

413

pretty today."

"Even though I waddle like a duck and I'm as big as the side of a barn," she replied.

"I like ducks and you're not as big as a barn." He didn't tell her he was concerned that she looked like she could give birth any moment. He took her hand in his and said, "Come on. Let's get married."

CHAPTER TWENTY-SEVEN

"Is it time for the cake?" Thorpe asked as soon as Stone kissed his bride.

"Are you hungry, Thorpe?" Stone teased.

"Yes, aren't you? We missed lunch."

"I agree with Mr. Thorpe. I want some of that cake," Jed said.

"Isabelle and Stone have to eat the first piece," Lily said. Earlier, she'd placed the cake on a table in the parlor along with plates, cups, and utensils. "I'll go get the coffee."

Thorpe watched Lily walk from the room with Blue right beside her. He thought she looked so pretty in her pink dress that he wouldn't mind nibbling on her instead of cake.

She returned with the coffee just as Isabelle and Stone sliced into the cake. After they enjoyed the first bite, Isabelle started filling the plates. "Thank you so much for the cake, Lily. It's wonderful." Isabelle handed the first plate to the pastor. "We appreciate you coming out here to marry us."

"It's my pleasure and I wish you the very best for the future," the pastor said.

Lily poured the coffee and was just about to hand a cup to Thorpe when she heard a knock on the front door. Thorpe was digging into his piece of cake and he didn't hear the knock.

"Thorpe, I think someone is at the door," Lily said.

The pastor was closest to the front door, so he said, "Eat your cake, Thorpe. I'll get it."

Before the pastor reached the door, it burst open and in strolled Evelyn Tremayne. She looked across the room and when her eyes landed on Thorpe, she ran to him.

Totally surprised that Evelyn was in the room, Thorpe spread his arms in question since his mouth was full of cake. Evelyn took that gesture as her invitation to wrap her arms around his neck. She stood on her toes and gave him a kiss on his lips. Thorpe backed up and swallowed his cake, nearly choking in his haste to speak. "Evelyn, what are you doing here?"

Blue started growling, and in seconds, Spirit had come to his side and joined him. The puppies thought their mother was sensing danger and started yapping, adding to the earsplitting cacophony in the room. The sound was deafening.

"Shhh, Blue," Lily said in an effort to quiet all the animals.

Evelyn glanced at the vicious-looking animals and moved closer to Thorpe's side. "Oh, Thorpe, I had to see you," she said in a low, sultry voice. Evelyn looked around at the strangers in the room. "Who are all of these people?" She glanced at the pastor who was supposed to marry them when she skipped out on the wedding. She pointed a finger at him. "And what is he doing here?" Her gaze landed on the blonde woman standing nearby holding the coffeepot, and instantly she curled her lip in disapproval. She looked at the cake in Thorpe's hand before she eyed the woman again. "Is that a wedding cake? Did someone marry?" Surely Thorpe did not marry that woman.

Stone was the only one that seemed to maintain calm. "We are celebrating, ma'am." He saw no reason to reveal more information.

Thorpe finally got his thoughts in order. He glanced at Lily to gauge her reaction to Evelyn, and her face registered the surprise he felt. She was holding on to Blue's fur as if she feared he might attack. His eyes

snapped back to Evelyn. "What are you doing here? Why aren't you in England?"

So this was the woman that left him at the
altar, Lily thought. She was lovely in her
expensive velvet cape with a fur hood and a
matching fur muff. Just as she imagined,
Thorpe's ex-fiancée was a very beautiful
woman in her expensive clothing. It was
easy to see why Thorpe hadn't been able to
get her out of his mind.

"Thorpe, I need to speak to you in private," Evelyn said.

"Evelyn, you are interrupting our party,"
Thorpe told her curtly.

She placed her hand on his chest and
leaned close. "Thorpe, honey, I know I've
hurt you, but it was exactly as you suspected. Please, can't we talk in private?" she
whispered. "I'm sure you don't want everyone to hear what I have to tell you."

Thorpe was curious about her statement,
and knowing Evelyn as well as he did, he
was certain she wouldn't leave until she accomplished her mission.

"We'll go to the kitchen," Lily said.

Everyone took their cake and coffee and
headed to the kitchen. Spirit and the puppies followed Lily and Blue.

"That is Evelyn Tremayne," the pastor
said as soon as they were seated at the table.

"Is that the woman Mr. Thorpe was going to marry?" Jed asked.

"Yes."

"He certainly seemed surprised to see her," Stone said.

"I know he is." The pastor didn't think it was his place to discuss Thorpe's business, so he redirected the conversation and asked the newlywed couple about their plans.

"What do you want, Evelyn?" Thorpe said when they were alone in the parlor.

She turned her dark eyes on him. "Could we sit down?"

Thorpe pointed to a chair for her, but she sat on the settee. Thorpe placed his plate of cake on the table and walked to a sideboard across the room and grabbed a bottle of whiskey. He poured a generous amount in a glass and took a healthy swallow before he walked back to stand in front of her. "Well?"

She reached for his hand. "Please sit beside me."

Thorpe sat down, but kept some space between them. "Evelyn, what do you want?" He was growing impatient.

Evelyn pulled a handkerchief from her reticule and dabbed at her eyes. "Oh, Thorpe, I don't know where to begin."

"Just say whatever you came to say."

She inched closer to him and placed her hand on his thigh. "When you came to Kansas City, I was afraid for you. You see, Ainsworth threatened your life."

Thorpe thought he did see tears in her eyes. He set his glass on the side table and grasped her shoulders. "What do you mean?"

She stared into his eyes. "He . . . he did force himself on me." She nearly climbed into his lap and dropped her head on his shoulder. "Oh, Thorpe, I didn't know how to tell you. I was so afraid he would kill you."

He wasn't certain he believed her. "You sounded pretty convincing when you told me you wanted to go to England and be the wife of an aristocrat."

"I had to make you believe me. He said if you followed us he'd have you killed. I couldn't let him do that. I knew he would follow through on his threat. He knew how much I loved you."

"When did he force you?"

"Right after he came to the ranch," she whispered. "He came to my room in the night and I didn't know . . . until he . . . well, he was in bed with me and had me pinned."

"Why didn't you tell me then? Why didn't

420

you go to the sheriff?"

"I didn't know what to do. He knew about you and he threatened your life. I knew you would confront him. I was so scared for you. I couldn't let anyone know or I would have been scorned. I couldn't do that to you or Father."

"Why didn't you tell your father? He would have shot him on the spot."

"Can't you understand he threatened me? Why don't you see what I was going through? You never had anyone force you to do anything!"

Thorpe was furious. "Where is he?"

"I don't know. I guess back in England by now."

"When did you have your baby? Did he take your baby?"

"No, there is no baby. He shoved me down the stairs at the hotel when he found out you were there." She sobbed into her handkerchief. "I lost the baby and I came close to dying. Father traveled to Kansas City so I wouldn't have to travel alone."

Thorpe moved away from her and jumped to his feet. He stalked around the room, stopping only to pick up his glass and down the contents. What kind of man would shove a woman down a staircase? He couldn't travel to England to kill him. What was he supposed to do?

Evelyn walked up behind him and wrapped her arms around his waist and placed her cheek on his back. "I came as soon as I could to tell you what happened. You have to know I wouldn't have left you at the church without cause. He told me he would kill you if I didn't leave with him."

Thorpe turned around and she held on to him. She'd removed her cloak, and he noticed she was wearing a deep blue dress that flattered her curvaceous figure. Unless he'd seen for himself that she was pregnant, he would have never known. She was more voluptuous now, a very enticing package to any man.

"Thorpe, I'm so sorry. I just didn't know what to do. I've never stopped loving you."

Thorpe was a man who always knew what to do, made decisions, and followed through. But right now, he didn't know what he was going to do about anything.

"Please hold me, Thorpe. I've missed you so," Evelyn said softly.

She sounded so sincere that Thorpe couldn't help himself from trying to console her. He wrapped his arms around her. "Shhh . . . we'll figure all of this out." His thoughts went back to that night in this very room when she'd undressed for him. It was the night when he lost his head and took her to his bed. He couldn't think about that night. He needed some time alone to think. "How did you get here?"

"I had our foreman drop me off. I knew you would take me home." She pulled back and looked up at him. "Or I could stay the night with you. That's what I want to do, Thorpe. I want to show you how much I love you. I've missed you so much."

Her offer surprised him almost as much as her account of what had happened with Ainsworth. "I have a houseful of guests." He pulled away from her. "I'll go tell them I'm taking you home. I'll just be a minute." He glanced at the plate of uneaten cake. Lily had gone to so much trouble to make that cake, and his first bite was delicious, but he'd lost his appetite. He walked to the kitchen without enthusiasm. He'd been so happy just a few minutes earlier, celebrating with his friends. Now he had no idea what he felt, but it wasn't joy.

Everyone was sitting at the table drinking coffee when Thorpe entered. He glanced at Lily and said, "Sorry for the interruption. I'm going to have to take Evelyn home. Their ranch foreman dropped her off so she has no way back."

The pastor stood. "Thorpe, I was getting

ready to leave and I can drop her at the ranch."

Thorpe liked the sound of that. "Are you sure you need to leave? I'm not rushing you."

"I told the missus I would be back in a few hours."

"I appreciate it. I have a lot of work left to do today," Thorpe said. "I'll go tell Evelyn."

Everyone walked to the front door with the pastor and Lily noticed Thorpe placing Evelyn's cloak over her shoulders. Evelyn turned and kissed Thorpe on the mouth again, and whispered something to him that Lily could not hear. She did hear Thorpe say, "I told you we'd work this out."

Thorpe walked out the door with the pastor and Evelyn, and after they rode away, he walked to the stable. He needed to go to work and try to think things through.

"Well, that was a surprise," Isabelle said.

"I can't say Thorpe looked too happy about her sudden appearance," Stone added, stealing a glance at Lily.

Lily didn't think he looked unhappy, especially when Evelyn threw herself at him.

Jed excused himself saying he was going back to work, and Lily was left alone with Stone and Isabelle. She thought she would give them some privacy so she went to her room to change her clothing. She needed to go for a ride.

Lily and Blue entered the stable and she pulled Blaze and Daisy from their stall to brush them down. She heard some voices at the other end of the stable, but she thought it was Jed talking to the horses. Once she finished brushing both animals, she saddled Blaze. "Yes, you get to come with us," she said to Daisy. She knew the mule would pout if she didn't get to go outside with them.

"You spoil that mule rotten," Thorpe said from behind her. He'd been listening to her talk to them the entire time she brushed them down.

Lily didn't turn around. "She's worth it." She mounted Blaze and headed out of the stable with Daisy and Blue trotting along beside them.

Thorpe had already saddled Smoke and he galloped up beside her. "You going for a ride?"

"Yes. I thought I'd give Stone and Isabelle some time alone."

"It was a nice wedding." *Until Evelyn showed up,* he thought. Evelyn surfacing like she did after all of these months threw him for a loop. He didn't know what to think about her story, but he thought she

425

was telling him the truth. Why would she make it up? He figured a woman who had been through such an ordeal would have been scared to death. Even though it was difficult for him to understand, it was possible she was too afraid to tell him about Ainsworth.

But then his mind centered on Lily and everything she'd been through. Lily fought her own battles. He remembered that shot she'd made when that killer was holding Isabelle. Lily would have taken care of Ainsworth herself. But Evelyn wasn't like Lily; she'd always had her father to come to her defense. She'd never been forced to protect herself. When he'd asked her to marry him, she looked to him to take care of her. If he could take time from the ranch he would go to England and settle the account with Ainsworth for what he'd done.

"I think Stone and Isabelle will be very happy," Lily said, pulling Thorpe from his deliberations.

"My mother and father had a sound marriage. My father never got over her death."

Lily was surprised that he'd shared that part of his life with her. She wondered if he was thinking he might be happy married to his ex-fiancée. From Evelyn's behavior when she walked in the door, it was obvious she wanted to resume their relationship no matter what had passed between them. But she wasn't going to bring up Evelyn if he wasn't. "My parents were happy together, too. As difficult as it was for me at the time, I thought it fitting they died together."

Thorpe appreciated how alone Lily must have felt losing her parents. It took an unusual woman to recognize that her parents would have preferred death together than continuing life without each other. More than ever he understood why she was determined to find her grandfather. She appreciated the importance of family.

"I think that was one of the reasons my grandfather left. He didn't know what to do with himself once my grandmother died. Finding his brother gave him a purpose, much like Jed. Jed told you he was a blacksmith, but what he didn't tell you was someone wanted his business, and basically the man took it from him. Jed had lived in that small town his whole life and he felt betrayed by the people. No one spoke up for him. He didn't have power or family. He was on his own. Finding his brother turned into his purpose."

Thorpe slowed his horse. "Did he tell you that?" Hearing what happened gave him a better understanding about Jed's comments earlier in the day.

"We talked about a lot of different things when we had watch together late at night. At first, Jed didn't say much, but we became friends, and he began to open up about what happened to him."

Thorpe told her about his conversation with Jed when he told him about the opportunity in town. "Surely he has to know I wouldn't let anyone take his business from him."

"People have disappointed him before. Maybe he's afraid it would happen again. I think he's hoping his brother is ready to leave the military and they can do something together. It makes all the difference to have family with you."

Lily was wise beyond her years. Thorpe had made a new family on his ranch with his foreman and workers. Not only did he consider them friends, they were his family. They all worked toward a common goal, and that was one of the reasons he offered houses to the men who married and had children. He wanted them to know they were his family. "I didn't know my foreman, Curtis, until I hired him to help me drive cattle here from Texas. He's been with me all this time, and the rest of my men have worked for me nearly as long. They became my family."

Lily remembered the first night they'd discussed what Christmas was like at Dove Creek. She'd thought he must get lonely, but now she saw he had many wonderful people in his life.

Thorpe reined in at one of the most scenic spots on the ranch. He wanted to tell Lily about the situation with Evelyn, but he hadn't figured out how to go about it. It was important to him to give her an explanation. "Let's give the animals a breather." He jumped off Smoke and lifted Lily off Blaze's back. Instead of releasing her, he pulled her closer. "Lily . . ." Gazing into her eyes, his only thought was how much he wanted to kiss her again, but he didn't want to be refused. She was looking up at him with those large blue eyes, and he didn't care if she turned him away; he had to try. When their lips met, he half expected her to push him away like she did the last time, and when she didn't, he took command and kissed her with unrestrained desire. Only when he realized he might not be able to stop with a kiss, he pulled away. He didn't go far; his lips found her neck and he planted kisses leading to her ear. He was perplexed by his reaction to her. For the life of him, he couldn't keep from putting his hands on her. "Lily . . . I want you."

Lily could barely collect her thoughts. Just a short time ago another woman had been kissing him, and here she was ready to give him anything he asked for. "Thorpe, what are you doing?"

Her question brought him up short. What was he doing? He wanted Lily more than he'd ever wanted another woman. Yet he knew he couldn't have her. Even if he was willing to think about marriage, Evelyn coming back in his life changed everything. He'd taken Evelyn to his bed and he couldn't forget that.

CHAPTER TWENTY-EIGHT

Thorpe closed his eyes and pinched the bridge of his nose. He took a deep breath and opened his eyes. "I don't know what I'm doing. When I get close to you, all I want is you. I can't keep from putting my hands on you." He cupped her face in his hands. "I want more. I want all of you."

"Aren't you forgetting about the woman you were kissing earlier?" She didn't intend to ask that question, but she wasn't sorry she did. She was jealous, and she'd never in her life felt that emotion. And when he kissed her, she thought about pulling away, but she couldn't, or wouldn't. Deep down, she wanted to know whose kisses he preferred.

If only he could put Evelyn out of his mind permanently. "She kissed me, and anyway, you kissed Anderson," he countered. He hated that he sounded like a jealous fool, but he couldn't help himself.

"He kissed me," she retorted. "I don't see Captain Anderson here, and I told you we were friends."

"Lily, I never thought I would see Evelyn again."

"It looks like she has other plans."

Thorpe began to tell her everything Evelyn had told him. It didn't surprise him to see Lily's eyes welling with tears. "The poor woman. I can't believe that man did those things. Why didn't she report him to the sheriff?"

"I asked the same thing and she said she was afraid." Thorpe was quiet for several minutes before he said. "I don't know what it means, but I still want you. It doesn't change that fact."

She looked up at him and said what she thought. "You're attracted to me. That's all."

Thorpe shook his head at her comment. "Any man in his right mind would want a beautiful woman like you. And I do want you." He wasn't sure what he was saying to her. He just wanted her to know . . . what? He was conflicted. While he wanted Lily, he felt an obligation to Evelyn. He couldn't be like Ethan Horn and use a woman and throw her away. Evelyn had been through so much that he couldn't in good conscience walk away from her.

Lily wanted Thorpe, but it was a lifelong kind of wanting. She knew it wasn't going to happen. She couldn't compete with a woman like Evelyn. "You want me in your bed." Her words were blunt, yet she thought when he said he wanted *all of her,* he meant more than just kissing.

He wasn't going to lie about that. "Yes, I do."

"I think you have some unresolved issues that you need to work out with Evelyn."

As much as he didn't want to agree with her, he had to face up to his responsibilities. "Yeah."

Lily slowly rode back to the ranch with Daisy and Blue. Thorpe had shared much more than she'd ever expected. He hadn't said as much, but it was apparent that he'd been intimate with Evelyn. He had to have been in love with her since he asked her to marry him. It was more than he'd said to her. *I want you,* was what he told her. No declaration of love or of marriage. He was obviously still in love with Evelyn. Knowing Thorpe's character, there was no doubt what he would do. He was a man who would always do the right thing.

By the time she rode into the stable she was cried out. She told herself she could handle staying at the ranch until Isabelle had her baby. Isabelle had Stone now, and she had no reason to stay after the baby came. Weather permitting, she could pack her wagon and take off, and that is exactly what she planned to do.

Thorpe rode into the stable and took the saddle off Smoke and started brushing him. He was right back where he'd started several hours earlier. All afternoon and early evening he'd done nothing but think over the situation he'd found himself in. All that thinking hadn't solved one problem. He thought he was in love with Lily and he couldn't deny it any longer. Somewhere in the back of his mind he'd known it all along, or at least about fifteen minutes after he'd met her. He wasn't a conceited man, but he knew he could have a few women if that was his nature. It wasn't just a physical attraction with Lily. Well, it was physical, but that wasn't all of it. He wanted her all right, but he also liked and respected her. He'd told her the truth; he wanted all of her, and that included her heart. He couldn't handle the thought of her waiting for Captain Anderson to appear. He didn't doubt her word that she considered Anderson a friend, but he figured Anderson might change her mind quick enough if he came calling.

Thorpe remembered his father had told him one time that the first time he saw his mother, he knew she was the one for him. He wondered if his father admitted it to himself right away, or if he came to the decision kicking and screaming. Frustrated with himself, he exhaled loudly. He had to stop thinking about what he wanted and start thinking about what he had to do. He couldn't be as foolish as he'd been before. There were consequences if he acted on his desires. His thoughts drifted back to Evelyn. He had to face the fact that what he wanted didn't enter into the equation. He had to do the right thing.

After he put Smoke in the stall and gave him fresh water, he left the stable. He was late for dinner so he figured he'd be eating alone. When he walked into the house he found everyone in the kitchen around the table. "Hello."

"Mr. Thorpe, I was just about to go looking for you," Jed said.

"Time got away from me," Thorpe said. He took a seat at the table and looked at Lily by the stove with her back to him. "Haven't you eaten?"

"No, we waited for you," Isabelle said.

Thorpe glanced at Stone. "Did you get a chance to move your things upstairs?"

"I hadn't talked to you about that. I wasn't sure you wanted another person under your roof," Stone told him.

"Nonsense, unless Isabelle doesn't want you to share her room, there's no reason for you to stay in the bunkhouse. When you two are ready after the baby is born, you can move to your home, but there is no need to hurry."

"Thanks, Thorpe."

Lily walked to the table and filled their cups. Thorpe took the coffeepot from her hands, saying, "I'll do that. Thanks for waiting dinner."

She couldn't respond for fear of crying again. She'd been emotional since her conversation with Thorpe, and when he didn't show up at dinnertime, she thought he might be with Evelyn.

Isabelle helped Lily carry the food to the table and after the prayer was said, Thorpe noticed Blue was lying at Lily's side. "Blue's been hanging pretty close to you the last several days."

"Yes, I don't know what's wrong," she said softly.

"But you think something's wrong?" Knowing how connected the two of them were, that concerned Thorpe. "Do you think he's sick?"

"No, his eyes look clear and he's eating well." Lily wished she could have a conversation like nothing was wrong, but she couldn't. She was worried about Blue, and she was heartsick thinking Thorpe had been with Evelyn. She avoided looking at Thorpe for fear of crying again.

It was obvious Lily didn't want to talk, and he didn't want to create more tension between them. He decided to leave it alone, and he turned his attention on Jed. He wanted to tell him about the plan he'd come up with earlier in the day when he wasn't thinking about Lily. Why was it he could find a way to help Stone and Jed, but he couldn't find an answer to his own problem? "Jed, I was thinking if you decide to stay here we might consider setting up a blacksmith shop in the old barn. We can get the equipment in here that you need and I'm sure the ranchers would come here with their business."

Jed gave him a look of disbelief. "Mr. Thorpe, are you serious?"

When Thorpe assured him he was very serious, he said, "That's mighty kind of you, and if I stay, you can bet I'd be interested."

Lily knew Thorpe had come up with that

plan after she'd told him about Jed's situation earlier. Thorpe's concern for others was one of the many reasons she'd fallen in love with him. His heart matched his bravery and she didn't think she'd ever meet another man like him. It saddened her to know that there would be no place for her in his life, but she was grateful that he'd helped the others. Evelyn was getting a wonderful man. She took solace in the fact that she would find her grandfather and they'd find a place to start over. She reached down and stroked Blue's head. She just prayed that Blue stayed with her; she couldn't bear the thought of losing him.

Everyone finished eating and Isabelle said, "There's more cake if anyone would like some."

"I would," Thorpe responded. He didn't get to enjoy his piece of cake earlier since Evelyn barged in on their celebration. He couldn't avoid thinking about her and the situation. He jumped up and walked to the parlor and grabbed the whiskey bottle. When he returned to the table, he held the bottle over Stone's cup.

Stone nodded and Thorpe poured some in his cup before he filled his own. He held his cup in the air. "Congratulations. I hope you have a long and happy marriage."

Stone tapped his cup to Thorpe's and said, "We will."

After everyone retired for the night, Thorpe sat at the kitchen table alone and had another cup of whiskey. It reminded him of the years he'd spent alone on the ranch and he had the whole house to himself. He'd always enjoyed his quiet time at night, but now that he'd had shared his evenings with friends, his solitude was dismal. He wanted to stop thinking tonight, particularly about Evelyn. He thought he was finished with her. He'd moved on. And then there was Lily. Why couldn't he get her out of his mind? He finished his drink and grabbed the whiskey bottle to take upstairs to his room. He planned to get a fire going and have one more drink before he turned in. When he passed Lily's door, he hesitated. *Keep walking,* he told himself. He couldn't. He tapped on the door with the bottle.

Lily opened the door thinking it must be Isabelle. When she saw Thorpe standing there leaning against the frame, she was so surprised, she forgot she was only wearing her nightgown. "What? Is something wrong?"

Thorpe stared at her, his eyes taking in every inch of her. Her hair was hanging over one shoulder and her hairbrush was in her hand. She looked so beautiful, he couldn't think of what he wanted to say. Who was he kidding? He hadn't planned on talking. He didn't want to talk. Yeah, something was wrong. She was driving him to drink. He stepped over the threshold, took her in his arms, and lowered his mouth to hers. She smelled so delectable and felt so soft nestled against his body that he wasn't thinking about anything other than his need for her. His hand moved up and down her back and he realized what she was wearing was so very thin that it felt like he was touching bare skin. His lips left hers and moved to her neck and his control was lost. He pulled her tighter to him.

Lily pushed him away. "You shouldn't be in here."

He backed up a step, but he didn't want to walk out of that door. "No, I shouldn't." He knew he should turn around and leave, but when his eyes drifted down her body, and he saw her barely there nightgown, a six-gun at his back couldn't have budged him from that room. He couldn't stand the thought of another man ever seeing her like this. She was driving him crazy. "Lily . . ." He wanted to take her in his arms and never let her go. What was he going to do? He couldn't let another man have her. Another man . . . *Captain Anderson* . . . He couldn't allow him to make love to her. He wouldn't let him have her. He moved to her again, but she backed up a step.

Lily glanced at the bottle in his hand. She thought he'd probably had too much to drink. "I think you need to go to bed."

"Yeah." His eyes slid to her bed. Another step forward, and she took another step back and felt the bedpost behind her. He threw the whiskey bottle on the bed and placed his hands on her shoulders, his strong fingers kneading the tension from her body. He leaned down and started kissing her neck again and he pulled her closer as his lips moved to her ear. He nibbled on her ear and whispered, "You're so beautiful. I want you. Let me love you, Lily."

It hurt to hear him proposition her like he would a soiled dove. She ducked under his arm and hurried to the door. She tried to control her emotions when she said, "Either you leave, or I will."

He wanted to be sorry he'd asked, but at the moment he wasn't sorry, and he knew later that would shame him all the more. Where Lily was concerned, he had no control. He knew she didn't issue empty threats and she would leave, so his options were limited. Grabbing the bottle from the bed, he walked to the door. He leaned over, his lips touching her skin just below her ear again. He wanted to feel the softness of her lips once more, but he didn't try to kiss her again. "Good night, lovely Lily."

His deep voice sent goose bumps over her skin. She quietly closed the door behind him and leaned against it, trying to calm herself down. She was hurt and she was angry. A tear slid over her cheek. How dare he treat her like that! She understood how Isabelle must have felt having fallen for Ethan Horn's passionate attention. Lily was so lost in the moment that she was close to ignoring everything she held dear just to be in his arms, in his bed. She came close to willingly offer herself up to a man before marriage. Grudgingly, she had to admit she was as angry with herself as she was with Thorpe. It wasn't his fault that she had no self-control around him.

When Thorpe reached his room, he started a fire in the fireplace. He picked up a glass and poured himself another drink. After he gulped it down, he walked to the bureau and opened the top drawer. He pulled out a small black box and opened the lid. His mother's wedding ring twinkled in the dim light of the room. He'd been so thankful he hadn't given Evelyn his mother's ring. Here he was again at that same crossroad months later. But this time it wasn't only his mind involved. Doing the right thing was much more complicated when his heart belonged to someone else.

He snapped the box closed, placed it back in the drawer, and grabbed the whiskey bottle. He didn't even bother with a glass. Pacing his room and drinking from the bottle, he contemplated his situation. He was no closer to a resolution when he removed his boots and holster before he slumped in his chair. He picked up the bottle of whiskey again and gulped the last of the liquid and closed his eyes.

Thorpe awoke a few hours later to the sound of howling. The fire had died down and the room was dark with the exception of the light shining thought the window. He rose from the chair and walked to the window. The full moon was so bright, it illuminated all of the buildings and land near the house. He looked around for animals, but there was no movement at all. The howling started again and he realized it was coming from inside the house. Blue. He walked to the door, stepped into the hallway, and quietly made his way to Lily's door. He leaned against her door and he could hear Lily speaking softly to Blue, trying to calm him. He started to knock, but after his performance earlier, he didn't think that would be a smart move. Blue finally stopped howling, and Thorpe walked back to his room and fell across his bed. Even though he'd only slept a few hours, his mind seemed clearer. He knew what he had to do come morning.

CHAPTER TWENTY-NINE

"Good morning, Thorpe." The doc opened the door and motioned Thorpe inside. "What are you doing here at this early hour? Isabelle isn't in labor, is she?" He rarely had visitors this early in the morning unless it was an emergency.

"No, Isabelle is fine. I need to talk to you."

The doc thought Thorpe looked tired, like he hadn't slept much in a few days. "Let's go in the kitchen. I'll make some coffee."

Thorpe followed him and grabbed some firewood in the corner and shoved it inside the stove. He had it flaming in no time. "It's a cold morning."

"Yep, and just the beginning. I expect we're in for a good snow." The doc set the coffeepot on the stove and walked to the table. He pulled out two chairs and indicated Thorpe should sit in one. "You want me to rustle up some breakfast?"

"No, coffee is fine."

"What's on your mind, Thorpe?"

Thorpe straddled the chair and braced his arms on the back rail. "Did you know Evelyn's back?"

"The pastor told me." So this was what was bothering him. He should have known.

"Doc, you told me Evelyn was pregnant, and I have some questions about that."

The doc shook his head. "Okay."

"I know I don't have to ask you not to let this conversation go further."

"Whatever you have to say will be kept between the two of us."

"When she came to you, did she tell you that Ainsworth . . . well, that he forced himself on her?"

The doc couldn't believe his ears. Evelyn hadn't acted like a woman who had been raped when he examined her. As a matter of fact, he'd thought she seemed angry when he told her she was with child. "Is that what she is saying now?"

"She told me yesterday that Ainsworth had forced himself on her the whole time he was at the ranch, and that he threatened to kill me if she told anyone." It hit Thorpe what the doc said. "What do you mean by, 'Is that what she is saying *now*?'?"

The doc rubbed his hand over his whiskers. "Thorpe, Evelyn told me you were the father of her child. I didn't think you were the kind of man that would bed her and not marry her, or if you did, you would soon marry her once you knew of her condition."

Thorpe thought about what the doc said. Evelyn knew he couldn't have fathered her child. But she might have been embarrassed, or afraid to tell the doc the truth. "Doc, I did bed her, but it wasn't my child. What happened between us was later."

"Did she bring the baby with her?"

Thorpe repeated what Evelyn had told him about Ainsworth pushing her down the stairs at the hotel and losing the baby.

The doc didn't normally discuss his patients with other people, but in this case he wasn't going to allow Evelyn to ruin Thorpe's life. "That's some story. Thorpe. When I examined her I saw nothing that would indicate she was forced in any way. If a woman has been raped, there are usually signs to indicate such harsh treatment. She had ample opportunity to tell me if such a thing happened. She didn't act like a woman who had been abused. I've seen them, I know how they respond."

"But it doesn't mean it couldn't have happened."

"No, it doesn't." The doc's dilemma was trying to decide how much he should reveal to Thorpe. He'd heard a lot of rumors about Evelyn, and he knew she was not the person Thorpe thought she was. "Thorpe, it is my professional opinion that no one forced her." The doc got up and picked up the coffeepot. He poured two cups and pushed one in front of Thorpe. "I should also tell you that I've heard she had a relationship with Tremayne's foreman."

That news caught Thorpe by surprise. "What? You mean Travis? Who told you that?"

"Thorpe, I'm afraid that was the talk for some time after you became engaged."

Leaning back in his chair, Thorpe digested that piece of information as he drank his coffee. "Doc, I never knew you to be one to listen to gossip."

"I'm not, and I'm usually not one to pass it along. But to tell you the truth, Evelyn is not the woman you think she is."

"I don't think she's perfect, I know she's spoiled, but I did bed her and now she wants me to do the right thing. She says she loves me and that Ainsworth forced her. She didn't want to leave me."

So that was it in a nutshell, the doc thought. "She came back hoping you would marry her now that Ainsworth refused to marry her. Everyone knows she left you at the altar to be with her lover. I'm telling you as your friend that woman was not raped." The doc knew he sounded harsh, but Thorpe was his friend, and he didn't want him to make a terrible mistake.

When Thorpe didn't respond, he said, "Look, Thorpe, why don't you go see old man Tremayne and ask him if her story about losing the baby is true? If it is, don't you think he would have contacted his friend in England to tell him what his son did to his precious daughter?"

The doc had a point. Tremayne wouldn't allow anyone to hurt his daughter. "Yeah, it wouldn't surprise me if he didn't take a trip to England and personally beat the stuffing out of Ainsworth."

"Exactly. It's worth talking to him before you sacrifice yourself the second time."

"Maybe I do need to talk to her father. I can't take a trip to England right now."

"There's something else you should know. Before Evelyn became pregnant she came to me and asked how she could prevent pregnancy. She told me she never wanted children. Of course, I told her at the time there was no sure way of prevention other than abstinence."

It surprised Thorpe that a woman would ask such a question unless she worked in a profession which required such knowledge. He could understand women who were with many men trying to avoid pregnancy. He stood to leave. "Thanks, Doc."

Lily opened the door so Blue and Spirit could go outside with the puppies while she prepared breakfast. She didn't realize Thorpe had already left, so she cracked a dozen eggs, the usual amount for the three men. When Stone and Jed joined her in the kitchen, Stone stoked the stove and Jed made the coffee. They tried to engage Lily in conversation, but they quickly noticed she wasn't her cheerful self this morning.

Lily walked to the door to let the animals back inside, but Spirit and the puppies came in without Blue. She walked outside and called his name, but he didn't come to her. Blue always came when she called. She had a sick feeling something was wrong. Snow was falling in large thick flakes and she worried if she waited to look for him, his tracks would be covered quickly. She walked back inside and said to Jed, "Can you finish breakfast? I'm going to look for Blue. He didn't come when I called."

"Maybe he went to look for Mr. Thorpe," Jed said.

Lily was surprised Thorpe was gone. "He's

not here?" She wondered if he went to visit Evelyn, but she wouldn't ask.

"No, ma'am, I heard him ride out early."

"I'll look for Blue," Stone said.

"No, I want to go," Lily said. She grabbed her coat off the hook and picked up her rifle by the door. As soon as she jumped off the porch, she saw Blue's prints and started to follow them. She walked for an hour, and she decided she needed to go back and get Blaze so she could cover more territory quickly. Once she was in the saddle, she followed Blue's trail until she could no longer see his prints. She refused to give up even though she wasn't dressed for the cold and snow. This wasn't like Blue. But Blue hadn't been himself for several days. Had he been trying to tell her that it was time for him to leave? She started weeping; Blue was all she had and she was desperate to find him. He'd helped her to get over losing her parents. He'd protected her on the way to Missouri more times than she could count. Blue was her family, closer than any friend could ever be. She would be lost without him. She called and called to him until she became so hoarse that her voice could no longer be heard above the wind whipping around her.

Thorpe thought he might stop at the Tremayne ranch before he went home, but he had a feeling he needed to get to the ranch. He'd go back to the Tremayne ranch later and talk to Evelyn's father. As soon as he opened the kitchen door, Jed and Stone were pulling on their coats.

"Did you see Miss Lily?" Jed asked.

Thorpe was taking his coat off and stopped midmotion. "What do you mean?"

"She went out to look for Blue. He didn't come back when she let him out this morning."

"We saw her come back and go into the stable to get Blaze," Stone added. "We were just going out to look for her."

Thorpe pulled his coat closed. "I'll go. The snow has probably covered Blue's tracks. Which way did she go?"

"North."

"How long has she been gone?"

"Going on three hours, but she took a rifle," Stone said.

Spirit walked to the door and started whimpering. "Stay here with your babies." Thorpe walked out the door and headed back to the stable. Over an hour later he'd caught up with Lily.

"Why are you here? Did Blue go back to the ranch?"

"I'm here to help you, and no, Blue didn't

come back." Thorpe noticed she could hardly speak, and he could tell she was freezing. She'd pulled her coat sleeves over her hands, but he could see the tips of her fingers where she was holding on to the reins were red. She wasn't dressed for this weather. He pulled an extra pair of gloves from his saddlebag and handed them to her. "Put these on."

Lily took the gloves and put them on her frozen fingers. "Thank you." She hadn't given a thought to the way she was dressed when she took off after Blue.

She didn't even have on a hat, so he pulled off the wool scarf he wore under his coat and gave it to her. "Here you go. Put this over your head."

Lily reached for the scarf and put it over her head and tied it under her chin. It was so warm and it smelled like Thorpe. But her shivering didn't stop.

They hadn't ridden much farther when Thorpe pulled Smoke to a halt. "Hold up." He was worried about her uncontrollable shivering. He unbuttoned his coat and leaned over and pulled her off her saddle and placed her on his lap.

"What are you doing?" Lily's voice was now a mere whisper.

"Getting you warm. I'm not going to let

you freeze to death out here." He opened his coat. "Put your arms around me."

She was too cold to argue. She wrapped her arms around his waist and he closed his coat around her. "You'll be warm in no time."

"I don't want to go back," she said.

He didn't want to go back either. "We'll keep going. Take the gloves off and put your hands under my shirt." He knew that was the best way to get her hands warm in a hurry.

She didn't question him and she tugged his shirt out of his pants. When her hands hit his bare skin she felt him shiver. "Too cold?"

"No, they will warm up more quickly this way." He wasn't sure if it was her cold hands or the fact that she was touching him that made him shiver. He took hold of Blaze's reins and kept riding. "Why do you think he left?"

"I don't know. I think maybe that's why he was staying so close to me. He was trying to tell me he was leaving, or it was time for us to leave. Maybe he didn't understand why we were staying here for the winter." Lily was warmer, but she was still shaking and she didn't know if it was from fear or the cold. "Maybe he wanted to go back in the wild and do what wolves do."

She continued to shake and Thorpe asked, "Are you getting warmer?"

"Yes. You put off a lot of heat."

"I remember you told me that when you changed my bandages," he teased.

She thought of caring for him and how he would tease her that she liked looking at him without his shirt. He'd made her blush with his teasing, but his comments were on the mark. She did like looking at him, and she liked touching him.

Many times Thorpe had thought of how her hands felt on his skin when she was caring for his wound. Nothing had changed; he liked the way she felt with her arms wrapped around him right now. Last night, he'd wanted to feel her touching him, but he'd been out of line and he needed to apologize. "I'm sorry about my behavior last night. I wouldn't have blamed you if you had shot me."

Lily had forgotten her anger, but she was too worried about Blue to think of anything else. "You weren't that bad. But if you do it again, I might consider it."

"I wish I could blame it on the whiskey, but that wouldn't be true. If things were different I would . . ." What would he do if Evelyn hadn't come back? No sense wondering about that now. The hard reality was Evelyn was back. He glanced down at Lily and her blue eyes were focused on him. "It wasn't the whiskey." He paused, then said, "I just want you, Lily."

She stared into his eyes and waited, but he didn't say more.

Like last night, Thorpe was tempted beyond reason to kiss her, but he kept his head. It was easier when he didn't have whiskey in his system and a more important mission at the moment: finding Blue. He pulled his eyes from hers and looked ahead. "I'm not seeing a trail anywhere."

"Why don't you go back? I know you have a lot of work and I can go on alone," Lily told him.

"No. You've already lost your voice. I'm not leaving you out here, but we should turn around soon. The temperature's dropping and you aren't dressed for this weather."

Another hour passed and as much as Thorpe hated to turn back, he had no choice. They hadn't eaten and they were unprepared for the conditions. He did take a different route back to the house, hoping to find some tracks, but no luck. When they reached the stable, he lifted Lily from Smoke. He asked one of his men to care for the horses so he could see Lily to the house.

They walked into the kitchen and Isabelle was waiting for them.

"Did he come back?" Lily asked.

Isabelle shook her head. "I'm sorry."

Spirit left her pups and sprinted to Lily.

Lily kneeled down and wrapped her arms around Spirit, but she couldn't say anything to console the poor animal. She understood her broken heart.

"Spirit has walked to the door a hundred times today, waiting," Isabelle told her.

"Lily, I'll heat some water and bring it up to your room. You need to get in the tub and get warm," Thorpe told her. "And you need to eat something."

"I'll bring a tray up to you," Isabelle said.

When Lily walked upstairs, Thorpe put some pans of water on the stove. "She hasn't eaten all day."

"Have you?" Stone had told her Thorpe didn't eat breakfast and they'd both missed lunch.

"I'll eat something after I take her some water."

"I don't know what she will do without Blue. He means everything to her."

"I'd go back out, but there's no trail to follow now." Thorpe sat down near the stove while he waited for the water to heat.

Isabelle placed a cup of coffee in front of him. "Do you think he will come back?"

"I don't know, but I hope so." It didn't make sense why Blue left, and he didn't know how to comfort Lily. He'd wanted to take her in his arms and just hold her, but after last night she'd probably think he wanted more.

When Thorpe carried the water to Lily's room, he found her standing at the window looking out over the ranch. He filled the tub and walked up behind her. "Why don't you get in the tub before the water gets cold? When you're ready, Isabelle will bring you some food."

Lily turned from the window. "Okay."

Thorpe heard her anguish in that one word. "Let me get a fire going." Once he had a fire blazing in the hearth, he left the room so she could undress. He walked back downstairs and Isabelle had a plate of food ready for him. "Thanks. Let me know when she's finished and I'll take Spirit and the pups up to her room to keep her company."

"She didn't eat much," Isabelle said to Thorpe when she came back to the kitchen.

"She's probably worn-out." Thorpe jumped up and gathered Spirit and the pups and took them outside for a few minutes before he took them to Lily's room. When he reached her room, the door was open and Lily was standing at the window again. After he placed the pups on their blanket, he walked to the fireplace and threw some more logs on the fire. "Lily, why don't you go to bed? I'll wake you if he comes back."

Lily turned, and she looked surprised that he was in the room. She glanced in the corner and saw the pups and Spirit. "I'm not tired. I thought about going back out to look for him."

She seemed lost and it broke his heart. "Lily, I would go if I could find his trail. But there's nothing to lead us to where he is going." He walked over to stand beside her at the window.

"But I have to do something."

He could tell she'd been crying. He didn't know how to offer her comfort any other way, so he wrapped his arms around her. "I'm so sorry."

Lily buried her head in his chest and sobbed. Thorpe picked her up and carried her to the chair and he sat and held her while she cried for her best friend.

When she could speak, she whispered, "I feel in my heart I will see him again, but that doesn't make the hurt go away, or the worry."

Thorpe rubbed her back, remembering the day she told him she felt it in her heart that she would see her grandfather again. He wouldn't bet against it. Jed believed Lily had a direct line to the Almighty and he wouldn't argue that point either. He'd never met anyone with her spiritual connection with animals. "It'll be all right, honey. It may not seem like it now, but things have a way of working out for the best." Now he just needed to listen to his own advice.

CHAPTER THIRTY

Hours later, Thorpe was lying in bed thinking about Blue. Perhaps Lily was right and Blue wanted to go back to the wild. Blue was young when Lily found him, but he'd obviously been in the wild before he was shot. He was debating getting dressed even though it was the middle of the night, when the howling started. He threw the quilt off and walked to the window. There was another full moon and the howling was such a lonely sound echoing through the night. He figured Lily was probably hearing the same sad sound. He got dressed and left the house. With the light from the moon, he figured he could see tracks if he found any.

Finding no sign of Blue, Thorpe started his workday three hours later. He had a lot of work waiting for him, and he'd miss lunch again. He planned on going to the Tremayne ranch before dinner to speak to Evelyn and her father. There was no reason for secrets; anything he had to say to Evelyn he figured he could say in front of her father and get everything out in the open. Since Evelyn had told him her father had traveled to Kansas City to bring her home, he had to know what was going on.

He'd given a lot of thought to what the doc had told him about Evelyn. He didn't give much credence to the gossip about Evelyn and Travis, their ranch foreman. Sure, Travis had brought Evelyn to his ranch on occasion because Evelyn didn't ride. But he certainly never noticed anything improper between them. Then again, Evelyn had carried on an affair with Ainsworth right under his nose, and he'd been none the wiser.

His thoughts moved to Lily. He wanted to be home in time for dinner to make sure Lily was eating, and she didn't take off after Blue again. Lily was an independent woman, and he wouldn't put it past her to try. Just like she took off by herself yesterday when Blue didn't return. She was some woman, not only beautiful but very capable. He admired her, but at the same time, she needed to learn she could depend on someone. He realized she had depended on someone for a long time: Blue.

Lily was sitting at the kitchen table drinking coffee while Isabelle chatted away about baby clothes. Isabelle was cutting patterns from the cloth Lily purchased and trying to keep Lily's mind off of Blue. They heard a knock on the front door and Isabelle jumped up before Lily to see who was calling. Before Isabelle reached the door, in walked Evelyn Tremayne.

"May I help you?" Isabelle asked.

Evelyn pushed past her and walked toward the parlor. "I want to see Thorpe." Evelyn had expected Thorpe to visit her yesterday and she wasn't happy that he hadn't showed. She didn't really expect to catch him at home during the day, but she was curious about the women staying at his home.

"Thorpe is not here. He's working," Isabelle said. Isabelle didn't like the way Evelyn just waltzed in like she owned Thorpe's home.

Evelyn stared at the pregnant woman. "Then get me some coffee. I'm sure he'll be here for lunch, and I'll wait."

"I'm not the maid. If you want coffee, you can come to the kitchen." Isabelle was fuming by the time she made her way back to the kitchen.

"Who was at the door?" Lily asked.

"That woman," Isabelle answered.

Evelyn was right behind Isabelle, and when she entered the kitchen, her eyes zeroed in on Lily. "My name is Evelyn Tremayne. And might I inquire who you are?"

"I'm Lily Starr and this is Isabelle Justice," Lily replied.

"Why are you staying in my fiancé's home?" When she'd barged in the other day, she had thought Thorpe was getting married and it was too late to get him back. After Thorpe's reaction to her story, she knew it was just a matter of time before she'd have him at the altar again.

"You mean your ex-fiancé?" Isabelle asked.

Evelyn glared at her. "Thorpe and I are going to marry soon."

"We are here by Thorpe's invitation," Lily said.

"How do you know Thorpe? I've never met you and I know all of his acquaintances."

Isabelle held her tongue, but she wanted to tell her it was none of her business.

"We met Thorpe on the trail to Wyoming,"

Lily said.

So that meant Thorpe met them after he left Kansas City. Evelyn glanced at Isabelle's belly. "I guess you are taking advantage of Thorpe's good graces since you are obviously unable to travel."

Lily bristled at her rude behavior. She felt sorry for Evelyn after Thorpe related everything that had happened to her, but that gave her no right to be rude. "We are not taking advantage of anything. Thorpe invited us here. It's as simple as that."

"If not for Lily, you wouldn't even have an ex-fiancé," Isabelle told her.

"And what do you mean by that?" Evelyn asked.

"Lily saved his life."

Evelyn's eyes roved over Lily. She'd never seen another woman who might tempt Thorpe, but she thought this woman could be a threat. She wondered if Thorpe had taken her to his bed. She doubted it, or Thorpe would feel compelled to do the right thing. She wasn't about to lose him to an interloper with long blond hair. She needed to rebuild her reputation if she was going to stay in this town, and that meant marrying Thorpe. No one was going to get in her way. She could handle Thorpe; she always could. She was confident he would believe any tale she told him. "Do you think you found yourself a rich rancher?"

Lily thought it was interesting that Evelyn didn't even ask what had happened to Thorpe. "I wasn't aware Thorpe was rich."

Isabelle didn't think Thorpe would appreciate Evelyn's behavior. "I don't think Thorpe would abide you insulting his guests."

"Thorpe cares about anything that affects me. Just so you know, Thorpe and I have known each other a long time. We're intimate and we share everything." She stared hard at Lily with undisguised loathing. "Everything."

Lily could hardly believe what she was implying. "Your relationship with Thorpe is no concern of ours."

"I will be sharing his bedroom soon and you will no longer be welcome in our home." With that said, she turned to walk down the hallway to the front door. Travis was waiting on her, and she had no intention of spending her time waiting on Thorpe to return. She had the information she wanted. She would tell Thorpe that she didn't want those women in his home and he could put them up in the hotel. She knew how to make Thorpe succumb to her demands; she'd done it before.

"Has that woman no shame?" Isabelle asked when they heard the front door close.

"She reminds me of Dora," Lily said. "She cares for no one but herself. She didn't even ask what happened to Thorpe when you told her I saved his life."

"Tell me he's not going to marry that harpy," Isabelle said.

"Isabelle! I've never heard you speak that way," Lily said.

"I'm sorry, but can you imagine Thorpe being married to her? What in the world did he see in her in the first place? My heavens, I can hardly fathom a worse fate."

Lily agreed, but it wasn't her place to tell Thorpe that the woman he was going to marry was seriously lacking in common decency, not to mention manners. "She does wear beautiful clothing." Lily felt so drab next to her. Her dress had to cost more than all of Lily's dresses put together.

"My father used to say, 'You can't make a silk purse out of a sow's ear,' " Isabelle said.

Lily shook her head. "That's terrible. But I guess I should be thankful Blue wasn't here. I was worried he was going to bite her the last time she was here."

"Too bad he wasn't here," Isabelle said.

Thinking of Blue, Lily walked to the kitchen window and looked out. She kept thinking that Blue may just be exploring the territory and would return.

Isabelle walked to her and put her arm around her waist. "Don't fret. Blue can take care of himself. I'm sure he had a reason to leave."

"I know he can, but I'm not sure I can go on without him."

Reining in at the Tremayne ranch, Thorpe tied Smoke in front of the house and loosened his girth.

Mr. Tremayne opened the door at Thorpe's knock. "Thorpe, I'm glad to see you. I heard you were back and I've been meaning to stop over."

Thorpe shook his hand. "It's good to see you."

"Come in, come in."

Thorpe followed him to the parlor and accepted his offer of a glass of whiskey. "Please, have a seat."

The two men sat facing each other and Thorpe said, "I need to have a talk with you."

"What can I do for you?"

Thorpe began to tell him everything Evelyn had told him when she came to the ranch. "I thought Evelyn would be here and we could talk about this together, but I

468

wanted to know if she is telling the truth."

Mr. Tremayne poured himself another whiskey, but Thorpe declined a second. He didn't want a repeat of his performance when he got home. "Thorpe, I went to Kansas City and I talked to the sheriff about Ainsworth. He told me there was a couple staying in the hotel and they were leaving their room and witnessed Evelyn arguing with Ainsworth. They said Evelyn was angry and she was the one landing blows on Ainsworth. Ainsworth did not strike her. She lost her balance and fell backward down the staircase. It seems Ainsworth didn't do anything wrong. As a matter of fact, he stayed with her until she recovered. He'd only been gone a day when I arrived. The sad fact is Ainsworth didn't want to marry her. He didn't think it was his child. Naturally, I wrote his father and explained the situation to him. I'm awaiting his reply. Am I right to assume that it was his child as Evelyn said?"

"Yes."

Tremayne nodded. "I thought as much."

Thorpe tossed back the remainder of his whiskey. Evelyn had been lying to him all along.

"Thorpe, I wasn't aware of what was happening right under my own roof." He gestured in the air with his glass and added, "Well, maybe I had an inkling if I wanted to admit such a thing was happening. But I can say Ainsworth didn't force himself on her. I'm sure of that much."

Thorpe just looked at him; he couldn't even form a reply. Evelyn was such an accomplished liar, yet her father was an honest man. She did him a disservice.

"This may sound strange coming from her father, but Evelyn doesn't deserve you. She tried to ruin your life once before. Don't let her do it again. I don't want you to marry my daughter. I like you, Thorpe, and I would have been honored to have you for a son-in-law, but Evelyn won't be true to you."

"Do you know when she will be back?" Thorpe wanted to talk to her one last time. She needed to know her lies would never work on him again.

"I saw Travis pull the buggy into the stable not long before you arrived. Go on out there and talk to her."

Thorpe thought it was odd that Mr. Tremayne didn't ask him to wait until Evelyn came into the house, but maybe he wanted to get back to whatever he was doing before he arrived. Thanking him for his honesty, Thorpe walked out of the house

470

and headed to the stable. He no longer had doubts about his responsibilities to Evelyn considering what Mr. Tremayne told him.

When he walked into the stable he heard voices coming from one of the stalls, so he walked in that direction. When he got closer to the stall, he recognized one of the voices belonged to Evelyn.

"If you had money, Travis, I would marry you. I don't want to be stuck here the rest of my life."

"Is that why you keep going to Turlow's? You think you'll talk him into leaving Wyoming? Or are you doing more than talking?" Travis asked.

"Thorpe will do anything I ask." She laughed. "Haven't you seen for yourself that I have a way of getting what I want?"

"Yeah, I've noticed. Are you back in Turlow's bed?"

Thorpe didn't hear her answer. The doc had told him about Evelyn and Travis and he didn't want to believe the gossip. But it looked like even Mr. Tremayne knew what was going on and that was the reason he sent him out here.

"When your old man dies, you'll have all his money then. You can go anywhere you want."

"But honey, I don't want to wait that long.

I want to go while I'm young and Pa is a healthy man. He'll live a long time. We could travel the country together."

"I know what you want me to do, but your pa has treated me kindly. I told you before you took off with Ainsworth that it ain't in me to do something like that. I know that's the reason you shared Ainsworth's bed, so he would take you out of here. Why did you come back?"

This time Thorpe heard Evelyn's response; her tone was meant to entice. He'd heard it before. "Honey, forget about Ainsworth. I missed you. We could make it look like an accident."

When they grew quiet, he started to walk back to the house to tell Mr. Tremayne what he'd overheard, but he wanted them to see him. He wanted them to know someone heard what they were planning. And he wanted Evelyn to know she would never deceive him again. He waited.

"Honey, just think, when we are rid of him we could go anywhere we want. You could have me forever, and never have to work again," Evelyn promised.

Thorpe knew how her promises were as shallow as her character. He wondered if Travis was buying her sweet words.

"I'll think about it. Now stop talking,"

Travis said.

Thorpe waited another few minutes before he walked to the stall's opening. Evelyn's dress was draped over the wooden slats and Travis's holster and shirt were six feet away from him. "Hello, Evelyn."

Travis rolled to face Thorpe and his eyes darted to his holster, but Thorpe said, "Don't. She's not worth the effort."

Evelyn sat straight and pulled the straps of her chemise up over her shoulders. "Thorpe, this isn't what it looks like."

"Are you going to tell me Travis forced you?"

"Yes, yes, he did."

Thorpe arched a brow at Travis. "Travis, you ready to get killed over her today?"

Travis jumped up and grabbed his shirt. "Nope. I got what I wanted. If you've been standing there long, then you know I didn't have to force her. You can have her."

"I don't want her." He realized he wasn't even surprised to hear Evelyn wanted her father dead so she could have his money. He'd heard enough to know that she'd been intimate with Travis before Ainsworth. "Did the baby belong to Travis?"

Travis's eyes snapped to Thorpe before turning to Evelyn. "What baby?"

"I guess she hasn't been totally honest

with you, Travis. When she left here with Ainsworth, she was pregnant. It wasn't mine."

Travis leaned down and grabbed Evelyn by the arm. "Evelyn? Is this the truth?"

Evelyn glared at Thorpe. "Yeah, it's true."

"Why didn't you tell me?"

"I told you I didn't want to stay here and waste away my life, but you wouldn't listen. I didn't want to be tied to this ranch with a baby."

"Was it my baby?" When she didn't respond, Travis pulled her to her feet by her arm and shook her. "Was it?"

"Yes, and he's dead!"

Thorpe doubted Travis loved Evelyn since he was aware of her relationship with Ainsworth, yet his eyes reflected the wound she'd inflicted with her emotionless words.

Thorpe looked at Evelyn and shook his head. He didn't want to hear more of her lies as she related her version of losing the baby to Travis. Before he turned to leave, he added a parting comment. "I heard what you two were scheming and I intend to tell Mr. Tremayne and the sheriff. It's up to you, Travis, but you should think about telling them first."

Thorpe left the stable, jumped on Smoke,

and headed home. It was difficult for him to come to terms with the depth of Evelyn's duplicity. The doc was right; she had been involved with two men, all the while pretending she wanted to be his wife. He figured if she had married him she would have continued her relationship with Travis. She knew all along it was Travis's baby, yet she was willing to deceive him and Ainsworth to get what she wanted. He could hardly believe how little he knew about her.

After he'd found her in Kansas City, he'd been so angry that he didn't think he would ever trust another woman. He was no longer angry; he actually pitied Evelyn. Yet he found himself asking the same question again. Could he trust another woman after this? Lily was the woman he wanted. Could he trust her? Would she ever betray him? Thoughts of Lily kissing Captain Anderson played in his mind. Logically, he knew it wasn't fair to compare Lily to Evelyn. Evelyn was a schemer and thought of no one but herself. He'd had weeks to observe Lily's character. She was honest, fiercely loyal, and put everyone's well-being above her own.

Thorpe hadn't made any declarations to Lily; she was free to do what she wanted with Captain Anderson or any other man.

Now that he no longer felt obligated to Evelyn, he needed to act on his feelings before it was too late.

CHAPTER THIRTY-ONE

"Where's Lily?" Thorpe asked as soon as he walked into the kitchen.

"She cooked dinner and then said she was going to lie down," Isabelle told him.

"We kept looking out for Blue all day, but there's just no sign of him," Stone said.

"Poor Miss Lily, she's plumb heartbroken," Jed said.

Isabelle intended to wait until she had a moment alone with Thorpe to tell him about their visitor today, but she knew that might not happen tonight. He had a right to know what happened when Evelyn visited. "Thorpe, your fiancée visited us today."

"I don't have a fiancée," he said.

"She said you were her fiancé. Be that as it may, she was here earlier today and she told us we were not welcome here. She said you two would be married soon and we would have to leave."

"Isabelle, if she comes back when I'm not

here, get one of the men to throw her out. You're welcome to stay on *my* ranch as long as you like. Evelyn is no longer welcome here. We straightened that out an hour ago."

"Thank you. You should know she made it clear that . . ." She didn't know how to say what Evelyn said.

"What?" Thorpe wouldn't have been surprised by anything Evelyn said.

Isabelle turned pink. "I don't know how to say it, but she indicated that you were . . . well, very close. I'm not quite sure why she would discuss your relationship with complete strangers, but I felt she wanted to make sure Lily . . . well, let's just say she was obviously jealous of Lily."

Thorpe got the gist of what Isabelle was trying to say. So Evelyn wanted to make it clear to them that he'd been intimate with her. He wondered what Lily thought about that. "I don't think she will come back, but remember what I said."

Isabelle smiled. "I have to tell you it would give me great pleasure to have her thrown out."

"Isabelle!" Stone said, but he was smiling. His demure little wife was showing some spunk.

"Well, you didn't see how she acted. She looked at Lily like she wanted to kill her. I think she took an immediate dislike to Lily because she is prettier."

Thorpe couldn't help it, he started laughing. It didn't take Isabelle long to see through Evelyn's motives.

There was a knock on the kitchen door and Curtis walked in. "Hello."

"Curtis, is something wrong?" Thorpe asked.

"No, I went to town to pick up supplies and just got back. The clerk at the telegraph office gave me two telegrams. One is for Jedidiah and one is for Lily."

Curtis handed Jed his telegram. "Where's Lily?"

"Upstairs." Thorpe stuck out his hand and said, "I'll take it to her; I'm going to get a fire going in her room." He pointed to a chair. "Have some dinner."

Curtis handed him the telegram. "I can eat in the bunkhouse."

"Sit. I know you must get tired of Charlie's cooking, but if you tell him I said that I'll fire you," Thorpe teased.

Curtis laughed and sat down. "Charlie only cooks a couple of things good, but I do get tired of having those few things over and over."

"Lily is an excellent cook and she makes

great cakes," Thorpe said. He was tempted to read Lily's telegram, but he stuck it in his shirt pocket. He glanced at Jed and saw a big smile spread over his face as he read his telegram. "Good news, Jed?"

Jed looked up at him with tears in his eyes. "Yessir, Mr. Thorpe, the best news. It's from my brother and he's going to come here in the spring. That Captain Anderson kept his word. He found him for me and got word to him where I would be spending the winter. Thanks be to God."

"That is great news," Thorpe said. He wondered if Lily's telegram was from Captain Anderson.

Stone slapped Jed on the back. "I'm happy for you."

"Me too, Jed. You never wavered in your belief that he was alive," Isabelle said. "You're just like Lily. She has never given up on her grandfather."

"Since your brother is going to come here, that's means you'll be here for a while. Why don't we set up that blacksmith shop over the winter?" Thorpe said.

"Mr. Thorpe, I think that is a fine idea. I thank you."

"If that brother of yours decides to leave the military, then he can work with you if he is of a mind."

"You mean we're going to have a blacksmith on the ranch?" Curtis asked, looking from Thorpe to Jed.

"It looks that way," Thorpe said.

Outside Lily's door, Thorpe pulled the telegram from his pocket. He glanced down and saw Anderson's name. Why did she have to hear from Anderson now, just when he'd found out he no longer had any obligation to Evelyn? He wouldn't read the telegram, no matter how much he was tempted. He tapped on the door.

"Come in," Lily said.

Thorpe opened the door and saw Lily sitting by the window. "I have a telegram for you."

Her eyes widened. "For me?"

She certainly looked excited to receive a telegram. No doubt she knew it was from Anderson. He walked across the room and handed her the piece of paper. While she read, he added some logs to the fire she already had going. He didn't want to leave, so he took his time at the fireplace. "Isabelle said she was going to bring you up some dinner." He glanced over his shoulder at her. She finished reading and was folding the piece of paper. Whatever Anderson had said made her smile.

He stood and faced her. "Good news?" Would she tell him what Anderson said?

She shrugged. "Captain Anderson said he would come visit if I am here in the spring."

Thorpe started to say he hadn't invited him to Dove Creek. "Is that right?"

"Yes."

"I guess you'll have to tell him you'll be on your way north."

"Yes." The last thing she wanted to think about was Captain Anderson. He'd been very honest about his interest in her, and she feared he would continue to hold out hope if she didn't dissuade him. She was in love with another man, and that man had a fiancée. "He said I should let him know where I will be."

Thorpe bristled at her comment. "I guess that would indicate you two are more than friends."

His accusatory tone frustrated her. "I'm not the one that has a fiancée while kissing someone else."

"I'm not either," Thorpe said.

"Your fiancée seems to be of a different opinion."

Thorpe crossed his arms and glared at her. "I don't have a fiancée," he ground out.

Lily had hit a nerve, but she didn't care. "She let us know today that you two were intimate and that you told her everything. Did you tell her you were kissing me? As a matter of fact, she said she would be sharing your bed again soon."

Lord help him. It was hard for him to believe even Evelyn would say such a thing to two strangers. He rubbed his forehead and closed his eyes. He was getting a pounding headache.

It was written all over his face that he'd been intimate with Evelyn. Lily jumped up and took a step toward him; their eyes met and held. "No response? You are taking her to your bed and you say she is not your fiancée? Wasn't that what you wanted from me? Isn't one woman enough?" As soon as the words left her mouth, she regretted them, but her temper had gotten the better of her.

He wanted to explain that what had happened with Evelyn was a long time ago, and he'd made a mistake, but he wasn't sure she was ready to listen. "Lily . . ."

"Dinner." Isabelle walked into the room with a tray full of food. Neither one acknowledged her, so she glanced from Lily to Thorpe. They were standing a few feet from each other like they were preparing for a shootout. She'd definitely interrupted something. "I can come back."

"No, stay. Thorpe was just leaving," Lily said.

Thorpe scowled at her. Did she think so little of him that she would assume he would kiss her and tell her he wanted her if he had a fiancée? He shook his head in frustration, turned, and stalked out of the room.

Isabelle had never seen Thorpe look so upset. "Lily, what happened? Did you see the look on his face? What did you say to him?"

"I just repeated what his fiancée said to us today." Lily started pacing. Guilt was flowing over her like a wave. She rarely spoke harshly to anyone, but she was angry. Or perhaps it was frustration and hurt. She thought Thorpe was being dishonest about Evelyn and the plain fact was it hurt to know he loved another woman. And then there was Blue. She was frustrated because she didn't know what to do to find him. She'd never felt so helpless since the day she found her parents dead after the raid on their farm. No matter what she was feeling, it was wrong of her to try to hurt Thorpe with her words. There was no justification for her actions.

Isabelle placed the tray on the table and reached for Lily's arm to pull her to a halt.

"Oh, Lily, Evelyn lied. I told Thorpe downstairs what she said and he told me if she came back to have one of the men throw her out. She's not his fiancée."

Lily stared at her. "Why would she lie about that?"

Isabelle shook her head. "I don't know. Maybe she wants to marry him and felt threatened by you. But she is lying."

"But I know they were intimate," Lily said.

"And I was with Ethan, yet you didn't judge me. Remember how upset you were with the people on the wagon train for judging us? Whatever happened between Thorpe and Evelyn was before he met you."

Lily was so ashamed, she started tearing up. She had never been one to pass judgment on anyone. "I was so mean to him and I said such terrible things. I don't know why I was so angry."

"You love him, and you believed Evelyn." Isabelle gave her a gentle shove toward the door. "Go apologize to him."

"He probably hates me for not believing him," Lily replied.

"After everything that man has done for us, for you, he deserves an apology. Lily, can't you see he's in love with you? He tore out of here so fast the morning Blue left and you were out there alone searching for him. Stone and Jed were going to go after you, but he wouldn't let them. And would a man go out before dawn the next morning searching for Blue if he wasn't a good man? Lily, open your eyes! I know he says he's not ready to settle down. Maybe that's due to his bad experience with Evelyn. It doesn't matter. Whatever it was, it has been resolved. That man is in love and I know you love him. Isn't it time you told him?"

Tears were falling down Lily's cheeks. "You really think he loves me?"

Isabelle threw her hands in the air. "Go! And don't you dare come back until you've apologized at the very least. If you're as smart as I think you are, you'll tell him you love him."

Lily looked for Thorpe downstairs, but he was nowhere to be found. Stone told her he went to the stable. Grabbing her coat off the hook, Lily headed to the stable. Finding it empty, she walked to Smoke's stall. He was gone and that meant Thorpe was gone. Instead of going back to the house, she brushed down Blaze and Daisy while she waited for him to return. She spent over an hour in the stable and it was getting late, so she walked back to the house. Once in her bedroom, she left the door ajar so she would hear Thorpe when he came back. Instead of going to bed, she decided she would work on her Christmas presents while she waited.

The hours passed and Thorpe didn't return. Lily set aside the shirt she'd been working on and walked to the window. She wondered where Thorpe was and why he hadn't returned. Had he been so upset with her that he'd gone back to Evelyn's waiting arms? Exhausted, she closed her bedroom door and crawled into bed.

Thorpe built a fire and once it was roaring, he threw his bedroll nearby. He hadn't planned to spend the night on the range; he just wanted to be alone to think. He tossed his saddle down and leaned back on it while he sipped whiskey from the bottle he'd brought with him. Lily was maddening. How could she hold what he'd done before he met her against him? She was angry with him, but she was the one receiving telegrams from another man. Anderson was obviously in love with her and he was planning on finding her in the spring. No doubt, Anderson figured he'd court her and talk her into marrying him.

He'd resolved his problem with Evelyn, and he'd planned on declaring his feelings tonight, but that plan went awry. Now, come spring, Lily would be gone and free to do what she wanted. If she left, maybe he would stop obsessing over her. She could go on and marry Anderson. He shouldn't care. *No way will I let that happen.*

He'd drank half the bottle before he headed back home. He didn't want to wake everyone in the house, so he tossed his bedroll into one of the empty stalls. After all of his thinking, he'd arrived at one conclusion: He needed to stay away from women and whiskey.

CHAPTER THIRTY-TWO

The next morning, Thorpe walked in the kitchen before dawn and Lily was already preparing breakfast. "Morning." He hadn't had much sleep and his whole body was stiff from sleeping in the stall. Not only that, but he was hungry and grouchy.

Turning from the stove, Lily looked at him. "I waited up for you."

Was she asking him where he'd been? He wasn't in the mood to argue. "Yeah?"

"Why didn't you come home?"

"I reckon I didn't want to," he said, not willing to give an inch at the moment. He grabbed the coffeepot from the stove. "Why did you wait up for me?"

Was he with Evelyn? She felt her indignation rising again, but she took a deep breath. She'd been wrong and she needed to admit that fact. "I wanted to apologize for what I said last night."

"I guess Isabelle told you what I said

about throwing Evelyn off the ranch."

"Yes, she did."

Thorpe arched a brow at her. "But you didn't believe me."

Lily threw her hands in the air. "It wasn't that I didn't believe you, it's just that . . ."

"What?"

She tried to summon the courage to tell him she loved him.

Jed walked in the back door. "Good morning," he said.

"Jed," Thorpe said. He poured two cups of coffee and handed one to Jed. Out of the corner of his eye he saw Lily turn back to the stove. He shouldn't have been so hard-headed since she did apologize.

Stone and Isabelle joined them in the kitchen, and while they ate breakfast, Thorpe told them the ladies from the ranch would be coming by later to help decorate the house and help with the cooking for Christmas Day.

"Only four more days until my baby arrives," Isabelle said.

Stone smiled at her. "You are still convinced this baby will arrive on Christmas Day."

"Yes, I am."

"That means you will be cutting a tree today?" Lily asked Thorpe.

"Yes." He wondered if she would like to ride with him, but he didn't want to ask in front of everyone.

Breakfast ended and Stone and Jed walked out the back door, and Isabelle thought she would leave Thorpe and Lily alone. "I'll be back in a minute to help clean up, Lily."

When Isabelle left the room, Lily saw Thorpe pulling on his coat to leave.

"Do you think I could go with you to find a tree?"

Thorpe smiled at her. "I was going to ask you if you would like to go."

Her eyes lit up. "Really?"

"Yes. The women will be here in the afternoon, so we'll leave after lunch."

Before he left, she wanted to try to apologize again. "Thorpe, I am really sorry. It wasn't that I didn't believe you."

Thorpe didn't let her finish; he needed to apologize, too. "I'm afraid I'm the one who needs to apologize." He reached for his Stetson. "I'll see you at lunch."

Lily felt better after he left even though she'd lost her nerve to tell him how she felt. When Isabelle returned to the kitchen, Lily told her about her plans with Thorpe.

"Oh, Lily, that will be so much fun. I hope next year I'm not in the family way at

Christmas so Stone and I can do that to-gether."

"Last year I spent Christmas alone," Lily said. She had never been so miserable in her life. "But then, the next day I found Blue." Just as Thorpe said, sometimes things turned out for the best even when they seemed the bleakest.

The remainder of the morning the women worked diligently on their Christmas gifts. Lily showed Isabelle the shirt she'd been making for Thorpe last night while she waited for him.

"It's such a beautiful blue. He will look so handsome in that," Isabelle told her. "It's much prettier than the black one I'm mak-ing for Stone. I made the brown one for Jed."

Lily wanted to make Isabelle a dress, but there wasn't enough time. Instead, she decided it was best to give her the pretty pink fabric as a gift and then she could make a dress after she had the baby.

"I wonder what Stone and Jed have been working on in the stable every night?" Isa-belle asked.

Lily was aware of the surprise they had planned for Isabelle, but she wasn't about to tell her. "Just don't you go snooping around."

Isabelle smiled. "I won't. I love surprises."

It was nearing time for lunch, so Lily ran upstairs to change into suitable clothing for Christmas tree hunting. She hurried downstairs and had just finished placing lunch on the table for the men when they walked through the door.

After lunch, Thorpe said, "Are you ready?" All morning he could hardly think of anything other than taking Lily with him to find a tree. It was something he'd always done by himself and he really looked forward to having her along.

She nodded. "I have my scarf, gloves, and hat."

"Perfect. Let's go." He looked at everyone still seated at the table. "We'll be back in a couple of hours."

"Bring back a real full one," Isabelle told them. As soon as they were out the door, Isabelle turned to her husband. "Still don't think Thorpe will ask Lily to marry him?"

Stone chuckled. "Honey, I already know not to underestimate your powers of observation."

"You two will be happily married forever. You already know it's best to agree with the wife," Jed told them.

In years past Thorpe probably wouldn't

have taken as much time searching for a tree as he was doing right now. But he didn't mind; it was a joy having Lily along. She would stop and dismount and walk around each tree he pointed out to make sure there were no bare spots. They'd been looking for over an hour and he was beginning to think they might not ever find the perfect one. Lily's cheeks were pink and he told her he'd have to select the tree if her nose started to fall off from frostbite. They didn't discuss the harsh words between them the night before; they talked about fond Christmas memories with their families.

He'd taken her to what he thought were the best places to look for a tree, but so far no luck. They were riding toward another clump of trees when suddenly she pulled Blaze to a halt. Out in the open, apart from all of the other trees, was a perfectly shaped pine about seven feet tall. Thorpe thought he knew his land pretty well, but he'd never seen this tree before.

Lily rode around the tree. "This is the one," she said, giving him a big smile.

"Are you sure?"

"Don't you like it?" She glanced at the tree again. She loved the tree and she envisioned it in his home in front of the window in the parlor.

"Yeah, I do. I was just making sure." He dismounted and pulled his ax from the saddle. He pulled off his coat and handed it to Lily and started chopping away at the trunk.

Lily watched as he swung the ax over and over. He was so strong that he felled the tree within minutes. Once they secured the tree with a rope to his saddle, he reached for his coat.

"It will be beautiful once it's decorated."

"Are you freezing?" He wanted her to say yes so he could wrap her in his coat much like he did when they were searching for Blue.

"Not too cold. Why?"

"I saw something not far from here just this morning that I thought you might like to see if you aren't too cold."

"I'm fine." She wasn't about to admit to being cold. She was enjoying their time together.

"Good." They rode for several minutes until Thorpe whispered, "Let's dismount."

He took her hand and led her to a group of cottonwood trees. He pointed to the largest tree just a few feet in front of them. "Look on that third limb from the top."

Lily looked at the limb and saw the most

beautiful snowy white owl. "Oh, he's lovely."

"I've never seen a larger one," Thorpe whispered as if he was afraid his deep voice would scare the owl away.

Lily pointed to the ground beneath the limb. "There's one of his feathers."

"Didn't you tell me feathers were gifts from the sky, and they come with a purpose?" Thorpe remembered what she'd told him that night she showed him her grandfather's carvings.

"Yes, that's what the Indians believe." She walked beneath the tree and picked up the feather. When she walked back to Thorpe, she reached up and removed his Stetson and stuck the feather in the band.

"What is the purpose of that one?"

"I don't know." She thought of Blue. She hadn't heard howling the last few nights. Hopefully, the feather was sent to tell her she would see him again. "Grandfather always told me when we show respect to all living things, they will respect us."

They watched the owl for a few minutes, as his golden eyes watched their every move.

When they mounted their horses, Lily said, "Did you know some Indians believe that owls bring messages from beyond the grave, or they may appear to give you a warning?"

"I'd heard they were the symbol of death," Thorpe said.

"I wonder how anyone could think something so lovely would be a symbol of death."

"I can't figure that one out," Thorpe answered.

"Thank you for bringing me along. I've had a wonderful time," Lily said.

"Me, too. I appreciate the help. I couldn't have picked a prettier tree."

They reached the stable and found Stone and Jed building a stand for the tree. Thorpe saw the buckboard in front of the house.

"I see the ladies are here," he said.

"Yeah, they got here a few minutes ago," Stone said.

"I'll brush down Blaze and go meet everyone," Lily said.

Thorpe took hold of Blaze's reins. "You go ahead, I'll brush Blaze."

"Thank you." Lily was anxious to meet the women on his ranch and thrilled that Isabelle would have friends once she was gone.

The women were popping corn and pulling out decorations from the box Thorpe had brought in from the stable earlier that morning, when Thorpe came in with the tree. When he placed it in front of the

497

window, the children clapped excitedly. The ladies commented that it was the most beautiful tree Thorpe had ever brought home.

Thorpe grinned at Lily. "You should thank Lily. She picked it out."

The women all looked from Thorpe to Lily and definitely saw sparks flying between the pair. Thorpe was no sooner out the door, when the women started asking Lily questions about her marital status.

Lily and Isabelle enjoyed the afternoon with the women and their children, but they were late preparing dinner. The men walked in right after the women left for their homes, and Lily said, "We'll have it ready soon."

"No hurry. We knew we would eat later than normal tonight," Thorpe said.

Lily appreciated the fact that Thorpe was so easygoing; little things didn't seem to bother him.

Isabelle must have been thinking along the same lines, because she said, "My pa would throw a fit if my mother was a minute late with dinner."

Stone hadn't heard Isabelle say much about her pa. "Seems like he missed an opportunity to watch his wife move around the kitchen. I can't imagine getting mad over something that is a real pleasure."

Isabelle blushed at her husband's words, but Lily smiled at him.

Thorpe didn't say anything, but he agreed with Stone. He enjoyed watching Lily in the kitchen, and it wouldn't bother him if his dinner was late every night. If he were married to her he might give her other reasons to have a late dinner. *Married?* A few weeks ago that thought would have scared him to death. But now the thought of seeing her in his home every day seemed very appealing. If he was married to her, she would be in his bed every night. Now that thought was more than appealing; it made his heart race.

After dinner, Lily left the table to slice the pie she'd baked while everyone continued to talk about the menu for their Christmas dinner. She thought she heard a noise at the front door and she glanced at the table but no one else seemed to hear anything. At first she was hesitant to see who was at the door out of fear that it might be Evelyn again. If it was, the perfect day would be ruined. *But maybe it's Blue.* She hurried to the door, but when she pulled it open no one was there. She closed the door and turned to go back to the kitchen, and someone grabbed her from behind. One arm circled her waist and a gun was pressed against her back.

"Shhh, unless you want me to plug you right here."

Harlow! He wasn't dead!

"Nod if you understand," he said in a lethal voice.

Lily nodded. "What are you doing here?" she whispered.

"Why do you think?" He moved forward, nearly lifting her off the ground.

Her mind was racing. If he made it to the kitchen, what then?

"Where's that wolf?" Harlow whispered.

"He's not here."

"Don't lie to me. He's always around you."

"I'm not lying. He left."

"If I see him I'll shoot him. Now move."

Lily saw no way out of the situation. His arm was clamped around her so tightly that she knew she couldn't escape. If she could make a move, she didn't think she could take the gun from him.

When she walked back through the kitchen doorway, Thorpe turned to look at her. He'd noticed when she left the room, but he didn't know why. By the look on her face, he knew immediately that something was wrong. Then he saw Harlow behind her.

He jumped up from his chair so fast, it skittered backward and hit the wall. Stone and Jed glanced at him to see what he was doing and then they looked across the room. Stone left his seat and grabbed Isabelle's arm and pushed her behind him.

Thorpe directed his steely eyes on Harlow. "What do you want, Harlow?"

"The money. And if you want to keep this pretty little lady alive, you'll give me what I want and I'll be on my way."

"I left the money at Fort Steele," Stone said.

"I know you, Justice. You wouldn't part with that money until you saw it returned to its rightful owner," Harlow said.

"I left it in capable hands."

Thorpe took a step forward, ready to tear into Harlow with his bare hands.

Harlow put the barrel of his pistol to Lily's head. "Don't do something stupid."

"Walk out that door, Harlow, and I'll overlook that you held a gun to Lily's head," Thorpe said menacingly.

"I want the money."

"Stone told you the truth. The money is with the soldiers at Fort Steele," Thorpe said.

"We heard you took an arrow," Stone said. He thought he would keep Harlow talking until they could figure a way out of this situation without anyone getting shot.

"Yeah, I did. The boys left me, thinking I was dying. They didn't know me as well as they thought."

Thorpe looked at Lily and her eyes were on him. She looked calm, but he wondered if she was as collected as she appeared. The first thought that went through his mind was the owl they saw that morning. Was it there to offer a warning, or was it a symbol of death? If Stone kept Harlow talking, he might be able to pull his gun before Harlow had time to react.

Lily mouthed the words *shoot him* to Thorpe and he gave a slight nod.

"Harlow, take Thorpe up on his offer. You walk out that door and you will have a good head start before the law gets on your tail."

Harlow sneered. "I'm not stupid. I know you will dog me for the rest of my life."

"Not me. I'm no longer a marshal. I'm ranching now," Stone said.

Harlow knew Justice was well-regarded for his honesty. "Is that a fact?"

"Yeah, I resigned when I got here."

"Now's your chance to ride down to Mexico and stay put for a while," Stone told him.

Leaning to Lily's ear, Harlow said,

"Honey, I might as well take you with me. I never wanted Dora, I wanted you."

His words revolted Lily. She tried to pull away, but he held her tight.

Thorpe had to force himself to keep his composure. All he wanted to do was dive across the room and choke the living daylights out of Harlow.

"Did you kill Dora?" Stone asked.

"Kip Young killed her. He didn't want to share the loot with another person."

Stone thought it was true justice since Lily had killed Kip Young. He figured things had a way of coming full circle.

Lily was sickened by Harlow's lack of emotion when he spoke of Dora. She didn't understand how a man could be so cruel.

"Let Lily go and be on your way," Stone said. If he released Lily, Stone planned to blow a hole through him.

"No, I like the feel of her," Harlow said. "If I can't get to the money, I'm taking her instead. A woman like her could make me a lot of money with the Comancheros when I get tired of her. They like blonde women." He started backing toward the kitchen doorway.

"You don't want to take Lily. If you do, we'll come after you," Stone said.

Shuffling to the door with Lily directly in

front of him, Harlow couldn't help himself from stopping long enough to taunt Stone. "You can try to find us, but I doubt I will still have Lily by then."

Thorpe wasn't listening to Harlow's words; he needed to keep calm. He focused on Lily, knowing she would give him a way to get a shot off.

Lily watched Thorpe, and when he shifted his body ever so slightly she knew he was going to act. Harlow was so much taller than Lily that he was crouched low to make himself more difficult to shoot. He was holding her so tightly that Lily did the only things she could to give Thorpe an ample target. She lifted her feet from the ground and shifted all of her weight on Harlow's arm around her waist and at the same time she turned her head away from the pistol.

Thorpe saw Lily's move and instantaneously drew his pistol and pulled the trigger in one swift motion. Harlow hit the floor and Lily stumbled to Thorpe's open arms.

"Are you okay, honey?" Thorpe asked, wrapping his arms around her.

She nodded.

Jed and Stone walked to Harlow; he had the vacant stare of a dead man. Stone picked up Harlow's pistol and tucked it in his belt. It was finally over. He thought of the woman and her little girl whom Harlow had killed. They also had their justice. He didn't have one ounce of sympathy for Harlow and the way he left this earth. "Jed, would you help me carry him to the buckboard. I'll take him to town to be buried. We don't want the likes of him on Thorpe's land."

Thorpe didn't disagree.

Before Stone and Jed carried Harlow out the door, Stone said, "One of these days you and Lily are going to have a shoot-off."

"Why is that?" Thorpe asked.

"You shot him smack between the eyes, just like Lily shot Kip Young. That's one heck of a shot."

Thorpe was so scared when he saw Harlow holding a gun to Lily that he prayed he would be accurate when he pulled the trigger. He was determined Harlow wasn't going to leave that kitchen with her. In that desperate moment, he recognized in an instant what was important to him. He had wavered about making a commitment to Lily, but that all changed when he realized he could easily lose her forever. He loved her and he wasn't going to let her get away if she felt the same way.

CHAPTER THIRTY-THREE

The next afternoon, instead of going to the house for lunch with Jed, Thorpe and Stone rode to the mercantile.

"Sadie, can you tell me what material Lily was admiring the last time we were here?" Thorpe asked.

Sadie remembered the lovely woman accompanying Thorpe on his last trip to the store. She was the talk of the small town. Everyone was wondering if Thorpe had brought home a new wife. "Of course, Thorpe. Are you thinking of a Christmas gift?"

"I am."

Sadie pulled out two bolts of cloth. "She was looking at this blue velvet and at this white silk. Now this silk wouldn't be suitable for anything other than a wedding dress, or a dress for a real special occasion." She looked at Thorpe, hoping he would give a hint if a wedding was on the horizon.

"This velvet would make a beautiful cloak. It's lovely material, but of course I don't carry fur like the one Ev . . ." She let the words hang in midair. She didn't intend to bring up his ex-fiancée.

Thorpe knew Sadie was referring to the cloak Evelyn had worn to his ranch. Even he'd noticed the soft fur trim. But he wasn't going to think of Evelyn; he was thinking how Lily's eyes matched the cloth.

She eyed Thorpe as he ran his hands over the material. It was soft and silky, just like Lily. "Of course, it would be beautiful without the fur. I have some new dresses if you want one ready-made."

Thorpe remembered how Lily felt in her thin nightgown. He'd like to see her wearing something made out of that white silk. "I like the feel of these. Give me enough for a dress and a cloak."

Stone walked over and looked at the material Thorpe was holding. "That's real pretty. That blue is the same color as Lily's eyes."

"That's exactly what I was thinking," Thorpe replied.

Stone held up an ornate sterling silver brush and mirror in his hand. "Do you think Isabelle would like these?"

"I don't know Isabelle, but any woman would love that set," Sadie said before

Thorpe could comment. "I hinted and hinted to my Jacob, but he didn't hear me."

"I think your new wife would be pleased," Thorpe said.

Stone liked hearing someone refer to Isabelle as his wife. "Isabelle didn't have much in the way of what he called frills, and I want to surprise her with something special."

Sadie wrapped their purchases and wished them a Merry Christmas. Thorpe and Stone jumped into the buckboard, but instead of heading home, Thorpe reined in at the bank.

Five minutes later he exited the bank and said, "I need to see the pastor now." He pulled the buckboard to a halt in front of the church. "I'll be right back." Thorpe was only in the church a few minutes and then they headed home.

Judging by the gifts Thorpe had purchased for Lily, Stone wondered if he was having a change of heart about settling down. "Have you decided you are about ready to settle down?"

"I've been giving it some thought." Thorpe wasn't ready to discuss his intentions. "Have you finished your Christmas gift for Isabelle?"

"It'll be done by tomorrow. I can't wait to

give it to her. She's really going to be surprised."

"She certainly will be. It's a beauty."

"Thanks to Jed. He's really a talented man," Stone said.

After dinner that night, everyone carried their coffee into the parlor and Thorpe lit the candles on the Christmas tree. When he finished with the candles, he walked to the fireplace to add some wood, and that's when he noticed the decorations lining the wood mantel. He recognized Lily's animal carvings at one end, but he hadn't seen the carvings at the other end of the mantel. She had arranged an intricately carved nativity scene in front of a large cross. In addition to the Holy Family with baby Jesus in a manger, there were carvings of the three kings. He had never seen anything so beautiful. He turned to Lily and asked, "Did your grandfather carve these?"

"Yes. It was the last present he gave me before he left."

Thorpe walked to the other end of the mantel where Lily had lined up all of the animals alongside a sacred totem pole. Thorpe picked up the wolf and studied it again. It was such a close resemblance to Blue. He missed that wolf though he hated to mention him to Lily for fear of making her sad. He picked up the pair of doves. "This is the only pair. There's only one of the other animals."

"My grandfather said he'd never seen a dove without a mate."

Thorpe's mother always told him that doves mate for life. He didn't know if that was true, but he liked to think it was. Thorpe thought it was interesting how her grandfather honored the beliefs of the Indians, while staying true to his own Christian heritage. "Thank you for putting these here. They look really nice."

Jed joined Thorpe at the mantel and handed him his coffee cup. "I've never seen anything as pretty as those carvings."

They talked while they drank their coffee for over an hour before Stone and Jed left to go back to the stable to put the finishing touches on Isabelle's present. Isabelle's back was hurting so she decided to go to bed. Lily carried the cups to the kitchen while Thorpe extinguished the candles on the tree.

Lily was still cleaning the kitchen when she heard Thorpe walk upstairs. She thought it odd that he didn't say good night, but he'd been so busy lately, she thought he must be tired. Once the last dish was dried and put away, she turned to Spirit and said, "Are you and your pups ready to go outside?"

Spirit and the pups jumped up, tails wagging in unison, and Lily laughed at them. She kneeled down and hugged them all as they jumped all over her. It would have been a perfect night if Blue had been there with them. "Oh, how I wish Blue was with us," she whispered to them.

Thorpe was standing at the doorway watching her play with them and heard what she said. A lump formed in his throat at the pain in her simple statement. How he wished he could find Blue for her. When he collected himself, he asked, "Are you ready to take them out?"

Lily jumped at the sound of Thorpe's voice. "You frightened me." She hadn't gotten over how Harlow was able to sneak up on her. If Blue had been there, Harlow would never had gotten close to her.

"I didn't know I was that quiet."

She walked to the door and reached for her coat. "It's just that I haven't been able to forget how Harlow caught me by surprise."

Thorpe held her coat for her and after she slid her arms into the sleeves, his hands remained on her shoulders. "Lily, I won't let anything happen to you."

Turning, she smiled up at him. "I know. It was the first time I felt like I couldn't defend myself. I always had Blue there. Harlow would have never entered the house if Blue was here."

"I'll protect you until Blue returns." He wanted to protect her even if Blue returned. In his mind, she was his responsibility and he liked feeling that way.

They walked outside and Spirit and the puppies followed. The moon and stars were so bright, they didn't need the lantern. Thorpe talked about everything but what he wanted to talk about. When they reached the corral, Thorpe told himself it was time to do what he intended. Both of them were leaning against the rail looking up at the stars when Thorpe said, "Lily, are you determined to leave in the spring?"

"Yes. I'm going to find Grandfather." It would be more difficult for her without Blue, and especially now that Jed planned to stay at Dove Creek, but she was determined.

"What would you think about me going with you?"

His question surprised her. "What about the ranch? How would you have time to leave when you've been away so long?"

"Stone and Jed will be here to help Curtis. I don't want you going alone."

She would like nothing better than to have Thorpe travel with her, but it was too much to ask. "I can't ask that of you."

"You didn't ask me. I asked you."

She didn't know what to say. It was more than generous of him to offer, yet she didn't feel right about taking him from the ranch. She had no idea how long it would take her to find her grandfather. One day she would have to say good-bye to Thorpe and she might as well do it in the spring. Whenever it happened, it was sure to leave a hole in her heart.

Uneasy by her lack of enthusiasm for him to go with her, he wasn't sure he should continue. After a deep breath, he decided he wasn't about to back down now. "There's just one hitch to my offer."

Puzzled, Lily said, "What do you mean?"

"I told you I wanted you . . ."

She couldn't believe what he was suggesting, and she held her hand up, indicating he should stop talking. "Thorpe, if you think . . ." She was near tears, either from outrage or sadness, she didn't know. But she refused to cry in front of him. She tried again. "If that is . . ."

He knew what she was thinking and she

513

was right. "Yes, I'd want you in my bedroll every night."

Lily opened her mouth, but nothing came out. She couldn't believe that he'd actually admitted what he wanted from her.

He reached into his pocket and pulled out the small box. His mouth tilted up at the corner. "I'm sorry if that shocks you, Miss Lily. But if I go with you, you'd have to be married to me because we will make love every night."

She looked at him and blinked. Her mind went blank. "What?" Surely she didn't hear him correctly. Was she hearing what she wanted to hear? What she longed to hear?

He opened the box to reveal his mother's wedding ring. "I'm asking if you would marry me, Lily. I want you, all of you, and I want you forever."

Each time he'd said he wanted her she'd thought he meant something else. "I thought when you said you wanted me that you meant . . ."

Thorpe couldn't disagree that it had been his meaning, but he wanted more. He gave her an irreverent grin. "Oh, I want that too, Miss Lily. Don't think I don't." He moved closer. "But I want you for the rest of my life. And if you say yes, I hope my life is a long one with you by my side."

"But what about Ev . . ."

This was a special moment between him and the woman he loved. He didn't want Evelyn's name even spoken. He placed his finger on her lips. "I told you there is no relationship there."

As much as she wanted to believe him, she had doubts. "But you traveled all the way to Kansas City for her. You had to care."

He saw no way around it; he had to tell her everything. "Lily, I went to Kansas City to see if the man she was with had forced her to his bed. Yes, I had asked her to marry me, but I had second thoughts. I was going to call off the wedding, but then . . ." He hated to tell her the reason he was prepared to marry Evelyn, yet he saw no way around it. "She'd shared my bed. One time." He thought he'd make that point clear. "We had been engaged for a few months before it happened. I had come to realize I didn't love her, but I had to do what was right. I was prepared to make her my wife. I only went to Kansas City to make sure she wasn't forced by Ainsworth. As it turned out, she had been intimate with Ainsworth before me. He hadn't forced her into anything. They were living as man and wife in Kansas City, though they hadn't married. I was free from any obligation. When Ainsworth refused to marry her, she came here and tried to change her story. Her father told me the truth." He saw no reason to mention Evelyn's relationship with Travis.

Lily had tears falling by the time he finished. "I thought . . . I thought you hadn't gotten over her or the hurt."

"You can believe I wasn't ready to ask another woman to marry me. I was angry and bitter after learning of her deception. To be honest, I wasn't sure I could trust another woman. Then I met you and you've changed everything. I want you. I want you to be mine." He pulled the ring out of the box and held it between his fingers. "This was my mother's ring and I've never offered it to another woman. You are the woman I want. I love you, Lily, and I want to be your husband." He held the ring to her finger, awaiting her response.

"Yes, I would love to be your wife," she said softly.

He slipped the ring on her finger and it was a perfect fit. He pulled her into his embrace. "Do you love me, Lily?"

"Yes, I love you. I have for a long time. Isabelle told me when I saved your life we would be bound to each other forever. I prayed she was right."

"You asked me about the past. It's only

fair that I know what your feelings are for Anderson."

"He wanted more than I could give. I was truthful when I said I considered him a friend. He planned to visit to see if I could feel more for him one day."

He nodded, satisfied with her response. "He's never kissing you again."

She gave him a smile. "I would think not. I do need to send him a telegram and let him know when we are married." She didn't want the captain to come to visit and be surprised to learn she was a married woman. She looked down at the ring. "It's beautiful and I will take care of it forever." It had belonged to his mother and she knew how important it was to Thorpe.

"It's not as beautiful as you." He felt so fortunate to have a woman like Lily. He'd never met another woman like her. It was difficult to believe, but her inner beauty surpassed her outer beauty. "You're positive you want to stay with me forever?"

"Positive. You know I'm a good shot, so I have no doubt you will be faithful."

Thorpe laughed. "That I do, Miss Lily. Even if you weren't skilled with a gun, there's no other woman for me." He lowered his head to kiss her and she wrapped her arms around his neck. He kissed her with a raging hunger he'd tried to keep under tight rein, and she returned the kiss with equal fervor. Their kiss sealed the proposal with the promise of a loving and passionate future.

He had to pull away from her before he picked her up and carried her straight upstairs. "I want you to kiss me like that tomorrow about one o'clock."

"Why one o'clock?"

"The pastor will be here at noon to have lunch with us, and by one o'clock I plan to be celebrating our wedding day in my . . . our . . . bedroom."

"You want to get married tomorrow? It's Christmas Eve."

"I spoke to the pastor while I was in town, and he'll be bringing his wife with him. I thought if you agreed, it would be a perfect day to get married." When he'd made his decision to ask her, he didn't see any reason not to marry right away. "Do you object to marrying tomorrow?"

"No, I just didn't want the pastor to be away from his family on Christmas Eve. But if he is bringing his wife with him for lunch, tomorrow is perfect." By this time tomorrow night she would be Thorpe's wife. Thinking about sharing his bed excited her and made her nervous at the same time.

They kissed again, and Thorpe was the first to pull away. "Stop kissing me like that or I won't be able to wait until tomorrow." He had his arm around her waist as they slowly walked back to the house. As soon as he opened the kitchen door they heard a wolf howl in the distance.

Lily stopped and listened to the mournful sound that filled the quiet of the night. "I don't think that was so very far away."

"Sounds in the night can carry a long way, Lily. Do you think that's Blue?"

"Yes."

He didn't miss the hint of sadness in her one-word response. And he didn't know if she was right or not, but if she was, he hoped Blue would come home before Christmas.

After they said good night at Lily's door, Thorpe walked to his room. Before he undressed, he sat in his chair and thought about his parents and how much they would have liked Lily. She'd saved his life in more ways than one. His heart had hardened after Evelyn's betrayal and Lily changed him. He gave thanks for the full life he was going to have with a beautiful wife and new friends. He didn't know how long he sat there before the wolf started howling again. He walked to the window and looked out. If souls could connect man and animal, he hoped Blue connected with his soul and knew he wanted him home. "This is your home, too." He grabbed his hat off the table and walked out the door. He wouldn't give up on Blue.

CHAPTER THIRTY-FOUR

Isabelle insisted on helping Lily dress for her special day and arranged her hair much the way she did the day at the fort when they'd dined with the captain. "I wish you had a real wedding dress."

Lily had the same thought, but even if she could afford that beautiful white material at the general store, she didn't have time to make a dress. She looked down at her dress; it was pretty and not threadbare like her other dresses. "This blue dress is my best one."

"It's pretty, but I wanted to see you in a white dress. But it doesn't really matter, Thorpe will think you are beautiful in anything, or nothing," Isabelle said.

"Isabelle!" Lily felt herself blushing.

Isabelle gave her a serious look. "I know you've never . . . well, never been with a man. Do you know what to expect?"

"I suppose. My mother told me some

things, and I've been around a lot of animals."

"Then you know the basics. There is nothing to be nervous about. I can only tell you, with the right man, everything will be wonderful. And I know Thorpe is the right man for you. I knew it from the start."

"Yes, you did."

"He knew it, too. He just fought the notion."

Lily looked in the mirror when Isabelle finished winding the ribbon through her hair. "It looks lovely. Thank you."

Isabelle stepped back and looked at Lily. "I've never seen a more beautiful bride. Now help me waddle down the stairs."

They walked into the kitchen and found Jed making lunch for them. "Miss Lily, you shor' look pretty."

"Thank you. We came down to prepare lunch, but I see we are too late. You didn't have to do that, Jed."

"I wanted to do it for you. You already made breakfast this morning and baked a cake. You've done enough work on your wedding day."

"Thank you, Jed. That's really nice of you." Knowing how much Thorpe loved cake, she didn't consider it work to bake one. Before dawn, Thorpe had joined her in the kitchen. While she was mixing the batter, he was standing over her, sticking his finger in the bowl. He smeared it on her lips and then kissed it off. She wasn't going to share that with Jed though. "What can we do to help?"

"You ladies can make the table look pretty. I'm not good at that."

"Seeing how delicious that fried chicken looks, you don't need to be good at anything else," Isabelle teased.

To make the table more festive, Lily made an arrangement in a bowl with the mistletoe Thorpe had brought in earlier, along with some pine cones.

"Is Thorpe back?" Lily asked.

"He's upstairs changing his clothes. He said he wanted to look handsome for his bride," Jed said, smiling wide.

"Yes, I do," Thorpe said as he stood at the doorway. He'd been standing there a few moments just watching his soon-to-be-wife. He could hardly believe this beautiful woman was soon to be his. "I don't want her to think she made a mistake."

Lily turned at the sound of his voice. He looked so handsome in his dark suit and white shirt that he took her breath away. "You succeeded."

He liked the look in her eyes. He hurried

across the room and took her in his arms. "You think you made a mistake?"

"No, you succeeded in looking handsome."

"I had to look presentable for the most beautiful bride in the world." He picked up some mistletoe from the table and held it over her head. "Now you have to kiss me." He didn't give her time to respond before he brushed his lips over hers. "I'll want some more of those later."

Stone came through the kitchen doorway. "Here comes the pastor and his wife."

Lily stepped away from Thorpe, her face turning a nice shade of pink, causing Thorpe to chuckle. He reached for her hand and walked outside to greet the pastor and his wife. After the pastor introduced his wife, they turned to go inside, but Lily abruptly turned around and looked off in the distance.

At first, Thorpe thought she was just enjoying the view, but he saw she was focused on a specific spot at least two hundred yards away. He looked at the trees, but he saw nothing. "What is it, honey?"

"I don't know. I just felt . . . something." She put her hand to her heart.

Thorpe was staring at her when her eyes widened. "Lily?"

Hearing the concern in Thorpe's voice, the pastor and his wife turned to see what was happening.

Lily took a few steps forward. "It's Blue," she whispered.

Thorpe looked out over the ranch. "Honey, he's not there."

Suddenly, Lily gripped her skirt in her hands and started running toward the trees.

"Lily!" Thorpe took off after her.

Isabelle, Stone, and Jed heard Thorpe's booming voice and ran outside thinking something was wrong. Stone had grabbed the rifle by the door.

"She thought she saw Blue," the pastor told them.

It only took Thorpe a few strides to catch up with Lily and he latched on to her arm and stopped her. "Honey, Blue's not here." Just as the words left his mouth, Blue came loping from the trees. When he saw Lily, he picked up speed.

Thorpe couldn't believe what he was seeing. There was no way Lily could have seen Blue before he came through the trees.

"Blue!" Blue ran to her outstretched arms. She crouched down and Blue started whimpering and licking her face at the same time.

Thorpe kneeled beside them and engulfed them both in his arms. He could barely contain his emotions. He'd missed Blue, and he'd prayed he would come back for Lily's sake.

"Oh, Blue, where have you been?" Lily asked him. "I've been worried sick about you."

Thorpe looked him over and the big wolf looked to be well-fed and he saw no injuries. "He looks great."

Seeing movement in his peripheral vision, Thorpe whipped his head around to see a rider coming through the trees in the exact spot Blue had exited. He didn't recognize the man or the horse. He'd left his gun in the kitchen, so he said, "Lily, go back to the house with Blue."

She heard the change in his voice. "What's wrong?" Then she saw the man on the Appaloosa riding in their direction. "Grandfather?"

Thorpe looked hard at the man as he approached. Though Lily had never described her grandfather, he'd envisioned him as a small man with white hair. The man on the Appaloosa was tall in the saddle and looked to be much younger than the age of a grandfather. A quick estimate said her grandfather should be well over sixty years of age. "I can't be your grandfather."

"It is!" Lily ran to him with Blue beside her.

Thorpe was just a half step behind.

"Grandfather!"

Ben jumped off his horse, and when he reached his granddaughter, he lifted her off the ground and twirled her around, much like he did when she was a small child. He put her down and held her from him and looked her up and down. "You are more beautiful than ever. You look so much like my Mattie."

"Grandfather, how did you know where to find me?"

"Blue led me."

Thorpe stared at the man who was almost as tall as he was, leaner, but he looked to be in excellent shape. His face was strongly sculpted, yet still possessed a youthful appearance despite the squint lines at the corner of his eyes. His hair was black with a smattering of white at the temples, but his eyes were as blue as Lily's.

"Grandfather, this is Thorpe Turlow."

"Am I in time for the wedding?"

Lily glanced at Thorpe, and Thorpe was staring at Ben.

"How did you know?" Lily asked.

Ben smiled. "The way we know all things. Have I not taught you to be still and listen?"

"You have. And you are in time," Lily assured him.

Thorpe knew there was no way the man could have heard about the wedding. When he went to bed last night, only two people knew he was marrying today: himself and Lily. He hadn't even told the pastor he was getting married. He'd just told him to be prepared to perform another wedding when he came to the ranch for lunch. They'd told Stone, Isabelle, and Jed this morning over breakfast.

Thorpe extended his hand to Ben. "It's a pleasure to meet you. Lily has told me so much about you."

"I've heard much about you. My granddaughter has made a wise choice."

Another odd response, Thorpe thought. "I'm a fortunate man." Thorpe planned to pull Ben aside after lunch to make sure they would have his blessing. He knew Lily would be pleased to have her grandfather bless their union. If Ben objected, Thorpe would be disappointed, but nothing was going to stop him from marrying Lily.

"Yes, you are a lucky man, and you have my blessing."

Thorpe stared at him, wondering if Lily forgot to mention her grandfather was a mind-reader. When he recovered from his shock, he said, "Did you find your brother?"

"I did and he is well. He has a wife and five children, they live in Montana Territory." He smiled at Lily. "Honey, you have a large family now."

"Grandfather, Mother and Father . . ." Lily didn't think she could tell him about her parents without crying.

Ben squeezed her to him again. "I know, honey. I'm sorry I wasn't there to help you."

Thorpe took hold of his horse's reins. "Let's get your horse in the stable. We were just getting ready for lunch and we want to hear all about your travels."

Thorpe and Ben walked to the stable and Lily took Blue to the kitchen. Blue ran straight to Spirit and the pups for a lively reunion.

When Thorpe and Ben came in from the stable, they all took their seats at the table. Thorpe glanced at the people around his table. He'd been fortunate to inherit this family and he was happy they were there to witness his marriage to Lily. He took Lily's hand in his, and when her eyes met his, he winked at her. He'd never been happier in his life. "Ben, would you like to say grace?"

Lunch ended and everyone gathered in the parlor. Stone had the fire blazing in the fireplace and the room was warm and cozy. The pastor stood with his back to the fire and Lily and Thorpe took their positions facing him with Blue between them. Thorpe declared his vows in such a deep, strong voice, it brought tears to Lily's eyes. She felt so much love for this wonderful man that she could hardly speak her vows.

After the preacher pronounced them man and wife, Thorpe took Lily in his arms. "It looks like you are bound to me forever."

The day they stood on that ledge on Chimney Rock flashed before her eyes. When he'd etched their names in that rock and carved the heart joining them together, she was filled with sheer joy at the thought of being connected to him forever in some way. Now she was the wife of this magnificent man, and she could hardly speak for the overwhelming love she felt for him. "Yes, I've been very blessed," she whispered.

Thorpe leaned over and kissed her tenderly. "I'm the one who has been blessed. I love you, Mrs. Turlow."

She was thrilled to be called Mrs. Turlow. "I love you, husband." She reached up and wrapped her arms around his neck and kissed him.

After they cut the wedding cake, Thorpe

joined Ben at the fireplace and handed him a plate. Ben was looking at his carvings Lily had displayed.

"I'm curious to know why you carved the wolf with the notch in his ear," Thorpe asked.

Ben turned his blue eyes on Thorpe. "Blue has a notch on his ear."

"Lily told me you carved that when you were a boy. She only found Blue last year and you had already left Texas."

Ben nodded. "This was my first carving. One of the elders in the tribe taught me."

"Did the wolf you had at that time have a notch in his ear in the exact spot?"

Ben smiled at Thorpe. "Yes." He saw the bewildered look on Thorpe's face, and said, "The Good Book tells us to have faith and believe. All things are possible."

Lily walked up and heard her grandfather's response. She wasn't surprised. She understood her grandfather possessed a spiritual awareness that often surpassed understanding.

Thorpe couldn't continue the conversation as the pastor and his wife were ready to depart. After the good-byes, Stone and Jed headed out to the stable to put the finishing touches on their projects. When Isabelle excused herself to go upstairs to rest,

Thorpe, Lily, and Ben were alone.

Thorpe had planned to spend the rest of the day in his room with his new bride, but now that Ben had arrived, his plans changed.

"What do you say we take Ben out to see the ranch?" he said to Lily.

Before Lily responded, she glanced around the room looking for her grandfather.

"He's on the porch," Thorpe said.

"I thought you wanted to . . ."

He arched his brow at her. "Why, Miss Lily, I think you can't wait to see me without my shirt again."

Her blush started rising slowly from her neck to her forehead.

Thorpe hugged her. "I do want to, you don't know how much. But I think we can make it until tonight. Unless your grandfather is too tired, let's show him around. You two have a lot of catching up to do and I want to get to know him."

The way she looked up at him, she didn't have to say the words; Thorpe shared her feelings. "Yes, Mrs. Turlow. I love you, too."

Lily pulled his face down to place a soft kiss on his lips. "I've never been so happy."

CHAPTER THIRTY-FIVE

Lily and Thorpe were cooking breakfast together on Christmas morning, exhausted from their wedding night, but filled with excitement for the day ahead. Thorpe couldn't keep his hands off his new bride, and he had her bent over the table kissing her when Stone came running into the kitchen.

"It's time!" Stone shouted.

"Oh heavens," Lily said when Thorpe released her. She looked at Thorpe. "Can we get the doctor out here?"

"I don't think there's time," Stone said.

"The women are usually here right after breakfast," Thorpe said, hoping their assistance would be enough to get Isabelle through childbirth.

Ben stood in the doorway smiling at their worried faces. "This is a joyous time. Lily, I'll finish up in here. You go help your friend."

Lily looked at her grandfather. "I've never delivered a baby. What if something happens?"

"I was the one that helped your grandmother when your father was born. If you need help, I'm here."

Lily was comforted by his presence and she started giving instructions. "Boil some water, get me some twine and some extra bedding."

"As soon as the ladies arrive, I will send them up," Thorpe told her.

Stone followed Lily up the stairs. As soon as she entered the room, Isabelle said, "Lily, I don't think it is going to be long."

Lily had always heard that the firstborn took a long time in coming. She hoped for Isabelle's sake that this birth would be different. Lily grabbed her hand and asked, "Is there anything you want right now?"

"Just talk to me. I think Stone is scared to death."

Glancing at Stone, Lily couldn't believe this big strong man had fear in his eyes.

Stone met her eyes. "It's just that I feel so helpless. She's in so much pain and I can't do anything to help her."

Lily smiled at him. "Go on downstairs and have some breakfast and a large cup of strong coffee. I will be here with Isabelle.

You can bring that water up after you've eaten." Stone left the room and Lily sat beside Isabelle. "Are you in a lot of pain?"

"It's not too bad. Truthfully, I think riding in the wagon all those days was worse."

Lily laughed. "I don't know how you did that."

"Lily, I really want this baby now. I hope God forgives me for the way I behaved after I found out about Ethan. When I think of all the terrible things I said and what I was thinking . . ."

Lily squeezed her hand. "Hush now. I'm confident God understood your feelings and forgives you if you've asked. It's not an easy thing to forget betrayal." She thought of Thorpe and how his heart had been hardened after being deceived by Evelyn. "Isabelle, if you forgive Ethan, you will be blessed in ways you never imagined. Let Ethan's wrongs go and think of them no more. If you can't forgive Ethan, how can God forgive you?"

"You are right, and I do forgive him." Suddenly, she clasped Lily's hand, hard enough that Lily thought she might break her fingers. "Lily, I think it's time."

Forty minutes later, and before the women arrived to lend a hand, Riff Carson Justice came into the world screaming loudly.

Lily wrapped him in a blanket and handed him to his mother.

Stone came into the room to see his new son, and Isabelle said, "Meet your daddy."

Stone leaned down and kissed Isabelle tenderly and took his son from her arms. "Hello, Carson."

Tears welled in Lily's eyes as she watched the new family. She glanced up when she heard the tap on the door.

"Can I see the new baby?" Thorpe asked.

Stone walked over to Thorpe and pulled the blanket aside so Thorpe could see his son. "He's a fine-looking strong boy."

Thorpe was in awe seeing something so tiny. "Why, he's not much bigger than the pups we found. What's his name?"

"Riff Carson Justice," Stone replied. "We're going to call him Carson." He looked at his wife and added, "Isabelle liked that better than Riff."

"It's a good name," Thorpe said.

Thorpe and Lily left the room to give the new parents some privacy. "Does that make you want one?" Thorpe asked Lily.

"Yes." As soon as she saw that sweet little's baby's face, she felt a longing to have Thorpe's child.

"Me, too. I guess we'd best work hard at having one." Thorpe grabbed her and kissed her before they reached the staircase.

"Behave yourself. Someone will see us."

"I'm sure they've kissed a time or two."

The remainder of the morning was a flurry of activity. The men left the house to attend to the ranch while the women were cooking, and the puppies kept the children busy. The Christmas meal was planned for late afternoon to give the men time to complete their work for the day.

Isabelle was too tired to come downstairs for dinner, so Stone ate dinner with her in their room. Everyone that lived on the ranch gathered around the table and Thorpe said the prayer. After dinner, the children opened their gifts from Thorpe before everyone left for their own homes.

Stone left Isabelle's side long enough to go to the stable with Jed to get Isabelle's gift. When they returned, each man was carrying a wooden cradle. Stone carried the one for little Carson upstairs to give to Isabelle, and Jed placed the one he was carrying in front of the Christmas tree.

"Jed, this is beautiful," Lily said, admiring the craftsmanship. "But why did you make two?"

"This one is for you and Mr. Thorpe," Jed said proudly.

Lily turned her wide blue eyes on him. "But how did you know we would even marry?"

"Miss Isabelle was so certain, we just decided she was probably right." Jed pointed to the carving on the head of the cradle. "Your grandfather carved this for us this morning."

Thorpe and Lily leaned down and saw the words *Dove Creek* perfectly carved into the wood.

"Thank you, Jed. It's a fine cradle." Thorpe pulled Lily to his side and added, "And I intend to have a little one in it as soon as possible."

Everyone settled around the fire and opened their Christmas gifts. When Lily opened Thorpe's gift, she was surprised he'd purchased the exact blue velvet she had admired in the mercantile. "This is the most beautiful material I have ever seen."

"I heard you say that in the store the day we went to town. Sadie said it would look beautiful on you."

Lily removed the paper on the second package and saw the white silk. "Oh, Thorpe, this is lovely. I love it, but it is so impractical."

Thorpe grinned at her. "A husband shouldn't give his wife practical gifts. He should give her things he wants to see on her."

Lily gave him the shirt she'd made for him and she was thrilled with his response. "It's too pretty to wear. It's the color of your eyes," he told her.

Jed was moved to tears by the book Lily gave him. "Miss Lily, this is a wonderful present."

Thorpe asked Jed if he would accompany him to the barn. Jed was speechless when Thorpe gave him the tools he'd purchased from the banker. It was everything Jed would need to start his blacksmith business.

They didn't have a gift for Lily's grandfather, but Thorpe resolved that problem by asking Ben to live with them for as long as he wanted. Ben was moved by Thorpe's kindness, and said it was the best Christmas gift he'd ever received. He'd missed Lily, and now that he'd found his brother, he wanted to settle down and enjoy his family.

Lily had mentioned to Thorpe she didn't have a gift for Stone the day he went to town. He told her not to worry, he had a plan. Thorpe and Lily joined Stone and Isabelle in their room and Thorpe handed Stone an envelope. It was a bill of sale for two hundred head of cattle. "Lily and I wanted to help you start your ranch off right."

If Lily hadn't already realized Thorpe's generosity, she saw it that day in so many ways. Looking back on everything he'd done for all of them since they met him in Missouri brought a lump to her throat. She'd married a man without equal. She felt her heart would burst with pride each time she looked at him.

Thorpe glanced her way and saw her staring at him. He winked at her. "Don't get too tired, wife. I want you to go for a ride with me later tonight."

She couldn't wait. She wanted to be alone with him, feel his arms around her, and tell him how much she loved him.

Thorpe and Lily were at the back door pulling on their coats for the late-night ride.

"Where are we going?" Lily asked.

"I'm going to show you a Christmas miracle," Thorpe replied.

She didn't know what he had in mind, but it sounded exciting. He'd told her they would be taking the buckboard so she could sit next to him to stay warm.

Before they walked out the back door, Ben handed Lily a small package wrapped in brown paper.

"When you stop tonight you can open this present. It's a gift for both of you."

Lily looked down at the package. It was wrapped just like the ones he'd given her each Christmas, the ones that always held one of his special carvings. "Thank you, but how do you know Thorpe plans on stopping?"

Ben kissed her on the cheek. "He's showing you his Christmas miracle."

Blue jumped into the back of the buckboard and they rode slowly in the direction of the entryway to the ranch. It was a cold night with a full moon. The snow continued to fall, lighting up the landscape, making it easy to see where they were going. Lily wasn't cold; she was snuggled close to Thorpe and he'd placed a blanket over her legs to keep her warm. When he reached the gate he rode through and turned the buckboard around to face the gate. He pulled the horses to a halt and pulled Lily in his arms.

"I ride out here every Christmas night. I wanted you to see what I call my miracle." He leaned over and kissed her.

When their kiss ended, Lily said, "Thank you for a wonderful Christmas. You've made everyone's dreams come true. It means so much to me that you asked Grandfather to stay on the ranch."

"You've made me the happiest man on earth. I think I've been waiting all my life to share this day with you. This is the best Christmas I've ever had."

Lily pulled her grandfather's package from her pocket and handed it to Thorpe. "We're supposed to open this."

He unfolded the brown paper and held up Ben's carving. It was a replica of the entryway to the ranch. There were two doves carved atop the rail over the words *Dove Creek Ranch* with their wings spread wide, as though they had just descended from heaven. Beside the base of one log was a carved wolf. Blue. Thorpe looked at Lily and her expression reflected the same look of amazement. "This would have taken months to carve."

Lily nodded. "He'd work for months on all of his carvings. He rode in with Blue from the north, so he hasn't even seen the entryway."

Just then, Thorpe heard a familiar sound, one he heard every Christmas. He pointed to the sky. "Look." Blue stuck his head between them and they hooked their arms around his neck as they all looked up at the sky. With wings fluttering in the hallowed silence, two white doves descended from the midnight sky and landed on the gate in the same spot they did every year: above the iron forged letters of Dove Creek Ranch.

"And I saw the Spirit come down from heaven as a dove . . ."

John 1:32